# ONE SMILE MORE

## CHARLOTTE PLATT

GRENDEL PRESS

Cover design by www.trifbookdesign.com
Edited by Kasey Kubica

Published June 2024
ISBN: 978-1-960534-13-2 (Paperback)
ASIN: B0D5DPQWHY (eBook)

Written by Charlotte Platt
www.charlotteplattwriter.co.uk

Published by Grendel Press LLC
www.grendelpress.com

# ONE SMILE MORE

SANDS OF ETERNITY

1

CHARLOTTE PLATT

For Bear, Crowley and Dearheart, who were always patient when I was rambling about the aftermath of immortality.

# Chapter 1
## London, 1862

London and Edinburgh were not so different, I discovered upon arrival, though London was busier. More bodies, a constant scrum of people I had to fight against while scouting a route to avoid a gang of sharp-eyed young men with grins that were too practised to be anything but bad news.

Even dressed as a man, I was going to stand out as new in this place—jostled out of the station, a monument of tracks and steam; huge, arching rib cages of steel filled with glass and metal lattices—carrying my bag on one shoulder to avoid highlighting what I hid beneath my shirt and jacket. I didn't need a thief finding there was more than a handkerchief at my breast pocket.

An alley in one city looks much like an alley in another too, though I had to commend London for its sheer dedication to red brick and fucking dust. Everything was red, or a ruddy, muted brown from the build-up of dirt and soot. It also meant they all looked alike, which did not help my search for a college. I ducked into a covered close, trying to lose my potential admirers, to find a small square yard, the loading space for the shops that backed onto it judging by the number of closed doors before me. And a man.

He hadn't even groaned when I'd stumbled into him, this bloodied man, laid on the floor like he'd been tossed out the back of the buildings. Bleeding too much—for a long moment I thought he was already dead.

But his chest rose, and that blood was still fresh and metallic hot in the back of my throat, not the sweet rot of death. He had a chance.

Throwing a look over my shoulder, I leaned closer, taking him in: dark brown skin, curly black hair, a broken set of glasses askew on his nose. Nice suit. His eyes were open but not seeing, though he blinked, and a deep brown like peat water. The tattoos on his wrists were that of the ritual schools, a collection of circles and script dark against the thin skin.

He was a mage. Well, shit.

I was shedding my bag and jacket like a fucking fool. Slapping his face, I pressed the bundled material against his chest, leaning my weight down to stem the flow. There were two deep slashes, angry against the white of his shirt. More blood pooled at his throat, which could be the way he'd fallen, and his temple showed a gash that spoke of impact.

"Can you hear me? Pal, I need you to talk to me." His blood was hot on my hands, seeping through the cheap jacket I'd lifted before I got onto the train. I slapped harder, the glasses going sideways onto the cobbles below. "Say something! I'm not a healer, but I can get you somewhere if you tell me where to go." I didn't know London. I didn't know the healing houses like I did in Edinburgh. There had to be them though, city this big, there would be somewhere, or we could get to his college.

My hat fell to one side, brim bouncing off my bag as I leaned more weight on him, my pinned hair left exposed and obvious to anyone looking—but there were limited choices, and he was bleeding too much. The rasp to his breath wasn't a good noise, and I pulled up, unsure how best to help. I could put air in his lungs with a word, keep him breathing, but there was so much blood, and I didn't know if I'd be pouring more pain onto him. He'd not made a sound, still, despite slaps and my pushing on his wounds.

"What are you doing?" Hands were on my shoulders, pulling me backwards off the man below, and I span on my knees to shove whoever it was away. He was dressed well, a smart coat and small hat on top of neat, thick hair, the same rich brown skin as the man below us. "Arif?"

I went for his arm, pulling a sleeve up to look for matching black patterns—not willing to trust the coincidence—and instead met the cold rush of old energy. Not human, too sedate to be one of us, but the slow pulse of hunger and magic meant vampire. My heart yanked, fear solidifying as I met anxious brown eyes. I knew there'd be more of them down here, people mixed with them given the accords, but there was no way I was going to pretend this was safe.

"You get the fuck away from him." I should have kept a knife handy; all I had was my heel blade, that was no use against a bite. But I wouldn't let a vampire finish this poor bastard off.

He blinked at me, glancing at the man below. "I'm a doctor."

I scoffed, struggling into standing and shoving myself between them, one hand on the vampire's chest to keep him back. "Aye right, a vampire doctor just passing when there's magic blood to be had. I might not be the same school as him, but I'll defend a fellow mage."

"Miss, I know the man." He tried to step close, and I brought my hands up; ready to swing. All for show, really. I wouldn't stand much chance except with magic; vampires were fearsome strong, but he didn't know that. I'd scratch his eyes out before he got his teeth into either of us.

A shout went out behind him, then a rush of footsteps getting closer. I had to get gone; there was no way to know if that was company for him, or for me, or the police. If my voice wasn't an issue, given how I was dressed and the blood on my hands, the accent would be. And if the college had reported me as missing, I'd be a sure find. I hadn't put up with second class carriage travel for three days to get my collar felt.

I glanced at the mage—still breathing, but it was wet now, close to death—and back at the vampire. Limited options. If I ran past him, that was a straight line into whoever was coming, and while I could fight it meant delays, more chance of being found and questioned. Blamed.

I had to go.

I shifted on my feet, shoving an arm up to get my hand skyward, towards the sliver of dusky pink visible between red brick and crossing ropes. *"Teine."*

A column of fire shot up, hungry for the sky and anything else it could consume, the magic enough to drive it past the slates and high—so it would look like a problem. Something that needed attention, police. I screamed too; the noise squeezing from my lungs like a wrung-out cloth. The vampire stumbled back, wary of the fire or me, I didn't care which, and I took the chance. Grabbing my hat and bag, I ran, muttering an apology to the mage as I left.

I shot to one door, twisting the handle on impulse. For my boldness, the thing opened: no need to break the lock. I slipped inside, shutting it quickly behind me and leaning my weight against it.

# Chapter 2

I plonked the hat on my head, checking where I'd landed. The room was dim, rather than dark, a selection of lamps burning low and whisper quiet. It was solid wood at my back, enough to block the noise from outside, and the windows were so heavily curtained no one could see through.

This was a mostly open space: a neat desk and till at the longest wall, and the centre taken up by a thick slab of shiny, red wood topping the counter. It ran the length of the shop, an eclectic variety of pieces sat on display. They were all some sort of art or antique, well maintained by the shine of the metal items, and the thick sweetness of beeswax and lavender hung in the air. Polish for the wood.

I skirted to the side, to a corner where I could press into the heavy curtains, checking myself over. Blood on my hands and shirt. Jacket lost, left behind. I swallowed against my guilt. I couldn't take him with me, but abandoning a fellow magic user sat poorly. I'd stopped him being fed from before dying, at least, that was the best I could offer. Tears would do him no good and I shook the beginning of them away. I had to get to a college.

I pulled my shirt loose from my trews, whispering for water so I could rinse my hands off at the same time as sluicing the blood. The cloth was slick and clinging as I tucked it again, little use as a disguise, but I tugged the shoulders and chest to create boxy space, enough to hide my cramped chest, bound under my undershirt. If I kept my bag on one shoulder, I had a chance of passing, and I could grab a jacket off a line. I only needed to get far enough to find somewhere to hide for the night.

No one investigated the slammed door, and there'd been no voices despite the air of a shop, so I would try to slip out another exit. I walked towards the open threshold at the far side of the room, hat tugged down and chin up like I knew where I was going. Best pretend I did.

I emerged into a bigger chamber, this one well lit with a selection of portraits and paintings studded along the walls. A gallery.

It had a low bench in the middle so one could sit and admire the work, with a mix of tall lamps and mirror boards behind them and small roof windows, so the room got light every which way. The walls were a neutral white to reflect the light back, giving an impression of a flickering sunlight rather than hissing gas.

The room also crackled with energy, a low buzz that started off like the tug of a stream about my ankles and changed to the insistence of the tide when I got closer to the pieces. A magical collection? I'd heard of collectors but not exhibitions. At least in Edinburgh.

There were some statues too—a searching-eyed woman in marble, easily nine foot tall, with a shield and sword; a marble couple entangled on a slab; a sandstone sphinx about the size of a strong bull, low on a plinth. My eye caught on that, something about the almost smile on the human face drawing me closer. It was only a few feet into the room, which was easily ten foot wide itself, and I could bolt back out if I had to.

Approaching the statue, I found a hunger in the stone, the yearning of something far from home. The familiarity between that yearning and my own was enough for its energy to brush up, a brief tremor of power pushing out before I could step away.

*"I used to be resplendent. They worshipped me,"* it whispered in my mind. There was no anger, not even the promised hunger, but I put a shield between me and it. No need to be finding new things so early in my

arrival, especially after that poor man. I bowed my head to the impassive face, to show no harm meant, and stilled when I heard someone else enter the gallery the way I'd come.

"My apologies for the late call in. I'm looking for Matteo." Of course, the peace had lasted too long.

I turned to look and met a startling creature—well into six feet, dressed in a long frock coat and dark gloves that spoke money. A little set of glasses sat high on his youthful face, dark lenses like those the fire users wore sometimes, protecting his eyes and contrasting with his shockingly white hair. He could have been my age, mid-twenties, but he wasn't holding himself like that. He had the air of being older. None of the parts quite matched, and I stood dumb as my mouth opened to respond, but no words came.

"Are you closed? I thought I'd made it in time, but there's a commotion outside." He pulled a pocket watch out of his coat, flicking his wrist to open it. It didn't work as planned, though; the piece slid from his grip and skittered along the floor.

I went down on one knee, grabbing the watch so it didn't smash and damage the glass or innards against the squat little sphinx. Standing, I looked at the man, who now had his head tilted as he checked me over. I went to him and held the watch out.

"Thank you." He smiled, nose wrinkling as he inspected the broken chain at the end of the fixing. "How careless, Matteo will scold me."

I nodded, eyes down and jaw clenched—trying to seem as unfeminine as I could in my wet shirt—and flinched when he laughed. Risking a look up, I found him with crossed arms, watch safely in one fist, and a grin. I raised my brows, still biting my tongue.

"Are you hiding from someone?" he asked.

I sighed and nodded again. He clicked his tongue expectantly, clearly a queue for me to speak. "Yes," I said eventually.

"An unusual spot to find sanctuary."

"Better than being outside with the police." And a body.

He laughed, his smile easy and quick. "I suppose so. And you're disguised as a man?"

"Men get less hassle when they travel."

"So they do. If you want to get out, the front door is through that curtain and the second door on the left. There is a little porch to pass through, then you'll be on the main street. I can show you if you wish?"

"Thank you for the directions. I hope you find your man." I bowed my head to him like I had the sphinx, walking to the curtain he'd mentioned.

"May I have your name?" I could mistake him for a fae the way he asked it, like it was a contract, something essential to get before I left. Not that they existed. Just stories for the children. I knew that. But it was such a strange thing to say that I stopped, peering at him.

"Why?"

"I should like to call it if I see you again." There was magic about him and for a quick flash, the thought he might be from one of the other schools flared. Those little glasses, hiding things. Someone had attacked the dying man in the alley. I wavered on if I should warn him, but that would reveal more, and if he was magic he'd not mentioned anything to me, either. My guard was tight.

"It's a big city," I said.

"So I'd count myself lucky if we were to cross paths a second time." Oh, that line had to be dug out from somewhere, magic or no.

"You can call me Ena. It's Scottish." It was almost true, only half a lie, and close enough that it would be believable to a man in London. There was no escaping my voice; I'd never picked up that skill.

"I thought so from your accent. I'm Addison, and I'd be glad to meet again."

I hummed, ducking through the curtain before he could speak more.

The corridor was brightly lit once you got away from the curtains, the walls rich red with more paintings dotted along them. These were mostly war portraits, the sort families kept after someone had been lost.

Slowing to examine one, I found the names; old family lineages displayed in careful script at the frame. They were born vampires—a few with names I recognised from studying the Immortal War—and my breath caught at all those golden eyes looking back at me. It had been less than a hundred years since the accords. There was no way these were relics. Someone was very bold to have these away from the families, or this was a very dangerous little shop.

I started back along the corridor, clutching my bag. The two dark doors on the left stood a few feet apart. I went to the second, opening it a crack to check what he'd told me.

A small rectangular porch greeted me, the heavy door closed and the little semicircle window above crooked open to change the air. The white-tiled floor had a circular pattern inlaid in black, a labour of love from someone.

The lock was open, so I stepped out, wrinkling my nose at how much darker it was now. I'd lost time in there, another fae thing, though the man was probably just rich. They never valued time right.

The layers of smoke in the sky made it hard to discern if it was truly dusk or simply dusty, but I made my way down the steps with one eye on the large clocks studded into the churches around the burgh. The chimes chased after each other, a joyful echo as they tripped over their own responses and signalled it was seven o'clock. I'd been waylaid, but there was still a chance some colleges would be open.

Taking a breath to settle myself, I walked down the steps, searching for more church spires to find my way. The colleges were further out than the city centre, but they were in the populated areas, and if my rough bearings were right, I wasn't too far turned around. Another alley ran beside the corner of the building, the mouth open and lit with an overhanging lantern. That should take me back to the previous street, the one leading to the alley and the square, so I could avoid any growing crowd.

I tugged my hat lower as I reached the pavement, to keep my braid in check. I should have redone it in the gallery; my scalp itched from the pins.

The sun was painting the sky as red as the bricks when I turned into the alley, which ran the full length of the strange gallery. It wasn't a good omen, but there'd already been a death and a vampire, and I was not one to look for more misery. They came in threes. It was always threes you had to watch out for.

"You took your time." A man stepped out from a doorway in the opposite wall. He was older, than me at least, and the same height, scraping six feet. He had a hard-knocked face—ruddy cheeks, a nose broken more than once—and everything about him seemed to sag, from his worn clothes to his mouth and the loping bouncing of his eyes up and down my frame.

"You waited it," I said, crossing my arms. "Do I know you?"

There was enough noise behind me I expected company, but I wasn't going to take my eyes off the grinning fool in front. Bait, but bait with bite.

"You lost me some money, getting the police to that mage. We offer a particular service, and my patron will not be happy that we've been unable to provide it."

"Dreadfully sorry to disappoint, pal, but the man was dying. Mages look after their own." I backed into the wall closest to me, so I could check each side without him leaving my sight.

"It means less money to feed my lads. I don't enjoy having to feed those who can't earn their own way."

"Maybe you should practice more charity."

He laughed, stepping into my space. I stared him down, chin up and shoulders wide so I could square up. He was broader than me, but I wasn't a small thing—that's how I could pass. I could hold my own with someone scrapping for a fight too.

"I don't find that my line of work lends itself to charity."

"Collecting kids? I think most find that charitable. Maybe you need to find some nicer ones than the jackals over there." I pointed my thumb to the three lads hanging off each other, too-thin necks craning to get a look at what the man before me was doing. One of them had a burn at the eye, pink flesh where the right orb should have sat, a shiny scar whorled with healing. There were other bodies milling around at the end of the alley, smaller boys playing lookout, but the closest three had heads perked up like dogs beside a table.

"They're all hard workers. And you've made it so they'll have to work harder to make up for the loss. How are we going to fix that?" He slammed a hand up beside my face, leaning in close enough that I could smell his breath.

I laughed, unfolding my arms so I could shove him off if I needed to. "I have nothing worth stealing. If you want my bag, it has clothes and papers in it. Nothing you'll be able to sell."

"I think my lads deserve something nicer." His hand was quick, grabbing my hat and yanking it off. The pins snagged but gave with his insistent tug, letting my braid fall. It was darkened with sweat from being under the hat, near black in this gloom. The three nearby laughed, shoving each other around as they inched closer.

"If you're expecting me to beg for mercy, you're seeking in the wrong place. Fuck off before I do something sharp."

"And what's that then, pretty thing?" His hand went up towards my neck and I bared my teeth as I caught his wrist.

"I've warned you already."

"Grant, company," a boy at the front called, running back in. "A man off the coach is coming."

He growled; wrist still in my grip. "Get in the way. This won't take long."

"We can take her somewhere else," one jackal said, a skinny thing with too much ankle showing at the end of his trousers. The red head beside him nodded, leering closer with a pecked kiss.

"I won't warn you again." I shoved Grant's hand off, scowling their way, too.

"Don't be so mouthy, pretty." Grant clipped the side of my chin, grip tightening to turn my head, and that was more than enough.

*"Teine."* Words of power slip off my tongue in a whisper, I'm that good at them. There's no need to shout them unless you're making a show of things, like when I'd screamed earlier.

Grant didn't recognise the word, but fairly began screaming when the fire started on his hand. It ran up his arm, wicking along his loose jacket, and curled lovingly around his neck and face like a cat rubbing itself against him. I shoved him away, so I wasn't singed by his flailing. I knew how these deaths went.

"Grant!" The skinny lad shot towards him, yanked back by the boy with the burned face—smart, that one—as Grant stumbled into the wall at the other side.

"Get water!" someone shouted. It wouldn't work unless they had a trough to sink him into. Grant was pushing himself up off the bricks, trying to reach out for me. I batted his hand away as the fire ate down his shape, chest engulfed and legs shaking as it raced lower.

He opened his mouth, shrieking high and angry like a pig, and the fire flooded in with his breath, lips cracking open at the seams as flames ate into the new cavity. His burning hair smelled awful, worse than usual, and I covered my mouth as I bent to pick my hat up. He was on his knees, curling in on himself as the fire rippled like the wind on water, leaping high before it extinguished all at once.

The three youngsters flinched back when I kicked him to be sure he was dead. The fire wouldn't lie, but sometimes people were hardier than expected.

"What's that?" the one missing an eye asked.

"Magic." It was obtuse, but they didn't deserve to know anything more about me. "Are you going to try to hurt me, too?"

They shared a look before bolting towards the road, not even stopping to check the body. Couldn't say I blamed them; the meat and dog smell from the burning was rotten even for this unfriendly city.

I brushed myself off, ready to make for a college again. The vampire from the alley was beside me between one breath and the next, much too quick, and his grip on the back of my head was strong. "Please excuse me, but I must ask you to talk to someone. Sleep."

The wave of influence hit me at the same time as the bricks: vampire thrall and a whack to the head. Well, that was bloody unfair.

# Chapter 3

"Did you have to hit her so fucking *hard*, Garrett?"

The ceiling of wherever he brought me was hideous. Not ugly, not neglected, actively hideous. It was done in the French style of baroque plasterwork, a scrum of wreaths and round-faced cherubs grinning down at me, but they looked like the sculptor had been in training. Someone must have enjoyed themselves in doing the plasterwork. It was too big a job to be sheer spite. The edges were undefined, or over defined, and they crowded together in an ungainly flurry of activity with squint gazes and leering mouths.

They were not unlike my abductors in that sense, with their hissed little whispers. Not at all subtle.

There were six men in the room, which was far too many, all spread out between another settee and a smattering of chairs at the far side of the space.

If Ben were here, he'd do something incredibly fucking stupid, like smash a window and leap out of it, or spit out an incantation for fire and hope it hurt them without actually checking what they were. He'd give all his advantages away by slapping his metaphorical dick on the table and be surprised when it got sliced off because he didn't know the extent of his enemy's power.

I was not going to do that, unless I really had to.

I didn't even know if fire would hurt them—it wouldn't kill them, necessarily; vampires were hardy, but it would hurt. That could be enough to buy time if I did need the escape. They only knew about the fire, too. They hadn't seen the other things I could do. I wasn't going to give them an inch until I knew what was going on. There was no reason to make myself more tempting to keep, if that's what was happening here.

Tiffany would say I should be charming until they gave me a reason not to be. For a fleeting moment I was glad I hadn't tried to talk her into running with me. It wouldn't have worked, we'd parted soft company too long ago for me to tug at her heart, and she might have turned me in, convinced I was moon-touched and a risk to myself. No point lingering on that little bruise on my heart.

Equally, I'd find no answers propped up in the corner of this settee glowering at those ugly cherubs. They hadn't bound me—that was either stupid or arrogant. Fine. I'd play nice until they didn't.

"Where am I?" The closer three jumped up from their seats when I spoke.

"Are you well, miss?" A tall man with blond hair peered over me, face pinched as he leaned closer. He was lean as a fieldworker, whippet thin, but his green eyes were full of worry. "Is your head alright?"

"It hurts."

"My apologies. It was a crude way to bring you here." The vampire stepped forward, ducking his head. Looked like the nose had been broken before—it wasn't terrible, a bump you could see amongst the freckles dotted over his rich brown skin. An experienced face.

"You clocked me one after the thieves ran."

"I saw them attack you. The man tried to grab your throat." He attempted a smile, but it didn't form. "Please, about Arif. He would have died anyway, even with help, someone had taken his organs. There was nothing you could have done."

Oh, that was either manipulative or desperate, throwing that out just when I'd woken, and I liked neither. I shoved myself back into the settee, one knee up close so I could go for my blade if I needed to. "Where am I, and why am I here?"

"He put you asleep and brought you back here for cover." The third close man stepped in, a lazy smile tugging his lips. He'd been the one asking about me being hit, by the voice. A touch taller than me, he was pale as milk and with a mess of brown hair that curled in near-ringlets, like a pig's tail. Water-grey eyes, quick despite the warm grin. "Can I check you over?"

"No, you can stay right there."

"We're not going to hurt you. I'm a doctor." The third man came closer, hands up.

I shot up, away from the seat and plastering myself against the wall to keep out of his reach. "You knocked me out."

"In Garrett's defence, he saw you set a man on fire, after nearly setting *him* on fire." The blond patted the vampire on the shoulder. Garrett was the vampire then, alright.

"I never sent the fire his way, I shot it up for attention."

The third man snorted a laugh. "Certainly got that."

"Chance, you're not helping," the tall one said, worrying his lower lip between his teeth. He crackled like he'd set alight, all nervous energy.

"I'm explaining things." That was the third man again, so he was Chance. My head span, the scrum of their overlapping words making my attention swim. Too many bodies. Were they all vampires? I could check their energy but that would show what I used, and if any of them were trained they would recognise it. Probably. That would single my school out, lose the cover of the elemental work. Was it worth it? Not yet.

"I'm Haddley, by the way. My apologies for the rudeness." The blond smiled briefly, rubbing Garrett's back. "I'd come closer to shake hands but I don't think you'd like that."

Polite, at least. "Why am I here?"

"For your safety." Chance walked closer still, hands going to my shoulders so he could twist me to look at him.

"Stop touching me," I said.

"I want your focus, petal. You're scared, and the blow could make you confused."

"Stop touching me."

"Just focus on me." He gave me a slight pull from the wall to turn me, and my head struck the dark wood.

Pain lanced out across the back of my skull, sharp as blood in the air, and my hands shot out to grab his shoulders, yanking him up against my chest as my knee landed between his thighs. He yelped as it made a solid connection, doubling over, and I sank my hands into his hair before pulling down to bounce his face off my knee in a second quick sweep.

I shoved him away and he groaned as he tipped onto the floor, hands over his crotch, and let out a disgruntled "oof" when he landed. The room went silent as I shuffled to the side, out of his reach.

It was quiet for a long beat before a new man from the cluster at the back burst into laughter, slapping his knee as he stood.

"I like her." He came over to me, hands up at his shoulders to show they were empty. He walked with the gait of a marcher—legs swinging with easy practice, his chest relaxed—and his bright red hair caught in the candlelight like a little flame. It was shaggy, thick enough that it pushed out to wavy curls as it hung at his ears. "I'm Edgar, miss, and I would love to see you do that again."

"Fuck off," Chance said from the floor. Edgar offered him a hand up, pulling him into sitting.

"If I could interrupt?" A black-haired man stepped into the centre of the room, holding his hand up as well. He was neat—hair short enough to be regularly cut, you could hide it under a hat, and his nails were clean. First of them that had that.

"By all means." Edgar stepped back, setting against the wall a few feet away from me. Giving me space. It should be reassuring, and yet...

The black-haired man came closer, smiling a little. "Garrett brought you back here because someone is hurting magic users in London. Our patron has helped other mages and is on his way back now."

"Must I be unconscious for him to assist?"

The man laughed, shaking his head. "No, but Garrett was afeared you would spark him up."

"He went for that man's blood. I don't care what excuse you're giving me, doctor or not. I know what happens with vampires and magic." This was a trap, everything about this screamed trap. Too many of them against me, even with magic. Too many hands.

"I understand you're afraid." The man inclined his head, almost bowing like I did in good company. "I'm Jonathan. I assist the house and I am human. I can't say much to make you feel better, but I can answer questions. Without having hands on you."

"You fuck off 'n' all," Chance said. He'd sat back against the wall, and was rubbing his face as if testing if I'd broken any teeth. Only one of them had said he was human.

"Fuck me, no," I groaned, covering my face with my hands so my shoulders crept up to cover my neck. This was a nest. Alright, reasonable plan was not going to work then, this wasn't a reasonable situation. I needed a way out, forget hiding my skills I needed the best ways to use them on an entire den of vampires.

"You're all behaving very poorly." Peeking through my fingers I spied the remaining man at the back, now standing, grinning like he knew something the others didn't.

He was taller than the rest, with shoulders broad enough, and barely contained by the shirt he wore, to be a worker. That had to be deliberate, showing himself off—he was too grown to be wearing the wrong sized clothes. Longer, reddish brown hair that sat in a mop over his ears shone in the lamplight, glinting as he stretched his back out.

As he came closer the lamplight showed his eyes were gold—a deep amber, almost like a cat. He was a true vampire, one of the immortals like the paintings in the gallery. That would be the head of the nest then. Walking straight at me.

I'd always thought my death would look like a woman.

"Oh hell, now one of the daddies is getting involved." Chance pushed himself up and scuttled over to the others, letting the taller man through. He was deeper toned than Chance, a warmth to his skin that spoke of sunshine and work but not the darker brown of Garrett.

"I hate it when you call them that." Haddley grimaced, going back to Garrett as the last man came to stand before me.

"My name is Tobias." He held out a hand, and I shook my head, swallowing against my fear like I could shake my voice free. I had to get out, the thrall of the sired was one thing but an immortal had the real blood magic, the sort that could compel worse than sleep. Thralled humans killed themselves if their master died; I was not about to die for anyone else when I'd just got free of my college.

Fuck that.

"I'm very sorry about all this," I said.

He shook his head. "You don't need to apologise, it's alright."

"It's absolutely not. *Adhair.*" I shot air at the human, enough to shove him off his feet and send him stumbling backwards, upending a chair as he went over.

Chance moved after him, and feeling Edgar reach for me, I shot the same at his legs, thumping him onto the floor as I launched off the wall. That made two distractions, one moving, and Garrett was putting himself between me and Haddley which was exactly what I needed him to do.

Tobias stepped closer and I ducked, muttering, *"Uisge."*

Water smacked into him, face-first because I was not letting fangs get anywhere near me, and I was shoving past him and towards the door.

Hammering into it I broke it with a word, the wood shattering out into a corridor that was lit by bright gaslight. Night-time then, maybe still the same evening, that was good.

The corridor stretched out either side and I tossed myself right out of habit, looking for a set of stairs. A big house like this—and it had to be a big house from the stupid bloody ceiling—had to have servants' quarters, which were almost always near a backdoor or trades entrance. I could shatter that and get out, get onto a road and run until I found a village or could hide.

# Chapter 4

"Fuck me, she's fast." That might have been Edgar, there was the same laugh in his voice as I shot through the corridor. It was all very beautiful—and expensive—dark red carpet to cushion the boards, large paintings, the occasional set of flowers.

Something about it felt like a warren. The broad corridor had doors leading off only on one side, and while I'd passed several windows on my left, confirming we were on the ground floor at least, there were no openings, nothing to branch the house out like a hall or a pantry.

Someone was behind me; footsteps chased my own as I finally found a large staircase and went up two steps at a time. The carpet was clearly hammered down well enough that it didn't slip under my weight charging up it, none of the flimsy rugs and pins of the college rooms.

Apparently vampires liked quality, but I didn't wish to die in a pretty cage any more than I did in a back alley.

Upstairs did nothing to dispel the impression of a warren either—the rooms all seemed to bleed into one another, the same shape of corridor snaking around the outside of the house as if there was something in the centre to be avoided. The air crackled with magic too, little motes of it sparking as I dashed through.

Servants were usually stuffed into the back or the side, something like a rear corner would be normal, so I sped past the half-open doors here and there until a large window on the wrong side of the first turn stalled me.

Why would they have a window on the inner wall?

Tugging the curtain back the answer became clear—the middle was empty. A courtyard stood where the rest of the inner rooms should be, making a house a square frame with a large arch leading out, what I presumed the back, from how I was running. I blinked at it, mind scrabbling to make it match up. No wonder the corridors were so big: it was a perimeter.

"Could you stop, so we can speak?" Tobias appeared at the top of the stairs, hair sodden from my efforts, and I ran again.

I didn't need to know why vampires made strange house-building choices, I needed out. There was an out, going by that shape, so I could get down the back stairs and be gone into the night.

Not that I knew where I was, or how safe it would be out there either, but I could take my chances with thieves and scoundrels on the road rather than fangs and thrall.

I clipped into the wall at the next corner, almost tipping over a beautiful painting that had enough familiarity to one of the Solomon Seals, and I paused, grabbing it before it fell. That was a protecting sigil, clearly worked into the painting to be effective without showing it off. It was quite well done, really. What the fuck did a vampire have that for?

Not that I needed to know; they could have magic connections, not my concern. The stairs must be somewhere nearby. I'd done two corners now and there hadn't been any other way to go at the top of the large staircase so I was almost at the opposite side of the house.

Rattling around the last one, my heart sank when I found flat wall, a large tapestry filling most of the dead end beside a small marble statue of a sphinx. It was glancingly familiar to the one from the gallery—maybe vampires liked them too—but wasn't big enough to hide behind.

The footsteps were still approaching, slow and clear so I knew he was there, and I knelt to get my heel blade out before I turned.

Stabbing an immortal wouldn't do much good, I was aware of that, I was leaning towards the Ben activities and not intelligent choices. But my choices had slammed into that wall as surely as I pressed my back against it, trying to find an option.

The rooms I'd passed ran back far enough that they'd probably have a window too, but that put me in the middle of their courtyard and I didn't know if there was a gate on that back arch. Smashing one on the outer wall would be better, though it meant embracing the fact I was going to have to do the fucking stupid thing. Gods above.

"I'm not trying to hem you in, but there's nowhere else to run. Can I come closer?" Tobias peered around the corner, not approaching.

I kept my knife up. "Why does your house have a bloody great hole in the centre?"

He laughed a little, walking slowly around with his hands up. "It's not actually my house, but it is a funny little place, isn't it? Where did you get the knife?"

"It's mine."

"Garrett will get scolded for not checking you for weapons." He stopped at the far end, not approaching.

"I'm rather glad he didn't."

"If you're afraid that we're going to bite you, I can assure you there's no risk. We abide by the accords. The nest has an agreement with a feeding house in the city, none of the sired are hungry. They won't touch you."

"Two already did. One to get me here and one to grab me."

Tobias chuckled and gave a small shrug. "And you saw him right. Chance is over friendly. Like a trail hound who falls for treats."

"I'm not one of those." I held his gaze, slowly checking his energy. I was right, about the eyes—his was an immortal energy, deep as a well. It was like standing at the edge of a cliff, peering over to hear the waves crash and hoping the ground didn't crumble away under my feet, even at this distance.

Begrudgingly, it was impressive. My college never dallied with vampires, they were the worst sort of risk; but it would be idiotic to pretend the sheer magic of it wasn't like a force of nature.

"I would say you're quite the treat, princess, but not one we'll be sampling." He winked, and I gripped my small blade tighter. Did he think he was charming? "What can I do to put you at ease?"

"Oh, if you could give me directions to the front door that would be most helpful."

"Where are you going to go?"

"Why would I tell you that?" My shoulders sagged at the banality of the question, knife dipping. This was a distraction, of course it was, but the stone at my back was solid and no one else had come around the corner.

"Fair comment. Have you been around vampires before?

"Of course not."

"I thought so, most people don't try to drown us. You'll have to get used to it if you plan to live in the city. There's more of us than up your way."

"I know you don't drown, it was to get you out of the way. I could have set you all on fire if I wanted it to hurt."

He smiled, and it was much too handsome. They were all supposed to be like that—a little too enchanting, a lure to distract someone until their throat was open and their breaths burbled with red foam. This was exactly what we were supposed to avoid.

"The owner of the house wants to speak to you, and once that's done, if you still want to leave, you can. Though I would ask you to stay the night; travel in the dark can be dangerous."

"More dangerous than being in a nest?"

"A nest that has promised safety," Tobias said.

"That's hardly a comfort. I know the stories." We all did. Mages eaten like roasts in the war, magic blood used to fuel fearsome battles. Yes, those on our side had won, and the accords were there to protect humans, but it was not wise to linger in a house of fangs.

"Of the war?" His voice was soft, and if there was a dimming in those golden eyes, I wasn't about to fall for it.

"Of course about the war. My college doesn't work with vampires, and I don't have any reason to be here. Now, I'm sure you're lovely and all, pretty face like that, but I need to leave. Will you let me past or do I need to be drastic?"

"Pretty, hm?" He laughed, almost like it was a real one, and slipped his hands into the back of his belt. "I don't know if I've had anyone compliment me while holding a knife at me before."

"You must have boring friends, then." I made for the window before he could continue, shoving the curtains back. *"Briseadh."*

# Chapter 5

The glass was cold against my hand as it fractured—spiderweb-white lacing through it like cracking ice—and then burst out, the metal latticework gnarling like angry tree branches with the force of magic. I could have knocked it out, but this was quicker, and skipped slicing up my palms as I scrabbled onto the windowsill. Drop down, buffer myself with air before I broke something landing on whatever was below, run like a mad horse.

Excellent fucking plan. Gods above.

"Wait!" Hands were on me, Tobias seeking to pull me back in as I made to jump, and I wriggled in his grip, teetering on the edge. "You'll break your neck."

"Let go!" I shoved myself forward, tipping out with all the grace of a birthing foal, and for a horridly clear moment saw the ground below like a waiting pit. My angle was wrong, even with using my air, I'd smash my shoulders in the landing.

Then, I was being grabbed, pulled against a chest that challenged the material around it unreasonably, and Tobias was falling with me.

We landed hard, and the crunch of his head into my nose was met by the crack of his ribs making noises they shouldn't.

Pain flared, hot and white and taking over my vision for a few beats as I struggled to sit up. We were sprawled on a gravel drive, the summer air cool compared to him below me, my legs tangled with his, and my blood pouring between us.

He gasped, one hand on a lump in his lower chest that had not been there before. Broken rib, at least one. That would kill someone.

I wasn't going to watch a man drown in his blood twice in one night. "Can you breathe?" I asked. He blinked at me, face pinched in pain. "I can give you air if you can't breathe, with my magic."

The scuttle of footsteps behind us jolted me out of my questions and I twisted, still on top of him, to see the other men coming around the side of the house. My blade was out of reach, glinting on the gravel a few paces away, and my head was throbbing with more than the impact. Fuck.

Tobias sat up, taking me with him and slinking his arms around my waist to keep me anchored in place, as he shook his head. "Haddley, blood."

The blond gave a little gag and ran back around the other side of the house, Garrett following him, though Chance and Edgar still approached.

"What on earth did you do? She's bleeding again!" Chance pointed at me.

"What sort of a vampire runs away from blood?" I asked.

"Haddley has a delicacy, it makes him unwell. Will you come and speak now?"

"Your man should look at your ribs." Clearly he could breathe if he could talk, and hug me for some unknown reason, but still. I wriggled in his grip and he stood, scooping me into a wedding hold that made me grab around his neck to stay in place. "Put me down!"

"My ribs are fine, they're not broken anymore. But you need to speak to Addison."

"Wait, Addison? Posh fop, white hair, fancy little glasses?"

Edgar howled with laughter, bending over himself with a bray like a donkey. "Oh gods, you have to tell him she said that. Can I tell him she said that? That's a new one!"

"Edgar, behave. You've met Addison already?" Tobias asked.

"Hush up and let me look at her, you've broken her bloody nose." Chance pushed Edgar aside as he came closer and I shook my head, pressing back against Tobias.

"It's not broken, just bleeding."

"You don't know how thick his skull is, petal, I'll have to have a look."

"I'll kick you if you come any closer. Just give me a hanky and let me bloody walk."

Tobias hefted me up a little, making me squeak, and began walking towards the house. "You heard her, let her be, Chance. Edgar, make yourself useful and bring me a bowl of water and a cloth to his study."

"Want Jonathan to bring tea?" Chance appeared at his side, fussing like a hen, and I scowled at the lot of them. I should try to run again, especially given I'd broken myself out in pretty terrible fashion.

But my face smarted, and I was feeling sick from swallowing blood, and if he wanted to drain me then he wouldn't have come out of the window with me. It would be easier to let me fall and string me up. There was a logic I could cling to there.

"Yes, I think that would be good, too. I'm surprised Addison didn't invite you back to the house directly," Tobias said.

"I left shortly after meeting him because I have places to be. Now will you please put me down?" I dropped my hips for emphasis, entirely ineffective, but he chuckled.

"I will, once we're in the study, and we can check your face."

"Jonathan's cakes are worth staying here for, if nothing else," Chance added. He stepped ahead of Tobias, opening doors for us as we went through the house again. I'd never have found the front door, evidently. While the large outside corridor did snake around the outside, there were offshoots here and there on the lower floor I'd have been lost in.

My heart sank as we went on, a pit carving into my stomach. I'd attacked first. Self-defence was a necessary act, I wouldn't apologise for not baring my neck for them, but it had been foolish to do that first, without testing if they were wanting to negotiate. Yes, it was a nest, and it was the worst place to be, but rushing to violence was reactive, not responsive. I needed to find another way to get out, and I needed to get a better read for them—to think like Tiffany, or myself, not use the lads' aggressive styles and rely on my fear so readily.

Tobias walked us around to a small door, the dark wood carved with a pair of wild-looking lions. They seemed to move in the gaslight, the detail on their manes making the shadows leap like they flapped in a breeze, and he opened it with a dip of his hip that had to be practiced.

The room was as packed as a library, and the walls were filled with a mix of books and timepieces; some whole and working, others in parts, spread out like a regiment of soldiers in training. He had clocks and dials, sand turners, pocket watches. There was a collection of calendars and candles marked out in burning segments on one of the many desks that studded the walls. Even the college had forsaken those bloody candles. It was like a museum had spilled into a spell shop.

The walls had been green at some point, from what I could see between the layers of books, and a small bed was tucked at the back of the room with a blanket folded neatly on the pillow. It was all carefully put together as a space for working; nothing standing out in the scrum of detail, so it all blurred into a natural mess.

Another hideous ceiling, too. My vantage point from still being carried like a sack of potatoes let me admire the vicious detail.

Addison, now without the gloves and glasses, his coat cast over a chair as if he'd not long gotten back, stood from a desk. He still wore the same little waistcoat, the broken chain of his watch hanging from the breast pocket. With a bewildered smile he pulled a high-backed chair from beside the fire, setting it before Tobias.

I was deposited into it with more grace than I might have given a captive, the two men standing before me.

"Ena, I didn't realise it was you. You should have mentioned her eyes, beloved, I would have recognised her immediately." Addison batted Tobias's shoulder, leaning closer to peer at me. He bent from his hips like an appraiser, and I pressed back into the seat despite myself when I caught the gold in his irises.

"You had the glasses on to hide your eyes, in the gallery. I knew there was magic about you." Another vampire. Another immortal, at that, two of them in a nest. My throat tightened at the thought of them being a pair, given the sweet name, and I licked my teeth to find something to barter with.

"Tobias, give her a handkerchief."

"Edgar is bringing a basin." Tobias did as he was asked though, passing me a little square and nodding that I could use it.

"Thank you." My shirt was sodden down the front, clinging wetly at the top of my chest, and I gingerly wiped my chin. Much as I hated to admit it, his carrying me had let the blood stop, and though I was tacky with the residue, it would have gone on longer.

I'd have left a trail going after me through the dark like a wounded deer.

"Now, lambkin, I'm terribly sorry about this. You've not had the best introduction to the house. Usually I'd welcome you first but I was waylaid in the city, I'm sorry I couldn't greet you directly." Addison stepped away, pulling two more chairs over so we were a little triangle, then brought over the table to sit next to me.

Tobias sank into one, tutting at the smears of blood on his own shirt, and smiled at me. "You threatened to kick Chance in the face."

"I didn't want him to touch me. Too much touching already here."

"Are you sensitive to vampires?" he asked.

"I don't know. You feel..." I licked the back of my teeth, struggling for the words. I could tell them the truth, but I'd already wrecked a door, a window and a shirt. Being rude on top of it all might not assist. "I'm not used to being around your energy. My college doesn't deal with you. Better to slit your throat than be captured by a nest." Should have done that with the heel blade, but I wasn't for dying yet.

"Why would you say that?" Addison came beside me, kneeling at the side of the chair to gingerly cup my face. "This isn't a place of pain."

"Gods above, take your hand off me." I pressed myself back into the seat.

He sat back too, hand up and open. I shivered as I flexed my hands, shaking them out to be rid of the feeling, stamping my foot to dispel the tingles going through my legs.

"Are you well?" Tobias asked.

I blinked at him for a furious second, the stream of curses I wanted to spit tangling in my mouth, before looking back at Addison. He wasn't only a vampire, or a kind-hearted homeowner. "You are ancient." He was silent for a beat. I sucked my lower lip in before I smiled. "Forgive my outburst. I was so shocked I forgot my manners."

It was a lie and a diversion, and a poor one at that, but I could be forgiven for being rattled. What knelt there like a cat before a fire was not just an immortal, already bad enough, but something incredibly dangerous on top of the fangs, and the nest, and all the rest.

"Sweet, you don't have to lie." He set a hand on my wrist, skin warmer than I expected from a vampire, and I knew that the sweet surge of power must be thrall. He was beautiful, undoubtedly, impossibly so. You could sketch him for years. People probably had. Gods, this had to be thrall.

"Are you sure about that?" I asked. Catching that golden gaze I could see the tiniest bit of confusion, the flicker of a flame in the wind, before it was lost to curiosity. I shook his touch free. It felt like being drunk, being around him, the swirl of power too much to keep your head above the hungry tide. I was absolutely going to die here, if I was right. Gods above.

He moved to sit in the chair before he spoke again, the pair of them like stone lions before a tomb. "Why would you need to?"

"Because we'll have to have a conversation, if I don't lie. I don't know you, either of you, beyond smashing up your house and breaking your ribs." I tilted my chin at Tobias who laughed, fingering the part where I'd seen bone pushing at.

"I smashed your nose, it's a fair exchange. Thought you'd break your neck going out the window like that."

"I had a plan." It was a bad one, but it was a plan. "You're more cautious than a broken bone," I said to Addison. His room was filled with pieces of eternity because he held more power than anything I'd found in my studies. He sang with it, a quiet strength like sand dunes shifting with a storm. I was so far out of my depth.

He inclined his head, hair falling loose a little, working his jaw like he was unsure of his own words. It made him slightly more human, which was a lie, too. "I promise I will not hurt you, whatever your fears. You must be distressed, and confused, but I give you my word I won't cause you harm."

I watched his face: the press of his lips, the small furrow at his brow. Uncertainty. I'd bet he didn't bump into that too often. "I believe you. I hadn't anticipated you would be... old. You smell like time. You're steeped in it. The room reeks of magic. I'd guess you were one of the archmages from the war, which makes you very special indeed."

Addison held very still as he looked at me, only his uncertain blink portraying anything but calm. Cold gold, not predatory but not friendly either. Tobias reached across and threaded their fingers together. "Now, lambkin, what are you that you can tell all that?"

I smiled, all teeth and nerves. "I trained at the College of Nicnevin. My skills usually keep me safe."

"Usually?" Tobias asked.

"Well, it's the first time it's landed me in a house full of fangs, but it makes my curiosity sharper. I spot things. Edgar was a soldier, Garrett and Haddley are entangled, someone's trying to be an artist going by the ceilings and the art littered everywhere." I bit my tongue to stop any more venom, shaking my head. "But none of that is the shining beacon of magic that an archmage is, so you must be very well hidden. You are a surprise."

Addison grinned, almost preening, mouth open to respond when a knock interrupted his mirth.

# Chapter 6

Chance and Jonathan came in, basin and tray in respective hands. Jonathan set about putting the tea at the little table beside me while Chance went over to Tobias.

"Your face alright?" I asked out the side of my mouth. Jonathan's eyebrows went up. "I tried to aim for the chest so it wouldn't hurt."

"I'm quite alright. Never had that done to me before." He winked and passed me a cup of tea, turning the handle of the milk jug my way before he went to pass cups to Addison and Tobias. I'd have been less ruffled if he'd be annoyed.

"Did you tell him what you called him?" Chance appeared in his place, a hand at the top of my chair and his head tilted Addison's way with a slack grin.

"No, we've been much too polite," Tobias said from somewhere behind the scrum of them.

Chance twisted on his heel, so he was half facing Addison. "Posh fop. She had your number from the off. Daddy here is the head of the nest, and all the other things, but I think your assessment's much more concise."

"She liked your glasses too, if I heard Edgar right," Jonathan added.

My face burned in embarrassment and I swirled the tea around the cup, checking for a flash of oil to betray a tincture in it. The English were always on about their tea but I wouldn't put it past them drugging a pot.

"You're both being very poor hosts. Ena may have evaluated my status from the short interaction we had at the gallery, but that shows observation skills that surpass yours."

I snorted, regretting it immediately when pain shot through my face and I yelped.

"Move yourself, Chance." Tobias nudged his way forward, setting the basin down on my lap. I kept still, holding the tea in place rigidly. "I know you said it's not broken, but we landed hard, and he'll fuss until we know you're alright. May I?"

"Let me put my guard up first. His is too much for me." I closed my eyes, pulling my energy tight like I was wrapping myself in a bundle, then nodded.

Tobias's grip was careful, holding my chin loosely while he swiped the drying blood in little semicircles that left an unpleasant buzz rather than stinging pain. The contact was sparking, certainly, but his energy seemed to flow differently to Addison's. My guard was enough to keep it challenging rather than overwhelming.

"Thank you both for bringing these, but I'd prefer to speak to Ena alone," Addison said.

"Is that with or without nursey here?" Chance asked.

"I believe you promised to help Edgar find her knife, did you not?" Jonathan asked. "To return it to you, Ena. Edgar works with a weapons shop and he thought you would like it back."

"Thank you." I tried to wave one-handedly in thanks but it wasn't the most successful effort between the tea and Tobias's careful attention.

"Shoo, the both of you." The shuffle of shoes and material told me Addison was indeed seeing them out, and I sighed, energy dropping a little.

"Tired?" Tobias asked.

I looked up at him. "It hasn't been my best day. Dead men and vampires weren't what I envisaged when I got to the city, but here I am. Smashing your windows and failing to get away."

He hummed, nodding, as he finished. It was better to not have the blood dripping there, I could admit that. "The city is a poor place for mages at the moment. Addison's been helping some. Have you been around bodies before?"

"What do you think?" I pulled my chin back, shaking him off.

He set the cloth back in the basin, resting his hands at the edge. "Not everyone does well with death."

"I'm plenty versed in it. As I imagine you two are, if he's from the war."

"We both were. Tobias fought just as well as I." Addison reappeared at his seat.

I looked between them. "Not magic, though."

"Absolutely not, I don't mess with any of that." Tobias laughed, taking the bowl away to somewhere behind me. Maybe near that little bed.

"How could you tell?" Addison asked.

"I didn't notice you, the gallery. I don't know if that was because the energy there is so unusual or if it was deliberate on your part. Here, you're less subtle, it sparks off you. His doesn't feel the same. There's the same age but none of the lightning."

"Did you hear that, beloved? I'm not often accused of being bold."

"I don't believe you." I laughed, shaking my head. "Steeped in time, a nest house full of your own, clearly magic but living in a quiet spot, that's all deliberate. If you aren't known for who you are, it's because you're careful not to be."

He glanced to his cup, looking at me under his lashes. "Is that your magic's assessment, or your own?"

"Mine." I took my cup in both hands to avoid his eyes, the weight of his question rushing into focus. They could still want to silence me. I should get to the point. "Might I speak plainly?"

"By all means," Addison said.

"I know the stories. I know what happens to mages like me, in places like this, in most instances. I don't want to die."

"War stories." Tobias appeared at one side of the tall back of the chair and I shrieked, bolting out of the seat and nearly clattering into Addison. I threw a hand up to stop myself, leaving me splayed half over him, and turned to scowl at Tobias. My teacup was in his hands, slops of fluid over the chair.

"You didn't move that quiet before."

"I was trying not to scare you. Sorry." He set the little cup and saucer on the table, all reasonable like he hadn't frightened me half to death and my heart wasn't trying to choke its way out of my throat. I sighed.

"Gods above." I wasn't sure if the tears were exhaustion or the ricochet of their energies, the swirl and ebb of them overwhelming me. I was too strung out from the whiplash of their emotional scrum, Addison's influence. I couldn't separate from their pushes and my own. "Yes, war stories. Mages bled and mutilated, passed around as pets for the immortals to fuck and feed from until nothing is left. Plucked out livers and tourniquet bound legs taken into battle to augment your magic." I hiccoughed around a sob, screwing my eyes shut. "No one wants that death. And here I am, wedged between the pair of you, no one knowing where I am because I fucking ran, nowhere for me to go because I stopped running when I saw your stupid broken rib and thought it might kill you, which of course it can't because you don't *fucking* die, and I can't even slit my neck because I lost my knife."

I pushed away from Addison's chair, covering my face with both hands. This was pathetic. I couldn't afford to have a breakdown now,

I needed to find another way to make this work, I had to get myself together.

"Princess, no, we weren't those men." Tobias's voice came closer, then he was tugging me against him. For the second time that night I was pressed into his chest and a vicious little part of me twisted with the want to shove him away, but I was so tired, and sore, and I couldn't stop the sharp push of fear in my throat. "Please don't think that's what will happen here. No one in this house would ever do so."

"If I may?" Addison stood, Tobias shuffling back a few steps with me still connected to him, and Addison came to stand before us. "Watch closely."

Addison unhooked his broken watch, setting the timepiece in the palm of his hand and the chain along the spread of his fingers. With a whisper of something I couldn't understand, and a faint glow to the gold in his eyes, the chain slid back towards the watch like a little bronze snake, the links knitting together before me, until it was whole again.

A mist of citrus and sea breeze flushed out, dusting over me, and I shivered at the blatant power. "Time magic?"

With a little smile, Addison held the watch up by the chain, letting it swing like a pendulum. "A very basic form of it, yes. You don't need to worry about the window, or the door, lambkin. I can fix all of those. No one is angry at you."

"Less worried about angry and more about murder, but thank you."

"I healed my own ribs, if that reassures you?" Tobias offered.

"You keep squashing me into them, I thought you might be testing their strength."

It was a miserable joke, but Tobias snorted nonetheless. "Such a sharp little thing, no wonder you had a knife hidden on you."

I batted at his shoulder, attempting to detangle from him unsuccessfully. It only pressed me towards Addison, making us a strange little triangle of bodies nudging together. "I'm neither little nor a thing, thank you. And I much prefer having a knife."

"A wise approach for a lady on her own," Tobias said.

"You assume I'm alone."

"You would have called for help for Arif, rather than run, if you weren't alone," Addison said. "Garrett told me what happened, when I got back."

I disliked that he was right. "Maybe my colleagues have sense not to go after vampires. Most users don't want to risk being a party favour for some kingly sire."

Tobias chuckled, his energy still close enough that I had to keep my guard up, but he was preferable to the thunderstorm of Addison. "You said that you ran. Fleeing your college?"

Shit, so I had. "That's not important. How do I leave here? If I believe you, that I'm not about to be strung up like meat, can I go?"

Addison tutted, putting his watch away. "In the morning, of course you can. I'd like to discuss if we can help you, before you go, but this is not a gaol. That's a talk better had after sleep, though, I'd suggest."

"Instead of pressed between the two of you?" I asked.

Addison tilted his head at me. "You may not have encountered it before, from what you've said, but vampires like contact. It's not suggestive, if that's your concern."

"Politely said, Addison, I'm being hemmed in by the two of you and I know neither of you. Given you two are as you are I'm not so worried about the carnal, but you're still terrifying. I'm afeared to even touch you, and he's hugged me twice despite my best efforts."

"As we are?" Tobias tilted his head now, arms still at my waist. I suppose he thought it was charming. They damn near glowed in the gaslight, skin catching the tone like a jewel. It was inhuman, an easy reminder that they were predators. Like cats cuddling up to a rabbit before they eat it. I half wondered if they'd purr with a petting, but this was not my intended escape.

"He's calling you beloved and Chance said he was the sire, so it's his best. So I suspect you're his partner, rather than a sibling or a relative. Spouse? I don't know your marriage conventions, but it seems like that. You look like you've a hook in your heart, each of you."

Addison's shoulders bounced with a laugh, barely audible, and he leaned closer to stroke my hair. "A visceral way to describe love, lambkin, but true. Though we both have dalliances with the fairer kind, too."

Oh. That wasn't reassuring, but at least I'd been right on the read of them.

"Addison." Tobias sighed in frustration, his head bumping onto my shoulder. "That's not the way to make her feel safer. Neither of us will harm you, Ena, I promise you that. The sired will leave you be tonight, and there's a separate room for you to use so you don't need to worry about proximity."

"That's less assuring when you're both hugging me." Truthfully, Addison was more hovering like a clucky hen, but still. These shallow intimacies did not soothe me like they seemed to expect.

"Are you sensitive to touch, as part of your magic?" Addison asked.

"With you, yes. It's like being a stone in the tide."

"We overwhelm you?" Tobias asked.

"Without guards, yes. And much as I appreciate your fussing, I'm not used to you. Picking up more than I should won't help. To that end, given that I've said I'll stay the night, we should set parameters." I set my hands on Tobias's shoulders, pushing him off so I could back away from both of them and have my own space.

It sent shivers through me to be away from the swirl of their energy and I backed up towards the fire, basking in the heat licking up the back of my legs. Fire, I knew. Elements were constant, a friend in the gale, and my chest loosened for the first time since I'd gone out the window.

"How do you mean, lambkin?"

"I can pick things up with my skill. Some people think loudly. You're both old, and powerful. I don't want to upset you." Or learn things that guarantee a death rather than simply risk it.

Addison hummed, stepping a little closer. "That must be distressing, to have knowledge you haven't consented to."

"Such is the way of it. You must face similar difficulties, siring folk."

"There are certain emotional overlaps, yes. The intimacies of a nest can be complex."

I smiled, glancing around the study. "Is that why your space is so neutral? To give you a safe spot to feel just yourself?"

"What a pointed thing you are."

"I'd say I'm sorry, but I can't help it any more than you can help crackling like a storm. I didn't mean offence." I shrank back a half-step, my body reacting despite my words. The ricochet of his energy was damn near physical, worse than the peat moors back in Caithness.

"No, lambkin, it's no bad thing. I hadn't expected to be laid bare so readily, but it's refreshing to fine one who can do so."

"It beats the usual fawning he gets; I'd love to see more." Tobias chuckled, stepping away to go over to the small bed again.

"Because you're a sire? They aren't too rare, from what I know of." Which was only books; I'd read everything in our library twice to be sure I could navigate the city without much trouble. Which was working out so well for me.

Addison coughed, wrinkling his nose. "I have dealings with a number of people in the city, is all."

"You're a fucking prince, love, just because she's ignorant of it now won't save you later."

"Prince?" That seemed like relevant information to present early, such as when making introductions. "What?"

Addison stepped closer, taking my hands. "It's a title by birth, not by choice. It means nothing. I'm simply a magic user now, the same as you. We don't have a system anymore, the accords did away with it. You must know that if you know other things of siring and nests?"

I nodded mutely, panic seeking between my ribs. Was this worse than being an archmage? Possibly not, but it did mean he was important as well as powerful.

"Ena. Look at me, lambkin?" Addison tugged me closer, enveloping me in a hug. He huffed a quiet laugh, stroking my hair. and I suspected it was a vampire form of showing affection, but it was charming. A little familiar, but charming. It distracted me for long enough that the screaming worry of death and blood abated. "You're very easy to hug."

"I'm sure you say that to all the ladies." I breathed in his scent. Underneath the magic and power there was something else, a subtle citrus. It was nice. The nudge of the scent warned me this was thrall again, a calming influence.

"I can assure you I'm nothing but cordial with other ladies. And you, I hope."

I risked a glance up to him, his perfect face close enough to count his lashes. "I imagine you're very easy to be cordial with, with a face like that."

"Oh?"

"You both look like statues. Much too pretty to be human. Was it the gallery that hid you, or was it you?"

"Both. I'm surprised you could sense the gallery."

"Some of the art near talked. That sphinx did, in a whispery little voice. Said it used to be worshiped."

He stilled. "You heard that?"

"Yes. It was irregular. But the magic here seems to be different to what I'm used to, so I'll have to learn about it. And whatever it is you keep doing, those little pushes of power, you should stop that."

He pulled back, frowning as his gaze inched over my face. "You can feel that, too?" I nodded and he laughed bashfully, shaking his head. "I'm sorry, then. I didn't expect it would be like that, I merely sought to ease your mind."

"How would magically influencing me make me less worried about your magically influencing me?"

"She has a point, my love." Tobias came back over, clearly having decided he didn't need to hover at the bed any longer, standing beside Addison. They made a good pair.

Addison nodded, nose wrinkled in contrition. "A fair point. It's intriguing that you can detect vampire magic itself though, rather than simply the effects of it."

"I don't know if it's unusual, you're my first immortals. We stay away from you." And here I was, hugging them, agreeing to stay the night. This was a disaster. *I* was a disaster. George would kill me twice over if he ever saw me again.

Which almost made it worth staying here, in all truth; at least death here might be quick.

Addison scrunched his mouth in thought. "Magic's like water; it always finds a way to more of itself. Yours has brought you here. I do wonder what it was seeking that it took you to Arif, too."

"Mages look after other mages. I couldn't leave him to die. Then I thought Garrett was going to finish him off, and..." The tears of before prickled again and I forced out a harsh laugh, shaking my head. "I couldn't do anything but shout at him. I couldn't give that man respect, or heal him, I could just make his death peaceful. It was so useless. But it was all I had."

Addison squeezed my hands. "And you did it anyway. Against the risk of what you thought was a hungry vampire."

"Sometimes you have to face danger despite your best wishes. Trust it will bring you right."

"I hope we can earn that trust from you." He stepped back, almost smiling. "Now, we've kept you long enough. You should have supper and take rest. In the morning we can discuss what to do next. I could introduce you to some of the mages I correspond with, I'm sure they'd assist you."

"You're being very generous. I don't have means to pay you for my stay and I don't like being in anyone's debt."

He shook his head, white hair flashing in the firelight. "Nonsense. It would be a pleasure to share your time. It may have escaped your notice, but you are the only woman here and I've missed fair company."

I faltered. "Is there a reason for that?"

"I have a female sired, but less women return to a nest after their change. They strike out on their own, experience their new selves, I cannot blame them for chasing that freedom."

My heart sang at the freedom that spoke of. "It must be wonderful being able to travel without fear. They can protect themselves so readily."

"You protect yourself quite well," Tobias said.

"Women must. While we may live lives of compromise there are certain things that cannot be given."

"Lives of compromise?" Addison repeated the phrase back like it was new to him. It probably was, with this much power.

"Show me a woman who is not living a life of compromises and I'll show you a liar. Maybe one of your vampire ladies, but I imagine they have the same thing in their own way. Rich, poor, even the undead, we must always weigh our choices. Find a path forward that harms us the least. And even then, we risk irking the wrong man and it gets us killed." I'd burned Grant without knowing who he was, because self-defence was necessary. He didn't care enough to know how I was before he threatened me.

"Sharp. I like her. You rest up." Tobias gave a little nod, patting Addison on the arm. "If you come with me, I'll take you to the kitchen for food. And a knife."

I blinked at him, sure I'd heard him wrong. "You're going to give me a knife?"

Addison nodded, tugging me closer again by a half-step. "If it makes you feel better. We have rooms that are safe for mages. There are wards to keep the magic of the house at bay, so it's easier for your own magic. You're elemental, yes?"

I licked the back of my teeth, wrinkling my nose. "Mostly." I didn't know if he could tell that I was lying, but I didn't owe him anything other than what was safe, for now, and it wasn't a lie. Heart was my real skill, my trained skill, but other than either of the vampire's emotions spilling out and overwhelming me, I wouldn't put anyone at risk.

"Mostly is enough. Now, come here." He tugged me close again, turning me in his arms so we dipped like dancers. I let out a delighted shriek of laughter, clinging to him as we stood back up.

"Where did that come from?" It was so silly I couldn't help but laugh, and his smile reached his eyes this time.

"You're a menace, my love." Tobias sighed, shaking his head but his smile was clear too.

Addison tutted at him, stepping back. "I wanted to see if I could make you laugh. And show I'm not upset. Now, much as I would enjoy keeping you here further, you need to eat, and sleep."

"Thank you for the hospitality. Tobias, can you let me walk this time?"

He folded his arms in mock thought, smirking at me. "Will you threaten to kick me in the face if I pick you up?"

"Yes." I nodded.

"Walking it is, then."

# Chapter 7

The corridor was like walking into sunshine, skin tingling at the contrast between Addison's little pool of peace and the rest of the house. It was only noticeable after the absence, but it spoke of the power of his enchantments. I'd be interested to see if the rooms were the same. At least until I could run. There had to be a catch, some price, even if it was not being stated plainly yet. Maybe it would come in the morning. I would simply have to survive the night and see what they sought tomorrow. Costs always fell due.

It was different to the college, or the houses I visited—they were never as soaked in magic as it was here. It could be nice not to hide my magic all the time. Not that I was doing a good job of that anyway. I probably sounded like a horse stomping through if they were all as quiet as the immortals.

"What are you pondering?" Tobias asked as he led me on.

"The magic here. I saw some sigil work upstairs too, it's all different sorts."

"Surprised you noticed it with how fast you were going."

I laughed, shaking my head. My nose grumbled with pain but it was passable now, no fresh blood since he'd tended my face. "That doesn't seem like a compliment from you. You didn't get from the corner to the window in that short a time without your following me being deliberately slowed down."

"We can move quickly, yes. I didn't want to frighten you, so I made myself obvious. Was that wrong?"

"The consideration is sweet, the execution lacking. Especially when you then pop up behind me like a ghoul in a kirkyard."

He laughed at that, clear as a bell in the night, and even if I disliked this place, that was a nice sound. It twisted in my chest like back home. "It must be scary, here. For you."

"I've been scarier places, but nests are to be evaded at all costs. We'd abandon a job, in some instances, if there were vampires." It wasn't often the college was willing to drop coin but vampires meant risk and risk was to be avoided.

"I suppose it makes it a safe place, if you're running from your... colleagues? Brothers-in-arms? Friends?"

I grimaced, folding my arms low across my abdomen. "Are they friends if you've just been pushed together by training? I don't know. I grew up with them and I know them but we're all just tools to the college." I loved them too, but not in the right way, and that was a noose about my neck.

"I think sometimes it can be both. Addison and I trained together, before we were together. I don't love him any less for that."

"That's sweet. I imagine not everyone was so lucky as to come back with their love."

He hissed air, sinking his hands into the back of his belt again. "No, there were a lot of losses. We lost another."

He stopped, covering his mouth for a moment. His chest wavered as he spoke, remarkably like crying. Shit. Crying men meant unsafe women, in my experience. Crying men led to beatings and revenge if you weren't careful. How did one diffuse that with a vampire? What was comfort to an immortal creature? They'd been all over me earlier, in an offer of comfort, maybe that would work?

After a quick couple of breaths, I stepped closer and hugged him low around the waist. That brought his chest against mine with no skin touching, my head planted on his shoulder. He stilled, rigid in my grip.

"I didn't mean to upset you," I said. I did not trust those cat-yellow eyes, but real or fake, the tears were there. "Sorry, I sounded callous. Pain is pain."

"Are you so aggressive with everyone you hug?" he asked.

"I don't usually hug new people. But you tried to comfort me with it earlier, so I thought it might help." It's what you would do with a human, at least. It's what I did to the children in the college. I didn't know about a vampire. They might rip your throat out in a temper.

I held still, silently begging him to speak.

"Are you concerned for me?"

"I'd be worried about anyone in pain. Kindness is a short currency."

"What an odd creature." He pet my hair, making me frown at him again.

I licked the back of my teeth before I asked what lingered on my tongue. "Was it another someone you both loved?"

"Yes. Is that scandalous to you?" He grinned but I knew those half smiles, barely keeping teeth back, like a beast in pain not wanting to show it had a wound. I wasn't going to sink my fingers into anything bleeding again tonight.

"Love has a lot of flavours. We need all sorts of love. If yours had more before and is now two of you, that must hurt. Bittersweet, perhaps is the word." I shrugged. "It's not my business, sorry I pressed."

"You speak like someone who yearns."

"It's natural, to want to find the love that suits you."

"Have you left someone behind?" His voice was soft, a gentle enquiry rather than pushing for an answer.

"I haven't found a type that suits me. Which is fine, I have time yet. That probably sounds ridiculous to you, tumbling around forever, but still." It was the truth, mostly. It was my truth. Ben would disagree. "Anyway, Addison said you both liked variety so I imagine that's more common when you don't die. As long as all involved know the agreement I don't think I have a place to judge."

"Very modern for a school that hates us."

"I'm not judging how you love, that's hardly groundbreaking."

He frowned a little, eyes tracking over my face before he nodded, stepping away and starting to walk again. "Can you eat, with your face hurting?"

"It's not so bad now. My nose got broken as a wee one and the cartilage got smashed up. Now, outside of a cracking punch, it'll swell then go down again. Your thick skull won't have managed that much."

He kept his eyes carefully forward. "That would have been a hell of a hit, to do that to a child."

"It was."

He frowned, nodding a little. "I'm glad to hear it won't have broken now. A sandwich, then, maybe, not too heavy on your stomach? Addison will feel better if he knows you've eaten something."

"He's fussy?" It wasn't that I didn't expect it, given his little pushes to make me feel better, and hosting a nest, but it seemed irregular for a war mage. They weren't known for warmth.

Tobias chuckled, the sound a rumble against my side. "He's a mother duck, dotes on those under his care. Thinks he can make up for old harms by putting new good into the world."

Ah. Guilt was always one of the treasures of war. "I'll try not to worry him."

"Good. And I'd prefer you used the door in the future, rather than leaping from windows."

"I did ask you for directions."

"At knifepoint, after calling me pretty."

I'd slap him next time. "Oh, aye, I bet you have no problem with that."

"How do you mean?"

"Pretty-faced man like you, immortal and smart? There's no way you don't have acres of invites from eligible young things."

"There's certainly attention, doesn't mean I welcome it. You, however, are certainly welcome to fling yourself on me whenever you like."

# Chapter 8

We had reached the kitchen, dim from the dying fire and low candles, and he pointed me to a chair.

"You grabbed me, if I recall." I went to the nominated seat, beside a large kitchen table

"You were falling out a window, I think that sets us on equal footing."

"Jumping out of a window, until you caught my shoulders and threw my angle off." It was sullen, and I was being rude, neither of which befitted my training. Manners until you knew they weren't worth it.

"Your angle was off. You'd have snapped your neck."

"You sound like a doctor."

"There's three here, if you consider academic as well as medical. Chance was one before he turned, still works. Haddley's a scholar. Garrett trained with the army." He stepped away, rifling through cupboards like a bee among flowers.

"How about you, you just lurk around here looking pretty?"

"I'm the one trying to be an artist. I did Addison's door, and the little sphinx I saw you debating throwing out the window."

"It looked heavy." Those were impressive feats, to give him his dues. I hadn't pinned him as an artist.

"It is, I'm glad you used the magic. Haddley will want to talk to you about it, he's enthusiastic about magic."

"How much do you know about magic?" If there was one archmage, there could be more. He'd said he didn't truck with it, but not practicing was different to not knowing.

He didn't turn, still gathering pieces of things to a long table near a backdoor. "A little bit but nothing like enough. I've read a lot, and I'm always curious, but I never sought to practice. Addison is tricky enough without me wandering into that as well."

"Reasonable. Your magic is different to ours."

"How do you mean?"

"Well what humans draw on will be different to what vampires do. Your souls will be... hrm. I wonder." I closed one eye, trying to see if I could spy any hint of an aura on him. Nothing, too much pain to focus properly.

"What do you wonder?"

"This is complicated but simply put, most souls are the same but not all of them. I wonder if yours, as in vampires, are different. Either way what you get in touch with for magic would be different to what I do."

"Does it have to be?" he asked.

"Probably. Training fixes you on a certain path, for how you access it, it's hard to break out of that once you're established. It's part of why untrained users are dangerous, nothing to structure or anchor them." Like my words of power being forbidden at the college.

"And trained users run away from their colleges because...?"

"Because of things I'm not going to tell you."

He nodded, setting to make the sandwich. There was a careful distance about his movements—avoiding hemming me in like they had in the room I awoke in. "That's fair. If there's anything you would like to share, or ask, you can do so. I know Addison and I feel like a threat to you, but we're not, and if there were indelicacies you wanted to share, I'm less scary than him."

Ha! "Such as?"

"You haven't asked much about Arif."

I half watched him move around the table, stomach twisting at his comment, Tobias whistling to himself as he worked. The busy display let me turn a question over in my mind a few times, until I settled on what I was comfortable asking.

"About him." Tobias stilled, nodding for me to continue. "Who was he to you all?"

Tobias hummed, turning to look at me, sandwich pieces abandoned. "He stayed with us a while. He was a powerful mage in the city, high up in one of the madras colleges, and he and Addison shared correspondence. When he needed somewhere to stay due to a conflict at the college, he got a room. Addison always finds a room."

"I'm sorry for your troubles."

"You tried to help."

I had, but it felt very little in the reflection of things. "I don't even know if he was there, really. I thought I'd get him to a healer."

"He'd had organs removed, princess, you couldn't have done anything more. Garrett couldn't have done anything, even with his training. If there was any of Arif left, he would know people were fighting for him." He went back to making the food and I sat with the answer, heavier than the blood I'd swallowed.

"You said there'd been others."

"Yes, a few. None as well-known as Arif. His loss will shock people."

"Did you know the others?"

"No. This is our first loss of a human in a long while."

"It's not news outside of the city. Not enough to reach us, at least. Prejudice against mages isn't new, but usually the training gives you a level of protection." Memories of water and screaming stirred, and I pushed them away before they could get a hold.

"People have always killed people for a variety of terrible reasons. I watched it with the war, same as others in the nest did in their own wars. You did all you could to help, that's all that can be asked from anyone." He brought the plate over, setting it on the table beside me.

"Thank you."

"Let me see your face." I looked at him, taller than me, given I was sat down, and he winced a little before he nodded. "You're bruising up, but otherwise your nose looks normal."

"Charming." I took the plate, setting it on my lap. "I'll look like a ghoul tomorrow, I always bruise easy."

"Sounds like you have experience."

"Do you think I'm sent in as the charmer in my school, looking like this?" I indicated my shoulders, the broad span of them in the white shirt. "Of course I'm used to bruising. It'll fade off, it always does."

"What sort of school beats its children?"

"I'm twenty-seven, I'm not a bloody child." I laughed, half choking on a bite.

"You weren't when you trained, though."

"Aye." I swallowed, eating a few more bites before I spoke again. "It's a hard thing to learn, for some of us. I was always too wild for it, truthfully, but I'm also very good, so they kept me. What's a few beatings in the face of excelling at a skill?"

I didn't believe it, and from the way he looked at me he knew that too, but he shrugged. "Well given you knocked half of our lot over with a few words, you clearly took well to it."

"Course I did. Do you want to see a trick?"

I was being foolish, this was an old yarn I span when I was tired or nervous, but it didn't exactly put me at risk.

"Of course. I'm always curious."

"Alright, stand there." I stood, stepping away from the table to stand straight as a railing, my arms by my side. Visualisations were good for teaching younger students; this wasn't too far from that. I closed my eyes, picturing my energy and the leaping, bright sparks of it looming around me. Careful as I could, I began to wind it towards me, drawing it closer as I pulled it into my centre and hid the jumping light. It was blue now, almost a turquoise, which meant I needed to rest.

"That's quite the trick," Tobias said. I opened my eyes to find him close, staring at me like I'd grown a second head.

"What does it look like to you?"

"It's like... it's like you're retreating, even though you're sat still. Like you make yourself shrink."

"Yes. I'm shrinking my energy in, holding it close. That's a way to hide in a crowd, or keep your energy close to make sure people can't tell what school you're from."

"Did you need to do that a lot?"

"We're..." Well. No real way to phrase that nicely. "It's better to blend in when you don't know someone's allegiance. And my work was such that blending in made me more useful. People say all sorts of things when they don't know you're there, it's easy to get a sense of their loyalties that way."

"You're very careful with your answers." He took my plate, taking it to a basin.

"What's a girl to do when she lands in a strange house, surrounded by vampires? Escape wasn't a roaring success, so may as well be curious."

"Instead of?"

"What would you have me do, beat my breast and scream and cry? How much do you think that gets someone like me? I've already let emotion overcome me once tonight, I don't need that again."

He twisted on his hip, resting against the table as he looked at me. "Are your feelings only good if they get you something?"

"I don't know, how do the dark nights of the soul serve you?" It was a sharper comment than he deserved, but he laughed.

"I have a long time to come back out of them."

"Humans don't have the luxury of time in that way. Bright sparks fading out, and all that."

"So cynical for a young one." He tutted, shaking his head.

"I'm going towards thirty. And I don't think it's cynical. Our time is too short and too long—joy flees, and regrets linger. That's why you have to cling onto it with both hands."

"That's more like I would expect to hear. Some agency in your life."

"I hardly feel like the master of my fate when I've wound up abducted into a nest."

"Understandable. But quite the story to tell."

"Assuming I'm so lax with my stories. No secret is free, I'm sure that's the same for immortals as mortals. If anything, the stakes are worse for you."

"How so?"

"Worst-case scenario, I die in the pursuit of knowledge. You don't have the luxury of death, you're stuck with the consequences of your actions."

"Quite right." He winked, a flash in those gold eyes. "Come, get a knife, and I'll show you to your room."

I went to join him and he offered me a selection of blades. Someone clearly took care to sharpen them, I'd gone out on work with blunter equipment, and I picked a shiny little paring knife that I could slip up my sleeve. "Thank you. I'll endeavour not to use it but I like having it."

"I'll tell the pups you have it, but try not to scare one of them out of their wits."

"There's things I could do to really spook them."

"Such as?"

"You want me to do something to you?"

"Depends what it is." Tobias stuck his hands in his pockets as if this was the most reasonable statement he could have made.

"I know I didn't set you on fire before, but it is still an option."

"How did you do it?"

I blinked at him. "The fire? Words of power. Useful in an emergency."

"Like someone accosting you in a dark hallway, or giving me air."

"Usually it's for something more immediate, but yes. I think it would work for vampires as well. It might not kill you, it's not magical in the real sense, but fire's bound to hurt." He laughed, shaking his head as he looked at me. I tried to smile, but I was too tired, and it probably came off as forced. "I think I'd best head to bed."

"I think so. Come on, I'll escort you." Tobias reached out and put an arm around my shoulders, pulling me closer for a moment. "It's been a hard day for you."

"Thank you. For ensuring I didn't break my neck."

"Least I could do. Do you have anything else to wear?"

I frowned at him, then down at my shirt. "No. I have a scarf I could make into a skirt in an emergency."

"Here." He tugged his shirt up over his head, handing it to me. "Mine's got less blood on it than yours."

"That's considerate. I would feel guilty taking this as well, though." I held his shirt. It was still warm from his skin, like Addison had been earlier. I didn't expect them to be warm, vampires, for some reason.

"I'll have it back when you're sorted."

I hummed, and the dull throb of pain it made was unfortunate. "Alright, then."

When we reached what was to be my room, he held the door open, pointing to the bedside table.

"There's a key there, and the doors are sturdy. If you want to feel a little safer you can lock yourself in."

"I know how to bar a door. And if a vampire turns himself into fog and comes through the keyhole, I'll throw a damp towel over him, too."

"We can't do that. Do they think we can do that in your school?"

"Some people do. Thank you, again, and good night."

"Night, princess."

I closed the door and grabbed the key, locking the mechanism. The metal slid into place with a reassuring click, loud in the quiet of the room.

It would not do to linger. I had to evaluate matters. I knew the next steps—secure the perimeter, get a safe spot to sleep, waken early and make a plan. No point churning my mind into the mood with trying to make much of a plan now, I was fit to drop.

Turning around, I was welcomed by a very neat, if much too grand, room. It had a large bed with a trunk at the end, beside a long row of windows which provided a view of the darkness outside. A dresser with a small mirror sat at the wall opposite the door, with a chair in front of it, and two wardrobes took up the back wall with a set of long, deep drawers in between. Any guests would be well catered for here, it was clearly intended for more than one person.

A peek into the bathroom, where a large tub and toilet took up most of the room—they even had pipes. Better than a lot of the big houses back home, they still needed water carted in. This was good. The tub was good: I could sleep in that and press my shield out, that would let me know if anyone was coming in. For all their assurances, and I did feel better for the knife, I still wanted to be safe.

I took a pillow and the cover into the bathroom, making a nest in the tub. The sides were high, making it deep enough that I couldn't be seen if the bedding didn't give me away, and the little window was broad enough for me to squeeze out of if needed.

I dragged the chair over, propping it underneath the door handle so it couldn't be opened even if someone else had a key. It was an old trick, one born of travel and the need for privacy. Little barriers to keep myself.

I lingered to inspect the wards. Carved into the doorframe, the marks were not Solomon Seals, they were more the madras school's work: a fluidity to the intricate lines that spoke of organic growth. Vines and brambles, not shapes and formula. I tapped them, smiling at the little pulse of power they gave in response.

He'd been honest about that, then. They were protection marks, as the painting had been, and they were a buffer. A barrier between the room and vampire magic, and all the seething, steeping, lingering parts. Interesting.

I turned, searching around for a candle to mark the bathtub with. Between my own wards and those in the room, I might be able to sleep. Maybe I could put a glass at the edge of the bathroom door, so it would break if someone opened it too.

# Chapter 9

I awoke with the light streaming into the room, the dawn a bright and easy thing in this strange new house. I let myself blink into the vibrant sunshine for a few minutes, still scrunched up like a body in a coffin, trying to pull awareness back together. My little nest had lasted the night, and I was swaddled well, though my legs ached to stretch out.

A small rectangular window was on the wall above me, brightly lit by the daybreak, but part of it was blocked by a shape. Rubbing my eyes I tried to focus, sitting up so I could peer closer.

My heart spiked as I realised what the large, rounded shape was, tapering into a thinner, stalk-like part that disappeared below the edge of the windowsill. It was a head.

Someone was outside the window.

We were a storey up.

I struggled up into standing, nearly pitching over the tub until I caught myself on the edge, and the head vanished down before I could disentangle myself to open the window.

Staggering out of the bathroom, I went to the long window of the main bedroom. In the cool dawn I could see a long drive of gravel and dirt stretching out from the yard, and trees lined the far-off boundary as well as a thicket or wood to one side. There were some closer too, drooping willows and decorative hedges whose teased shapes betrayed the effort put into them.

Someone was stomping off down the track. I couldn't see who it was—too far off—but they were tall, and the hair could have been red, or that could be the sunlight.

One of the sired was red, if I remembered them right. Edgar, the soldier. Impressive if he'd managed to climb a floor up to check I'd not run. That would have to be asked about.

I shook myself out of my musings, going through to the bathroom to wash up. I passed Tobias's shirt and smiled, trailing my fingers over the material. Not the most auspicious of meetings, but it was sweet of him to give the shirt off his back after I'd broken his ribs.

After washing and debating how corpse-like I looked with the bruising already blooming across my face, I dressed in the shirt Tobias had given me, checking how low it sat on me before I pulled my trousers on too. It could have been a dress in the dormitory, possibly a bit too shocking for this household. I didn't know their levels yet, better to play careful with the sired. The immortals would have seen worse, no doubt, especially given their comments about broad horizons.

I braided my hair up as normal and ventured out, pocketing the key and aiming for the kitchen. After a few steps I pulled my guard up, the magic of the house floating past me like seaweed in the tide. Best not to get tangled.

No one else was in the kitchen when I arrived so I set about making my own breakfast, slicing some bread to make a sandwich. I would even consider venturing into some of the cold meat.

I had a kettle boiling on the stove when someone else appeared, a tall form filling up the doorway in the edge of my vision, and I flinched away in habit. I turned to find Addison there, frowning slightly.

I coughed to try and hide my embarrassment, squeaking more than I'd like. "Good morning. I have the kettle on, would you like something?"

Addison remained silent, stepping into the room and slowly coming closer. The small frown deepened as he stopped in front of me, fingers catching my chin to tilt it up towards him. He studied my face, the shadows of blue and purple snaking under my eyes, and angled me lightly this way, then that, to get a better view. I held still other than following his motions, the weight of his scrutiny being matched by a similar one in the pit of my stomach, the only balm that his energy fizzed, but did not rush. A concession to my fear.

The heat rose in my neck and cheeks as he clicked his tongue, eyes darkening. "Addison?"

"Your bruising is quite substantial."

"It'll fade off."

"Did you sleep at all?"

"Yes, your bathtub was excellent. There's wax on the outside now, but that will come off, I didn't carve anything in." The knife was in my back pocket, but he knew about that. That should be alright.

"You slept in the bathtub?"

"Bed could have been vulnerable, and it's bare on three sides. Bathtub is only bare on one. Though someone seemed to be peering in the window when I woke up, any of your lads fly?"

"Haddley makes attempts, though the results have been lacking. Did you really sleep in the tub?"

"Truly. You can go and check the tub if you wish, I've put the bed back together but the wards will still be on the metal. What has you so vexed about it, you must have had other mages being cautious?"

His brows pinched. "None quite so dedicated to their fears."

I laughed, licking the back of my teeth to keep my immediate response in. "I'm certain their schools were less afraid of you. Can you take solace in the fact I didn't leave in the dark? I could have got out that bathroom window."

"I suppose I must. Would you sleep in my room, in the bed you saw last night?"

I blinked at him, pulling away to take the kettle from the heat when it began to whistle. "Did you just ask me to get in bed with you?"

"The bed in my study, it's a spare. Well, I sleep in it sometimes, but it's not my main bed. It's beside a wall, if that would feel safer for you? I could get you some other clothes while you sleep. Much as Tobias's donation suits you, you should have your own." He said it so simply.

"I can't repay you."

"You don't need to. It's a gift. An apology for lack of care, given you were so frightened."

I was still frightened, but at this rate I was going to die of concern rather than being bled like a hind in the hunt. "I would appreciate it, since I'm lacking other outfits until I find somewhere else to stay."

"We can see to that this morning. When it's a kinder hour."

"What time is it?"

"A little after five o'clock."

Oh no. "I hope I didn't wake you?"

"Not at all, I'm an early riser."

"Someone else must be, given the company at the window."

"They might have been checking on you, if the bed was empty, though most of them are still in bed."

"Most?"

"Some go off early. I don't keep a leash on them, they're free to come and go as they please."

"You're better than many, then. Are you sure I can't tempt you with some tea?" I nodded to the kettle, sat cooling. Addison said nothing, watching me carefully like I would vanish. "Are you alright?"

"I'm concerned," he said after a brief silence.

"What troubles you?"

"You."

I raised my brows at him. A pot of tea was going to be necessary, evidently. I turned, finding one big enough for both of us and taking two cups from the cupboard I'd seen Tobias root in last night. "And why am I prompting your concern?"

"Things Tobias said, about your discussion last night."

"Worried I'm not human? I'd say take a bite of me to check, though I imagine that would be considered rude. My blood must smell human."

"Not that, sweet. Can you look at me?"

If it was fear that lingered at the base of my back, at his question, I would shake it off like a wet cat. I was still myself, not some pitiful stray. "Can I make the tea first?"

"Of course."

I fished a small jug out for some milk and found sugar cubes at the front of the cupboard, setting both on the counter before I gave the pot a final stir. Once the tea smelled right, I poured us both a cup, pushing Addison's his way.

"I like strong tea."

"I'm sure it will be lovely. I want to ask you some questions, if that's alright. You don't have to answer if you don't want to, but they are coming from my concern rather than anything else."

My stomach twisted at his tone, but I met his gaze. "You could have me worried."

"Tobias said you told him your nose couldn't be broken."

"It was broken when I was a child. You can push right onto the bone; the cartilage is wrecked."

"That takes quite the strike. Were you hurt?"

A vicious grin pulled at my face, all teeth, and I took a sip of tea to wind myself back in again. He was not asking out of malice or this would be more pointed. He did not know what a sharp tool I could be; it was natural to be wary. "What are you asking?"

"Did someone hurt you, and your magic manifest?"

The angle of his questions suddenly crystallised, and I choked on my tea as I tried to suppress a laugh. "You're worried I'll react instinctually with magic if I get spooked? Not be able to control it?"

Addison inclined his head, a small smile on his lips. "Not solely that, but yes. We are a house where there could be unfortunate consequences. Vampire magic can be reactive, that's why I have the wards on the guest rooms."

"Much as my magic protects me, it is very much mine to use. I was trained well."

"Did they hurt you?"

"Very much so. But I'm not there anymore." I brought my tea up to my chest, holding the cup close as a shield while I drank a sip.

"I'm sorry that was the case."

Much good that did me. "My thanks for the sentiment. I don't find much solace in dwelling on it."

"No. Should you wish to speak on it, your company is welcome in my study."

"Are you a priest as well as a prince?"

He laughed, head tilted back as he shook it. "No, thankfully. The immortals don't have religion in quite the same way."

"Are you really a prince? I know your lot had royalty, but it all stops with the accords. The records are secretive about what happened, other than that your old king is sleeping under the mountains, but he's pretty much just a legend now. Same as humans have King Arthur as a legend."

"The old sleeping king would be my father."

I blinked at him, hoping it was a joke. There was no laughter. "You're the prince? The one that stepped back?" Not 'a' prince, not some bastard who was living well off a wise mother who bedded a king, '*the*' prince who went missing after the war. That was excellent blackmail material to know, in most instances, it would get me through many doors. I didn't think there was much point on that in a house where they could just kill me, but it was useful.

"Would that be a bad thing?" His voice was so soft. I hated that, felt it turn over in my gut like disgust. It wasn't at him, though—I'd not room to blame someone for regret.

"It would be a big fucking surprise. I'd expect a prince to have more... I don't know. Fanfare. You snuck into that gallery the same door I barrelled through, and I'd run from a body. You don't seem fancy enough to be royalty."

He laughed, taking my cup of tea from my hands and tugging me into a quick hug. "What a kind thing you are, separate to all that bite."

"You can put me down." I patted his back uselessly like a seal on a rock, entirely ineffective as I was squashed into his waistcoat. Different pattern today, he must like those.

He did so, still gripping my shoulders. "Thank you. I was concerned you would be afraid of us. Or hurt."

"Less hurt than I would be elsewhere, I assure you." Much less than if the college found me and took me back. I'd never be forgiven for landing here, of all places.

He seemed satisfied, giving a little nod and picking up his tea. "I trust your knowledge of that."

"Thank you. Though I probably should get some sleep if it's still that early. If your spare bed is free, I'd take it. Or a settee. I can curl up on one of those no bother."

"You can use the bed, lambkin, it's alright. Consider it a thanks for being so gracious about my circumstances. Not many are so calm about my previous position."

I raised a brow at him. "It's only fair. I believe in being fair."

"I believe in being more than fair when I can. And I intend to be, with you." Typical rich-man mentality, even in an immortal, underline their excess. At least he was nice with it.

"That's kind of you. I'm in your debt already."

"None of that." He stepped closer to me, catching my fingers and tugging my hand close to press a kiss on my knuckles. "I've welcomed you into the house. You are one of my guests, and under my protection. Even if only for the night."

Our eyes met, his lips still brushing my skin. The room was full of a low tension, a mix of my upset and his agonising gentleness. I believed it came from a good place, this softness that was so unnatural it set my teeth on edge. I did. But one could never trust so much being given freely, there was always a cost, somewhere. He pulled up, still keeping hold of my fingers. "Thank you."

"Are you alright?" he asked.

I blinked away the unease. "Yes. Tired, you were right."

"Of course. Shall we go back to my study?" Tobias was right about him being fussy. It made sense, as the master of a nest—they were all like cats, if you believed the stories, in both their affection and their cruelty.

"That would be lovely, then. And do you have any arnica cream, or witch hazel? It won't make the bruising vanish, but it will help get it out of my skin sooner," I said.

"I'm uncertain if we have those but will check with Jonathan, or Chance may have some in his rented room in the village. If not, we can procure some. Now, shall we? It would be best to go now before the others awaken."

"So we don't disturb them?"

"And so they don't see you in Tobias's shirt. Between that and your escape attempts, I think the household may combust with curiosity." He offered me his arm and I took it, walking to his study.

# Chapter 10

The fire was cooled, only ashes and the faint scent of smoke, but the sunshine illuminated all the timepieces stood around the walls. The sands slid quietly in the hourglasses, the barest glint of lights reflecting off the grains in a sparkling curtain. The clocks clicked together like a small army marching.

"Why so many ways to keep time?" I asked.

He bit a lip in thought, eyes going over the rows of them. "All of them are to do with my magic of some variety, though most indirectly. Marking the passage of time becomes a stronger ritual when you can donate time more freely than a human could."

"I said to Tobias I thought it would be different for vampires."

He caught my hand again, giving my fingers a light squeeze. "If you would like, I can work in the library."

"I'm not going to chase you out of your study, for goodness' sake."

I shook my head at him, going to the little cot. It was barely larger than a dormitory bed, tucked snug into the corner of the space, and would be fine for me. It probably fit him, though I wondered about his height. He was certainly over six feet tall, just about, but maybe he slept curled up. The thought was sad, but it was not my problem to take on.

"Eyes front for a minute." I glanced to him as I said it, judging his stance. I was not blind to the fact I was alone with him, getting into a bed, with no one likely to challenge the head of the house. He did as I said, looking away, so I slid my trousers off and folded them up. The knife went under the pillow in sharp reassurance. "Thanks."

"You're welcome, oh my—" I turned to see he had looked around and then covered his eyes.

"You alright?"

"I had thought you were done changing."

"I am. This shirt's long enough to wear as a tunic, seems alright to sleep in." He brought his hand down, glancing at my legs before he looked to my face. I would swear there was a blush up on those high cheekbones. "You're an immortal. You'll have seen much more daring things than a set of legs."

His face twitched between a few different expressions before he settled on giving me a small nod. "I'm flattered you consider me so experienced. However, for my peace, could you retain the shirt?"

"That was my intention, yes."

"My thanks. If you can't sleep, or if you need anything else, let me know."

"Thank you." I smiled before I slipped into his bed, cool enough to let me know he hadn't been in it.

I wrapped myself in the covers, wriggling lower to tuck in close into the wall. Always better to have something solid at my back, be it a person or a pillar, and despite my earlier fears, it was easy to get my breathing regular and even.

I would drop away if I made myself do this long enough—kept still and breathed deep—tricking my body into something like safety. I trusted that with him, the same way I trusted the lock in my door. Maybe I should have put a chair under him, just to be sure.

I was beginning to get the hazy tendrils of sleep around me when I heard the door open, immediately followed by a shush.

"I have company," Addison said, voice soft as a prayer.

"In your bed? Addison, I'm scandalised." There was more of a laugh than shock in Tobias's voice.

"She was in the kitchen before the larks. I wanted to know she had rested at least a few hours before we establish if she'll be staying. She slept in the bath last night, rather than trusting the bed."

I did my best to keep my breathing even, taken aback at the frankness of Addison's words. There was a sweetness to the open worry.

"Smart lass. I don't think she'll stay. Sounds like she's from one of the stricter schools, it can be hard to break out of that structure."

"You mean the gaols."

Tobias made a non-committal noise, walking closer to the bed. I kept myself still, breath as smooth as I could manage. "Her poor face."

"She asked for arnica cream, to help with it."

"That should work. She hinted bruising wasn't unusual, but still."

"She confirmed they hurt her in her studies. If it's anything like with some of the others, I don't expect her to lay it bare for us when we're still strangers."

The experienced tone in Addison's words made my chest lurch. I knew he'd been handling me gently in the kitchen but my heart thudded that he was aware of the college's tactics. It made sense, the vampires were as ancient as our powers. But it didn't mean I liked violence against me known.

"Well, I won't go prying unless she offers. She was careful with us, we can offer the same indulgence."

"Indeed. She asked about me."

"And did you tell her?"

"Yes."

I assumed it was Tobias who whistled. "Feeling generous?"

"She knew enough of us that it felt appropriate to share."

"You are notable, beloved."

"Hush, you menace."

They had to be married. It was almost sweet. I turned over in the bed to avoid laughing, or them seeing anything on my face. Back to the room and face to the wall was less safe, but I also knew it was rude to listen in like I was.

"Did you speak to her about travel, today?"

"Not yet. Though she assured me she was fully trained, so there shouldn't be any danger in making introductions. I question if my clumsy enquiries were much help, she was far ahead of me when she realised why I was asking."

"If she knew that then she'd know it was for safety. Same as we assure people we won't bite them. It might sting to have to say it, but new meetings mean new warnings." I may have hated that Tobias was right in that regard. If I'd had the energy to hate things. But the bed was soft and warm, and their voices were a surprisingly gentle lullaby.

"I hope you're right."

"Careful, Addison, you could sound fond." There was a sing-song to Tobias's voice that made me certain they were together, a willingness to needle that was full of such affection. I could have been jealous, at the idea of being able to love someone so readily, but they'd had hundreds of years to get so familiar.

"You're a menace." Addison's voice was equally fond, a warmth full of experience.

"No more than you, old dog. Getting attached already?"

"As if you haven't? I'm sure it's just your shirt I could smell beside her door when I went past this morning."

Tobias laughed, but it wasn't as nice as the laugh he gave me last night. "I might have stayed a little to be sure she was alright. I was worried she would cry more."

"I'm sure that was all it was."

"I felt poor, scaring her. I didn't know what else to do but stand guard."

"We are always good at falling into old habits."

There was something so final about the way Addison said that, certainty that made my heart yank against my ribs. A curl of guilt tried to push against me, at hearing such a private exchange, but I plucked it like a weed. Guilt did not assist in strange new places.

"May we always be able to be so useful." I wanted to peek over and see the expression on Tobias's face, but I was still traipsing along the edge of dropping away.

"That's dangerously close to a curse, you know?" The amusement was back in Addison's voice, rich with a withheld laugh. "She must have had reasons to flee her college. If even half the tales in London are true..."

"By that note, are you still going out this morning?"

"Yes, when it's a more decent hour. I'll have to visit the school to extend our sympathies. See if there is any word of the funeral."

"We should warn her."

"You told her of Arif being with us. I don't think there's anything further to say for now. Though, she did say someone was at her window this morning."

"Addison." It was almost a bite, the snick of teeth clicking together in condemnation. "Someone stalking around the outside of the house is a new boldness."

"Let us not add more worries to her shoulders yet. We don't know Arif's connection to the nest caused him to be targeted, and it could have been one of the sired." He didn't sound convinced.

"Peeping in her window? Tosh. She should know there is a risk." The thump of weight on the desk almost made me jump. I'd never been glad for George's shouting temper except that I was controlled in my reactions now.

"Then I will speak of it with her. Baseless conjecture does us no good, but a discussion of the dangers in the city is no more than safety, I suppose."

There was no response except the click of the door closing.

# CHAPTER 11

"Lambkin, can you waken for me?" Hands were on me, shaking my shoulders, and I lashed out with the knife in my hand as quickly as I could, throwing myself backwards.

My head struck the wall before the rest of me, a spiderweb-lace of black flashing over my vision as I blinked awake.

I was in Addison's room. His spare bed, he'd offered me it because I'd slept in the bathtub last night.

There was a knife in Addison's shoulder.

*Fuck.*

"Gods, I'm so sorry." I sat up, shoving the covers off so I could stand and twist him around, sink him down onto the bed. "Addison, can you look at me? We'll need to take that out but I need to be sure it's not hit anything significant."

Couldn't be in the bone or the knife would have snagged. It was a short blade, I'd have felt that. Could a vampire bleed out? Could he have a long-term injury or would his flesh try to heal around the wound?

"Ena, please stop panicking." Addison took my hand, no time to pull my guard up.

*They were three men together, rising and growing through teens into adults. Students, then soldiers, men with duty and love entwined with family lines and expectations. Meant to lead the future in wisdom and opportunity. Unbridled potential. Then the Immortal War.*

*A man with hair like sunshine, and a heart like a dragon. A smile that would melt snow.*

*Only two returned, a grief joining them like bloodied silk binding their wrists.*

I wrenched myself back, tripping over so I sprawled backwards and landed hard on the bones of my arse, pain flaring up my back like the memory of a beating. I froze, mouth open and eyes stuck on his stricken face, trying to find something enough of an apology. Tears stung my eyes, the throb of impact a punishing penance.

"I'm so sorry. I didn't mean to see him." It was rude to pluck memories out unbidden, we must never let someone know that we know. We had to keep secrets silent.

"Do you always bring the memories forward, when you brush against them?" Addison remained where I'd set him, hands on his knees, still as marble.

"No. Usually it's silent. I can pull them forward, if needed, but I didn't mean to see yours. The touch, before I had my guard up, I couldn't stop it. I'm sorry." Would he kill me? Would he use thrall to make me compliant, silent, while he did it? Tobias had mentioned it with weeping, and Addison hadn't offered—it was such a betrayal to take things out unbidden.

Addison hummed, a sad smile on his face. "You have to do that all the time? Your guard I mean."

"Yes. Closing off completely isn't easy but with practice you can do it. I think, as an immortal, you might be harder to stop. There's more of you, pushing at the surface."

Addison tutted, glancing towards the roof as he considered my words. "I don't know if that's the case or if there is simply more life behind us, given we don't die. A broader stream to dip into. It's an interesting philosophy to contemplate."

Maybe he was too shocked to do anything yet. "Addison, there's still a knife in you. I know you might not want to see me right now, but can I help you with that?"

"Ah, yes, quite." He took the knife, tugging it out with an easy little flourish. A handkerchief appeared from a pocket, wiping the blood down, and he set it beside him on the bed. "Don't fret on that, lambkin, I suffered worse before."

I blinked over at him, waiting for the inevitable anger. No one wanted secrets spilled. His eyes caught mine and he shifted, coming down from the bed to sit on the floor, so we were level and his legs sat beside mine. "You're afraid."

"People get angry when I see things. And I stabbed you."

"I was surprised. I thought to ask about your magic, but those reflexes are starling impressive. I apologise for not respecting your skill. And it's a while since I've spoken of Luc, but it's a good memory. Tobias said you'd discussed him, it was probably fresher for that."

"That's very gracious of you." I glanced down, grateful Tobias's shirt was tunic-long given I was sat here half undone. "I'll avoid further indiscretions."

"I asked you to rest."

I laughed a little as he caught my eye again. "It is a nice bed. Not big enough for you."

"How so?"

"You have to sleep at an angle, I can tell by your legs."

He shook his head, gave me a bashful smile. "I only use it when I get too distracted to go elsewhere. Sometimes my studies last late into the night and I'm loathe to wake others."

"I used to like doing that. When I wasn't on an active job, I researched whenever I wasn't training." Tim used to come and bother me in the archive, sitting on the tables like he'd been brought up in a barn. Tiffany brought me apples when she wanted to tempt me away into the stacks, or out into the daylight. I was never going to see her again and it stung like a lash across my heart. "I swear I'm not as much of a weakling as I seem."

"You don't appear weak. Disorientated, and confused, but those are understandable for a mage from a wary school in the presence of vampires. And a sore head, no doubt."

"I bruise easy. I can scratch my arm and it looks like I've had a fight."

"Do you get into many fights?"

I understood he was trying to walk me down, keep me talking until the panic had faded off and I could talk without stumbling into weeping. I could appreciate the care without liking it. "Depends on the company."

"Ah, you're adaptable."

"How else is a lady going to make her way?" I sighed, pulling my knees up close to my chest. He would have hurt me by now, if he was going to, the reaction would have come. I pushed at the fear in my chest, trying to unsnarl it.

"Are you running from someone, rather than something?" He tilted his right foot so it rested against my calf, and I let it sit there. A small concession to show I wasn't as afraid of him. I should be, but there was a calm patience that felt more like the tide than a threat.

"It's hard to explain." I wanted to be someone different to what the college needed. I didn't want to be a weapon, or a beast. "If I share things it could put you at risk."

"A mutually assured risk, given your knowledge of me."

I huffed a laugh, nodding a little. "Suppose you were somewhere that only saw you as a value, not as a person. Like with your position, that you're hiding from, they couldn't separate the fluke of your birth from who you are. Would you be able to stay? You didn't, you set your own place to be. That's all I'm trying to do."

He nodded, standing and offering his hand. I took it, blinking up at him while he looked me over again. "I'm sorry that doing that meant you had to run."

"It did for you too."

"But I had Tobias. You're setting off alone."

It hurt for him to say it, and my mind flashed to Tiffany's heart-shaped face, but I shrugged. "We have to make choices. Hopefully one of the other colleges will have me. Which we should discuss, though might I suggest I put on trews on for that?" My legs were cold.

"Indeed, though I'd like to provide something better suited. Even if you're not to stay with us, you should have proper wares."

"Thank you. It's considerate of you given my indelicacies."

He smiled, shaking his head. "Think nothing of it. I'll go arrange tea while you dress, if you would like?"

"I'm not expecting you'll be watching me change. I only have to pull on trousers."

"Do you think me so very noble?"

"That you wouldn't peep on me? Yes. I've been on your floor half undressed for some time, you kept your eyes on my face. You could easily have overpowered me and done as you like. You have thrall, too, you could make me."

"We're not men like that. Has someone hurt you, before?"

I laughed, pushing down the urge to cross my arms. "Plenty, but no man's made himself on me if that's the question. I've tumbled with both but the college didn't extend its punishment that far."

His brows pinched but he nodded. "I'm glad of that, at least. Some men can grow... possessive, of strong women."

"I had a sweetheart like that. She worried a pretty man would steal my heart away." He was a comely enough man, Ben. Objectively. Never was my type, though. Not that he listened to that. "We parted ways. And since I have my pick of pretty people, liking both, I'm sure I'll find myself someone who doesn't feel worried about the next pretty thing catching my eye."

"I didn't realise you partook of both."

"You were so busy assuring me of your own position I didn't think to mention mine."

"Of course, last night was a lot." He nodded, pecking a small kiss to my forehead before he turned and went back to his desk. "I'll go and find Jonathan, that should allow time for you to get dressed."

"Surely," I said, face burning.

"I shall return shortly. And I—" He stopped turning back to look at me as I sat up. "I kissed you."

"Just a peck. That's a rich person thing, no?" I bit my tongue before I said anymore.

"Indeed. A form of friendly affection. You're alright with that?"

"I'm going to have a lot of new things to learn, that's a sweet one."

Addison nodded, brows up high as he turned on his heel and fled the room. I grabbed my trousers as his steps disappeared down the corridor, one hand over my face. What was that? He'd clearly not meant to do it, or realised he had, until it clocked him a few seconds later. Maybe I could find books on vampire etiquette, or pin Jonathan down to speak about them.

Shaking the thought away I slid the trousers up my legs, cool enough to make me squeak, and I sat to pull my shoes on.

# Chapter 12

There was little else in the room other than his desk, the books, and all the pieces of time, so I set to examining them as I awaited his return.

I could inspect his desk—glean what I could from ink and paper—but I doubt he'd have left his correspondence in the open when I was a new person in his space.

Instead, I went up to one of the rows of hourglasses; a set of six stood together on the lowest shelf, one of them out of pace with the others. The magic in the glasses was deep and ancient, like a well in the cities back home.

I sat crossed-legged before one and felt my way around it. There was elemental energy, growling like the ocean hitting the shore, and there was that same thick scent of time and something more visceral. Decay, maybe? It wasn't blood, women knew blood, but it had the rich sweetness of copper and meat like it could be. I rocked up onto my knees, leaning in to get a better read. It had to be decay, that telltale promise of rot, but there was nothing to rot within.

"Please." The word rippled through the room; whisper soft. I flinched back. It wasn't the voice of one of the men in the nest, it was too papery, dry as dust and cobwebs. None of the life from the mess of the sired. It wasn't either of the immortals.

"Please." It sounded again. Oh, gods, it was behind the fucking glass. I screwed my eyes shut, mind cantering through options. It could be so many things: a prisoner, a curse, some murder cell underneath the house that he kept the access door hidden here. People did all sorts of horrors; the war stories were brutal. There was no space for someone to be stood behind there, flush to the wall, it had to be hidden.

"Hello?" I kept my voice low but firm, unsure if there was some trickery afoot. If someone needed help I'd need to keep them focused—avoid any screaming. "Can you hear me?"

"Please." It was firmer now, not even a plea, almost an invite, coming from the hourglass out of time with the others. It was almost run down; less than a palmful of grains left in the top.

A glimmer of something within caught my eye like a magpie to silver. I leaned close again, hand hovering above the glass, so cold my breath misted across it.

I glanced back to the door, checking for footsteps, see if I could get to the door and wedge a chair under the handle so I could investigate more.

"Please." It was so close in my ear, the sand sparkling like frost, and my hand made contact before I could think better of it.

The plummeting rush of falling hit me first: the same heart stopping fear as when I had fallen off a rock stack as a child. The certainty that nothing would catch me until death. Then, I stopped.

The scene before me was still, as if I'd been plucked up from my curious kneeling and set on a stage. It was a noble house—I could see money in the broad and open marble fireplace, the carpets and the dark furniture, the tapestry on the wall. A long table dominated the space, chairs thrown back and whatever papers had been on the table scattered around. It was filled with angry men.

Addison, hair black as a crow feather and eyes like stone, stood over a wizened, furious man whose flesh hung from him as if he were starved.

The man's face was a mess of lines and scars, dark eyes glaring up from his prone position. They were speaking but I could hear nothing, from any of the scrum. Magic crackled at Addison's hands, a sickly blue light that webbed between his fingers and reached towards the man.

Tobias was at Addison's back, sword in hand and fangs on show. The other five men, nobles by their clothes, formed a semicircle around the three, milling back and forth like a pack of beasts testing for weakness. They were all ages with each other, none like the creature on the floor, and though I couldn't hear the shouts they seemed outraged, pointing at Addison and baring fangs.

"Please." It was no longer weak. It was goading, a taunt from the thing beneath Addison. There was no other sound; none of the snarl I felt from Tobias, not even my own pulse in my ears. I was trapped with that word, a repeating demand.

Addison brought both hands together in a smooth sweep, palms flush, and a rush of that icy magic scooped the older man up. Grimacing, Addison spat at him before throwing his hands apart, stretched as far as they would go. The man was wrenched to pieces, splitting like a dropped mirror, and the shards hung suspended in the air. Addison stood panting, still and furious, as the colour drained from his hair and the magic flooded over him like lightning. My mouth fell open, no scream, and I grabbed my throat lest one try to escape.

Tobias leapt to Addison's side, yanking one of his arms, but was shrugged off. The other men surged forward as if to take them both, and Tobias put up his sword, slicing the first one down without warning. They pressed in and he gave no quarter, stabbing or slashing each with vicious certainty. He wasn't determined, though, not in the way Addison was, his eyes watered and wavered as he killed.

Once they were down he went quickly to each body: decapitating them, knocking out their fangs, and placing the bloodied heads in the open fire. It was so ruthless, like he was chopping wood rather than hacking bodies. As they burned, he added more fuel to the flames, boxing each in their own pyre; the bodies catching alight where they laid.

He returned to Addison, who had brought the shattered man down before him. His hands moved quickly, precise arcs and flicks that looked close to a ritual, and the pieces wound into themselves before condensing into seven small cubes of sand.

Tobias shouted at him—I think, from the way his arms waved—threw the sword down at his feet, then grabbed Addison up and pulled him close. He clung as if they were shipwrecked, marooned with each other's shoulders shaking with sobs. Addison stood still as a sculpture.

It was wrong to see this. I knew the nagging guilt of peering into someone's heart.

The scene went black, the dark twinkling like the sand in the hourglass, before it began to form again. I was back at the start, Addison with the wizened man below him, Tobias baring fangs. I turned away, covering my eyes so I didn't have to see it again, and my stomach twisted in on itself when the word came again.

"Please."

# Chapter 13

The burn of bile in my throat curled all the way along my nostrils, acrid sharp as I retched up the tea from earlier. I gagged and spat, lopsidedly led on my right side so only half my tongue was burning, and pushing up I found I was propped on a settee, in a morning room with wide windows.

I was cold despite the sunshine pouring in, and choking on the burning again, threw up into the space before me. I shuddered around a hiccoughed breath, which sent the burning further up my nose and I cried out at the sting.

"Ena?" A hand on my shoulder, pulling me up to sit. I screwed my eyes shut to force the tears clear of them, wiping them off to find Tobias staring down at me.

I shot away from him, jarring into the back corner of the chair, feet slipping on the large carpet like I could kick the settee back further. That failing, I held my hands out so he wouldn't come closer.

He nodded, showing he understood the gesture, then knelt on the floor so we were equal height. "Are you alright?"

I shook my head. I wasn't sure if I would throw up again, so shook it again to be sure.

"Can I come closer?"

I scowled at him.

He winced but nodded, shifting to sit cross-legged on the floor. "That's alright. I'm going to keep asking you questions, can we do that?"

I nodded. My stomach lurched again and I clamped a hand over my mouth.

"Easy, princess." He pulled a new handkerchief out and set it on the seat. "No rush. Only talk if you can."

I grabbed it, wiping my mouth and chin. "Alright."

"That's a good girl." He smiled but it wasn't real, wasn't in his eyes, and all I could see was the way he had clung to Addison. No wonder he cried when I mentioned the war. No wonder he was so achingly fucking careful with a new mage in the house. "Can you tell me what happened?"

"Addison used to have black hair. You're good with a sword."

He closed his eyes briefly, mouth open just enough to show teeth. "I was," he said eventually.

"You don't like talking about it. I should leave."

"I'm not having you run out of the house because of that. You don't need to leave."

"Maybe I want to. Gods, this is exactly what we are warned about, and I was thinking it wasn't." I spat it out, folding my arms close to my chest to hide their shaking. I was still cold, like the sand had taken all the heat out of me, and the sunlight did nothing to thaw it.

Tobias shucked his jacket off, tossing it to me. I frowned at it before taking it up, the warmth rushing over me as I slid inside it. I was collecting bits of him.

"If you wanted to, I would say wait until you can speak to Addison first, or Haddley." His voice was so flat, I knew that tone. That was the way I spoke to the children ready to run from the college. Doomed to fail but hurting, I never wanted to scare them worse than they already were, so I tried to be reasonable. "I don't know if that magic will have hurt you, but Garrett and Haddley come as a pair, and one of them is bound to know."

A mage and a medic. Made sense. "What was that? And don't say magic sand or I'll smash the fucking thing open with your face."

He snorted at that, sighing at the end of it. "Can I come and see that you're alright while I tell you?"

I worked my jaw before I could answer, two flavours of fear tangling. "Yes."

"Thank you." His smile was more like a real one this time. He shuffled over, graceful as a toad on ice, and pulled my right arm free to show my hand. A bright red blister bloomed from the heel of my thumb up to the meat of my palm like I'd gripped a scalding kettle. "That is going to hurt."

"Tell me what that was."

"Let me tend to this."

"Tell me." At least it was my right hand, easier for me to keep clean.

"You're an impossible thing, aren't you?"

"What's in the sand? Don't make me ask the other questions, Tobias, I don't know you well enough to be kind."

He stilled at the use of his name, catching his lip between his teeth. "It must be terrifying stumbling around the world like an open wound. Getting flooded with other people's pain. I'm sorry."

"I didn't get much chance to be scared once my college had me working."

"No. Of course not." He took my right hand in his other, gently squeezing them. "If I tell you, I have to beg you not to share it with anyone. Only Addison and I know of it."

"Whatever's in there knows it."

"No one else has found that out."

"That's why his study is neutral. It's not for Addison's benefit, it's to hide whatever that is."

"It's both. Addison hurt himself, with what he did. It changed him. Others would have died. This little oasis helps him."

"Tell me."

"What you saw was the last of a battle. The man on the floor was Henry, head of one of the older families. He killed Luc, as revenge for his sons' lives. But he didn't kill him purely as we ought to, no blessed fire and pitch."

The rush of Addison's memories pulled again, a surge of sand over the scribbled ink of this disaster, and I licked the back of my teeth before I spoke. "I saw him, in Addison's memories."

Tobias cupped the back of my head, looking at me like I was a precious thing. "You saw Luc. How did he look?"

"Beautiful. Pale hair, almost like Addison's, warm white skin, a smile that begs you to speak. Happy, I think. I only saw the echoes, it's not like I can interact with them, but he was happy."

Arms surged around my shoulders, Tobias crushing me to his chest like I would vanish. "You speak like you know him."

"Only the memory. I see what people hold close." It's why I was so useful in the college; passive powers make great tools. Dreg information, pull out secrets like a barometer of emotion. Politics and negotiations and evidence of betrayal.

Tobias shook his head, his chin now balanced atop of my head. "Luc was beautiful. He was golden in the alchemical sense, sure and true and always shimmering with light."

"I'm sorry he's not here." My face was pressed into the warm crook of his neck, the bruises stinging, and I tried my best not to tremble or cry as his pain sifted down over me like drizzle. This was all so rotten: broken hopes and promises haunting around the house like ghosts. I'd waded into them like a drunk at a low tide, stumbling towards doom.

"It's alright. We've had a hundred years to grieve, and we'll have a hundred more. But that doesn't tell you what you saw."

"Henry killed him?"

"In a sense. His sons had been mages, time users like Addison and Luc. They left some magical tools behind when we killed them, and Henry turned to those in his grief. Certain things are forbidden, even amongst us old monsters. Things considered like a sin, too wicked to be borne, and they are met with the forever death."

"Forbidden magics."

"You have them too?"

"Yes. Changing schools, or using methods out with your trained skills. It's enough to get you killed as a warning."

"I'm sorry they do that to you."

"Finish your story."

Tobias pulled back from hugging me but took a hold of my injured hand instead. "What they did to Luc was forbidden. An aberration of the skills those men had learned, twisted into something much worse by their father's grief. Luc's spirit was severed into pieces, and then scattered across time. Much worse than the forever death. Unending suffering."

"Gods." I swallowed against the threat of more bile. There'd be nothing left in my stomach.

He intertwined our fingers, anchoring me to him. I didn't pull away. "A brutality, even for the Immortal War. What you were warned of, the worst of us. Grief is a pointed thing. And it was sharp for Addison, too."

I knew where this would go. I felt like I would retch again as I spoke. "He did the same thing to Henry."

"Yes. He expected to be killed afterwards."

"But you protected him."

Tobias sighed, shifting to sit beside me while keeping hold of my hand. "I killed them because they would harm who I loved. I'd already lost the other half of my heart. It was my fault, I couldn't see Addison lost too. If that was protection, or selfish desire, I can't say."

"I can't think of any desire I have enough to take five heads. I've never even chopped one off."

He glanced over to me, eyes glowing in the low light. "Never?"

"I've stabbed, or sliced, or punched…" I trailed off, shaking my head. "I wasn't one of the proper killers, you know? I'm a spy, good at negotiations. See who was lying, see who was too good to be honest. Sometimes that got the wrong reaction. People thought knowledge was understanding, or that attention was interest. You had to deal with that. Sometimes more bluntly than others."

"Set any of them on fire?"

"Only threatened. Broke some necks."

"Good lass. I killed them and made sure it was clean, burning the heads in blessed fire so the bodies would follow. Then I fell on him. I think he hated me, for denying him peace."

"He had pieces instead. Are they all like that? The hourglasses I mean. Only one spoke."

"Spoke?"

"It said please. Like when he taunted Addison. That was the only part I could hear; it was like watching something with your ears stopped up."

"Your magic must have caught it. What an unusual creature you are."

"An open wound," I said.

"I'm sorry."

"S'alright."

He shook his head. "It's not. You're hurt. I'd have saved you having to see it, if I could, but no one else has felt it."

"Thank you. Is it part of him, in there?"

Tobias slumped back into the seat, spitting at the ground between his heels. "Yes. A shard of him, so Addison knows where he is. Knows that he hasn't escaped his punishment."

"That's risk."

"No one else has found it. And few would admit to knowing what it was. Means admitting to knowing the forbidden."

"You knew what it was, I saw it on your face." I twisted in my corner to look at him, ignoring the fact our fingers were still tangled.

"I'd wanted to know what had happened to Luc so I learned about it."

I nodded, laying my head on his shoulder. "Reasonable enough. Grief hurts."

"Speaking from experience?"

"The schools aren't good for children. You learn about all sorts too soon." Even when they were your salvation they were hard places.

"And we've made it worse for you."

"Are you going to kill me too?" I kept my eyes on our hands, not sure I could stand to see it in his eyes. He'd killed five immortals to protect Addison. What was one stranger?

He laughed, bringing our joined hands up to peck a kiss to my knuckles. "No. I don't think you're going to run off and tell anyone, or blackmail us, or any of the other things that would have been done by another immortal. Some others suspect, but do not know. My slaying those men helped end the war, and I was a very popular man for that."

"How obscene."

"Yes. But Luc's family had vengeance by our hands, and I had Addison, and that was all I could ask for. We were allowed to slink off."

"Had?"

"Had, have. We love each other. Love comes in seasons when you're like us, it draws blood as well as blush."

I blinked at him, unsure if I had the grasp of what he meant: that they were together but pained, joined in their grief as well as the rest. "Good?"

"Yes, good. Though, should you be fond of him, don't feel I should stop you. There's nothing untoward about such joys."

His suggestion caught in my throat, heat rising up my face. "I just watched you both murder people, and my hand's injured, I've not thoughts of fucking anyone right now."

He snorted, nodding at me. "Indeed. Will you stay here while I go find Garrett?"

"Yes. But leave your coat, I'm cold."

# Chapter 14

I sat like a duck on the settee, shuffling lower so I was almost laid down, covered in Tobias's coat. Like Arif yesterday with my jacket. I shivered at the memory of hot blood on my palms, better than the cold glass and the throbbing blister. That would hurt in the lancing.

I should run. It would be sensible, dart out the window and be along the path by the time they got back, have at least something of a head start, but I felt half wrecked, my energy lost to the sand. And, if there was some lingering poison in it, I'd no clue how to fix it, and no protection outside my magic. I could run all I liked and the ignorance might kill me. I brooded on it, closing my eyes under the jacket.

My mind was full of breaking glass and sand as cold as a burning winter.

"My boys were not fools."

I couldn't move—a weight on my chest like a millstone pressing me down. I'd seen men die like that. The idea of my ribs cracking, spilling blood out onto the carpet, raced against me. I'd die under those ugly cherubs, grinning down like they would lead me off wherever came next. A poor death.

The cold was so intense it stung to breathe. Snow on the long, dark road home, or the shock of water over me when I'd been left outside in punishment. I'd had enough nights in the yard, I could survive cold, but it hurt.

At least it was dark in the space behind my eyes.

"They took after their mother, though. Skilled but subtle. No venom." It was the voice from the hourglass, the haughty taunt that tipped Addison into violence.

A sharp nail ran across my wrist, real enough to make me whimper. I shook my head, chest swooping that I could manage that, though my limbs remained useless. My fingers twitched, though, and I flexed them like I was searching for a blade.

"I haven't had a level of freedom in decades, little thing. You struggle well for a human. Imagine what I could have had from you in the war."

Breath flashed against my neck, fetid, and I sank my fingernails into my palms until the blister on my right hand burst—the rush of pain let me scream.

The thing hunkered on my chest laughed, coughing around the sound. "Clever. You know the value of pain. Good."

Nails sank into my stomach, through the skin, then dragged down towards my thighs. Pain bloomed. I sucked in air, screaming it out again, my throat raw.

There was a scrum of noise at the door, bodies shifting as they barged through it. The wood banged off the wall as they spilled into the room, too many steps for me to keep track. I tried to turn but everything between my chest and hips hurt, burning bright with pain, hot blood.

"Ena?"

"Princess?"

"Fucking move!"

A jumble of voices overlapped as my eyes blinked open, still on the settee underneath Tobias's jacket. My clothes clung to me, the material too heavy to move; I could scream from the press of it against my abdomen.

"Ena, are you well?" Haddley was at the seat, hands flapping as he went to touch me then pulled them back, twisting away when he breathed in. "Gods, it stinks of blood."

Tobias and Edgar were next there, Edgar racing to the window to check it was closed as Tobias knelt beside me.

"What happened?" he asked. He grabbed my hand and growled at the burst blister, the wound bloody and torn from my nails.

I groaned at the movement, my whole stomach rippling with pain as I tried to push the jacket off. I was shivering and hot, too many things at once for me to speak properly, and Haddley shot forward to pull it for me.

The blood was a lot, I knew that from the fug of it, and a cold wave hit me from the wetness across my skin. I whimpered, hating myself for it despite the fresh hurt, and the men stilled.

"What's that?" Edgar was the first to speak, spitting it out as he looked at Tobias. "That's a wound, what's done that?"

"Go get Addison," Tobias said, pointing to the door. "Ena, what's happened?"

I shook my head, scared to say what I had seen despite Edgar's exit. I looked at Haddley, struggling for a reason to send him away. "My bag, please?"

"Yes!" Haddley shot from the room. Probably grateful to be free from the blood.

"Ena, I need you to talk to me, and I need to look at you. Alright?" Tobias asked.

"Henry." I got the word out as I tried to press down on the cuts, the material of his shirt slick and sticking to the wounds.

"What?"

"He was on my chest, whispering about his sons. And the value of pain. Fucking bullshit."

Tobias leaned closer, glancing to the door before he spoke. "You're sure? It wasn't a nightmare?"

"Do nightmares slice you open?"

He shook his head, lips tight as he looked back at the door. "We'll need Addison to assist with this."

"What is it?"

"A haunting. Of sorts."

"Never heard of a vampire ghost, they a common thing?" I punched the wooden back of the settee, once, twice, the cuts smarting like they'd been dosed with salt. "Gods, this is not something I want to know."

"I'm sorry, princess." He took my left hand. "I need to clean those wounds. It means you'll be bare when the others get here."

"I have underwear on, get on with it." A thrill of cold went up my stomach, the shock of it making me twist which made the pain worse. I squeaked, punching the frame again and tightening the grip I had on Tobias's hand. "We should get me on the ground before I fall."

"Alright. I'll lift you down. You must have done this all the time in your old place, yes?" Tobias pecked a kiss to my forehead before he stood.

"It was usually me patching others up, but yes. I've had wounds." He scooped me up like he had last night, and I cried at the fiery, demanding pain that rushed over me before he set me down again. His jacket was stuffed under my head, a makeshift pillow.

"Tell me about some of those." He fisted the material of my shirt, one large hand at the span of my ribs below my breasts, and I looked away before he started to tear it open. It wasn't like I had much to worry over, the top was already shredded and coated red, but something about the intimacy of him tearing my clothes off felt indecent when I was sodden in blood.

"This is a shit distraction tactic, you know? I used to do the same to the younger lads." Pain surged anew as he carefully peeled the material free, leaving my chest covered for my modesty, though any such soft thoughts slid away with the tatters. He was more utilitarian with the trousers, undoing the button with confident ease and sliding them off my legs.

"Tell me something else, then." He was bent low over me, sniffing at the wounds, and I cried out when he lapped, gentle as a kitten, at the side of one.

"Like what? How I plan to set your whole fucking house on fire when I get well enough to stand again?" The anger was good, a focus compared to the gnawing, hungry pain.

"It would need to be blessed fire to kill them, they're the born sort. Normal fire works for us, though," Haddley said as he popped through the door.

"I'll start with normal and see how we get on, how about that?"

Haddley snorted as he hesitated beside the door. "I can't get much closer, I'm so sorry. I brought your bag, though." He held it up.

"There's a little book in there, can you fish that out?" I asked.

"Yes!" He dropped to his knees, riffling through the pack as I heard other footsteps approaching.

"When you find it, pass it to Tobias if that's easier. You don't have to stay and feel awful with the blood."

"I want to know you're alright. Garrett isn't here, so I want to be able to tell him we took care of you. He won't be able to take losing two people in two days, I must help."

"He should be back soon, he was helping Chance with something," Tobias said. He was kneeling on the floor now, hands on my hips to keep me still as he lapped a little more blood.

I swiped for his head. "Why are you doing that?"

"Immortals can tell certain qualities in the blood—disease, thrall, those things," Haddley said. He skirted closer, handing me the little book, then retreated to the door. He kept sniffing, like something was bothering him. I was about to ask when Addison and Edgar appeared at the door.

"Ena." Addison rushed to me, a hand on my forehead as he peered at the wounds. They burned at his voice, the jolt enough to make me screw my eyes closed before I could reply.

"Well met," I said.

Edgar snorted, coming over to stand beside the window like he had to keep guard. "I've told Jonathan to keep an eye at the gate, he can tell the others what's happened when they return."

"Good man," Tobias said.

"Lambkin, what has happened to you?"

"A ghost, apparently," I replied, biting my lip at the tug of pain in my lower stomach. I had always hated the soft fold of skin I had there, but now I could have ripped it off me. Every time Addison spoke it was like I was being sliced anew, the cuts hot and angry.

"Look at her hand," Tobias said, not moving from his spot

Addison felt around for my right hand, holding it up to inspect. "Gods."

"Is this a branding mark?" Haddley hovered nearer. He had one of his shirtsleeves pulled low on his arm, over his hand to act like a handkerchief.

"In a sense." Addison frowned down at me, leaning in so he could look at my eyes. "You don't seem to be possessed, but for the fact he could make wounds on you, it's a risk."

"What?" I tried to sit up, fuck the pain, and Addison pushed me back down.

"What are you doing?" he asked.

"I know about possessions; I'm not staying here!"

"Princess, stop. You're bleeding."

"I'm going to keep bleeding if he's right, they leach you out until you're a damn puppet and wear you like a skin! Do you know what they do to us?" I knew I shouldn't be shouting at them, especially not Tobias who had been trying to help, but I had no hope of fighting off possession from a vampire. A ghost of a human was bad enough, they could do acres of harm in a mage's body, but the idea of a leaching soul eating me hollow was enough to spur me on.

"She's right, about mages," Haddley said, peering around Addison. "It's worse than with normal humans. What sort of spirit is it?"

Edgar set a hand on my shoulder, bringing my attention to him. "You're too hurt to walk, mistress. I know you're afraid, but you will hurt yourself more if you try to run. You have my word I will carry you if you ask me to, but wait."

"This will need to be removed directly. You'll need to fight it off," Addison said.

"How can I do that? It's—" I doubled over as I spoke, more cuts peeling down my stomach as a growling laugh echoed through the room.

"Is that a demon?" Haddley shot over to me, squeezing my hand. "Ena, if it's a demon you need to fight as hard as you can."

"It's not a demon." Tobias was glaring at Addison, still hold of my hips as I writhed on the floor.

"It may as well be," I said, thumping the ground. Blood squelched at my strike and I recoiled, redoubling the hurt.

Haddley touched my shoulder. "I know you said it's not a demon but if it is, there are a few things we need to consider."

"Why do you know so much about this?" I asked.

"They thought I had one when I was human, they tried to drive it out of me."

"Gods." I knocked my head back into the jacket, grabbing his arm with my hand. "I'm sorry, that's horrible."

"I wasn't a demon, though, so it's alright, but I know a lot about the process."

"Haddley, peace, it's not a demon." Addison set a hand on his shoulder, pulling him from me.

"What is it then?" He peered up at Addison.

"It's a dead vampire, seemingly, and I'm glad the prick is dead, but can we get rid of him?" The laugh sounded again, rich and dark, though no more cuts bloomed on my skin.

Haddley clapped a hand over his mouth, looking between Addison and Tobias. He shook his head, then shot up and out of the room.

"Edgar, go check on him," Addison said.

"Someone should stay for her."

"I'm here," Tobias replied. The grip on my hips hurt, but it was a dull, steady pain compared to the bleeding lines dug out of me.

Edgar frowned at him, crossing his arms, and I tapped his shin. "Go. I'll shriek if I need you."

"You do have a good set of lungs." He scowled at Addison then left the room, calling out for Haddley.

# Chapter 15

"This is your fault," Tobias said.

"I'm well aware. Ena, I need you to tell me exactly what happened." Addison knelt beside me, stroking my hair, and a surge of pain ripped along my wounds.

"Don't touch me, he doesn't like you." I ducked my chin towards the wounds, blood welling up. Addison blanched, standing. "The pain gets worse when you touch me. It's him."

"Clever little thing. Spirited little thing." The voice was a scratchy whisper, not as strong as it had been in my sleep, and both the immortals whipped their heads around.

"That's the gent." I grabbed the shredded shirt, pressing down on the new blood spilling at my hips. I was going to be striped as a damned harlequin if I survived this. *If* seemed a heavy word.

"He's not a gentleman," Addison said. "I don't know how this has happened. He's contained."

"Evidently not well enough." Tobias looked like he would rip someone's throat out, none of the bashful smiles or wavering lips from the night before, and half of me wanted to knock their heads together.

"We don't have ghosts, Tobias."

"Not a ghost, then, a soul shard, different thing." I tried to sit up, regretted it, cried out as I flopped back down.

"Stay down, princess."

"I need salt in these."

"Salt?" Addison rounded on me, frowning like I was speaking madness.

"It cleans the wound, and it makes the pain worse, which helps me focus, so I need salt."

"That's unwise," Tobias said.

"How often do you get bleeding wounds and infection, oh undying ones? I'm the one who has a risk of death!"

"Infection can't kill us, she's right," Addison muttered. He turned, inching around like he was looking for Henry lurking somewhere in the shadows.

"Rubbing salt into a wound is torture," Tobias said.

"So's a lingering death." I screwed my eyes shut, covering my face with my hands as I tried not to scream. The pain was a constant, pushing wave, a noise in my mind that drowned out all reasonable thoughts. "I'm not going to rot into the grave because you two are squeamish. These are deep, I need to know they're clean."

"We need to stop any more first. I'm not sure what the best course of action is. I could try to draw him out but it's not the same as a normal summoning. I could banish him, but as a shard I don't know if it would work."

"You didn't learn that bit?" My hands dropped from my face. Addison was beside Tobias but looked to me and shook his head. "What if it had gone wrong?"

"He planned to be dead either way." Tobias still hadn't let me go, an anchor in writhing, and I laughed.

"You'd think you'd at least want to be sure the job was done first." Addison recoiled, and Tobias winced.

"Quite." Addison came back to my head, hand moving to stroke my hair then pulling away.

"Go pet Tobias, I can see you want to comfort me," I said. I wasn't able to keep the blur of tears in, their betrayal hot and quick down my cheeks, and my stomach twisted as a fresh round of pain was pulled out of me. "You can fuck off too whatever you are."

"You know my name," Henry whispered.

"I don't care. You're not even whole, you're the dying part of a grieving man who lashed out because his sons were dead. I know plenty of men like you." I spat on the floor, no clear direction to aim for, and was rewarded by another laugh.

"I wish I could have had you in the war. You would have fuelled me so well." It was like he was at my ear, close and cloying, but the immortals bristled too.

"I'd have done myself in before you got a hold of me. Even if it meant gnawing my arm off like a dog in snare."

"Easy, princess. If you get too excited you'll bleed more."

"Excited? Excited! I'm going to set both of you on fire. I'm burning the whole fucking house down, except whatever books you have, and when you come to, I'm going to beat both of your heads in with the biggest one I can find."

Tobias was the first to laugh, snorting into the back of his hand which he had to dip down to cover. "You like threatening to burn us."

"It won't kill us, Ena."

"I know, that's the point!"

"I have an idea!" Haddley raced back into the room, flinging a pair of books before him. Addison caught them, rocking with the weight, and Edgar stumbled in behind Haddley with a scowl.

"He moves when he wants to," he said.

Haddley threw himself down, grabbing my hand. "I think I know what we can do but I need you to trust me."

"Haddley, what is this?" Addison had opened the books and was frowning at the messy pages.

"They're notes I made as a human, about magic. They're much improved on now I'm turned but I did a lot of research into spirits and how I could improve my skills through them before I met you."

"You're mad," I said. That was so dangerous. He could have been killed communing with spirits without any wards, and he had none of the ink of the Solomon Schools.

"I think what we need to do is scrub Ena of the possessing force, which truly she can do herself. She works with spirit, I think, from the smell of her magic, so she's better placed than most to do this, which I'm sure you already know." He stopped to breathe, smiling at me quickly.

"What do you suggest, then?" Addison asked.

Haddley rocked back on his heels, still hold of my hand. "That we do the inverse of what the vampires do. Proper vampires, the born ones. We overpower her."

"How do you mean?" Edgar said, peering over the edge of the book Addison held to look at the notes.

"We give her a large dose of power so she can, uh, flush her system, or flood it, so to speak, and that will mean she can purge the creature. It's not a precise method but it will work. There's nothing for it to cling to, this way, so it can't create a new hold, and it means her own power can regroup afterwards."

That was unspeakably dangerous, but if I was going to die either way then it was worth a try. "How are we doing this?"

"This is the bit you won't like: vampire blood. One of them." He pointed to the immortals. "Either through a turning, or purely donation. Though donation is distinctly untested, in my experience, usually in the case of only one party is giving blood—it's the human—but both should work."

"You want me to drink their blood?"

"I could sire her, the change would make it easier to shuck this off, certainly," Addison said.

"We are not turning her!" Tobias was up, off the floor and shouting, his hands fisted into Addison's shirt. He dragged Addison away from me, fangs out. "Addison, if you so much as try I will do more than take your fucking fangs, not one step towards her."

Haddley shot between them, shaking Tobias's shoulders. "It doesn't have to be turning! Turning requires mutual exchange, we can do this one way. She drinks of you. And it's not thrall, that requires repeated biting or influence by a vampire to a human. I looked into this a lot, how do you think I found Addison so readily? Or how the church thought me wicked."

"Will that work?" Edgar asked. He had one of the books, squinting at the script as he sat beside me, his knife out in front of him. I glanced to him and he winked. "I'll let none near unless you approve."

Haddley looked over to us. "I don't know, truly. Addison turned me so I didn't have to try and bleed him in experiment."

"Let's try," I said. My thighs were cold from the blood leaking over them, and my muscles were twitching without my direction. This was too much blood gone—I was lacking other choices but to attempt this. A fresh cut ripped into me, from mid rib to hip and I screamed, twisting on the ground. "Now, let's try now."

"We don't know if it'll work," Addison said.

"Nothing else has and she's bleeding too much. Christ, Addison, I can smell it, I know how much she's lost." Haddley looked almost brave, the nymph of man poking Addison's chest with a spindly finger, eyes blazing.

"It'll have to be Tobias," I said. They all turned to look at me. "He hates Addison. I don't think it would make it easier to be rid of him if I took in Addison's blood, and I'm not being turned."

"We know who it is?" Haddley asked. "That's better, we could do a banishing, or a summoning to draw him away, and—"

"It's not a demon, Haddley." Tobias pushed past them, coming to kneel in front of Edgar, who looked to me. I nodded. "I don't want to risk you turning."

"Then don't bite me, idiot," I said.

"I have a blade." Edgar held his knife out, still frowning at the book.

Tobias sighed at me as he took the knife. "We have no guarantee it works the same way."

"Keep your fangs to yourself and we have a good chance. That's how it works, right, Addison?"

"There is a need for mutual exchange in the turning, yes." Addison was pacing back and forth, fists clenching as he went. "The logic of the suggestion is sound but I've never attempted something like this. If it doesn't work, we still have the other choice, I suppose."

"I was going to do it, before you offered to turn me, if that helps?" Haddley asked. "I had a plan for draining you and using the accelerated healing for ensuring a continuous source of power, but the instabilities were too significant, and then when we talked I liked you too much to stab you." Addison stalled, but continued walking.

I shared a look with Tobias.

"Such foolish children." Henry's voice was wet on my neck, and I gasped as the sharp nails dug in there. "You don't deserve this little gem."

I grabbed at my throat as the wounds began to open, blood seeping between my fingers. "Tobias."

# Chapter 16

I knew the taste of blood. You learn it quick as a child, with training at the college. I always had it in my mouth when I was new there.

Vampire blood was less familiar. There was the same rich, metallic tone, coating my tongue and flooding my mouth, but the magic within was sparkling, almost like newly brewed beer. I gagged, but swallowed, forcing myself to keep sucking as the sting at my neck lessened. Tobias moaned like he was in pain, hands fisting at my shoulders to keep me in place.

"How much should she drink?" I thought it was Edgar asking but I couldn't look, my face buried into Tobias's neck, and a woozy, heady heat running along the backs of my arms, down to the tips of my fingers. A metallic thump sounded beside us, but it seemed far off compared to the draw of the blood.

"Ah. I don't know. Probably a few cups?"

I tapped Tobias on the shoulder, trying to signal he should stop but he cupped the back of my head and pressed closer. "Keep going, you've barely had any."

I groaned, unable to speak, but swallowed more and kept lapping at the red spilling over my lips. It was so hot, such a difference to the cold greed that had accompanied Henry, and I was flooded dizzy by the warmth of it.

Tobias made a noise between pain and something else, a pitch too close to fear. He pressed his face next to mine, the line of his jaw hard at my cheek, his breaths laboured as a workhorse. I took a final gulp and pushed away, shoving at his chest as I flopped back.

"No more, you need to heal," I said.

"Check her neck," Addison said. He was leaning on the end of the settee, the wood groaning as he gripped. Sunlight danced over his skin, marble bright and glowing like he could lure anything his way with one glance. I was drunk on the sight, a queasy distance from the pain, but adoring the new focus the detachment gifted me.

I lifted my chin, the skin tight but unyielding, and Tobias ran his finger gingerly along the flesh. "Healed."

I turned to look at Addison and found Henry peering over his shoulder like a ghoul, sad face pinched in a scowl. "Can you see that?"

"What?" Addison looked around himself, the looming face twisting with him.

"There's someone at your shoulder." It was a nonsense way to say it, totally wrong, but I stumbled up, towards Addison.

"Easy, mistress, you still have wounds," Edgar said. A hand hovered at the base of my back, careful not to touch but close enough that I knew about it, and I smiled over at him as I wobbled away from my bloodstains.

I kept my eyes fixed on the little face. It snarled, but no noise came, and when I reached out to pluck the straggly hair, it came to me like a hissing cat, twisting and spitting.

My touch seemed invigorating: it pulsed with enough energy to spit out a single word. "Please."

I shoved it at Addison's chest, dusting my hands off. There was no cloth other than my underwear, my trews discarded and top torn to bits, but they'd have to do. Anything to be rid of the clammy, cold touch of that thing. "That's yours."

"I think she's right to burn us down on reflection." Tobias was on the carpet, torn shirt pressed to his neck. "We should let her."

"What the fuck is that?" Edgar asked. He passed the book to Haddley, drawing another blade to point towards the little creature.

"Can I have one of those?" I nodded to Edgar's blades, still weaving on my feet.

"I'll return shortly." Addison vanished in a flurry, the head at arm's length, and I sat heavily on the settee.

"Can someone get me clothes, please?" I asked.

"I'll get you something," Edgar said.

"I'll find Jonathan, he knows how best to look after humans." Haddley was quick on Edgar's heels. I stayed on the seat, tracing the new lines in my skin with idle fingers as their footsteps faded off. The room was so quiet, in contrast to the shrieking before, and other than the unsteady beat in my chest, it felt barren.

"Are you well?" I asked, not turning to look at Tobias.

"Neck hurts." He shuffled over to me, hoisting himself to sit on the other side of the settee so I had space.

"Honey in tea helps with that, often."

"I'll ask Jonathan for some." He shuffled closer, tilting my chin a little so he could check my neck again. "How do you feel?"

"I don't know. Your blood was strange. Seeing Henry was strange." I glanced at him, those cats' eyes full of worry. "Don't look at me like that."

"Like what?"

"Like I'll break. I didn't break."

"I don't think you'll break. I fear we'll harm you. And I'm embarrassed."

"Why?"

I would think he was blushing if I could tell whose blood was whose. There was a lot of red all over us both. "Your drinking from me was... enjoyable. It's a dreadful thing to take pleasure in something done desperately."

Oh, that's what that noise was. I laughed, shaking my head at him. "You haven't had that before, when siring?"

"I don't sire, I have no pups." He shook his head, blowing air from his cheeks. "I don't want you to think poorly of me."

For fuck's sake. "Why would I? And why should you care? You did it to help, there's nothing dreadful in that. No more than someone feeling good after a sparring match. Don't be foolish."

"May I?" He put a hand on my thigh and my whole face heated, that new blood rushing around as well as the old. "I want to check your wounds."

"Alright."

He trailed his fingers carefully over Henry's scratches, the skin tender and prickling with the threat of pain under his touch.

"These will need more time than your neck. They're well on the way to being healed, but there's more of them to tend to."

I huffed around a sigh, swallowing my immediate words. "I'll just need to be gentle with that skin."

"What's wrong?" He looked at me like I was the moon, like he wanted to peer closer, and I glanced away.

"I almost fucking died on a nest floor, it leaves one a touch put-out. And your blood has left me irregular."

"What's it like?"

"What?" I frowned over at him.

"The feeling, you impossible thing." He threaded our fingers together again, stroking the back of my hand like he needed to be sure I was there. "Tell me about it, so you don't fret. We'll need to get you to see someone, to be safe, but talk to me until then."

I scowled at him, licking the back of my teeth before I spoke. "I've never tasted magic before. It tingled, on my tongue, and it was rich. Not as coppery as human blood."

"You make me sound like wine."

"I'm not much of a drinker of that, so I'd no doubt do you a disservice. The magic was like heat, a warmth spreading out. The feeling like when you step into the sun on a snowy day and it washes over you. I feel like I could race a horse, and win, but I'm so tired."

Tobias sighed, sitting back into the settee, the wood creaking again. Must be damaged from Addison's grip too. "It let you see Henry."

"Ugly git."

He snorted. "I saw immortals flee the battle rather than face him."

"He was probably more effective as a whole being. I only had a shard. And you two struck him down, you didn't run off." I reached up with my free hand, shifting his hair and to check his neck. He held the cloth away to show it was closing, lessening, then brought it back in place. A mar on the pale stretch of skin, which would vanish. Immortals were not known for their scars.

"The war made us all do strange things."

"Some stranger than others." Addison appeared back in the room, somehow paler than he was last night. "How are your wounds?"

"Healing, but she should see Margery." Tobias released my hand, standing to go to the window. The heat of his skin lingered and a part of me wondered if that was his blood or my own softness, everything else burned up in my fear. I pushed it away: no need to figure that out now.

"I am so sorry." Addison went on one knee in front of me, catching my hands in his. "I had no thought that he could do that. If I had even a suspicion, I would have destroyed every part."

"No, you wouldn't. You wanted him to suffer."

Tobias laughed from his spot, squinting into the sunshine. "She has the number of you, Addison. I wonder if my blood's making her blunter?"

"You're giving yourself too much credit there, beloved. Lambkin, I will ensure nothing of what happened here is repeated. I'll have him placed elsewhere."

"Do as you wish, it's not my business. I can't think it would do you much good having him whispering in your ear."

"He never spoke to me."

"Oh, he really hated you, then. Reasonable, I suppose."

Addison laughed, mirthless, groaning as he stood. "I have a friend in the city I wish for you to see. She is a healer, and she can check you over to be sure the blood has no interplay with your own magic."

"Is this what happened to Arif?" It was out before I could stop it, the chill of blood loss raising goosebumps over my skin. He'd lost so much blood. "Did something attack him too?"

Tobias sighed, head ducking down like a stone. "No, Arif's death was entirely of the city. That thing has never interacted with a human before. Or any of us, that I know of. I know it will be hard to trust but if nothing please mark my hands on Addison as evidence of that."

"You threatened to take his teeth."

"It's quite the threat amongst us," Addison said, sitting beside me. "It's evidence of the forever death."

"Like he did with those men, to protect you."

Tobias barked a laugh, walking over to stand at my other side. "Just like that. You should wash, before you visit Margery, so the wounds are clean. Jonathan can stand guard at your room if you wish."

"That, or give me a proper knife. And gin. I think I'd feel better with some of that in my stomach."

# Chapter 17

Jonathan had insisted, once I had been returned to my temporary room and he had finished shouting at the vampires, on checking my wounds over. He cleaned the drying blood and examined the scars, clicking his tongue.

"This will help keep them clean." He held up a small metal tin, the label worn off from handling. "Do you wish to apply it before you dress?"

"That would be grand, thank you."

He nodded, passing me the tin. It smelled like lavender and something minty, but the underlying sweetness was clearly beeswax. "I'll ask them to give you some time before the coach is arranged. I want to shout at them more anyway. What if you had died?"

"You'd have to help hide a body. Can't be too unusual in a nest."

"Never had to do it yet, though there's always a first time." He shook his head at me but there was a smile on his face, a fondness that seemed misplaced on me. "Chance wishes to see you, if you'll permit?"

"Why?"

"He's the nominated doctor. Garrett thought you might not wish his company, given recent events."

"Alright. Let me wash my face, first, then he can come fuss."

"Do you wish company?"

"No, if he tries anything I'll yank his bollocks off and feed them to him."

"Good to see you're recovering." Jonathan smiled as he went out the door, and I went to the bathroom to inspect the damage.

Once I was before the mirror my stomach quivered, the new scars a horrid chicken scratch over my skin. My mouth wobbled and I bit into my lip to keep the treacherous upset back. It was ridiculous to be upset. I was never destined to be clear skinned and beautiful, I was a tool rather than a piece of art, but something about the wounds made my eyes prickle. Like I'd been crossed out, or the spirit had thought better of having me present, scored me away.

It hadn't managed it, though.

My hands cupped the soft skin at my stomach, now segmented like I was a roast to be carved. The wounds were still raised little ridges, easy lines for being separated and portioned out. The thought made me gag and I dropped my hands, abandoning the shredded top and pulling on my stained shirt from yesterday. My skin erupted in goose bumps, and I rubbed them away, shaking the chill off. I needed new trousers, but they would have to be a donation. Probably from Tobias or Jonathan, the others might be too thin hipped.

"Petal?" The sound of Chance entering brought me out of my musings, and I grabbed the little tin to bring with me.

He was by the door, a hand on the handle as he held the other up, open palm towards me. "I want to check you over. I can get someone else to treat you, if you want. A human. They'd look the other way if you needed to leave."

"I believe I'm being taken to a healer."

Chance nodded, stepping a touch closer. "I know, but she's a vampire as well. A former nestmate. Good, she's stellar good, but you need choices, including human ones."

A sweet sentiment, I was surprised by his care. "Alright, you can have a look."

My lower half was still in drawers but I couldn't find it in myself to be worried. Doctors saw a lot, Chance had seen a thousand bodies, no doubt, it wasn't as if he would be surprised by my form.

"This balm is good, I recommended it for Jonathan after a bad set of burns." Chance had plucked the tin from my hand, sniffing it.

"He spoke highly of it. The cuts are on my abdomen and stomach, so will standing do?"

"Yes, come and stand here." He sat on the bed and pointed to the floor in front of him. I went, folding the shirt under itself so I could tie it at the arch of my ribs, showing the wounds without anything else.

He struggled to keep the frown off his face as he looked me over. "Can I touch you?"

"Where's that come from? You were all hands on me last night."

"This isn't the same. I don't want you to feel uncomfortable."

"Get on with it."

He tutted but gripped my hips carefully, avoiding the mottling of dark green and brown marks. Tobias had a broad reach; I hadn't considered that until I saw the gaps between the bruises.

"This is a lot of scarring." Chance frowned, mouth screwed up in one corner. "It could have an impact in the future. If you have a child, the skin won't swell as it should. It could risk you both."

What a sweet idiot. I shrugged, tugging the shirt down again. "I don't want a babe, and I don't even know if I can have one. I've not had a scare yet and I've had a few men in my bed separate to Tiffany. It's not a worry for me."

He blinked up at me like I'd said something in another tongue, before he yanked me hard into a hug: his arms around my waist so his face crushed into the newly scarred skin. It tipped me forward with a scream, which sent him backwards and both of us sprawled onto the bed. His grip didn't lessen though. I battered onto his head with the flat of my palm.

"I'm so happy." The words were muffled against my stomach. With a firm twist I popped free, rolling onto my back on the mattress, before sitting up and covering my legs with the blanket.

"What was that?" I shouted.

"I was feared you'd be so upset. I wasn't even here to help, we were both checking the grounds over. What good's a doctor in the house if you're left to die?"

"Ena?" Jonathan was through the door, as was Tobias, both shoving into each other and into the room. I blinked at them.

"My fault, chaps, I gave her a hug." Chance stood, shaking his head. "Couldn't resist."

"Throwing himself at me already," I said, going along with his line. It was a gentle, and very human, worry, to be fretting about me when he wasn't even in the house. I shuffled off the bed so I could stand too. "I'm going to need trousers from someone, and half of you are slimmer than me. Can I trouble someone to find me a pair before I go see this healer?"

"You should eat too. Your body needs food for healing," Chance said.

Jonathan stepped closer, catching my hand. "I'll make something light. A boiled egg, or crumpets?"

"As you like, I've no appetite but I'll have something small."

"I'll see to that, then. Tobias, if you could take care of the clothing?"

"Alright. You'll be drowned in mine but you can turn the hems up." He went out the door, followed by Jonathan, though Chance lingered.

"I'm glad you're hale, petal. We were so worried for you. Garrett's wrapped up in Haddley sobbing, because he thought he'd killed you, bringing you back."

"Well tell him to stop. I didn't die." I huffed, rubbing my arms again. "Thank you for your care. I've no means to pay you."

"Never a whit of that, perks of the nest. Quite the little hellion, beating something wicked at its own game. Do let me know if you need anything, I'll soon growl the oldies down too."

"I'm well, Chance, I just want to be dressed and get this over with. Thank you." I smiled at him and he seemed satisfied enough with it, grinning again before he left.

I slumped back onto the bed, bringing my knees with me to cover my legs with the shirt. Good thing I'd chosen a large one, to help hide my breasts, it was doing twice its work now. I gulped air, not even enough to be a laugh, setting my forehead on my knees. This was a disaster. I needed to get out, find a college with a healer.

They weren't human killers, evidently—they could have had a feast with me writhing around bleeding on their carpet, and here they all were caring for me like a sick cat—but I was at the end of my nerves. Whoever their healer was, that would be fine, but once I was in the city I would get away.

# Chapter 18

I sat huddled in the far corner of the coach into the city, hating myself for needing to be close to the door but doing it anyway. Such a blatant show of weakness was ill-fitting, even if I was ready to throw myself out of it.

Addison sat across from me, keeping a distance between us. "How are you feeling?"

"The skin isn't too tight, with the balm Jonathan gave me. And the healing has been quick." I pointed to the marks on my neck, now barely noticeable against the collar of my shirt.

He smiled wanly, swallowing before he spoke. "I'm pleased. I would like to have a discussion if we can?"

"What about?"

"Secrets."

"Ah. I don't know anything. I never do. I am both forgetful and stupid, they're healthy traits to cultivate."

"I don't think you're either of those things, sweet."

"It's often better if I am. Safer."

"I understand." He nodded, mouth screwed up in a little frown that looked silly on such a pretty face. "Firstly, I wanted to apologise again. I was afraid you would die, earlier. When I said I could turn you, it was thoughtless. No turning should happen without explicit agreement. But, the fear made me consider it."

There it was. Inhuman creatures with inhuman answers. I shouldn't have been surprised, despite the little kernel of it nestling in my chest. "Tobias stopped you."

"He knows me well. It's part of why drinking from him was wiser, there is a level of control there for him even if he wanted to bite."

I fingered the marks on my neck. "I wouldn't want to be turned. It seems a terrible thing."

"Because we're all monsters?" His eyes were dim at the question, burnished gold in need of a polish, but I had little comfort to offer him.

"Death has always been a comfort, of sorts. A reassurance you could get out if you had to. And while you're not monsters, from what I've seen, you're still all bound up in each other, aren't you?"

"How do you mean?"

"You're here putting good into the world because killing the bad didn't work like you wanted it to. Pretending to be a scholar because the blessing of your blood turns your stomach. Tobias is making art because holding a sword hurt too much now, and the pain has to come out somewhere." I laughed, running a hand over my scarred stomach. "A house full of ghosts and I found the only real one. Nearly killed me. But, if it had managed it, then at least it would have been over. You're all stuck together."

He raised a brow at me. "And you say you know no secrets."

"I see things. I'm trained to. It doesn't make me popular but it does make me very good."

"It can be lonely, yes." I nodded, about to turn to face the window when he reached for my hand. "I'd like to help you find safety, if I can. With a college, or even with us for some time, if needed, until you find a suitable spot. I know that may not be easy, given today, but you have my word we'd keep you safe as part of the house."

I blinked at him. The house that had tried to bleed me. The house I'd leapt from a window, poorly, to try and be free from. "I believe you mean that." It did not mean it was effective.

"Good. Tobias might forgive himself."

"He's nothing to forgive, it was an urgency." I bit my lip. He'd been careful to give me space, after the blood. Helping where he could but not crowding. Scared, even, when he'd had me on the settee, but still helping.

"How gracious of you, despite everything."

"I don't like causing harm. Self-defence is a necessary act but needless harm is pointless. You know that."

"I do. We should discuss if you'd like to stay with us a while."

"I don't like to make decisions off the back of disasters. Let us see if there will be any consequence to what happened, and I'll make a choice then."

"I meant no pressure, simply to reassure you that the offer's still there. Your knowing... unseemly things about my past does not sway me wanting to share your company."

"Thank you. I'll consider it."

He gave my fingers a little squeeze, but no push of power; it was a purely physical touch, a reassurance. "I appreciate it. Now, the place we are going is a sired companion of mine, an apothecary, and a healer. I'll leave you with her while she sees to you, so there's no chance of influence."

"Won't there be anyway, with you siring her?"

"I don't sire my nest to be surrounded by fawning, pretty things." He chuckled, shaking his head. "Pretty as many of them are, I offer what I can to those I value."

"Three of whom would stab you, it seems."

"Three?"

"Tobias threatened your teeth, Edgar set his knife out, and Haddley had a plan to bleed you."

"Ah, yes." He wrinkled his nose, the brush of a smile coming out. "Haddley's very skilled magically. I don't believe he'd have done that, but he'd defend someone well. So yes, at least three indeed. Chance would too, if that brings you any comfort?"

"He did offer to get me a human doctor. Then chucked me onto the bed, so I hit him."

"That may be considered encouraging, for him. But yes, my nest is a place for growth and learning, not fawning and worship. Much as I share intimacy with my sired in certain ways, they're all their own souls. I don't sway them with thrall."

"That seems..." I trailed off, huffing air. What was the point? I was leaving, no need to have the argument.

"Seems?" His prompting needled something petulant in me, teeth flashing at the edge of my smile, and I pushed on.

"It's different to what I've been taught. Sires are the head of a nest and supposed to be doted on by their blood-children. Here yours are threatening your neck."

"Oh, how I despise that term!" Addison grimaced, shaking his head like a startled cat. "That's an old curse, they still use that in your college?"

They did. "I didn't know it was a... an uncomfortable term?"

"It's pejorative. My sired are their own people, not simpering whelps to be thrown into battle." Ah. The war.

"Apologies." I squeezed his fingers this time. "I know you wouldn't want that. You fuss like a clucky hen; I wouldn't think you'd do that."

"Thank you." He batted his lashes, leaning back in his seat. Our fingers parted and I was reminded of Tobias, earlier, his careful disentangling. "I'm not certain I enjoy the comparison to fowl but there is care in my concern."

"Hence you're taking me to see a healer. Who I will not tell anything other than what you want told, because I never know anything until I'm told it."

"Do people often believe you?"

"Depends on who it is. Do you?"

"Naturally." He winked, folding one leg over the other so he could turn on his hip, watching the outside slide from the green of the country to the reds and browns of houses, the dusty certainty of the city. "Should you feel uncomfortable at any point simply let me know. There need be no more discomfort."

# Chapter 19

The coach took us through the city and into a practical area, a small square dotted with shopfronts set away from the pavement by steep, neat steps.

They were all busy, but less so than the main streets, or those I had been winding through on my arrival yesterday: people with definite business rather than browsing. Addison took us towards a tall green door, paint the colour of ivy in the winter. He knocked quickly before turning the handle and letting us in.

A jingling bell sounded as we stepped over the threshold, and the smell of medicine and herbs swept us in as the door closed. The air was thick, pungent and pushing into my lungs no matter how shallowly I tried to breathe, overwhelming enough to make my head spin.

"Just a moment," called a female voice.

The shop was compact, narrow as a galley with low ceilings to match, and dimly lit from the thin stained-glass windows either side of the door. There were lamps but they were crowded in with assorted scales and discarded containers, and a small fireplace held glowing coals.

Rows of bottles and boxes lined the shelves behind the counter, which ran the length of the wall, with more scales and paper notebooks sat at intervals along the wood. Only the packing space beside the till was left clear—canny that.

A door at the far end was cracked open with no small amount of smoke coming out. white at least, not the building going up.

"Are you well, Margery? That's a lot of incense to be burning."

"Something went a little wrong, this is a better smell than the other options." A formidable woman came out of the door, wiping her hands on her skirt as she approached us. "You have company. Bruised company."

She was my height—taller, with being behind the counter—and built like a ship, broad across the front tapering down into a narrow waist, but with heavy-set arms that promised strength within the confines of her blouse. Creamy skin, almost sallow in the dim light, but quick little eyes. They were probably brown but seemed hazel with the stained-glass light. Not that I had cause to care. Her lips were painted a red too bloody to be anything other than deliberate but it suited her, brought a life to the pallor hanging about her cheeks.

Addison sighed, taking his hat off. "Worse than bruised. There was an incident at the nest, and she'll need your care."

Her smile dropped, leaning forward to peer at me. "What's happened?"

"She was attacked by the consequences of one of my spells, and the manifestation caused significant injuries."

"Cuts across my stomach, sides and neck." I tilted my chin up to show the marks.

"Those look healed."

"I necked his other half." I pointed my thumb to Addison, who blinked a couple of times but nodded. "At Haddley's suggestion."

"You drank from a vampire? My dear, that's the wrong way around."

"Rather."

"I must be elsewhere, but can you please tend to Ena? I trust your eye on these things more than the others, given her magic."

"What does your school say?" She ignored Addison as he departed us, tinkling in his wake.

"My college wasn't detailed on anything vampiric except run in the opposite direction or kill it with fire."

Margery nodded, red lips screwed together as she frowned at me. "Were you on college business?"

"With a nest? Of course not. Garrett abducted me after I set a man on fire."

"Well, that would get Garrett's attention, yes. Your reason for setting someone on fire?"

"Said man wanted to beat and ravage me. Or have some of his thieves do that."

"Had it due to him, then." She leaned on the counter, chin propped in her folded hands as she evaluated me. It wasn't the light; her eyes were hazel. She was stunning, especially with the wicked smirk she wore.

"Can I leave out your backdoor?"

She pulled up from her lean, frowning at me. "Pardon?"

"I didn't plan to end up in a nest house. I'm sure they're lovely, but I nearly died on their floor and I need to be somewhere else. With humans. His influence is overwhelming."

"He can be a lot, too much power tied up in one place. They do help a lot of people, though. Addison's very focused on rebuilding what was lost. Doesn't win him many friends in the hungrier circles but most humans like him for that."

"I'm sure he's charming. I don't take well to being scored like meat."

"Where are you going to go?"

"The Solomon Schools, or one of the other older colleges, anywhere I can claim sanctuary. Stay a day or two then see where I can go next."

"Running from your school?"

"Aye."

She took a deep breath in, looking towards the door. "He'll be disappointed if you do that. Can I check your wounds over before you vanish?"

"Unless you know how the blood will impact them I'd rather not strip again."

"Given you're magically attuned already, in theory, it should mix well. The cuts will have healed, and the bruises will shift overnight. Most likely."

"Likely?"

"In all honesty, my dear, other than the dotty mage he has, I've never heard of someone being so foolhardy. And yet Haddley was right about it, because here you stand. I'll get screeds from him about this."

"He can talk to Addison about it too, I'm sure you'll not get all of it."

She gave a shocked little laugh, slapping the counter between us. "You know what he is."

"Was. He stinks of magic."

"Sharp. I like it, very sharp. Though, Addison doesn't talk to anyone about his magic. He's sworn off it since the war."

I opened my mouth to disagree but closed it again, shaking my head. I'd forced his hand a little with my escape attempt, and the pushes of power. Better I had gone out of that fucking window. "I'm sure he'll indulge Haddley. He did threaten to bleed Addison like a stag this morning so I presume conversations will be had."

"I must ask the man what he was doing, this is chaotic." She sighed, exaggerated and long as she looked me over. "Will you come back, if you can't find safe harbour?"

"Mages look after their own. Even when we're desperate there's a spot by the fire for another mage."

"And are you? Desperate I mean."

"Desperate enough to run from Edinburgh to here."

She set her elbows on the counter to lean her weight over it and look at me more closely. Reaching out, she caught the end of my braid, playing with the tuft. Her cheeks were high and full; she'd be lovely if my skin wasn't itching to run. "Hiding with the nest would give you cover. No one would expect it."

"They wouldn't expect me to run either, but I did. They would be open-minded about my next steps."

"You're lying."

I snorted, tugging my hair free. "And you're stalling."

"I am. If I do let you bolt, he'll be most upset with me."

"Say I threatened to set you on fire. I'm good at it. I can show you, if you like?" I pointed to a nearby candle, almost burned out and overlayered with drips and runs of wax, so it looked to be melting down the side of the counter. "Or the hem of your skirt, to look like it was a struggle."

"I'll pass, you little wildcat." She laughed, standing back from me. "Promise me you'll come back if they refuse."

"They won't."

"But if they do, will you?"

"Yes. I promise if I can't get in, I'll come back and you can gloat about it while you take my shirt off."

"Alright. Through that door leads you to the backdoor. The close is obvious enough to get out of, it'll lead you to the street the coach turned in from. There are some colleges nearby."

"Thank you." I bowed my head, out of respect and in case she liked the look of me, then went for the door.

# Chapter 20

The colleges were easy to find, signs jutting out from the bricks above their doors like doctors and pawnbrokers. It only took a few streets before I found a Madras School, judging from the golden sigils glinting on the sign. It was an imposing building; the heavy door flanked by two carved pillars and the arching windows covered with a cross-hatch of metal to dissuade any attempts at entry. Not that we were much better, but at least Edinburgh had saved the barred windows for inside.

The dark stone steps were wet from someone washing them, given there was no rain, and I trotted up them quickly.

Inside I found a waiting desk with a neat, small woman sat behind it. Her hair was dark and straight, fallen forward to half cover her face, and her clay-brown skin glowed in the lamplight—the nearby window too small for much real sunshine. She was older, judging by the lines on her brow, and her eyes were outlined in heavy black make-up. It was startling, but charming, giving the impression you took all her attention as she looked at you.

"Can I help you?" she asked. Her accent was all here, broad, and clearly London, and I bit my tongue at how thick mine felt. I closed the door and stepped up to the desk, coughing before I spoke.

"I'm here to seek sanctuary. I've had to flee my college to avoid a forced marriage and I'm looking for shelter," I said. "I'm fully trained, and I'm willing to work for my cover until I find somewhere else."

"Is running why you look like that?"

I grimaced, half laughing. "No. I, uh, ended up spending the night in a nest house. One of the younger vampires took me back after seeing me use magic."

"And beat you?"

"No, this was from something else. The magic in the house was hostile, I got injured in a power interplay." It was only halfway a lie. I had no reason to lie for them, there was nothing but guilt in the bloody place, but...

She pressed her lips and brows together, slim face compressing even further. "You look dreadful."

I winced. "So I keep hearing."

"I'm sorry." The frown stayed in place. She crossed her hands over each other, baring the back of them to me, and I saw dark ink circles creeping from the edges of her sleeves. Looping patterns, not the geometrics of Solomon Schools; I'd been right about the signage.

"Do I need to speak to someone, about claiming? I'm from far off so our rules might be different. I didn't know if I should bring anything, but I had to travel light when I ran."

"It's... it's me who you would speak to about that." She swallowed, and wiped her eyes quickly with the back of one hand. "We're not permitting anyone to enter the school currently."

"Excuse me?"

"The school is closed." She took pity on my raised eyebrows. "I don't know if you know about the recent murders?"

"The dead mage, a day or so ago, a young man?"

She gasped, letting it go with a shuddering exhale. "Arif. He evaluated new entrants. We can't be sure it wasn't a deliberate choice to kill him so someone hostile could gain entry. There was a mage spotted near him, when he was killed, though no one knows who it was."

"Are your schools so base that you go about killing each other?" I should not have shouted at her. I knew that as my volume tipped up, as my throat constricted like I'd swallowed glass and my voice cut until it cracked. But there were agreements about this. Standards. We were not meant to abandon those who had trained. We didn't cooperate with other colleges, exactly, but they were all afforded professional respect.

Mages protected their own.

Her face hardened, briefly, then crumpled like she would cry, eyes screwed up to stop the tears. "There have been eight mages lost in the last year. The colleges are afraid. We cannot risk our school suffering more. I will not lose another of our own."

"And I'm not one of yours. No ink."

Watery eyes opened to regard me. "Yes. We're not the only ones, it's the same across the city. Arif was the most senior to be killed. It's made everyone afraid."

"Right." I looked away from her, the streaks of black tracking down her face. A closing of the ranks—I'd not planned for that. We didn't bar the door when one of ours died, but we were an old college. We knew our worth beyond one dead man. Equally, we'd have hunted someone down and pressed until they spoke. There were bright and bloody ways to fix a mage killer.

My plans crumbled around me as I considered their stance. I was alone in the city. I'd relied on seeking sanctuary because that was a certainty, a guarantee we all gave each other, understood between us. And now, nothing. I was fucked.

"Are they chasing you? Your college?" Her question broke me out of my contemplation, brought my gaze back up to her kohl-stained eyes. A little roil of sympathy bubbled in my chest, her sadness contagious, and I couldn't find it in me to spit more bitterness at her. It must have been diluted by the vampire blood.

I nodded. "They will be."

"How do you know?"

"I've brought folk back before, I know what we do. The price of leaving is steep."

She wrinkled her nose, wiping her eyes again. "I'm sorry. If they come to ask, I won't have seen you. And when the doors are open again, please come back. I'm Cynthia, ask for me and I'll be sure to come and assist."

"If I'm still here I will."

"I hope you do. Where will you go?"

My stomach sank. "I don't know. Back to the vampires, I think."

"The ones who kidnapped you?"

"I've nowhere else." I shook my head. Any option was better than home, and I'd been hurt enough to play on sympathy for a night or two. I could shut myself in that warded room and try to make a plan.

"There are human-friendly nests in the city. I know some mages are still wary, even with the accords, but most of them are harmless. There's one outside the city that has a connection to our school, I could give you the name if you wish?"

"Would you trust to stay with them?"

She stared at the desk for a long beat, twitching into response after a deep sigh. "I would. I trusted them with my own, once, and he was safer there than here. The nest head's name is Addison Jagger. The surname's totally incorrect for his age, I suspect it's one he's adopted for convenience, but he's well-studied. Respectful."

Several things rushed together and my stomach curled like a cat, pushing for a way out. "Was Arif your son?"

She smiled, but it was not a thing of joy. "How did you know?"

"Lucky guess. Son or love, for the sake of the tears. Love takes as much as it brings. You must have loved him very much."

"I did. I'm sorry we can't help you."

"It's alright." I shook my head. There was fuck-all else I could do. I could run again, but if the college were looking for me there'd be a reward, and I didn't know that the blood was settled yet. No one here owed me anything, and coin was coin. None of them would expect a nest. Even for a few days, until I knew I was safe, it could be cover. "Sorry for your loss."

# Chapter 21

I entered Margery's shop by the backdoor, as much for my own pride as any chance of Addison spotting me. She was already in the small backroom, eyes fixed on a concoction she was making like she'd dash it against the wall. She had the decency to ignore my slinking in.

"Does glaring at it help?" I asked.

"Welcome back. Are you well?" She didn't look up to me, swirling the fluid in a fat-bottomed container until it began to change from a dull brown towards sumptuous red.

"They're 'closed'. None of the colleges are taking anyone in while there are mages being killed." I flicked my hair out, combing my fingers through it until it was soft and smooth. Braiding it again was quick work, automatic.

"It has been a lot."

"She said eight. Last man down was a senior in their school, so it's shut the door. Doesn't help it was her fucking child, naturally."

"I don't follow?"

"They suspect it may be someone trying to get entry, another mage was seen near him dying."

She blinked up at me, eyes taking in my form. "So they suspect it's a set-up. Understandable."

"I was the mage."

"Excuse me?" The beaker went down.

"I found him dying. First day in London and I find that, hardly a bloody welcome sight. I tried to stop his bleeding, see if I could get him to a healer. Then, when Garrett went for him—" I sighed, shaking my head. That wasn't fair. "When I thought Garrett was going for him, because he was a vampire and there was magic blood, I threw some fire to get attention. I couldn't stop him dying, but I could get his own people to him, was the thought."

She looked me over like a cat gauging if a rat would fight back. "Very considerate for someone you didn't know."

"Mages look after mages. I couldn't heal him but I could defend him from worse."

"Poor Garrett."

"I didn't know! And while I apologise for any undue suspicion, all my tales of vampires are you get fed from, fucked, and left for dead."

She snorted, a wicked little wrinkle forming on her nose as she shook her head at me. "Your place hated us, hm?"

"Yes. And now I have to go back and bide with that lot because I have nowhere else to go other than try to get a ticket on a boat, and I have no money." I crossed my arms, perilously close to sulking. My skin itched with regret and adrenaline, and my stomach had settled low in me like a weight.

"Is it coming after you, what you fled?" I nodded, propping myself against one of the walls. "You can always stay with me if it doesn't work with the nest. I live above here, the shop could always use an extra pair of hands. I scare apprentices off. One bed, though, you'll have to put up with that."

"Welcome as the thought of bedding with you is, I don't want to bring anything untoward down on your head. Addison or otherwise."

"He'll not give me trouble. I'm his favourite. First one he made." She grinned, near rolling her eyes. "He was quite the darling thing about it, too. We were together before he turned me, and he was very careful to be sure I knew what would happen, how I would have to feed. It's easy, in a city, there are arrangements to be made all over, but he was cautious. Tender."

"Together, together?"

"I was in his bed, yes. Is that so scandalous?"

"Were you and Tobias also...?"

"Ah, that pair are impossible. So, no, though he was precious sweet about it too." She leaned back in her chair, tapping her nails along the wood for a moment. "Addison loves, and indulges, widely, he's open minded with that. Tobias, for someone who was never human, has a very human heart. I've seen them both take up with various folk, but Tobias is more guarded. He still hurts."

"He's been good to me. Other than the headbutt."

Margery cackled a laugh, clapping a hand to her face. "He didn't! Did you catch him sleeping?"

"I leapt out a window and he went with me. Landed on him, broke his rib, he whacked my head. It settles off in the round."

"You went out a window?"

"I'd been kidnapped, one usually tries to escape such circumstance."

"I must come visit soon, this sounds delightfully disastrous. They're a terrible pair, and perfect together, when they do go together. You'll be safe with them if you go back."

"I wasn't earlier."

"The others make up when the older ones lack. He did collect a lot of doctors." She winked, shaking her head. "In all the telling, Addison considers his duties well. He is kind to his sired, and honours his guests."

"The accords do encourage that."

"I think he would have been before them, but, well. Who knows how he was before the war. Tobias and him are tight-lipped about it and I trust it's for a reason. In the sixty years I've known him, he's always moved to be protective of it." She barely looked thirty.

"Is that why you moved out?"

She shook her head. "I wanted my freedom. I can run this shop myself, live above it and have the whole of my circumstances in my own control. In a city like London that's a huge boon."

My heart sang at that thought. The freedom of your own terms. "I see the appeal."

"Yet you don't want to live with them."

"Were you trained in magic, before you were turned?"

"No. I learned all of mine afterwards, between Haddley and others. I rather like being a healer, but I'd not have been able to get training as a human."

"We're trained about what happened in the war. Better dead than a battery."

She shook her head. "They're not that type."

"I'll have to take my chances either way." I could break things even if I couldn't kill them. Let them try to bite me with a broken jaw.

"I think it'll be a good match. You can hide with them and they can be terrified of you. If you want to—" She was cut off by the sound of the jangling bell, before Addison called out.

"Hello?"

"Back here," Margery shouted. "Come on."

# Chapter 22

"Are you well, Ena?" Addison asked. The carriage was rattling along at a pace, bumping with a gait closer to a boat than horses.

"Hm?" Disappointment sat around me like a shawl and I hadn't found how to say what was on my mind in the passing scenery. It would be pointless to delay it, but my words had run off with all my hope of escape.

"You're quiet."

I smiled at him, running my tongue along the back of my teeth as I struggled with what to say. In for a penny, and all that. "I find myself in a bit of a predicament, if I'm to be honest with you."

"Tell me what it is, I'm happy to help if I can," he said.

"The colleges are closed, which leaves me unable to hide. I'll be looked for, and seeking sanctuary was my way out of that. At least temporarily. If the colleges are closed, then I'm limited in my options."

"Ah. Did Margery tell you they were closed?"

"No, I threatened to burn her shop down if she didn't let me run off, then went out the backdoor."

His brows went up and he clicked his tongue before he spoke. "You could have come with me. I went to pay my respects for Arif, you could have spoken to them at the same time."

"And I'd feel so enthused going to one you had approved, absolutely no chance of influence."

"I marvel at the powers you think I have. Our influence isn't so vast."

"Thrall victims kill themselves if their master dies. I nearly died on your floor. Spare me the outrage." I glared at him, and he nodded, looking away.

"Forgive me, lambkin. I find your... concern about my influence unusual, but of course you would be afraid. Did the college upset you?"

"I upset them. I managed to find Arif's mother."

"Cynthia?"

"Aye, that's the one. Big eyes, pretty. Weepy. As she would be, her son was killed."

Addison was quiet again, threading his fingers together on his knees. "He was well-known in the city. As is Cynthia. She was setting him up to take the school on, be her replacement. He was young for it, and it caused some disquiet with them, that's how he came to be with us. He'd not been back long."

"They think another mage did it."

"Ah." His brows popped up. "Your fire, to scare off Garrett?"

"You see my predicament. With the police, it was one thing, but if the colleges suspect me I'm stuck."

"Have you considered venturing into detective work?"

I flared at his glib response, irrationally angry as Arif's face flashed behind my eyes, the watery run of Cynthia's make-up a condemnation. "Fuck off, if you're going to mock me, at least be considerate of the dead."

He startled, blinking at me like I'd struck out. "I'm quite serious, sweet. I appreciate you may not want to say it was you that found him, a new face makes a fine one to blame. However, my suggestion would allow two avenues into the colleges."

"Go on." I hunkered back into my corner but turned towards him.

"Someone is harming mages and you have no haven. Staying with us until the killer is found means you've somewhere until they reopen. You could simply wait, with us."

"I don't want to be in your debt."

He held his hands up, palms out. "The second option, which aligns well with the first but doesn't have to happen, is to be seen openly as part of the nest. Not so openly that whatever you're hiding from could find you, but be seen with us. If someone is targeting users with an association to my nest, you would be sought out. Whoever has done this can be captured."

"Why do you think it's connected to you?"

He leaned forward, catching my hand in his. "I don't know for certain it is. If I knew, I'd offer you something else, a house in the city or one of the villages nearby. Arif was the only mage who had been with us who has been killed, and we've had others keep our company who are alive and well. However, three of the mages killed were known to me."

"Less than half but more than a coincidence."

"Yes. I keep correspondence with many scholars, and those who have been taken were of the larger academic schools. It could be simple coincidence."

"You don't believe that."

"I'd rather be cautious. If you are willing to play a role, it may mean less deaths. And more chance of you being able to go where you wish."

"Or get killed too." The words sat between us, the silence worse when his eyes looked so pained.

"Arif was no fighter. None of them were. He was trained, certainly, and he could hold his own in a debate, but he wasn't a fighter. I suspect he would've been less capable than you of defending himself."

Arif's glassy eyes came back to me, brown irises almost swallowed whole by their pupils, the empty stare. "He didn't say anything, when I tried to get him to speak. I even slapped him." I took my hand back, cradling it against my chest like it was marked, hurt from the hurt I'd inflicted. "I fight, yes."

"So, I trust, between yourself and those in the nest, if anyone tried to harm you, they'd be much the poorer for it. And you could evidence that to get you into a college."

I'd played bait before. There were all sorts of plays we had in college work, pretending to be staff, or a cousin, a new charge brought into a rich house. Anything to let us get in and blend with the folk, working people over. Seeing who lied and who was devoted, which contracts were to be trusted.

My colleagues may have made better bodyguards than me, but I was excellent at blending in. There was a perverse familiarity in the idea.

I sat up, leaning forward to speak to him, eye to eye. "If I do, I'll need to be able to trust you. And we'll need to set some boundaries."

"Such as?"

"I want some sort of exchange. I won't be in your debt. You can promise me as much as you like, I need something more substantive than that."

"Is kindness so strange to you that everything must be transactional?"

I laughed as I shook my head. He wasn't wrong, and it needled in my chest to admit it—I couldn't trust something freely given. I pulled back a touch, enough to check him over properly, dressed in the same frock coat as I'd met him in, though no gloves given it was daytime. He blended in so well it would be easy to forget who he was. What he was—immortal, never human, never limited in the choices as we were. Never having to balance a knife edge of compromises and hope your path was right.

"I can trust an exchange more readily, yes. I prefer being able to make my own choices, and a debt's an obligation. Especially around someone who has magical influence, which I've had to knock back."

"I give you my word that I will not do that again. Are there any other terms you would wish?"

"I need a way to earn my keep, other than being bait for you. I can cook and clean, we kept our own space in the dormitory. I can lay my hand to several tasks around a house, and I know how to mend and stitch."

"You don't need to do that."

"I want to do something."

"What about magic?" I blinked at him. "Clearly you're skilled in more than one way, to throw elements around and pluck up memories. I'm aware your colleges don't approve, but I find it fascinating. We could trade knowledge, like I do with my correspondence in the city. You ask, and I ask. We both learn."

I frowned, biting the back of my lower lip and worrying the flesh. It was an attractive offer. "I thought you didn't share your magic. Margery said you didn't."

"I would for a scholarly endeavour."

"Alright. I also want to have somewhere to be alone if I need to be. Somewhere with a lock."

"For your safety?"

"In a way. Haddley, and his aversion. I don't know if he's been around women a lot since turning, but I'll have my moons. And while I can certainly be crabbit on them, more pressingly the inevitable comes with that." I didn't want to hurt the twitchy, worried man who tried hard to be nice, and had reasonably, done a better job saving me than his sire.

"That's thoughtful of you. I must confess I don't believe he has been. Margery didn't experience them once turned and Haddley has lived with us a considerable time."

"I want the option lest he's not alright."

Addison nodded. His smile was more than polite, almost like he was enjoying the negotiation, and I didn't have it in me to push at it more. "Agreed. Anything else?"

"I might need to run at short notice."

"Your college?"

"Aye. They'll be enraged at what I've done."

"Killing that man?"

"That won't be a shock. Running, living with a nest, that'll be seen as reckless."

"But not the death?"

I bristled, tilting my chin at him. "Self-defence is a necessary act. Do you know how many magic users get killed, fangs aside, in some places? Petty scores settled in lochs and on gallows hills, users singled out even when they're untrained. Fuck that. I wasn't going to get raped because some prick didn't like my defending myself."

"I can see why Margery took so well to you."

"I threatened her."

"I'm certain." His smile told me he didn't believe it but I'd stick to the line. "I agree to all you request."

"Right." That was much easier than it should have been. "Do you have any rules in exchange?"

"I'd like an undertaking. If you're in a position where you feel the need to run, please let me know. I want to help you." He took my hand in his, squeezing a little. I looked at the way our fingers sat together; mine rough with work, his smooth other than a smudge of ink.

"Can you see why it might be hard for me to believe that?" I asked, refusing to meet his eyes.

"That some people wish to help?"

"It's asking me to bear my neck to a snare every day, living here. And I don't know what else you're not telling me, but I know some things I shouldn't already."

His grip tightened on my fingers, fingertips tapping against the side of my hand. "Hopefully we can earn your trust. I'm content to talk about what you saw, if you wish to, but on your own terms. Is there any way to make you feel safer meantime? I could give you a recipe for blessed fire, that would kill an immortal properly."

I blinked at him. "You just keep that about your house?"

"All the immortals know how to make it. The war would have gone on a lot longer if not."

That would get me in a lot of places in the future. That would mean death if one of them went for me, too, which was more than I had otherwise. "I'd like that. I don't think I have the skill for it, my fire isn't blessed, but it would be fascinating."

"Then we'll do that. And can I ask one other thing?"

I looked up at his question, so soft to be almost a whisper. "What?"

"I don't want you to feel like you must fake things with me, but I would dearly like, at some point, for you to feel safe enough with us that you could also be happy. My house doesn't have to be a monstrous place."

"I don't think it is. The lack of choice can be, but that's not your doing. I knew I had limited choices when I ran."

"But it was better to do so anyway?"

"Yes."

His face rippled, briefly, a sadness in his eyes that looked deep as the ocean. A sea of gold, old and hungry in the worst way. Longing. What did a creature with all the time in the world long for? "Then I'll try to support you getting as many options as possible when the colleges reopen," he said.

# Chapter 23

"She didn't run," Haddley called as Addison and I walked back into the house. He was peering out of the drawing room doorway, perilously close to falling at that angle, with Garrett stood propped behind him.

"Was there a betting pool?" Addison asked. He cast his eyes around the entryway, the various sired lazing around like cats in sunlight. The only missing members were Jonathan and Tobias, conspicuous in their absence.

"I started it, thought she'd be away from you and into the city," Chance said. He was sat on the steps, leaned back so he was propped up on his elbows and with his legs skewed out in front of him. It was so foolishly young, like lads on the college steps, melting in the summer heat and whistling for pretty things going past, and I could have hurt my neck at how different he was to earlier.

"He actually bet she would break out the shop window at Margery's," Edgar said, sat at the top of the steps and slightly above Chance. "I said that'd be too obvious."

"One of you is not entirely wrong, but I won't say who unless I get a cut of the winnings," I said. I shed the coat I had been loaned, an ivy green wool blend that was surprisingly light for the summer warmth. Addison took it on one arm with a slight bow.

"By your face it was the window and you fell out of it." Garrett raised a dark brow at me.

Addison scoffed, leaning closer with a conspiratorial wink. "That's from beating Tobias last night."

"Is that all she did?" Chance asked. "He's been sulking in the library since you left."

"Might be feeling faint because I drank so much of his blood."

"It was barely anything, they all took more from me in our turnings," Addison said.

"I bet they did, strapping man like you." It was out before I could stop it, much too much like the dormitories, but I'd said it now so I flashed my sharpest grin and hoped not to be cast out immediately.

Haddley did drop to the floor at that one, Garrett's hand coming up to cover his face as he howled with laughter and Edgar smothered his like someone in trouble at church.

"His blood must have done this, yesterday she's cracking me between the thighs and today she's taking strips out of daddy here?" Chance folded his arms in faux disapproval, shaking his head.

"Did Addison manage to get a drink in you or do you simply like inflicting harm on the helpless?" Edgar asked. He perched the toe of his foot at Chance's shoulder and shoved, sending the lower man tumbling down the steps into a heap.

"Aye, right, a flock of lost lambs here looking for guidance." I shook my head at them, settling my shoulders. "And no, he didn't even offer to buy me a drink."

"I at least got a drink." Chance dragged himself up into standing. "Your standards are slipping, old bat."

"Peace, all of you. You're to let Ena rest. She's going to be a guest of the house until other matters are settled, so she needs time to get used to it. And your rambunctious behaviours."

"She's staying despite nearly being killed by whatever that was earlier?" Chance frowned at me, and I shrugged.

"Your charming company convinced me."

Addison smiled, dipping my way. "Edgar, I'll also need to speak to you for getting a new blade for Ena's travels."

"You're arming her too?" Chance asked.

"Just physically." I winked at him. This was easy, I knew how to roll about with lads who had training. I wasn't entirely sure what Chance was trained in, other than medicine, but the others still had that give and take of being in a group.

Chance sighed, bumping shoulders with Addison. "Not that I'm not delighted, but why are we keeping the angry mage that threatened to burn us down twice?"

"You keep Haddley, no offence," I said. Haddley shrugged from his spot beside Garrett, arms tangled as they hung off each other. It was a sweet, if an odd, embrace.

"He's different. He only throws himself off the roof, no one else at risk."

"Except those below," Garrett said. He nuzzled into Haddley, who batted his shoulder with no real force.

I turned back to Chance, nodding. "Noted. I'll be sure to only pick one person to do that to as well. Is Jonathan about?"

"In the kitchen. I'll take you." Edgar came down the steps, bumping past Chance to lead me.

"Thanks." I went after him, falling into step with his easy gait. "So what does the winner get, in your bet?"

"Nothing, truly. We're glad that you didn't run."

I choked down a laugh, shaking my head at the thought. "You may change your minds on that."

"We won't. Addison always has a plan. Not always a smart one, but a plan nonetheless."

"That why you got your knife out before?"

"That was in case it was a bad plan." He chuckled, rolling his shoulders. "Tobias has the ruling of him but knowing others disagree lends weight. A knife wouldn't kill him, but losing an eye tends to dissuade one from actions. Even when the eye comes back."

"It's a direct objection."

"I can get you a knife like mine. Addison will say to get whatever's best, so if you have a preference let me know."

"I need to make it hurt if someone tries things."

He snorted, shaking his head. "I reckon you'll be alright enough on that mark."

"Reckon all you like. Chance isn't that wary after me clocking him, is he?"

"He's a funny 'un. He was a doctor, still is, and that's as much as he's said to any of us but the immortals." He glanced back over his shoulder, giving me a low shrug. "Well-travelled for a doctor."

"Some of them are, they're always needed."

"Yes, I think needed is the term. He worked hard. A lot of folk here did. I was in the army, Garrett too, Haddley... I'm not certain. I try not to think about it."

"Not keen on magic?"

"No, that's fine. He sometimes gets this look, when he's watching one of the masters of the house, and it's awful like he's trying to figure out if he could take them. Then that comment, before, when you were bleeding. I don't think he would, but there's a look." He tapped beside his eye.

"Sizing them up."

"Aye. That. Would be an unwise thing, to do that."

"I'm sure Garrett will keep him right, he seems solid." Too solid, for the fact he took me here, but I couldn't fault that he seemed to mean well.

"As a cliff before the shore. Good-hearted man. Have you forgiven us yet?"

"No."

He chuckled, and it was all the field, all the sort you heard between commanders getting ready to talk dirty and get things settled. "Thought not. You're not army, what are you?"

"I'm a mage." I snorted at his raised eyebrows. "My work covered a lot. Negotiations, companionship for travelling ladies, contracts. We're a versatile place." Hired bodies were always flexible.

"As you say. Here we are." He stopped beside the kitchen door. "You can get out to the quad through that door too." He tilted his chin to a door on the opposite side. "Haddley doesn't often come off the roof. Just when he gets ideas. He's determined to fly."

"I suppose falling is a close second." I gave him a nod and turned into the kitchen.

Jonathan was stood at the counter, kneading dough like it was a face he disliked. I refused to believe he'd earned his muscle solely through beating bread, but he did it with an experienced vigour.

"Do you bake every day?" I asked as I came to stand at his side. The counter was neat for a baker, the flour not straying away from his little spot near the sink.

"Most of them. There are a lot of mouths to feed."

"On top of the blood."

"They don't often mix them, but yes." He paused his beating to wipe his brow with a small cloth that had been tucked into the back of his belt. "We get deliveries every couple of days from one of the feeding houses and I make food regularly."

"What can I do to help?"

"You're staying?"

"I was going to run off in the city but the colleges are shut." I portioned off a little segment of flour to trace shapes with. "Turns out I'm stuck."

"Are you alright?" He bobbed his chin my way, watching me out of the side of his eye as he began to knead the bread again.

"Can't say I'm delighted, but it's here or under the hedge. I need a way to earn my keep and you seem to be doing that, so I thought I'd join you."

He thumped the dough, folding it into itself. "Well, half of them have a sweet tooth and the other half lie about it. Very fond of scones, if you can make them."

"Course I can."

"Then we have the first thing you can do. I have a jar of sultanas in the pantry, you can make a batch to go with supper."

"Alright. You like baking?"

"I'm better at it than some other things."

"Did you work in a shop? You know what you're doing."

"My dad was a baker a long while, he taught me and Teresa to do it too. The plan was for me to do the same, but it didn't work out."

"Teresa?"

"My sister. She was never going to take the place on, of course, but I was."

"And now you're down here."

"Hm?" He twisted on his hip, looking around.

"That accent's no more local than mine."

He laughed as he turned back to the dough. "Aye, travelled a bit. Now if you want to get the scones ready I'll let you have the oven while this is rising, so they have time to cool as well."

"Gracious of you."

"Save that 'til I see your scones. I'm not easy to please in matters of baking."

Right then.

# Chapter 24

"Ena, are you available?" Addison appeared in the kitchen door while the scones were cooling. He took a deep breath in, sighing happily when he spotted the cluster of them beside the window. "Fresh scones? We don't usually have those except for company. What's prompted these?"

"They're not mine, that's a set by her. A bit rough in form but they're lovely and light."

"You can show me how you get yours so neat, then." I near stuck my tongue out at him, the preening little sod, but Addison scooped one up before I could.

"I'll look forward to more. I am rather fond of a scone." He broke it in half, then did so again, popping a small segment in his mouth. "Come join me. Could you bring us tea as well please, Jonathan?".

"Of course." Jonathan nodded, sharp as a soldier, and went to the kettle. I followed Addison out, resisting the impulse to grab a scone myself.

Addison led me down the corridor towards his study, taking us around the quadrangle and the lazy afternoon sunlight spilling in through the little windows which studded the walls. It was an odd sort of house, with a space carved out of the middle, but there was a decent basement underneath from the size of the staircase leading down into the damp earth. It did mean the house was wonderfully light too, sunlight coming from somewhere whenever it was out.

It suited the place, with all that dark wood to make up for.

Once we were in the study, Addison directed me towards the same chairs as last night, now before the fireplace properly with the little table between them for the tea. I sank down in one while he shifted papers around on his desk, finally plucking one up in victory.

"I wanted to give you this." He handed me the paper, the dark ink in neat little lines.

"What is it?"

"A recipe for spiritual, or blessed, fire. I said I would give you something proper. This should be accessible to you as a human, rather than our methods."

I looked between the page and him, the paper wobbling in my grip. "You're giving me this?"

"I'm a man of my word."

"This isn't that hard to make. Would take a little time, yes, but it could be done. I could do it, I mean." I put the page down on my lap, crossing my hands over it. "I understand the knife but why this?"

"I want you to feel safe. You've agreed to help us with something that could risk harm to you, so this goes some way to protecting you in a different way to the knife." He sat across from me, eyes flicking over my face before he spoke again. "And, truthfully, the idea that you would run off with no warning, that you did without my realising, upsets me. I won't be able to settle all your fears, but this should at least let you sleep? In a bed?"

"It wasn't the fear of you lot keeping me from sleep." The door opened as Jonathan came in with tea, setting the tray down on the table. He'd also brought a few slices of fruit cake which he put on my side of the tray, with a small nod.

"Thank you, Jonathan," Addison said.

"You're welcome. I'll be stepping out for shopping, do you require anything?"

"No, thank you, but do take one of the others with you rather than carrying it all back yourself."

"He looks like he can lift a cow with those shoulders," I said.

"Addison likes to be careful with us weak and frail humans." Jonathan gave me a wink as he took the tray back. "I'll ask Garrett to come with me once he's done assisting Haddley. I think they're planning another experiment."

Addison's face pinched. "The roof again?"

"I expect so."

"He really jumps off the roof?" I asked. I'd thought it some inner joke at my earlier threat.

"Haddley believes the right application of magic will allow him to levitate. Why he doesn't start from the ground, like geese do, I don't know, but I haven't an ounce of magic so I may be an uneducated swine," Jonathan said.

"I can't imagine many colleges approving of that."

"Haddley isn't a member of one, given he lives with the nest," Addison replied.

"Right." I took a slice of cake so I had something to do with my hands. He'd break his neck, surely. At least a leg. "Does he see Margery a lot?"

"Chance sets anything significant so it's easier to heal, but a sired vampire can regrow a bone in a few days. He may need some extra blood to assist. Best had arrange that while you're shopping, Jonathan."

"Already on the list." Jonathan tapped his shirt pocket and made for the door. It clicked closed and I took a quick bite of the cake.

"May I ask an indelicate question?" Addison asked. I chewed, slowly, but nodded. "If it wasn't us, and I would understand if it were, especially with what happened, what else makes you feel unsafe?"

I swallowed and huffed air, running my tongue across my teeth as I mulled my answer. "The lack of sleep was not connected to the lack of safety. I can see why it could be, but I don't sleep well anyway."

He coughed, pressing his lips together. I took another bite of cake so he had to speak instead of me. "I don't intend to pry into anything you don't wish to share."

"But?"

"Is it something I can assist with?"

"No." He didn't need to know what haunted my dreams any more than I needed to know what kept him researching through the night.

"Will the knife help?"

"It will help with the feeling safe while we see if your potential stalker tries to kill me."

"Quite. We have a lot of experience, between us, in the nest, so if there is anything you wish to talk about please do let me know. Though, if you are practicing that spell can I ask you warn Tobias and I."

"To save you the fright?"

"Yes. I would offer tips, but it might seem a bit self-aggrandising."

"Could be a vested interest, indeed." I sipped some tea, letting it sit on my tongue for longer than necessary before I swallowed. "Can I say something indelicate?"

Addison's brows rose. "You don't need to ask."

"You did, only seems polite. I very much appreciate what you have done for me, but my lack of ability to repay you is a clear thing."

"I've said you don't need to do so, given you're assisting us."

"And I've heard that said many times, often with a catch. Talking to Margery, it seemed like you do just... give things away. Offer safety for those you take interest in. She's a great example of it."

"Margery is a force of nature."

"And your first sired."

"Haddley and her were turned very close together, but she was my first, yes."

I nodded, tearing the rest of my cake into little chunks for something to do with my hands. "So I do trust her word, and she trusts you. As did Cynthia. When she wasn't crying she said you were safe."

"You told her you were staying with us?"

"No." I barked a laugh, heat in my cheeks at how harsh it was bouncing back at me. "She mentioned safe nests, when I said I was staying with vampires. Your name was raised. I didn't say I was with you."

"Why not?"

"If they suspect I killed your lad it would hardly help either of us, would it? Risks your nest getting burned and risks me getting blamed. We'd both lose. I didn't want to bring you more risk. Even if I'm unsure of the long-term view of the matter."

"You're worried this is an investment to me, to be called on later." He almost smiled.

I blinked at him, nodding a little. "The thought had occurred."

"Is that what your school would do?"

A startled laugh shook from my throat, and I drank more tea to cool my anger. "Yes, it's exactly what we would do. One way or another. Everything is thought of long term. Your long term would be very different to theirs, but I imagine there's an overlap. You have enough sired here that it must be deliberate, it's hardly a knocking shop."

"I won't deny it is myself who asks if one of my charges or friends wishes to turn. All the residents in the nest have been contacts or companions of mine or Tobias."

"Quite the extended family."

"A family by choice. No one here was turned through coercion. Or indebtedness."

I swirled the dregs of tea. "Good. You didn't seem the type but generosity has strings. Pimps and scoundrels, lords and pastors, there was always an expectation. The college was at least straightforward in its terms."

"I prefer being upfront as well."

I scoffed, barely able to keep a scowl down. "That's less reassuring when I know that you're lying."

"Am I?"

"Do the other archmages hide in nest houses in the country, or was it being royalty that spurred you to bolt?"

He sighed and shook his head, selecting a slice of cake and taking a bite before he spoke. "In that regard, I am exclusive. Both in my actions and that I am the only one remaining."

"Pardon?"

"The war was vicious. The only other, towards the end, was Luc. Your mages may look after one another, ours kill."

I winced, ran my tongue along my teeth as I took that in. "Sorry for your troubles."

"You weren't even alive, you don't need to apologise."

"Pain's pain, new or old. I keep bumping into yours."

"As you said earlier, I have more of it than some. Your concerns are not unreasonable." He drank more tea, bobbing his head a little before he spoke again. "While I am almost hurt you find me so suspect, you're still giving me your company. And have openly discussed your concerns with me. I hold that as a mark of trust."

"It is. I trust this to be the safest place for me to be, even with your circumstance."

"Have I convinced you already?" He finished the cake slice off in a couple of quick bites. Mine was still in the plate on my lap, torn into pieces, and I couldn't stomach having more.

"Without belabouring a point, I was in your bed, confused and without guard. If you wanted to do something to me you've had opportunity. If nothing else, that makes me feel safer."

"Would having an escort help? One of the sired would be happy to accompany you if there's a worry about Tobias or myself, and we won't be sending you out alone."

"It's not that I'm any more afraid of you than them. I'm looking forward to getting to know them. Carefully."

"They're all good men. Impulsive, yes, some of them. Haddley does jump off the roof, Edgar is protective. Chance has old habits he flexes when someone new is around. Garrett has a wonderful heart." He smiled, lopsided, before he shrugged. "They all sought the change for good reasons, or I wouldn't have turned them."

"That's private business, I don't want to pry." I held my hands up. "Just please understand it's not you I fear. There are worse things than you."

"I would assist you with those, if you wished me to."

My heart twisted at his words. I suspected he meant them, and that didn't make it hurt any less. "Thank you. Do you mind if I go now? I think I'd like to lie down."

"By all means. We should also discuss arranging you a better wardrobe at some point."

"Let me be sure I'm healed up, less chance of getting blood on things."

# Chapter 25

"Ena, can I ask you something?" Haddley was propped against the wall beside the study door, immediately at my side as I stepped out. It was all I could do not to shriek.

"Were you waiting for me?"

"Yes, I wanted to speak to you about your magic but you were busy with Addison so I didn't want to be rude."

I blinked at him, a breath stuck in my throat as my mind tried to catch up. "Right. Yes."

"I wanted to speak to you about which college you're from, because you smell like spirit magic but you use multiple elements which is very forbidden from what I've read but you also don't use a ritual, and that would usually mean you were very well attuned but you don't have tattoos." He tapped the inside of my wrist, the thin skin showing only veins.

He was loquacious. "I think this would be easier over a drink," I said.

He blinked, frowned, then crossed his arms. "Hrm. I don't drink a lot."

"You do look like I could lose you in a wine bottle."

"Is that because I'm thin?" He bobbed his head at me, like a bird examining a bug.

"Yes, Haddley."

"I like that one. Can I use that as well?"

"Absolutely. Can we go find some wine and talk more slowly?"

"Yes. I'll get some and meet you in the garden? It's nice in the sunset, there's a good spot you can watch the colours change."

"That sounds lovely." I glanced around for which way to go. The backdoor was somewhere near Addison's study.

"Follow me." We walked through to the kitchen in merciful silence, though he kept glancing over to me and nodding to himself.

"You alright there?" I asked.

"I want to ask you a lot of questions, but I won't do that until we get to the garden. I'm trying to keep track of them in my head."

"You really like your magic, hm?"

"Yes! I can't ask Addison much about his, he goes very quiet. Tobias hasn't got much other than the natural stuff, with being an immortal, and Margery is patient with me but she's only healing so she doesn't have the same questions I do so she listens to me theorise but she doesn't have many answers." We reached the kitchen and I waited inside the door as he went to find a bottle of wine.

"What school did you study with?"

"All sorts, I've looked into ritual and elemental, but also some of the more dedication-based ones like the Solomon Schools." He paused as he went up on his toes to pluck two glasses out of a cupboard. "They're not too different to your traditional rituals but they're less careful on the components, whereas when you get into the focus of the Christian branches you're looking more into alchemy which I like, but it's very dangerous, and I haven't even looked into healing yet."

"Haddley, do vampires need to breathe?" He poured a glass for each of us, capping the bottle with a heavy metal stopper from one of the drawers. He frowned before he answered, bobbing his head side to side while he thought. I walked closer, hand out for the glass.

"Not really, technically, but it's a habit for most of us. Why?" He passed me the glass, only half full but that was fine for the afternoon.

I smiled at him. "Just checking. You didn't answer me, though. Where did you learn, to begin with, before you were turned?"

"Oh I wasn't allowed in any of them."

"What?"

"I was, uh." He smiled, all teeth, shaking his head. "I wasn't the right sort for them, in the schools. Too enthusiastic, and too, well. Odd."

"Oh." Shit. Untrained mage. "Odd."

"You have that look."

"What look?" I drank a quick gulp of wine.

"There's a look people get when they learn I'm untrained. It's like a mix between them being angry and scared."

"I'm not scared of you, Haddley." I set the glass down before I drained more. "Untrained magic use can be dangerous. Risky. But that doesn't make me afraid of you. You helped me."

"How could I learn if they wouldn't let me in?" His voice was so small, well-worn words tripping off his tongue.

"Sometimes there's good reason they don't let you in. I was late to join mine, they nearly didn't take me because of that."

"But you did get in."

"They thought I could be useful. My college wanted bodies they could hire out, once trained, so we could earn for them. It wasn't a good place."

"I could have been useful."

"I'm sure. I know…" I trailed off and drank more wine. "I know a lot of people hide their powers and live normal lives. The idea of going off and training with no support when you had the chance not to, to seek a struggle like that out, it's unusual. Normally, it would make you dangerous."

"You left your college because it was dangerous."

I bristled, shoulders going high around my neck on reflex. "You don't know why I left. Don't speak for me."

"I didn't mean that." His whole face flushed; his lips pressed together. "They're not helping you, is what I mean. You're here hiding with people you hate because the people from your college will hurt you."

"Kill me, possibly, yes. I don't hate you, though."

"You don't pull knives on people you like."

"Nor do I like many people who knock me out and abduct me, but I'm still here."

He screwed his mouth up, frowning deeply. "Isn't that only until you run away?"

"Not anymore."

"What?" He looked up at me, eyes watery.

Gods above. "I was going to. I tried, earlier on. The colleges are closed. Too many murders." I shrugged, raising my hands so I could spin the empty glass between my palms. "So, since I have to stay, I'm going to try and make the most of it. Like discussing magic with you."

"So this is alright?"

"Us talking magic?"

"Me being like I am."

"Haddley, no don't say it like that." I set the glass down, putting a hand on his and running my thumb over the sharp peaks of his knuckles. "I'm sorry I said that. It's surprising for me, given you're so learned. You knew exactly what to do before, when I was being hurt, so I thought you were from one of the colleges. I suppose I was taking some comfort in that."

"Someone who would know how you felt."

"Yes." I smiled at him. His face was blotchy from trying not to cry, and I fumbled for something to help. "Do you want to see some of my untrained magic?"

He sniffed, wiping his eyes. "What?"

"I told you I was late to join the college. I was seven, and they usually have you in at three or four."

"That's very small. To be away from their mums. So little." Haddley wrapped his hands together, worrying the knuckle bones of his left with the fingers of his right. My heart tugged at the motion, guilt warring with wanting to make up for my clumsy upset.

"People notice elemental powers early. They didn't notice mine because of what I use." I tapped my chest, above my heart. "Not as obvious as setting fire to the nursery."

"Do they do that?"

"Some of them. One of the men I worked with, he was fire right from the start, he went through two sets of drawers in his parents' room when he was a baby. Caused all sorts of trouble." Ben had never stopped making trouble.

"Do their mums stay with them?"

"Sometimes. Sometimes the nuns looked after them, if it was too sore for the mums. But that's not what I'm going to show you. Do you have a handkerchief?"

"Five." He gave me one, patting his pocket with the others. "I like having spares."

"Good man, you're who I want at an emergency. Let's go by the sink." We shifted over while I folded the material into a little pyramid, standing it up on my palm. "Garrett told you how I used my fire, yes?"

"Yes."

"It's not always that big, it can be delicate, too. Watch. *Teine.*" I whispered the word, watching the tip of the material light like a candle. It wavered, gentle as a caress, then began to eat its way down the material.

"Spontaneous manifestation? That's what that is, isn't it? I've not seen someone do that in person before!"

"I don't know what they'd call it properly, but they're my words. They're my natural gift, separate to what I was trained in. Very naughty, but they never managed to get me out of the habit. The words summon energy to you and direct it in one way, quickly. So that can be calling down fire or water, or it can be breaking something, or air to your lungs. They're narrow tools."

"Like when that man attacked you in the alley."

"Or if a man goes overboard on a boat and you need him to breathe."

He made a little noise in agreement. "That would be wanted in a coastal place, yes."

"Stand back a touch for me."

He did as I asked and I tossed the material up, kissing the same word on the air. The fire flared bright at my invitation, consuming the linen square in a sudden flash, then the ashes were floating into the sink.

Haddley was immediately over my shoulder, face into the basin to look at the fragments. "That's how you did what Garrett saw. And you can vary it with intent, as well. That's so curious!"

"Thank you. I'd prefer you kept it to us, as I don't know how the local colleges will be about it. But it's untrained magic, all wild. So, you know I don't think you're bad, yes?"

"Very much so. Oh Ena, I have so many more questions." He clapped his hands together, bouncing on the balls of his feet like he'd found a treasure.

"We can speak about them another time, I'll need to tidy this up and I might go lie down."

"You go do that, I'll tidy this." Haddley put his hands carefully on my arms, at my elbows, and turned me away from the sink like he was guiding me in a waltz. "I want to examine the ash."

"Alright. Thank you." I ducked my head, ignoring the heat in my cheeks and neck at his enthusiasm. It could also be the wine.

"It's no problem. I'll make a list of my questions too, so we can speak another time. I find people like it better if I'm organised."

"That'll be nice." I retreated from the kitchen, aiming for my room before anyone else wanted a chat.

# CHAPTER 26

*"D on't say a word, Ena!"*

*"Mam!"*

*"Listen to me. It's all alright. But you mustn't say a word, do you hear me?"*

I woke with a dry face, the fear too familiar to prompt tears. I swallowed the creak in my throat; must have been shouting. I'd need tea.

I rolled up from my curled position under the sheet. I didn't scream often anymore but it was no real surprise—everything was still unsettled after the vampire blood more than a week since, and magic was unpredictable.

Scrubbing my hands over my face to shake the dregs of the nightmare off, I slapped my cheeks twice, quick and hard to get the blood pumping. I stood, stretching my spine out, and huffed a deep breath. No point in dwelling on it. It was flashes of back then, it wasn't as bad as the full dream I used to have. That was a blessing.

After dressing, I wandered down to the kitchen, alone again. I'd found a sort of routine since I agreed to stay, helping Jonathan with meals or the sired with tasks in the grounds, taking trips into town with the men as suited. It gave cover in case of any unwanted attention and felt more useful than rattling around the house. Or being volunteered for experiments with Haddley.

It was such a strange house, sprawling in uneven ways I was still mapping in my head. It had been added to as it was owned, one could track the changes in stone or the way the floor dipped between two rooms, but such was the way of big houses. They grow with the family. Or the nest. Some of them certainly seemed to share rooms, but the overlap was unclear to me yet.

I pilfered an apple and some cheese from the pantry, slipping it into my satchel for my wandering. It shouldn't have surprised me that vampires liked food—it would have been a miserable life only supping blood—but it made me smile to see their indulgences. Good cheese, fresh produce. The jovial relationship Jonathan had with the butcher. Bet he bought a lot of blood pudding.

I met Edgar at the door, his smile quick as the creeping dawn.

"I'm glad I caught you, I wanted to give you the blade you were promised." He held up a leather sheath, a short handle sat in his hand.

I took it, sliding the leather off so I could examine the metal. It was about the length of my middle finger and shiny from polishing. The cutting edge was keen, and a thin line was etched into the length of the blade on the blunt side.

"Good cleaning spot." I ran my thumb nail along the little dip, the metal cool.

"Ronald's fond of making sure maintenance is easy. Terrible way to run a shop, but good for those who like weapons."

"Means you're sure he knows what he talks about." I smiled at him, switching the knife between hands. "Thank you. I know Addison's paying but I appreciate it."

"You seem trained, thought you'd appreciate something more useful than a cooking knife."

"I do. Are you away to the shop today?"

"Yes, being kept busy. I was thinking you might like to come visit, one afternoon? Ronald's not got your accent but his family's from that way about, if you miss the sound of it."

The idea was curiously sweet, if misguided—I didn't want to be spotted by anyone. But it was a lovely thought. "I'll think on it."

Edgar walked with me until we diverged, him along the drive and me towards the trees. The sky was a watery pink, like rose petals left in sugar to crystallise, and in the quiet I could think I was anywhere. An irregular peace. I ate silently, biting into apple and cheese in turn. I didn't have a trip planned today so there was an opportunity for me to explore.

The grounds were significant. Not an estate like you saw up north, by any means, but there was a good few acres of woods and open field. I'd seen still water, like a pond, in my brief excursion into the woods—accompanying Tobias to get flowers—but hadn't the chance to go out investigating properly.

It was mostly made up of older trees, this place; oaks that tangled out with grasping branches, sweet chestnut and ash with leaves that sagged in the late summer heat. It was lacking the pines we had back home, but still beautiful.

Walking whichever way the path took me, I wandered until I found a thick bank of brambles, the tangle green and hungry in the morning light. The berries were as ripe as they'd ever be, heavy on the stems, and I plucked one up. It was almost as big as the pad of my finger, warmed by the sunlight and shiny with juice. I savoured the way it burst in my mouth—different to the taste of home, but they'd bake up well.

I tipped my cap off, splaying my fingers open to support the base. It was maybe the size of a small plate, with my fingers underneath, and certainly enough to get a good haul of blackberries. I filled the space inside, shimmying around the snarling vines.

I sang as I went, some of the old songs from the halls: Orkney giants, faithful hounds, sleeping bairns. It was easy to seem far off from everyone—like I was back home in Caithness and the trees were a bit funny in the sunlight.

A branch cracked as I drew a breath, the sound off to the side of me. I kept singing, twisting my hip a little so I could glance that way. If it was someone stalking me, they'd been very patient, and anyone from the college would have moved in before I had my cap half full.

"Anyone there?" I asked. I kept picking brambles. The dark juice was staining the brown of my cap. "I have a knife."

A deer wandered out from one of the trees, pointed ears flicking this way and that. She had big black eyes, rounder and darker than any of the fruit in my hat, and lashes to kill for. Tiffany came to mind, briefly, and I smiled despite myself. Of all the things to miss, she was a nice one.

"Off with you, mistress of the woods. I don't need you for the pot, but I don't doubt some of the gentlemen would." I walked towards her and she shot off, springing away like a lamb gambolling. I chuckled at her flight, the laugh tangling in my chest. The instinct to run was strong in all of us.

# Chapter 27

The crumble was, largely, a success. Certainly enough to justify the stains to my cap, which now soaked in a large mixing dish.

"I must admit it smells rather lovely," Jonathan said. He'd inspected it as soon as it left the oven, found it adequate, and bestowed it pride of place beside the window to cool. This was a high honour.

"Thank you. It should do most folk, it's not over sweet other than being fruit and—"

A knock on the doorframe caught our attention, Tobias peering in and sniffing the air. "Can I borrow you for a word when you're done, princess?"

"We're about finished here," Jonathan said.

"Alright." I gave him the pot towel and followed Tobias.

He stepped away from the threshold to let me pass, leading me to one of the smaller rooms at the back of the house. He opened the door and let me through, following in but hovering at the door. "Is this alright?"

"Speaking? Yes. What was it you wanted?" I stayed stood, walking over to one of little square windows so I could keep my back to a wall.

"I wanted to apologise. I know I've been avoiding you the last while and it's been foolish of me."

He had? "I assumed you had your reasons. You've been very careful with me, after things."

Tobias nodded, face straight as a new gravestone. He didn't come further into the room either, none of the closeness that had been his way since I landed here, back pressed to the door like he might bolt. "I was worried you would fear me. And some of us in the house have been worried about you."

"How so? I think I'm doing remarkably well for an abducted woman. I have a new wardrobe and a knife too, paid for by someone else. It's better than most get, turning up somewhere new."

"Did I frighten you, when I gave you blood?"

I crossed my arms, eyes rolling at his careful stepping around. "Nearly dying frightened me more. What are you not managing to spit out from between those fangs of yours?"

He sighed, shoulders slumping. "Can I come closer?"

"You can bloody hug me if it gets you to speak plainly." I bristled at the careful handling, like there was something going on around me that I didn't know about. I had negotiated my precarious position too much to want secrets that involved me.

He stepped into the room fully, off the door, and came to stand before me. "I'd like it if we could hug, so I can know you're alright."

"Come here." I stepped into his space to hug him close, arms up against his back, resting my head on his shoulder. "Better?"

"I suspect you're indulging me but it does make the next part easier. You've been screaming at night. I was concerned it was because of me, and the feeding, the way I went to your neck. And the other part."

I snorted at the comment, but it was a mean laughter through me, twisted around the guilt of old things. "You can say you messed your trews, I'm hardly a delicate flower."

"It's embarrassing to have done it. I don't want you to be scared of me."

"It's a touch prideful to assume it would be you I was feared of, and not that horrible hobgoblin, no? But it's neither, so take peace. You did not bite me, if that nuzzle against my cheek was an attempt at biting then no wonder you have no sired."

"Do you wish to talk about what it is?"

"No. It's old pain, and if it disturbs the others tell them to hammer on the wall. In the college I could go and bed in with someone if it was too bad, but there's none of that here, so best waken me up."

"I'm sure there are some as would share their bed with you if you asked."

"Aye, and have all the complications of that? Addison's already paired me up with them for going anywhere, it could make things difficult."

"You could share mine then? Seems the least I could do to apologise."

I pulled back, blinking at him. "Are you offering to tumble me as an apology? I can't tell if that's more pride or a terrible advertisement."

He snorted, shaking his head at me. One hand came up to toy with my hair, almost brushing my cheek but not lingering. "I can share a bed without any ill intent, you little wildcat. Nothing done unless invited is any easy rule. But if you would like a body beside you I would be content to be that. My door would be open for you if you needed comfort."

The sigh I huffed was equal parts bemused and annoyed. "I'll think on it. And hammer on the door if I'm keeping you awake. Women screaming can be hard. We had boys in the dormitory who would cry and shake when they heard it."

He stepped back, catching my fingers. "Why did they hear it?"

"Lots of things happen in a college." I shook my head, pulled my hand away. "Best not dwelled on when you're already throwing your chivalry around so carelessly."

"If you say so." He stepped aside so I had a line to the door. "Do think on it, please. I'd feel better knowing you had some comfort."

"Other than my nice new knife?"

"Other than that."

His eyes were crinkled at the edges, like he was holding things back, and I couldn't offer him the same comfort he was so ready to give. "I'll consider it. I'm going to go find some peace elsewhere if that's alright?"

"Of course."

I stepped around him to get through the door and into the corridor. Gods save me from well-meaning vampires, I was tripping over them in this place.

I doubled back along the corridor, towards the staircase, hoping to make it back to my room so I could lock the door and sit in peace. Being close to him was no longer the shock of power it had been; I suspected the blood was the cause of that, but he was such a maelstrom of a man. The roil of emotion caught in my throat was enough that I wanted to be alone until they passed.

## CHAPTER 28

I found solace in my room for all of an hour before someone knocked on the door, disturbing what was perilously close to a doze.

Rolling off the bed I found Chance at the other side, immediately tossing a coat at me. "Get dressed, I want to talk to you."

"I'm fully clothed."

"We're off out, come on." He grabbed my wrist, barrelling down the stairs and through the corridor, grabbing my bag from beside the front door. He tugged his own coat on with a practised grace, shaking the tails. "Ready?"

"Off where?" I pulled the coat on, admiring the wool blend. There was a lingering sweet scent like old perfume clinging to the material.

"I'm going to show you one of our great English traditions. The local pub."

"We have pubs in Scotland."

Chance shook his head. "But we have conversations to have, petal, and that requires privacy."

"The privacy of a room full of drunkards?"

"Many's a man that can be lost in the crowd, you know that. And none of the others will bother us there, so we can speak plainly." He winked at me, already going through the door.

"Oh aye, clearly something you have trouble with."

"All that venom and you're the only one without fangs."

"Jonathan doesn't either."

"Damn near does. Come on."

The pub was in a smaller village—all dirty yellow thatched roofs and wattle and daub white facades—a couple of miles out from the nest. We had a smattering of that stark white-and-black covering back home, ours was mostly plain stone; better to weather the changing seasons. This was more gentle, more attractive, than the soot and brick and shouting crowds. It sat ill on my skin, like I'd upset the place by being there.

"Did you want company, or do you just not want to drink alone?" I asked. We were walking there and back, it seemed, no coach called. I'd expected this would be the time for Chance to interrogate me, but he was quiet.

"It can be nice to soak up the company. Listen to what's being said here and there."

That sounded more than passing familiar. "You're a gossip."

"No more than anyone else with an ear for things. You have little room there, petal."

A spy didn't out themselves to another without good reason, be that making friends or establishing common ground. I thought we were far enough into common ground already, given our now mutual benefactor, so maybe this was a sign of friendship. I wondered briefly if Addison knew about Chance's skills before siring him. Must have, given the mention of old habits.

"Whose coat is this, by the way?" I stretched one arm out, pushing the other topic away. "It's a bonny thing, shame to have it off someone."

"It was a gift. One of my patients is convinced I have a wife back home that I don't mention. Her daughter had been very sick during her pregnancy, nearly lost the babe, but we got her right again."

"No wonder they were grateful."

"I'd have accepted thanks in whisky too."

I grinned at the comment, and the thought of a proud new granny finding the nicest thing she could to celebrate the babe getting here safe. "That's lovely. You must be very valued, as a doctor. It's not cheap work."

"I charge as little as I can get away with. We have to pay for the medicine, but Margery helps with that when she can, and it's not like I have bills other than rent for the treatment room. You can do a lot of good with very little, in some places."

"Then they're lucky to have a bleeding heart." I wrinkled my nose at him, the tease clear in my smile. He wasn't an old man, at least not in visage, but he had the lines of worry deep on his forehead and the pinched little crinkle at the edge of his eyes.

He caught my stare. "You're one to talk there."

"How?"

"Throwing air and water around instead of fire when you were trying to escape? You were pulling your punches."

"It's a foolish fighter who gives away all their secrets from the off."

We'd reached the pub, a squat structure that only just had an upper floor underneath the heavy roof. The thick thatch was messy with birds and stray bits of hay, and the windows were small enough to be little use, but it was a familiar sort of building. Would be good in a village, keep people together.

I let Chance enter first. "This isn't as grim as I was expecting. You were talking like we had troubles."

He led me to a little table, intimate enough to look like we were company, and pulled my chair out. "There's no saying we won't when we're done. I'll buy the drinks if you answer the questions."

"Trying to get me drunk?"

"As if I'd have a hope at that!" He barked a laugh, quickly covering his mouth when the smatterings of others looked at us. "I bet you've been sipping whisky since you were on the hip."

"I drink gin, you oaf. But I'd see you under the table, right enough."

"As you say." He did a half bow and a flourish of his hand before heading up to the bar counter.

It was a nice pub, cosy; the sort where I could imagine a gaggle of old men spending their evenings, games running around in the background. There had to be packs of cards for lending stashed behind the bar.

Places like this were spots I could slot into the background of, blend like I belonged for a while. But only a while. How would that card game go if they knew they had a magic user around, never mind a trained one? If I told them I knew who held grudges and who was thinking they would go home early, to ponder over fucking their friend's wife as he ambled back. I didn't belong in nice places.

I shucked the coat off, taking a deep breath of the perfume. It was certainly scent, rather than pressed flowers used to keep something fresh, and that was not something that smelled grandmotherly. Maybe there was a sweetling he hadn't mentioned.

"You've got a thinking face on." Two drinks were set on the table, a gin mix and a whisky.

"Wondering who else had worn the coat."

"Assuming someone else has?"

"Not sure florals are your scent." I held the coat arm up to him.

His brows knitted together as he breathed the smell in, eyes falling to the table. "I know that one. I think it's Angelica."

"One of your many mistresses?"

"One of the schoolteachers. I check the children if there's been an accident. She's a daunting lady but she uses rosehip oil on her hands, to keep them soft. I'd not even noticed that, good nose on you."

"You'll be used to it." I set the coat over the chair, adjusting it so it ran down my back as a cushion. "So, what's the story here?"

"I want to have a level discussion."

"Go on then, doctor."

He grunted, taking a deep sip before he shook his head at me. "No pulling titles, petal."

"Why? You're hardly bashful."

"You're working me like I'm a job, which I don't appreciate."

"I don't know what this is." I raised my glass to my mouth, watching him over the lip as I drank. It was strong enough, potent despite the mix. "Maybe you're here to scare me off."

"Me?"

"A well-travelled doctor with an eye for weapons, and massive flirt to boot? I know what that is where I'm from."

"I dread to think what you're meaning." He pouted, stretching his shoulders under his shirt. Thin, but muscled, he'd be called wiry in Caithness. Strength underneath the smiling façade.

"I doubt there's much you dread except memories."

He coughed around his drink, setting the glass down. "I don't plan to talk about me."

"I'd bet you undertook not to. Is this because Edgar gave me the knife, you're nervous of me?"

Chance swirled the liquid in his glass, slow so the ice span in its own little pattern. "Edgar's a funny one. Good man, very serious. Regrets the army. He hears you shout at night. A lot of us do." He raised an eyebrow at me and I met his stare with a very nice, very toothy smile.

"I doubt I'm the only one in the house with nightmares."

"You're the only one who screams."

"You've probably had longer to get used to them."

Chance laughed, glass going down on the table as he covered his mouth with the back of his hand. "Look at the claws on you coming out."

"I'm playing nice." I pressed my palms into the cool glass, focusing on the swirl of the two fluids mixing.

"Then let's get to the point so neither of us has to play. You landed with us in very poor circumstances, and we've made them worse. It'd be understandable if you were on your last nerves."

"Tobias has already had this talk with me, and I had to hug it out of him. I'm alright."

"There's nothing putting worries in your mind?"

"Other than the college I ran from and nearly dying?"

"Aren't you as dry as kindling?" Chance sat back in his seat, snickering to himself. "Alright, that's fair comment. But there are other areas that could cause you concern. The two oldies like you."

"Bullshit." I shook my head, cradling my drink close to my chest as I sat back in the chair.

"Oh gods, you don't see it?"

"You're so keen to flirt you see things that aren't there. Firstly, Addison clearly has his pick of you lot, which seems to be welcome."

He nodded, shrugging a little. "In one way or another, yes. Other than Haddley, he's only eyes for his beloved."

"That's sweet. Secondly, the immortals are devoted to each other. There's no room between them and their ghost."

Chance's brows shot up, his glass snatched away from the intended sip to cradle against his temple. "You know about the third."

He looked like I'd spat in his mother's face, all levity from before drained into the tumbler. I took a burning sip before I replied. "Aye."

"Not many do."

I scoffed. "The immortals must."

"Tosh, they don't count. They all know each other inside and out, incestuous little pack of rabbits. But ones like us, and mortals, don't tend to know about him."

"You sound like you've been trying to find out."

"I might have been." Chance took a sip, setting the glass down on the table before he poked the wood with his index finger. "How did you get that out of him? Addison's tight-lipped as a priest after confession when it comes to the war."

I sighed, hanging my head for a beat. "It was an accident. I was sleeping in his room, the first morning I was here, and he woke me up. I stabbed him. There was some crossover."

I looked back up at him. Chance blinked rapidly at me before his face erupted in a grin. "Sleeping in his room? Stabbed him?"

Oh no. "Shut up."

"The sly dog!"

"I will drown you in your own drink if you don't be quiet." I knocked back the rest of the sharp spirit, ready to escape this indignity.

He caught my wrist, grip soft as butter, tugging me back. "No, tell me. I thought you'd growled everyone off. If you're set to be one of the elder's partners, that's a whole different matter. I'll have to tell Edgar to swallow his feelings, for one."

"Get your hand off me."

His hand sprang back, fingers wide to show his retreat. "Sorry. Are you with him, though? Daddy himself?"

"Recall the part where I stabbed him? He had me in his bed because I was terrified. His room's like a bit of a magical... lake maybe, would be the word. The energy is old and slow, all to do with time, it feels peaceful. I could sleep there in a way I couldn't in the house yet." Then Henry attacked me and things changed, rapidly.

Chance raised one brow slowly, clearly weighing my story. "And he touched you?"

"After I stabbed him. Well, before as well, but that was on my shoulder. While I was panicking about the knife, he caught my hand and we entangled. I saw things I shouldn't."

Chance pouted. "How boring."

"You're remarkably calm about the stabbing part."

"He's given you a knife, it can't have been that bad. I thought the old man had got some life back. He's been so withdrawn the last while, with things."

Dead friends would prompt that. "He's plenty of life, but I don't expect he's keen on mortals. We're like pets, or fond gifts that will wear out."

"Rubbish. We were all mortals before we chose to join the darkness with him, and most of us trading hearts with him too. He's full of love for humans." He wiggled his eyebrows at me, glancing around the pub. "I revel in being around mortals, too—so many delicious options."

I rolled my eyes, naturally he was enthusiastic about mortals. Horny little goat of a man. He was sired though; it would be different for immortals. "I'm going to head off, this place is noisy."

"Stay a bit, I'll buy you another drink."

"Only if we sit outside."

Chance leaned around me to peer at the window before giving a little nod. "I'll get the drinks; you find a seat in the sunshine."

I stood, weaving between bodies as I made for the door. It was a nice enough place, and a good way to waste an afternoon, but between his mysterious questions and ridiculous suggestions I was getting tired. Soaking in some sun would be a good reprieve.

<h1 style="text-align:center">Chapter 29</h1>

The village was quieter now, the little crowds dissipated with the afternoon heat. I stood beside the door for a second, pulling my shield tight and tucking my energy away, so we could sit and talk in peace.

I found a bench beside a dusty pink rose bush that still held straggling blooms. They let off a perfume despite being overripe, on the cusp of shedding their wilting petals. Intoxicating this close, an overwhelming sweetness on the edge of rot swirled around the seat. It could almost be the gardens back home, bushes and buds dripping with scent in the late afternoon heat. Honeysuckle pushing through as the day wore on. Walking through the Edinburgh Gardens was always a good way to kill an afternoon, immersing ourselves in the milling people of the city. The memory tugged at my heart for a sharp moment.

"Are you curious about plants?" A voice interrupted my introspection as a shadow obscured the sunlight.

A tall man took up the space before me, backlit by the sunshine. Quiet on his feet to have gotten so close. He wore traveller's clothes, a thick coat that had mud spattered over the lower hems, despite the warmth of the day.

"Hello," I said.

"Hello. You seemed interested in the roses." He was nearly seven feet, easily, and had a short beard that glinted in the light. His hair was a deep red, almost brown, in contrast to the lightness of his facial hair. That had always been a warning back home, to be wary of a man whose beard and hair were different colours.

I shook off the dizziness of his proximity, looking back to the blooms. "I like them. It's a shame they're almost gone, but at least we get to enjoy them right to the end."

"A sweet sentiment." He reached close to my face, knuckles near brushing my cheek as he slid his hand deep into the bush and plucked a rose free. There was enough stem to fit across his palm and a hint of red, like one of the thorns had caught him in the intrusion. "Do you think their death makes them more enjoyable?"

"I don't know if I'd say that." I sat back, crossing one leg over the other so I could kick him if he got much closer. "The imperfections of decay can make the beauty stand out more. The scent of the roses is all the sweeter before they drop."

He brought the bloom up to his face, resting it against a cheek. I frowned, almost squinting as I tried to focus. Between the light and the bloom, it was like looking at fogged glass, his features swimming as I peered. It wasn't the light stopping me from seeing him, though, it was deliberate. I pressed myself back against the wooden bench, shivering at the display of magic.

"Who are you?" I should drop my guard, see if I could feel him out, but something screamed not to. The idea of him peering back, also unguarded, made my spine tingle.

"A curious traveller." His voice was rich with a smirk.

Two could play that card. "Me too."

"You're certainly curious. Here." He held the rose out, the bloom now freshly open, barely past the budding.

"That's quite the trick." The words were dry, the thud of my heart loud despite the sounds from inside the pub. I accepted the rose from him, settling it in my crooked palm. It was cool and fresh, back to its first blush of life. Time magic. What a very pretty threat.

"We're all full of tricks, aren't we?" He tilted his head to one side, hair falling to his shoulders. He could have tied it up, it was thick enough to do so, a texture to it which would braid well if he grew it out more.

I shifted under his gaze, glancing to the tavern door. "I'm here with company."

"I won't keep you unduly. I wanted to get a closer look at who was causing such a ruckus in the house. And scaring deer in the woods."

Cool certainty beaded in the sweat prickling like dew at the back of my neck. Either he had been around me alone, or knew someone who had, and I hadn't seen them. Neither boded well.

"You know them, at the house?" I asked.

"We're acquainted. And if you're going to stay there much longer, I have no doubt we'll get acquainted too."

"What's your name?"

"What's yours?"

"Ginny."

"You lie so easily, Ena, what a shame." He grinned, a flash of teeth that I couldn't keep for more than a beat. I shook my head, tightening my grip on the rose stem so the pinpoint pain of the thorns anchored me.

"I have no reason to trust you, and you have me at a disadvantage. Why can't I see your face properly?"

"Sharp as those thorns, aren't you?" He laughed, a musical sound in the close space.

"Maybe you're just blurred at the edges."

The laughter stopped, his chin tilting up. "Maybe you're right. What would cause that?"

"I can't say." Torture, loss, grief, rage. In theory, anything that could grieve you enough to touch the soul could cause a wound on it. I'd done it, taking people back up to the college with a slit in their spirit so they couldn't use their magic to fight back. But I'd never encountered one that wasn't precise; that blurred or fuzzed rather than bled. All of mine could be repaired. I glanced to the door again, weighing up the steps. I could slip off the bench, bolt for the door. Spit a word and hope I could make it.

"I don't believe you." He bent closer, his mouth beside my ear. "I think you don't want to say."

"I'd probably get an idea if I could see you better."

"Why don't you check, little spy?"

"Why do you want me to?" I turned my head, ghosting my lips against his ear as I brought the bloom up between us and pushed it against his cheek, a barrier of his own making. "You don't need magic like mine to tell you that, you're far ahead of me."

He sucked in a breath, his beard almost scraping against my chin. "How bold, darling."

"Charm won't work either. What's your name?" He smelled as sweet as the roses, cloying at this proximity, and I bit the inside of my cheek with the effort to keep my breathing even. I would stand my ground even if my back was against the wood.

"You can call me Mark."

"Thank you, Mark."

"I like the sound of my name in your mouth." Our cheeks never brushed, the rose petals gradually heating as we both refused to move. Not that I could move far, but I wasn't going to give him an inch.

"Why don't you tell me your real one, I'm sure it'll sound better."

He laughed, taking in a deep breath, before he stepped back to straighten up. "You're quite the little spark. I think we should speak again sometime."

"Do I get a choice?"

"No."

"What have you done with Chance?"

"One of my colleagues will have spilled a drink on him, kept him talking while they buy him another. They're good at distractions."

I nodded, shoulders up around my ears as I burned what I could into my mind. No face and a false name, vampire magic; what else could I get out of him? "There are worse distractions."

"Like lighting people on fire?"

"Like using ancient rites for party tricks." I held the rose between us. "Beautiful as it is, magic like that is usually reserved for something more significant."

He smiled, I think, there was a flash of white against the blur of his face. "Perhaps you're special, so I wanted to show you something special. Please do keep the rose, it's a beauty." He stepped back again, turning away from me.

"You could have cursed it."

He twisted a little, looking at me over his shoulder. "You know I haven't. Until next time, darling."

The door to the tavern burst open, a roar of laughter spilling out as Chance and a short man with vibrant red hair barrelled outside. He was young, barely out of his teens by the looks of it, and pressed a giggling kiss to Chance's cheek before running off. Mark was gone when I looked back.

Chance shook his head, swinging his face around to find me and making a line for the bench. "You alright?"

"Who was your friend?" I asked, grabbing the drink and downing it.

"A pretty little face, who it seems was much too interested in me."

"Distraction."

"And here I was thinking my charming good looks had struck again." He knocked his drink back too, setting the glasses down on the wood. "Tell me about it as we walk home?"

"Let's." I tucked the rose behind my ear, save risk crushing it in my clenching fists.

# Chapter 30

"Well, that's fucking ominous," Chance said. We were almost at the house, the story told as we walked, the rose still hanging at the edge of my ear.

"He knows about the alley."

"Your tinder man? Could have been anyone did that. You weren't spotted other than Garrett grabbing you, and you were dressed as a man."

"Probably recognised Garrett if he knows you lot."

"You're sure it wasn't one of the ones looking for you, trying to make you run?"

"We don't have time magic. And the closest they get to subtle is a sack over the head."

"No wonder you got out." He flashed me a grin, knocking our elbows together. "Try not to look so grim, petal."

"Someone using old magic for party tricks is either deranged or determined, and I like neither. Checking for my college is bad enough, Addison being right in his hunch is worse."

"They that bad, to grab you?"

"Yes. A few of us are skilled at returning strays, as well as the other work."

"Us?" I shrugged, fingering the petals of the rose. I didn't want to be diving into old memories on top of new worries. The bloom was cool and soft, still undeniably alive despite the earlier back-and-forth between Mark and me. "Gods help the oldies if they piss you off."

"I'm much more likely to punch someone."

He snagged my elbow to stop us, shifting to stand before me. "I don't know who your mystery man was, but you should let the old ones know. I'll see if I can shake anything out around the town too, but have one of us about if you're out. Safety in company."

"And if my good brethren come seeking me, and injure one of you?"

"You think too little of us."

"I'll trust your word." I stepped around him and he stepped in turn, blocking me.

"Plus, the lord of the manor would rip someone limb from limb for laying hands on you. He's very protective of his guests. He'd have their heads."

"I don't think he'd go quite that far, but he is... doting."

"Exactly. Addison will look after you." He ducked his head to catch my gaze, smiling at me with what I had to assume was a pout.

"Aye."

"Good. No unnecessary risks."

"As if I'd risk my skin for your dead hides."

"Undead, you'll get us a bad name."

I scoffed, pushing past him to continue on the road. We were almost back at the garden of the house, and while the sky was still bright, the chill of evening was creeping in.

"Are you going to talk to them before we eat?"

"Yes, I will. Happy?"

"Ecstatic, petal."

"Why do you keep calling me that?"

"Means I'm not calling you something someone will have an ear out for."

That was a tolerable reason. "Alright."

"Thank you, petal." He winked, linking our arms for the last short mile.

"Why?"

"If the mystery man is watching us maybe he'll target me next time."

"Are you hoping for an encounter?"

He shrugged, tightening the grip. "Might be fun to see what tricks he'll do for me."

I rolled my eyes, unwilling to indulge in such imaginings.

We were rapidly approaching the house when a figure came bolting out the front door, followed by another on its heels. Was that Jonathan?

"What on earth?" Chance shoved me behind him, one arm out to cover me. Sod this. I nudged the back of his knee to tip him sideways, hopping back out as he went forward.

The first figure was almost at the gate, which was standing open, and as he reached it, I kicked the metal back into the gap at the wall, jarring him and the gate together with a solid clang.

"Shit!" He shoved one arm through the metal while he was trying to right himself, a gloved hand splaying out to seek balance. I grabbed hold, hugging it to my chest as I sank to my knees to pull him hard against the bars. His head bounced off the metal, lodged close as I pulled tighter.

"In a rush, pal?" I asked, glancing up at him.

"You!" It was the scarred young man from the alley, frown creased by the bars crushing into him. I curled down so my face was covered. I hadn't set him on fire, at least.

Jonathan barrelled into him, fisting a hand in his hair before he yanked the man's head back. "What do you think you're doing laying a finger on her?"

"I grabbed him, he's not hurting me," I said.

"He's lucky I don't break his wrist." Jonathan slammed the youth's face into the gate, a spurt of blood smattering my cheeks as his nose gave in.

"Easy!" I got up, and Jonathan dragged the man away, shoving him up into the wall.

"Let him handle it," Chance said.

"He's really angry, the guy's bleeding." More blood on me, rapidly cooling across my skin. At least it was someone else's blood.

"He will be. You'll remind him of his sister, no doubt. I'll stay with him, you go speak to the oldies." Chance gave my hip a little push, sending me along the path, and I turned to go up it despite the twist low in my gut.

I trotted up the gravel, eager to get into the house and check for any further upset, and collided with Edgar as he came to the door too.

"Sorry," I said, grabbing his arm as we separated.

"Are you well? You're bleeding."

"It's not my blood, it's the chap Jonathan has against the wall down there. Do you know where Addison and Tobias are?"

Edgar squinted over me towards the gate. "They're at the courtyard."

"I'll go, you help those two." I smiled, hoping it was some comfort, and shuffled past him while he went out the door.

The dark wood panelling was as oppressive in the daylight as the night, and I plucked the mysterious rose from behind my ear to have something in my hands.

I found the kitchen with both outside doors open to let the air flow through, and the spike of voices floated in along with the dying light. The men sounded close to cross words, snips tight as a duel, and I hesitated at the threshold. I should wash the blood off my face instead of eavesdropping.

"You don't give the young ones enough credit," Addison said. "She'll be protected."

"And you trust in the goodness of those who haven't earned mercy. It hasn't been that long since the fighting ended and we know they dislike your new habits."

"As if either of us has the right to speak of mercy." There was a moan of impact, the sound of a body hitting something. I took that as a sign now was as good a time as any to interrupt, brandishing the rose before me.

"I have a problem." I stepped into the courtyard, steps stuttering out when I realised Tobias had Addison up against the bricks, fists buried in Addison's shirt to hoist him up. "This is intimate."

Tobias blinked, mouth agape as he looked to me. "Princess, this isn't what it appears."

"I'm certain." I struggled to say more but the heat between them was oppressive, like an oven door left open catching you unawares. I stared at them and Addison slumped a little, shaking his head.

"Ena, you have blood on you."

I shrugged, grip on the rose tightening. The thorns pressed sharp against my palm, enough to keep my focus. "It's not mine."

The men shared a look and Tobias let Addison go, stepping away. "I'm sorry you saw that."

"You said you had an issue, lambkin?" Addison stepped forward while Tobias lurked back near the wall, face darker than the encroaching twilight.

"This." I held the rose out, loosening my grip a little. No blood.

"It's a pretty bloom. Young for the season," Tobias said.

"You look at it." I passed it to Addison, folding my arms as he accepted it.

He frowned as he turned it around in his hand, bringing it closer to sniff. "Magic?"

"I watched a man turn that from a fully blossomed flower back to nearly a bud. Only I didn't see him do it, because I couldn't see his face." I wiped my face with one sleeve, the spray of drops tugging where they'd begun to dry. I'd need to wash properly.

"A mask?" Tobias stepped off the wall, coming beside Addison to peer at the flower.

"No, it was like his face wasn't there. Had to be magic, as does that flower, and you're meant to be the only one left."

Addison looked at Tobias, who glared at him before looking back to me and the bloom.

"He approached you?" Tobias asked.

"I think he was trying to scare me. Made a show of knowing my name, that I was here in the house. That he'd ensured Chance was distracted so I was on my own. He must have been waiting a while."

"Watching the two of you, waiting for you to part." Tobias spat on the hard earth, kicking the stain with his boot.

"There aren't many who would have that skill. You couldn't read him?" Addison asked.

"I didn't want to. I'd put my guard up not long since and the thought of him looking back at me was..." I shook my head. "I've been seen by others like me before, but he felt worse. Like he would hurt."

They shared a look, Addison drawing me in for a hug. "I think you were wise. Could you recognise him, if you saw him again?"

"Are there many men around here without faces? That sticks in the mind."

Tobias snorted. "That's an old tactic against humans, part of a thrall. He must be strong to do so without having influence over you."

"I think..." I couldn't pin down how to say it, my tongue as con-fused as my eyes. I ran it along the back of my teeth to search for the right words.

"Yes?" Addison stroked my hair, sending my shoulders up around my ears. I stepped back to settle myself, and Tobias came closer to nudge Addison away.

"I think he wanted to influence me. He was goading me, telling me to look at him. Then he turned sweet when I wouldn't, pressing up close and giving me the rose. It was like he was working through ways to needle me."

"Probably hadn't anticipated you could resist." Tobias stroked my shoulder, shooting Addison a cruel smile. "That means one of the families. As I said."

"I thought you all got on now." Forcibly. It had been agreed that everyone, even the previous human killers, had to behave around the humans, abide by feeding agreements and restrict their violence. That was the main point of the accords.

"The truces are complicated. I can think of a few who would enjoy having a spy in the camp of a family they disliked, but we are not that," Addison said.

"You're still a prince," I replied.

Addison smiled like it hurt, and Tobias sighed. "Much as we're still a nest we're not a family, as far as they'd see it."

"What about yours?" I looked to Tobias, who grimaced.

"Mine were on the wrong side. Well, some of them."

I opened my mouth and closed it again, words jumbled. "You fought with Addison. I saw you."

Tobias nodded, hands sliding into his pockets. "My brother switched sides part way through. Someone got his ear, and he got my father's head on the way out."

"Gods." I wrapped my arms around myself again, pulling my energy tighter. "I'm sorry."

"It was a long while ago. The war took Edmund too, so it balanced out in the end."

"Your mother?"

"He couldn't manage to kill her. And she couldn't manage to save my father. Pain all around for my sisters and me."

"Tobias, I'm sorry." I went closer, pulling him into a hug with too much force to be decent.

He coughed, patting my back a little. "Easy, princess. It's old pain."

I gave him a light squeeze before I separated. "Is this what you were fighting about before? Those who haven't earned mercy?"

"That was about something else, though it may be related." Addison stepped closer. "This may be connected to our concerns about the nest being targeted but it's not certain. So, I must ask you to keep one of us nearby when you go out."

"Chance already said that. Speaking of which, you had a break-in."

"Pardon?" Tobias snagged my shoulder, turning me towards him.

"Some lad was bolting out of the house when Chance and I got back from town. I got tangled in the catching of him, this is his blood. Chance and Edgar were helping Jonathan with him."

"Do we know who he is?" Addison asked. He leaned closer to sniff my cheek, tongue darting out to flick over the blood. I flushed hot at the action, a wave of embarrassment creeping over me.

I coughed to force the words out. "He's one of the pickpockets."

"Who you set on fire?" Tobias asked.

"Not the same one. But yes."

Addison clapped his hands together, catching both our focus. "We should see what's going on. Do you want to go and wash your face, my dear? Any of the men will worry it's your blood."

"And Haddley will shriek if he sees you," Tobias added.

That was fair comment. "Alright."

# Chapter 31

I washed my face in my room, studiously ignoring the mirror. My healing was fine, I'd stopped noticing the marks at my neck, but I was ground down between the encounter with Mark and walking in on the immortals arguing.

Tobias had a fury on his face I'd only seen when he was chasing Addison away from me, when I was bleeding on their floor. I didn't recognise him like that. None of the warmth or friendly words—infuriating words—I'd come to expect from him.

A knock on my door brought me out of contemplation. I dried my face, crossing to the door to open it.

Tobias stood on the other side, propped up on the frame, fiddling with his hands. We blinked at each other for a few moments, his face serious in the dim corridor, half shadowed with the lengthening dark.

"Can I come in?"

"Of course." I opened the door to let him past, fixing the lamp beside my table so we had light aside from the sunset.

"I was worried about you," he said.

"That looked like a fight." He snorted, sitting on the end of the bed so I could perch elsewhere. I took the chair before the dresser, so we were on equal level but apart.

"It wasn't much of a fight compared to other things we've done. It can't have been nice to see."

"I've seen plenty of not nice things, don't fret. You seemed distressed."

"You have the knack for finding me in all sorts of ways."

"I was worried that something was hurting you, but you have hundreds of years up on me, you'll know yourself well enough."

"Hm?" He looked over, eyes flicking across my face like he would sketch me, like I was something other than another lost soul rattling around this house. My chest throbbed, once, an urge to give him some comfort that I had no real place to do.

"If you need comfort, you know how to seek it. And much as you had him pinned to a wall, I reckon Addison would offer it."

He covered his face with his hands, sighing. "We've known the worst of each other. We still come back together."

"I doubt you leave those you love easily." I shifted from the chair, going to sit beside him on the bed. This was... off. Unsettled. And it was none of my business, but I didn't want him to hurt. "Are you alright?"

He turned and yanked me into a hug. I squeaked at the touch, the force of his grab pulling us over onto the mattress, his face in the crook of my neck. I held still in his arms, blinking furiously into the mop of his hair.

"I can't stomach the idea of someone trying to manipulate you, or turn you, to hurt Addison and me. The families are terrible creatures."

"I'm alright, Tobias. I'm doing this willingly." I gingerly patted his back with my free arm, the other pinned underneath us. "I'll set fire to anyone who gets too close anyway."

"All sparks, you are. Furious little thing."

"So I can find my way in the dark. Light your own path and all that."

"Sounds lonely." He stroked my hair a little, ever soft. This close he was not the same sort of handsome as Addison, but he was comely: strong jaw and sparkling eyes. I wondered, briefly, how I looked to him—messy and flustered this close, too human and difficult, to be as beautiful as an immortal.

"No more so than anyone else. I don't need rescued." Not unless the faceless Mark showed up again; I'd take a rescue from that.

"I don't think you do. But I would be glad to share the ship."

"Always nice to have company. Did they send you up here to distract me?"

He laughed, loud next to me, and flicked my ear as he shook his head. "Yes. He worries you'll be worried. His indecision makes my fangs itch."

"Sounds unfortunate. We should go and see what's happening."

Tobias smiled, hugging me closer for a beat before he pushed us up, keeping me against him. "I'll happily accompany you down."

I pressed my lips together, trying to find the right words for the flutter in my stomach. "The lad looks young."

"Addison won't hurt him. Edgar might tie him up by the ankles for the impertinence, but he'd do that with anyone."

"You do have a good selection of guard dogs. Is there a way they get picked?"

Tobias tucked my hair back again as he worked his jaw. "I don't sire them. You should ask Addison. He makes his choices."

"You want him to be well. Hook in the heart." I tapped his chest, smiling. "I don't even need magic to see that, it's on your face."

"The others at least don't comment on it," he grumbled.

"He's their 'daddy', probably don't want to risk him being mad at them."

Tobias shuddered. "Please don't call him that. I may never sleep again."

"Must have picked it up from Chance," I said, disentangling from him to stand.

"There are worse to sound like. Good heart, that one."

"You're sweet on him?"

"He's nice to have a cuddle with."

"Is it a sired thing to be touchy? He had his arm in mine on the way home. I'm not exactly used to it from you two, but it at least makes more sense."

"How so?"

"You're pack creatures. You need high levels of contact. It'd make sense if the sired were like that too, hence the nest."

Tobias caught my waist, hugging me against him. I tipped back into his lap, squirming at the embrace. "You're just like watching a puzzle solve itself sometimes. I love seeing you break things down like that. We're all hopelessly needy. Quite inappropriate, causes outrage with well-mannered humans."

"Good thing you got me, then." I looked over my shoulder at him, his face close to my neck.

"Yes. We're very lucky to have you."

I batted his wrist. "I'm certain you're a distraction now, you know?"

"Only in case the lad was vicious. I've heard no shouting so we should be safe to go."

We arrived downstairs to the thief in the morning room, my spine tingling at his being perched on the settee. My stomach tightened as if I could still smell blood. The whole brood was in the room once we joined, Tobias separating from me to stand near the fireplace while Addison knelt before the boy, staring into his face like an artist examining a sketch.

"I thought you were distracted." Chance appeared beside me, tugging me to one of the seats.

"I wanted to see the lad was alright."

"Addison's busy doting on him."

We sat, back from the others, and I swallowed the tightness in my throat away. "He can't be much over sixteen. I killed his mate."

"And Jonathan broke his nose, I'm sure he'll not hold it against you. If he even remembers once daddy's done with him."

Addison's gaze glowed, his power like a mist through the room as he whispered, low and steady as a stream, to the boy. He was glassy-eyed, near drunk, nodding or shaking his head like someone in the pub.

"Are you sure you want to be here?" Chance asked, eyes flicking between me and the settee.

Addison wasn't a bad man. There was no reason to think that he would do something like George in the college would. Just because the whole nest was here, surrounding the child, easily able to overwhelm him, didn't mean they would. Nothing so far had shown they were as bad as us.

I focused on the thrum of my fingernail back and forth on my thigh, turning my wrist this way and that to scratch. "I've seen his thrall before."

Chance threaded the fingers of one hand into mine. "If you change your mind let me know, we can go into the garden. Or the kitchen, steal food before dinner."

"Are you happy to speak to me now, Leo?" Addison's voice was different, a rich lilt to it that pushed up against me like a cat seeking to be scratched, begging to be indulged. I pressed back into the seat, but the lad looked up, nodding.

"Yes."

"Good. I want to ask you some questions and then you can go home. It won't take long, and when we're done, I'll have a carriage take you back to the city, so you don't get cold. Is that agreeable?"

The lad, Leo, nodded, his single eye glassy wet. It wasn't tears but it was close enough for me to sit taller to watch. My gut twisted, half queasy with the skill on show. It wasn't like we didn't use influence in the college—there were a thousand ways to make someone come around to what you wanted. This was like watching a bird lay down for a cat to paw at it.

"I need to know why you broke into my house, and why you tried to take this." He set a small notebook on the boy's knee, leading one scuffed hand to touch it.

"The man said there was stuff to take, and we could have anys we wanted, so long as I took that. He pays well. We need the coin."

"That must be hard for you." Addison's hand unfurled from the spot on Leo's knee, cupping his chin to tilt his face, making sure there was eye contact.

"It's not so bad for us, but the younger ones get a beating if they're caught, so it was easier shifting bodies an' that." Gods, strike me. It was no shock, they'd get the same in Edinburgh for being thieves, but hearing about children getting a beating was no good thing.

"Did the man offer to help you other ways?" Addison asked.

"Naw. I don't like him. I can't see his face right, it's like you're looking at him but it won't stick in your head. That's magic and I don't like none of that. Gets you killed."

The breath I held was burning in my lungs, chest too tight.

"That's our gent, then. Setting up a distraction with us while the lad lifted things." Chance's voice was low and close to my ear, his curls brushing the shell. It would make sense, rattle us so we brought a com-motion home and Leo got away.

"Is he part of your group?" Addison was gripping the back of the settee, so he was crowding Leo in, only the two of them in their little bubble. It made my fingers itch, my magic begging to react to such a saturation of power, to yank Addison away from the boy. I balled my fists into my skirt, tugged my energy close as a cloak.

"No. I thought he would move in to take over from Grant but he ain't. He just told us about here. And said to be careful for the bitch that killed Grant."

I squirmed lower in the chair, Chance's hand shifting to squeeze my knee.

"We can go," he said.

I shook my head. I couldn't speak; my voice hiding somewhere in the pained knot at my chest.

"Why did you need to look out for her?" Addison asked.

"She might do the same to us. Grant was for hurting her, to be fair, toss her to the lads. But it's magic again. He said she lived here."

"Do any of your friends want to come seeking revenge?"

Leo shook his head, a laugh bubbling slowly up. "No. Grant was decent, but he was a brutal fucker. Some might spike her if we saw her, but I wouldn't."

Addison gave an approving hum, the hand on his chin move to cup Leo's cheek, keep their gazes locked. "That's good. Do you know the name of the man who told you about here?"

"Mark. Doesn't sound right with his accent, he sounds fancy."

"Thank you, Leo." Addison's other hand came down, so he was cradling the lad's face, like blinkers. My chest tightened, creaked with anxiety.

"What's he doing?" I asked Chance.

"Thrall."

It wasn't like that when he tried it with me. He'd touched me, yes, but not my face, or neck. Panic twisted my heart, the closeness of his neck.

"You've done very well, Leo. Now listen carefully. You couldn't find this book. You are never going to come back here, and you don't want any of your friends to either. Do you understand?"

Leo nodded, leaned in closer in rapt focus as he stared at Addison. "Yes."

"Good boy. Now, this might hurt." Addison's hands slid quickly to the boy's neck, and I was up on my feet.

"Stop!" I hadn't screamed in a while. That was why my throat hurt, and why the other men were looking at me like I'd drawn a blade.

"Are you alright?" Chance was up with me, an arm around my shoulders. It was only when his grip tightened I realised he was helping me stand; legs shaking like I'd drop.

"No need to thrall the dead, princess," Tobias said from his perch. A hot flash ripped through me, tears in my eyes, and I bit into my cheek so I didn't spit venom at him.

"This is to make him sleep," Addison said. He didn't look over to me, taking the slumped lad and handing him off to Jonathan. "You thought something else."

"I thought—" The words broke off, and I coughed. "Yes. I thought something else. I need some air, excuse me."

I shook Chance off, making for the door.

# Chapter 32

I closed the door behind me, marching down the corridor, eyes burning.

It was stupid of me to think Addison would snap his neck. There was no need to thrall the boy, to warn him off, if that was what he had planned, it would be a waste of effort. But the blur of his hands had looked like things I'd done. Seen done. The boy was young.

It was like I'd been drinking too quickly, my stomach tight and high against my lungs, solid as a ball. I could go off into the garden around the front, but they'd see me, all those windows an easy lookout. My blood itched, fizzing like I should run, but I needed peace.

The woods would do, somewhere plain and safe and bare of influence. I pivoted towards the kitchen, slipping out the open door and running towards the huddle of trees, keen to be in their darkness.

There was a commonality about wild spaces, a promise of being able to blend if you were careful. I'd walked the woods a few times now, never seeing my little doe again, but I could find my way through to get to the pond, sit beside the still water. I shivered at my lack of coat, the damp air between the tress pressing in against me, through the expensive cotton blouse Addison had purchased for me. It would be better not to get it muddy, but the skirt would face the worst of it. I could add it to my apologies.

I stumbled a few times but was sure-footed enough to find my little oasis, the water barely rippling as the lazy breeze puffed around me, full of the wet promise of rain. I hunkered down before a tree, tucked low into the trunk, a thick carpet of discarded leaves and twigs seeping cold underneath me. My legs would chill, so I pulled my knees close to my chest, wrapping my arms around them and tensing against the shivers that were pushing insistently now.

The air wasn't cold, just chill and damp, and the ground was a steady stillness that was easy to sink into. I closed my eyes, letting my guard slip lower with each breath out.

The guilt crested with my dropping the energy, and I folded down so my forehead was against my knees. Tears came and I wiped them off, nothing but the fruit of temper. Why did I have to scream like that? Addison had been nothing but kind to mortals around me, and he'd fed the lad. They wouldn't offer hospitality just to kill.

Unless it was a trick. Unless it was to lure someone into a false sense of security and get them to share more, like we would. Like I thought they would with me, before. He was not that. They were not us. I knew that deep in my chest, but the fear lingered like a bruise against my ribs.

I should apologise. Even if I still had doubts, Addison had been welcoming, as had the house, and we had an agreement. It was a poor way to behave as a guest. And I didn't like the idea of hurting them.

I let my head rock back, face up to look at the pool of sky between the trees and the open gap about the pond, the stars cold-silver and bright. There was a bonny moon somewhere, the sky was bright with her light between the leaves and branches, and there was a swooping wonder about looking at all those sparkling points and thinking how much bigger the world was than any one problem. How much more there was out there. Places with different stars, new ones to me, spots I could run off to and learn new patterns in those pearls and twinkling lights. The yearning was a froth in my chest, bubbling up only to burst. Plenty of time to find new stars. I could ask the immortals about that too, how much they knew about the great blackness above given how their magic played with things.

A branch snapped off in the distance and I ducked, hunkering into myself. Mark had mentioned being in the woods. Or someone he knew, given he was using the little gang, maybe there were more than Leo and the redhead. It would be sensible to run, but let them come at me. I was already rotten; I'd be happy to serve them as poorly as my mood.

"Ena?" Tobias's voice carried through the trees, loud footsteps bouncing back across the little clearing. "Princess, are you there?"

"Here." Edgar appeared across from me, the other side of the pond, smiling like he had bad news. "I won't come closer if you don't want me to."

I nodded, clocked Tobias coming in from the left side and making a show of it, noisy as a hog rooting for truffles.

"You had us worried there." Tobias stopped a few feet off from me, not crowding me in. "I thought we agreed running off at night was dangerous."

I snorted a dry laugh, shook my head at him. "I didn't run off, I needed to be away from that room. You've dragged Edgar out into the cold."

"Thought you might like the armed company."

I shook my head. "You can come by, Edgar, I'm not going to run."

He nodded, walking the perimeter of trees rather than across the rich mud of the pond edges until he stood close by, back against the tree beside mine. "You alright?"

"I was scared."

"Can I come closer?" Tobias asked.

I shook my head, and shivered as a fat, cold drop of water hit the back of my neck, the promised rain threatening more.

"We can take this slow." Tobias shed his jacket, tossing it to Edgar who draped it over me. The warmth rushed over me as I slid it around my shoulders. He was a warm man. My chest burned at being handled so carefully, a useless frustration in recognising their care.

"I'm not a wee ain, I don't need swaddled up."

"It's cold, miss. You'll catch something none of the rest of us can. Or get Jonathan sick, then what will we do?" Edgar toed one of the thick roots of his tree, working his jaw a little.

"Be on your own a bit. I bet you can cook, being in the army."

"I could, you know." He grinned, and just for a minute he looked like one of the lads in the dorms, easy smile and about to tell a story. "I was better at it than a lot of my lads, we took turns when there was a chance but half of them cooked like it was pig swill."

I tugged Tobias's jacket closer, the cold below me leaching up my back, fingers of it creeping against my spine. "So you'd be alright. I bet you can cook too."

"I like a few things, none of them as good as Jonathan makes." Tobias was still lurking beside the tree and I cocked my head, indicating him closer. He smiled but I knew how he faked them now.

"I'm not scared of either of you, stop acting like I'll flit."

"You ran off into the dark, after being approached by an immortal who knows you come here. Forgive my wariness, lovely, but it's not safe," Tobias said.

Edgar knelt, one knee in the dirt, hand beside my hip but not touching. "I can walk you back, if you like. We both can, but he thought you'd prefer me."

"Why?"

"I'm the baby of the house, so they tell me. Most recently human, only been turned twenty years. Jonathan's engaged getting the lad returned to the city, and Chance is riding with them, or they'd have sent him."

"Jonathan'd just tell me off."

"He's sick with worry," Tobias said. "He'd have gone out the window after you if he'd seen which way you went."

"I'm sorry to cause him trouble."

"You spooked us all, with that scream." He shook his head, half a laugh dying on his lips, glancing back towards the path out. "I'd rather we went back to the house to speak, lest there's company."

I pushed off the tree, legs thick and numb from cold, brushing them off as I stamped the blood back into flowing. "I'm keeping your jacket."

"As you like. Do you want Edgar to walk you?"

I shook my head, smiling to Edgar. "It's alright, we can go together. I never see you two together much."

The rain began as we were walking, fat drops bouncing off the leaves and smattering over us and the path indiscriminately. "That's because he's like a big bloody cat. You stay still too long he's asleep against you, then you're stuck," Edgar said, falling in beside me.

"You don't fancy a cuddle?" I asked.

"He's threatened to stab me if I do it again," Tobias said, matching our gait.

I smirked over at Edgar. "I believe he would."

"And yet Addison keeps buying him more knives."

# CHAPTER 33

Addison was waiting in his study, pacing back and forth like he had when Henry attacked me, his jacket discarded, hair mussed as if he'd been running his hands through it. His eyes seemed to glow in the low light of the fire, popping wide as they took me in.

"Ena." He rushed forward, stripping Tobias's soaked jacket off me and replacing it with his own, checking over like I had been gone for days. "Are you chilled? You should come before the fire. I can ask Jonathan to bring tea, or soup."

"Down, old dog, she's barely through the door." Tobias set a hand on Addison's chest, pushing him back enough for us to get into the room, steer me towards one of the tall-backed chairs.

"I'm well, Addison. You don't need to fret."

He pinched his lips together, walking off to pluck the blanket up off his bed and tuck it about me, petting my hair lightly before he stepped away again. "You dashed off and I couldn't follow."

I looked at my hands, stomach twisting. "I was spooked, is all. I'm sorry I shouted at you. I should have known that you wouldn't hurt him."

"He's on his way back to the city, with Garrett and Chance accompanying him. Jonathan refused to go, he wanted to know you were safe."

"Edgar's off to let him know she's back." Tobias flopped into the chair Addison usually took, one leg hooked over the edge so it soaked the material upholstering that arm. He was soaked through, no blanket for him, and water dripped from his trouser hem.

"Sorry for the trouble, too," I said.

"Stop apologising and come here." Addison came back before me, holding his hands out, and when I took them, he yanked me up into a hug, curling around me like smoke does a fire. He pressed me into his chest, one arm against my back as the other stroked my wet hair. "I'd never want to scare you like that. I asked Tobias to distract you thinking it would be enough but of course you wanted to see he was alright. You're so viciously careful that people are protected."

"It's only what anyone would do."

"You're a terrible liar," Tobias said.

I fizzed at the comment, hot to my bones. "It's uncouth to assume wickedness when shown kindness."

"Don't fret on it. I'm glad you came back. Between the dangers in a forest and another immortal seeking influence, I was scared Tobias would find you hurt."

"I was just by the pond. I like looking at the stars."

"We can go out onto the roof some time, when Haddley isn't using it, then. I would like that. But please take one of us with you, I was so worried."

"Peace, Addison, I'm alright." I pulled back, laying my hand on his cheek to make him look at me. His eyes still seemed to shine, like candlelight on dull metal, and I smiled at him. "I'm here. Don't fret. Also, may I bunk with one of you, if that's alright?"

"Oh?" Tobias pitched up in the question, coming to stand beside us with brows high like an angry cat's back.

"You said I could bunk with you if I was upset, and I am. And I'm cold. Nothing funny, I don't want to drag either of you onto your backs, but having some comfort to feel safe by would be nice." They shared a look, and my worry tangled like a snagging thorn. "Or I can ask Jonathan, but he might take it funny, given I ran off."

Addison shook his head, still cupped by my palm. "Jonathan wouldn't lay a finger on you for anything but care. You remind him of his sister. But if you're sure, of course you could share our bed."

"Our?" I blinked between them. "You sleep together?"

"When we manage to overlap, yes." Addison smiled at Tobias, his eyes dimmer but still full of something. Love must be so strange, when strangled with grief, even for creatures like them.

Tobias looked at me through his lashes, a retroactive attempt at charm. "He has a ridiculous bed, and mine is covered in sketched and toils for my works. So we share. Sometimes."

"There's no harm in seeking comfort," Addison said.

I wrinkled my nose at the thought he was right. "I trust you both, but I want to be upfront. Your kindness to humans is clear. You don't fight a war on shallow beliefs. But I can't be certain of things yet." *Yet*, I should not have used that word. I bit my tongue to shut it up.

"Is that what you think?" I looked up at Tobias, as he took my free hand and ran a thumb over the bones on the back. He sang with the need for touch, ready to tip into a hug, but I didn't want to push him where he didn't want to go, so I smiled and let him lead.

"Yes. I don't think you were some silly bucks looking for glory."

"Why not?" Addison asked.

"You can't die easily, given what you are. No need for a glorious death and songs in your honour. You'll be here to tell folk. So, you must have done it for believing in it."

Tobias grunted, tugging me closer so he could slip an arm around my shoulders. It folded us into an odd sort of hug, three bodies entangled, and the heat from them was better than the low fire, or my own burning shame. "I think you're too kind to us." His words were muffled into my neck, head pressed to my shoulder.

"Kind?"

"Finding goodness in such a vile thing. We believed in what we fought for, and still do, but some of it was an excuse for the families to spill blood," Addison said.

I nodded. "It often is. Politics is greased by blood and bile."

"So it is." Addison let go of me with one arm, tugging Tobias closer so we were a little triangle together, all pushed in. Tobias's grip on me tightened and he heaved a sigh.

"Tobias?"

"I want to know you're alright. Nothing more." He nuzzled my neck, breath hot on the cool skin, too desperate to tickle as it should. "After the war, I never wanted to sire anyone. Or thrall, or anything like that. I saw what was done to humans. The idea that we could change you, hurt you, it makes me sick."

I laughed, twisting a little to catch one cheek with my free hand. "I'm afraid I have some terrible news for you, then."

"You're mocking me."

"I am, you daft creature. We change people, it's part of being around folk. I change people, it doesn't mean I'm out here making them magical or setting them all alight. Your presence is cause for change the same way water running through the stream is."

"That's an awful flowery way of saying I'm an overwhelming prick." He buried his head in my shoulder again, shaking my hand free.

"No more than anyone else someone cares for. If my being around you means I change then that's not a dreadful thing, especially when you saved my life." I stroked his hair, just as soaked as mine but starting to dry. No one had ever warned us that vampires were fussing, touchy. Probably didn't have much experience of letting them be such. "Anyway, you've not managed it these few weeks past, so you're not doing so bad."

"Despite all the hugs," Addison added. Rich, coming from him.

"Do you mind it very much?" Tobias stroked my hair back, his fingers running gentle along my scalp, and I reached up to let it free of the tie I had around it.

"I don't mind it too much, though it's not what I'm used to," I said, laying my head down on a shoulder. Addison's, I thought.

"You deserve better than that," Addison tutted. "Affection should be freely given where it's welcome."

I huffed air, unsure what to say to such a sweet thought. "I'm a rotten thing, you know. Not sure how right you are."

"We know a thing or two about wickedness, princess. Don't be so cruel to yourself."

I shook my head, sighing as he continued to move his fingers. "As you say."

"Stubborn thing." His smile was loud, clear in his voice, and he squeezed me closer for a beat. "You should sleep. Can we hug you, too?" Tobias asked, head perking up.

"You're nothing but a giant cat, I swear it." I laughed, leaning up so I could separate from them. "Yes, you can hug me if you so feel the need. I might even like it, when it's you two, but nothing beyond a hug."

Addison smiled, a little glimmer in his eyes but nothing like the witch-light before. "You're good to hug. Soft hips."

"I'll sleep underneath the bed at this rate."

Tobias shook his head, catching my hand again. "Don't do that, it's much less comfortable."

# Chapter 34

Addison's room should have been in a painting. It was dominated by the bed, a massive thing that had to have been liberated from some palace or another. All in dark wood, the frame had a high-ceilinged top, though the canopy was only half the length of the same, and thick green curtains that were pinned back, giving a half-drawn feel at the headboard. That was carved with intricate, swirling vines and dotted with stars, an imaginary garden in twilight. More pillows than a man could need nestled at the top, with a thick quilt and cover laid over the mattress.

The surrounding room had some furniture, but not too much: a pair of chairs, a love seat beside one window, a set of drawers. No desk, no dresser, not even a mirror to reflect light from the two long windows. There were a few stacks of books at the walls but nothing like the study. Awful bare for the two men together.

A small door in the far corner evidenced a bathroom, but I'd not managed to escape into there for changing. Instead, Addison had loaned me a nightgown, tugged out of a drawer that squeaked with neglect, though the material smelled enough of pressed flowers and lavender that it must have been changed occasionally. They had retreated from the room, as if they'd not seem me half bare and bloodied on their floor weeks ago, and I was left stripping with my back to the door, the chill evening air nothing compared to the sparking in my chest.

It was ridiculous to be bashful. They were ancient. They'd have seen more bodies that I had living in the dorms. I rubbed my arms to dispel the goose bumps that had prickled along my nerves. I was being foolish.

"Are you alright for us to join you?" I turned to find Tobias with his head through the door.

"Has Jonathan finished shouting at you?" I asked. I plucked a small blanket up from the box at the bottom of the bed, sliding it around my shoulders as I perched on the edge.

"He still has Addison." Tobias sat beside me, tugging me onto his lap and hugging me against his chest. "Jonathan will be fine once he's done shouting."

"I'll make him scones to apologise. Are you hugging me to keep warm?"

"We can say that, yes." He winked.

"Alright." I smiled at him, pulling him closer for a beat. Foolish man, fretting over me needlessly, giving me warmth. I wanted this for a while, though. Let him have some of that softness he'd shared in the study. He so deserved some of that.

"You may want to check where you're pressing my head, princess" he said.

Looking down I realised he was pressed into the side of my breast, given how I was twisted into him. I batted his shoulder, all soft musing dispelled by the heat in my cheeks. "Behave. Despite the lack of female company, I'm sure you've been around a pair of tits before, they're not unusual."

"I might be fond of them."

"I'm sure you could go find a welcoming pair if you were." I twisted off his lap, going back to my procured blanket.

"What about yours?" he asked. His head plopped down on my shoulder, arms around my waist.

"They'll remain where they are, I'm rather attached to them."

"You're impossible."

I laughed at that, leaning into him. "You're daft."

"I must agree." Addison came through the door, shedding his vest and tossing it to one side before starting to unbutton his shirt. "I don't think I've seen Jonathan so incensed. I think I talked him down from standing watch at the door, but I'm certain speaking to you tomorrow will help."

"At least he's settled." Tobias began to strip as well, shirt coming up over his head. "Chance is going to be insufferable."

Addison went to the drawers to pull another nightshirt out, throwing one to Tobias too. I kept my eyes on the floor, stealing glances around the windows rather than the men undressing.

"Going shy on us, princess?"

"You had to see me for the cuts, before. This is not that."

"I would have thought you were used to changing with men," Tobias said.

"I am, but I've known them since they were lads."

"No fancy man back in Edinburgh?" Tobias asked.

I shook my head. "None proper. I've had fun with folk but no more than that."

"Don't tease her, she's had enough of a day." Addison came back to the bed, catching my hands to pull me into standing, and turned the covers down. "I would suggest you sleep in the middle but if you would prefer to take one of the sides that's fine."

"How do you two usually sleep?"

"Poorly," Tobias said.

"I prefer the left side of the bed," Addison replied.

"Alright, middle works for me, then." I got onto the bed, shuffling into the centre. "I also sometimes scream in the night. Sorry about that."

"Don't worry yourself, lambkin. Try to sleep."

I woke once in the night to moonlight on my face and Tobias shifting around like he would toss from the bed.

"He'll still in a few minutes," Addison said from his side. I looked over to find him tucked close, eyes on me and his hair in a tumble from sleep. He stroked my face with one finger. "Are you well?"

"Yes. Tired."

"You would be, after the night. If you wish to talk about it, we can do so whenever you need to."

"There are some conversations one shouldn't have. If this is one of them, I can do that."

"Do you always put up such barriers?" he asked.

I sighed, too tired to be anything but direct. "Barriers keep me alive, Addison. I know my life is much shorter than yours but I do value it."

"I meant that the constraint must frustrate you," he said.

"Constraints are more common than most would like to admit. I'm simply aware of mine."

"A dear lesson, but one you have made successful. You wouldn't have run if you didn't know the cost of the alternative."

I nodded, eyes inching over the canopy above us. The threads still dimly shone in the moonlight, fae bright and lingering. "Everything has a cost; most things come with a balance. On the balance, fleeing was better than staying. I don't want to become one of the nuns."

"They're dogmatic?"

"No. They raise the youngsters, that part isn't so bad. But you can't work jobs if you're a nun. You do research, care for the children, all that helps, but the Council come and pick who they like the look of. You can't refuse, you must earn your keep. I don't want to be a bed-warmer for someone because I can't refuse."

"I'm glad you left."

I turned my head to look at him, unsure of the statement. "You are?"

"Yes. You deserve to have a life you want, rather than one forced onto you. And I would never have met you otherwise." His smile was soft as butter, golden eyes almost silver.

"Not unless someone hired us to move against you, and I can't see if being taken on. Even the Council's terrified of born vampires."

"A wise choice, some would say."

"I don't think so anymore." I smiled at him, reaching over to tuck his hair back. "It's not fair to treat you like those who started the war. Even if I did scream at you."

"You've seen a lot of the worst of us, in just a short month."

"And I've not even burned the place down."

"I'm grateful for that too. I would miss parts of this house. We've been taking care of it a long while."

"Since the war?"

"Yes. It was a nice place to come and recover, and I never left. We stayed and new things grew."

"But you kept Henry close, despite all that goodness."

Addison sighed, looking at the canopy for a long while before he spoke. "It became a sort of penance. If I was reminded of what I caused, I couldn't deny what I'd done to others to sate my pain."

"Not content with the cruelty of the war, you had to be cruel to yourself too?"

"You think it cruel?"

"To only be defined by our worst impulses? Yes. We're more than our darkness. And if we weren't once, we can be. There's always a reason to change if we aren't pleased with who we are. Maybe you're bad at recognising that because you're immortal."

He shifted on his shoulder, rolling so he was facing me. "How so?"

"Too much time to get stuck in your ways. We have the reminder that it could all end, especially with our wars. When the world wants you dead, survival's an act of defiance."

"I don't want you dead. I would have been desperate if worse had happened to you when you ran off."

"I believe you." I kept stroking his hair, arm against the pillow so I didn't disturb Tobias. "Even if we must be like dogs to you, dying so quick."

"You aren't like that. For some immortals, yes, but I've never thought that. I've loved several humans, in many ways. We have longer to grieve afterwards is all."

"It changed your hair. Grief."

"Romantic as that would be, it was my own hubris. The spell was an undertaking beyond my powers. It weakened me. I'm surprised Henry wasn't more consumed by that when he did the same, but his sons had left him tools. I would have been much worse if Tobias hadn't intervened."

"I'm glad he did."

"Could I ask you something? It doesn't have to have an answer yet, but I want you to think on it."

"What is it?"

"I want—"

Tobias shot up, one arm on me, squashing me into the mattress, and one arm out like he was blocking a blow, peering around.

"Peace, beloved. All are well." Addison half sat up, catching Tobias's arm.

"Aye." Tobias kept checking around the room, shaking his head like he was sure the shadows would jump. "I thought I heard something."

"Me chunnering because you're crushing me," I said.

He turned to look down at me before pulling his hand off. "Sorry, princess. Old habits."

"Cuddle up if you're wary." I shifted onto my side, so my back was to him. "I'll hug him and you can hug me."

Tobias laid down, shuffling close. His chest was like a low fire behind me, cosy as anything I'd ever had in Edinburgh, and I took the hand that set itself gingerly on my hip, sliding it to rest at my waist. "Are you certain?"

"Unless you'd rather cuddle Addison. I'll not take offence but we'd need to switch around."

"I'm quite content with this position," Addison said. If the smile I saw in silver was smug, I'd blame it on a trick of the moonlight.

"Alright. Thank you." Tobias sank against me, lips close to the nape of my neck, and I closed my eyes to the ebb and flow of their breathing.

# Chapter 35

Addison and I shared a carriage towards the city some days later, his location to see Matteo again while I went to see Margery. Garrett was riding with the coachman, despite an offer to share the cab.

"Is he accompanying you?" I asked.

"I think he has his own tasks today." He shifted on his seat, pulling something from a dark leather satchel he had taken with him. "I have something to give you, and I would like to have a discussion, if we can?"

He had a habit of doing this in coaches. "What vexes you?"

"It's nothing so bad as that. I wanted to give you something to assist with your studies. You've been so thorough in what you're sharing, it seems fair to be sure you have an equally thorough response." He passed me over the thing he'd taken out—a small leatherbound book, almost like a notary's pad. The same book Leo had tried to steal. The exterior was stained dark from handling, and despite it being cold it was supple and well-worn.

"What's this?" I hesitated to open it, half afraid it might break. A low tingle of energy, like the air before snowfall, settled across my palms.

"It's one of my notebooks. From studying, early on. Do not ask me how old it is, I will lie." He smiled, shaking his head a little. "There's nothing within that's exceptional, so I have no idea why the boy was sent for it, but I'd planned to give you it already. I was a careful note-taker, and my writing is not too abysmal. Or, if it is, you can ask me about it. I would like if we could continue our discussions."

"Are you certain it's alright for me to have this?" I held the book between my hands, itching to open it. Time magic, the basics of it at least, had been fascinating, and the ability to get into the skill of it was between my palms. My stomach fluttered at the idea; holding history—time—and being able to pore over it.

"Yes. It means I can be assured I won't mistake telling you something due to overfamiliarity. When you come to know something well, you can forget the steps."

"Thank you so much, Addison. I don't have the words."

"There's something else, which I've been avoiding discussing." I blinked up at him, nodding for him to speak. "I find myself very fond of you, Ena. Immeasurably so. I know our arrangements are temporary until the city is safe for you, but would you consider staying with us longer?"

"Pardon?

"Not forever, you must have a life of your own. I don't want you to feel obliged. But if it were to suit you, I would like to have your company as long as you would share it."

"That's extremely generous, Addison. I'm not a particularly good house guest."

"We've done more to endanger you than you have us."

"I mean I'm happy to set someone alight if that would make you feel better. You or Tobias, probably, to save the others any embarrassment."

He chuckled and reached over to pat my hand. "Think on it. I'd be happy to have you with us and practicing your powers, if that suited you. I know you don't want to be cloistered up, or taken back to Edinburgh, and I won't push you out if you say no. The protection of my house is always open to you either way."

"Thank you. What's caused you to ask now?"

"The thought of not being able to speak to you brings an ache." He tapped his chest with his knuckles, just beside his heart. "Sentimental, I know, but I've come to value you. So I want you to have all your options, and the assurance that your choice will not sway my duty to you as a guest."

We were never warned immortals had such hearts. I'd burn the books in our library, that warned only of feeding and thrall, if I was ever dragged back. Write my own out of spite in the nunnery.

I coughed, shedding the angry thought. "May I ask something out of turn?"

"Of course."

"Tobias clearly has part of your heart. Plain as day. And you a part of his."

"I cannot call it untrue, though you always say it so viscerally."

"Love takes as much as it gives back, I imagine that's more so for immortals. You're both so kind to me, and I don't want to tread into areas that would be harmful without clear agreement from all."

"Despite our sleeping arrangements?"

I had continued to share their bed some nights. I frowned at him, licking the back of my teeth as I struggled for the right words. "That's you giving me comfort. I asked, and you acquiesced, and that's a kindness. What if I agree to more, and hurt you?"

He snorted, covering his mouth with the back of his hand for a moment. "I wouldn't fret on it, lambkin. We have done much worse to each other than you ever will."

The words twisted in my chest, a reminder of his impossible age. It wasn't that I forgot it, but sometimes he seemed closer to me than others. This was a distant time. "Alright, that's good. I'll consider it, then, though I'd like to speak to Tobias, too."

"Thank you. And, one other thing."

"Yes?"

"If you wished to share other intimacies with Tobias only, I don't want our history to stop you. The nest is open to openness, and he's a good man."

"You've both said similar things to me, you know?"

He chuckled, nodding a little. "That's no surprise. Sweet creature that he is." He turned to look out the window. His hand sat atop mine and he made no move away, so I left it there as I watched the countryside change from green to grey to red brick and busy streets.

Margery's shop had been quiet, and her advice useful, though cut short when we saw Garrett perched at one side of the door like a lost pup.

"Are you done already?" I asked as I exited. Garrett pushed off the wall to join me in walking down the steps, eyes flitting about.

"I wanted some time with you."

"You came into town for that?"

"I needed something from the shop too, for Haddley. Will you walk with me a little?"

"Alright."

"I'm obliged. I know a good place." He set off in a quick pace and I matched him, weaving between folk as we went away from the shops. He led me to a quieter street, one tall red brick wall running along the side of the pavement we were on. We went in a comfortable silence until we reached a substantial iron gate. I liked that about him, I decided; he was good to be quiet with.

Going through the gate, Garrett holding it open for me, we slid into a cemetery with neat lines of graves rushing down a hill away from us.

"Romantic spot," I said. Some of the graves were impressive—tall marble pillars with searching angels stood at the top, stone dogs with their heads forever down and waiting for their masters. Others were the usual fare, simple rectangles, or curved topped plinths, a few fully fledged tombs around the edges that backed into the walls.

"Haddley said graveyards might be good for you. That the energy was different. I was never much fond of them as a human, but I didn't use magic." We walked along the gravel path, passing the trails of family memorials with blank segments of stone awaiting those yet to go in the ground.

"They are, of a sort. It's like being beside a pond rather than a river."

Garrett nodded at the comparison, almost smiling. "It's also not somewhere Addison would expect to find us."

"I concur." There was no one else in the graveyard.

"So if you need to speak about anything you wish him to be unaware of, you could do so now."

I snorted, his subtlety about matched Haddley's. No wonder they were a pair. "Are you seeing if I need to run away, Garrett?"

"The thought had occurred to me. It would be a good spot for me to be distracted."

I smiled at him, joining our arms. He clicked his teeth but kept walking. "You're so kind. I'm not being held captive. And there's no thrall involved, I promise."

His jaw bulged but he nodded. "We've done a poor job keeping you safe."

"And someone in the city is killing magic users. At least you tried to help."

"You're mocking me."

"I'm not." I stopped, catching his free elbow with my hand so I could turn him to face me. "Truly, I'm not. I thought about my fear a lot, and I would prefer to stay where there's kindness. Right now, that's at the nest. I'm not saying I would stay forever but it's a good place to be now."

"With no offence meant, you are a strange lady, Ena. Is there nowhere else you would rather be?"

"Plenty. Back home in Caithness, or off in some sunny place on the continent. But I'd be hunted there as much as I would be here, with less places to hide."

He tutted, shaking his head. "What about your choice?"

"Choice is always tempered by reality. You were a soldier, you know that. Once I know where I'm going I'll have more choices. I might still come back to see you, though, even if I leave."

"Truly?"

"Naturally. You've been kind to me. I'm even, almost, used to you all being so cuddly."

He pursed his lips, frowning at one of the monument's stone faces. "Does it not trouble you? It's not very proper of them."

I swallowed a laugh, shaking my head. "It's fine. I grew up in a dormitory, there's plenty of mixed living in those. No one has tried to be untoward with me, and now that I don't think you're going to gobble me up it's less concerning."

"Would it be something we could do?" He was still fixing a stone woman with a fierce glare but there was a softness in his question. "You and I, I mean. I've seen the elders do it with you, and Haddley doesn't like it as much. I don't want to make him uncomfortable, but it would be nice to be gentle."

"As long as it was also nothing untoward, yes. It can be nice to have a body close by."

"I think I would like that, sometime. Yes, that would be nice." He nodded, as if to himself, before he pulled back a little. "We should get back to the coach."

"Alright. Thank you for your concern, Garrett. It warms my heart that you'd sneak me out."

"He's my sire, I owe him a lot." He took a deep breath. "I couldn't be as I am, without the nest, or be with Haddley. But Addison does have a blind spot. Too tied up in those he's avoiding to see what's in front of him."

"I think it comes with age."

"What's your excuse then?" he asked.

"Sheer stubbornness. I didn't get anywhere in my college being easily swayed."

He shook his head at me, starting towards the gate again. I lingered around the stones for a few moments, soaking in the peace of the place before we rejoined the bustle of the city. It was nothing at all like the ones at home—plague and burning pits, generations of lost family in the country. Horror. Here was nice. I could stand to come back.

# Chapter 36

Once we arrived home I went to my room, closing myself up in it so I could rest a while. I settled on top of the bed with a small novel—the notebook saved for the morning when I could give it full attention—and propped against the headboard so I could doze.

Heavy banging on the door interrupted my first line, Chance stumbling in before I could rise to open it.

"We have company, petal. I'm not entirely sure what we're going to do with you. We can't hide you in the garden, because the coach is already here, and we can't shove you in the attic because they'll smell you a mile off with your magic."

"What's going on?"

He grimaced, passing a hand over his face. "Some of the other immortals have dropped in. Unannounced."

"That's rude."

"It's damn near obscene in the old families, which has everyone in a ruffle." He leaned around to peek out the window. "Shit, they're nearly out of the coach."

"Why do you all need to make an appearance?"

"We're Addison's children, as far as these ones are concerned, so the full household has to welcome them."

"Right, I must too then. If Jonathan's there and I'm not, that'll have a look to it."

"He's not magic, though. I don't know if these are the good sort."

"Either way, hiding me will seem deliberate." I grabbed his wrist, tugging him from the window before I plucked up a ribbon too. I tied it into my hair as we trotted along the corridor, barrelling down the steps to catch up with Garrett and Haddley and pour in through the backdoor of the morning room.

Edgar was already at the main door, stood beside it like a sentinel, and Tobias was pacing between the windows and the seats. Haddley and Garrett perched either end of one low sofa, enough room in the middle for someone else to join them, and Chance went for a nearby love seat that kept us close to the back wall. I followed him, landing a respectable distance away.

"Is he alright?" I asked, nodding to Tobias.

"Hates the visits, he's sullen for days."

"Ena, a moment?" Tobias said and I went over to him. "Come with me."

He grabbed my hand and took me out the door I'd just entered, peering about before he slipped us into the scullery. Once the door closed, he pulled me to him, face buried in my neck, shifting my hair so he could rub against me.

"What are you doing?" I hissed. I yanked him back by his hair, eyes barely visible in the light from the book-sized window.

"Scenting you."

"What?" I let go of him.

"This couple are old-fashioned, and while they were neutral in the war, they retain certain views." He sighed, shaking his head as he ran his hands over me, patting my blouse, playing with my hair. "I wish Agnes had married someone other than my uncle."

I bristled under his touch, focusing on his eyes so I didn't fidget. "How do you mean?"

"She's a snob but she's not terrible compared to others. Oswyn brings out the worst in her."

"I imagine that's a danger, with your sort, bringing out the worst in someone. Too long together to fall into bad habits. At least with humans we die."

"That's grim talk."

"You're rubbing up on me like a school lad in a cupboard, how's my comment worse?"

"That should do." He gave a short nod, brushing my hair a little. "I'll check the door and you slip back in next to Chance. We'll try to cover you with the others. Be careful. You can never tell with these types."

"These types?"

"Those that come visiting." He sneered, scowling before he stuck his head out the door. "Right, let's go."

We darted back into the morning room, Tobias returning to the front as I scurried to my seat with Chance. Footsteps approached from the main entry and Addison's voice carried through the door.

"We alright?" Chance was doing his best impression of order, legs neatly crossed and hands positioned together on the top knee.

"Yes." I straightened my skirt, sitting up to look neat.

"Let us take tea in the morning room, it has the best view of the gardens." Addison led the pair in, directing them to the plushest settee. "Jonathan will arrange for tea."

They were an odd match; she was regal in her looks, a long, thin neck supporting a slim but lovely face, small nosed and clear-eyed. Her hair hung freely other than a delicate pin fixing some length back, away from her face, the deep gold like heather honey. He was a different sort all together, as broad across as the chest as Tobias but thick-set, and his jaw was as square as a shovel. His hair was dark and coarse, curling a little at the parts near his scalp but notlong enough that it carried through.

They dressed almost to match—her dress deep red with a golden pattern sweeping down the skirt, his tunic black with a front panel in the same ruddy shade.

Tobias stepped forward to give a bow, turning to each of them. "Agnes, Oswyn."

"Tobias." The woman smiled and it was such a cold thing I tucked my shoulders down, folding into myself. She held her hand out and Tobias kissed the knuckles.

"Well met, nephew. You sent your companion out to greet us again." Oswyn sat himself down without further pomp, glowering.

"Someone must corral the house into order when you drop by unannounced." Tobias took one of the high-backed chairs near the window, crossing one ankle over the opposite knee so he filled up as much of the seat as possible.

"Addison is most cordial, greeting us in your stead," Agnes said as she joined Oswyn on the seat. They left a more than respectable gap in the middle, like they repelled each other.

"It's always been his way. What brings you to our property? I wasn't aware you were in the area."

"We had cause to visit with another and it seemed unbecoming not to come here. It's been two years, has it not?" Agnes asked.

"We would have sent a message ahead, but our travel plans changed at short order." Oswyn barked a laugh and Agnes inclined her head in what may have been a nod. It was like she was in freezing water: every word carefully plucked out, every gesture worked through like a marionette.

"I'm sorry to hear your plans changed, that's bothersome." Tobias nodded, glancing around the room. "We should have a pot to talk over shortly, and I think you know most of our company."

"You have a new human," Agnes said. I smiled but stayed sat, hoping that would be all that was said on the matter.

"Yes, a recent addition. Who were you visiting?" Tobias said.

"We have tea for our guests, a lovely new blend I had imported, and refreshments for the group." Addison breezed into the room with Jonathan on his heels, a cart trundled before him.

A large pot sat on the top, four cups and a tea-set already prepared, and the lower shelves had a selection of bottles. I counted three or four wines as well as gin and whiskey. They'd been holding out on me in this regard, it appeared.

"Jonathan, could you pour for us please?" Tobias asked.

Oswyn spat a derisive laugh, "*Please*, he says."

"Manners cost naught, uncle, and yet you're so ungenerous with them."

"Addison, you have a new human," Agnes said again. Shit.

Addison glanced my way then back to them. "Yes, she's delightful, isn't she? I do love when she wears a ribbon in her hair, so precious." I kept my face blank other than a small smile, pushing my nails into my palms.

"Come here, girl," Oswyn said. He was peering around Jonathan's shape as he served the tea and passed around the cups, eyes like a dog looking for scraps. I stood, approaching them slowly with my eyes on Jonathan's back.

"Well met, mistress, master." I curtsied, low enough to have to tug my skirt a touch, and stood back up to meet their gaze. Her eyes were the same gold as her hair, old and rich. His were brighter, closer to the cat's eye colour Tobias had.

"What is your name, sweet thing?" Agnes asked.

"I am Ena Sinclair, mistress."

Oswyn leaned towards me, eyes flicking over my face. "Where's the accent from?"

"Scotland, sir. I came down for work, but the city has been unsafe. I'm obliged by the protection offered by the masters of the house."

"You have magic." Agnes beckoned me closer and I stepped into her appraising stare, shoulders low and chin high. I could not be small, but I could seem it.

"I do. I trained in one of the schools and was looking for a scholarly post."

Oswyn narrowed his eyes at my hands. "What sort? I don't much like magic."

I turned them over, showing clear wrists and backs. "Elemental, nothing from the ritual practices. We aren't as well-known as the Solomon Schools."

"Ena has been pleasant company for the younger ones," Addison said. He stepped close to my back, turning to draw me away, and Agnes caught my sleeve.

"Don't steal her yet, Addison. Come sit with us, Ena, I wish to speak more with you." She patted the seat between them, plenty of space for me to fit even with my stature. I bowed my head, squeezing Addison's hand briefly before perching next to her.

"You're too kind, mistress. I'm sure nothing from my history could be as interesting as my hosts."

"You have her well-trained, how long's she been here?" Oswyn brushed against me as he turned to look at Tobias, and Agnes caught my hand, entangling our fingers. No escape soon, then. I wound my energy tighter, like a corset against my form, and licked the back of my teeth. Edgar uncrossed his arms, brows low, but kept his position.

"A while now. A few months, is it?" Tobias fell back in his seat, glancing over at Addison.

"I think it may be as many as seven. Is that right, Jonathan? You keep me right on these things." Addison settled into the other high-backed chair, the two men like sentry lions guarding a gate.

"Yes, sir, seven. She joined us after the last snow in February." Jonathan had served everyone but me some form of drink and I tried my best to stare a gin into existence. He gave me a little shrug but produced no glass before he took his exit. Coward.

"And her accent is still so pronounced. It's quaint." Agnes took a sip of tea, eyes on me as I sat still and careful.

"Thank you." I ducked my head in deference, my hair spilling over one shoulder, and Oswyn reached over to stroke the lines on my neck. I froze under his touch, locking eyes with Tobias.

"Someone been having a share in her?" Oswyn asked. "I thought you were all too well-behaved for such things."

"She was attacked," Tobias said, sitting up.

"On her journey down someone accosted her," Addison added.

"What tosh, those are clearly bites."

"Nails, sir. Someone tore at my neck." I laid my fingernails on the marks, showing him how they spread out. "I healed well so I can understand how they would look like bites, but it was nothing like that. Everyone in the house has been most welcoming."

"I bet they have, pretty little sweeting like you." His laugh was knowing and lewd, a hand on my knee.

Agnes's fingers squeezed mine a touch more, a small shake of her head accompanying my panicked glance over. "He is fond of pet names for his humans. Pay him no mind. We won't be stealing you off from Addison or Tobias."

"'His humans', they're not animals," Tobias said. His tea sat abandoned beside the chair, discarded as he leaned forward. "You cannot treat them like pets."

"We don't need to have this discussion again." Agnes shook her head at him, turning to speak to Addison, but Oswyn's grip on my knee tightened.

"You're not still spouting this rubbish, are you? The accords protect them but there's little point pretending they are the same as us."

"As your good lady wife suggested, let's not have talk of back then," Addison said.

He set his own cup down, empty from what I could see, and I clocked Haddley and Garrett gulping their drinks as well. Wine, by the looks of it, lucky bastards. Chance had his glass of amber fluid up against his chest like he was ready to toss it in someone's face. I was going to steal a bottle from the cabinet at this rate, get drunk in the bath as I scrubbed myself clean.

While I was protected from their energy, I was steeped in their smarm; a cloying, unspoken expectation that hung around them like a haze of perfume. Rich people were the same between vampires and humans, at least.

"I know you get sensitive to it, excuse me, Addison. But you must see the difference." Oswyn gripped my chin, turning it away from him to bare my neck to the room. "Months of healing and she's still marred up. They're so much weaker than us."

"Oswyn, you should unhand her. Guest or not she is under my care, and I do not believe anyone should be handled unwillingly," Addison said.

"She doesn't mind it, do you, pet?" Oswyn asked.

"You can't help it, sir, it's a compulsion of your nature." I turned my smile to him. "I must say I was surprised how touch heavy vampires are. It was quite a lot to get used to, especially when I'd burned to death the last man that pawed at me. The nest has been patient with me, though." It was mostly true—I had burned the last man who touched me unwelcomely. Much as Chance had manhandled me when I woke up, he was a vampire and I'd only clocked him between the legs. He wouldn't take offence if the way he buried his face in his tumbler was anything to go by.

"Burned him to death?" Agnes repeated.

I turned back to her. "What's a lady to do when attacked? Even with my height I wasn't likely to be a match in strength, and some men get such terrible ideas when they meet a woman alone on the road. It was the only way I could be safe, and he still hurt me so." I tapped my neck, eyes downcast.

"She was most distressed when we found her. Magical fire always leaves a particular mark on a corpse, as you know, but on a human it's much more... disfiguring. You would barely have known it was a man but for the scent," Addison said.

Oswyn's grip slipped from me, back straightening. "That's quite the undertaking."

"Did you have experience, in the war?" I asked, catching Tobias's eye as I looked over to Oswyn again. "We learned a little of it in my college, but not as much as the better schools, so my apologies for any ignorance in my question."

"Not ignorance, sweet thing. It is better to stay away from such matters." Agnes stroked my arm, seeking my attention. "We were lucky to avoid most of the war, as all the sensible families did. The fighting took many great lives."

Tobias's eyebrows drew up, but he hummed in agreement. "A terrible time for all."

Oswyn nodded, loudly swallowing his tea. "Is there more?"

"Of course. Ena, could you, since Jonathan has left us?" Addison asked.

I stood, taking the cover from the pot and pouring more amber fluid into the white china cup Oswyn held out. There was an empty slosh as I brought the spout back level.

"I fear the pot is nearly empty. Shall I go get more?" I turned to Addison, eyes flicking to the door.

"Yes, thank you, lambkin." I twisted, giving another curtesy to the guests before I turned to leave. Addison caught my hip as I went to the door, pulling me close to the arm of his chair. He looked up at me through heavy lashes and pressed a kiss at the line of my belt, against the cotton at my hip. I burned at the gesture, my face flushing so quickly my pulse thudded against my neck. "Hurry back."

"Naturally." It was barely squeaked out of my mouth before I shot to the door. Edgar mercifully opened it for me so I could retreat to the kitchen.

# CHAPTER 37

I found Jonathan lurking within in the kitchen.

"You had better give me gin immediately." I dumped the pot out in the sink, still a cups' worth of the brew abandoned. I set the lid and base firmly on the counter as I turned to look at him. "They want another pot but I will need at least a double to go back in there."

He rushed up to me, hugging me close, and I squeaked at the force against my ribs. "Did they hurt you? I didn't hear the sound of a falling out but they're such brutes, I've had his hand down my trews more than once."

"No harm. Some light petting but I talked about murder and he stopped."

He pulled back. "Murder?"

"I did set a man on fire."

"Ah, that. Right, we must get the water on again and then we can have me take the fresh pot in, and you can do something..." He looked around the kitchen for inspiration.

"Cakes? You're always baking, do you not have some handy?"

"Just some parkin, I doubt it will be to their tastes."

"I'll mix some cinnamon sugar and sprinkle it with that, call it a Scots version. That's got to be hospitable."

"We can try that, yes. Let me lead." He took the cake from the tin, passing it to me, and put a fresh kettle to boil.

I found one of the nicer plates, setting it to one side as I sliced the cake into finger-sized segments. "Why are we telling them I arrived in February?"

"There will be a reason they wish to know, and a reason the masters have so carelessly forgotten. They must have been enjoying your company so much they have lost track of time."

"Of course. Easy to lose track as an immortal." I fancied the cakes up, laying them on the plate in a little circling pattern, pretty enough to look like effort, and followed Jonathan with his now steaming teapot.

He knocked on the door, which was opened by Edgar, just in time to see Agnes and Oswyn standing again.

"We brought refreshments," Jonathan announced. He stopped before the trolley and I held the cake plate close, in two hands lest I get bumped into again.

"That is gracious of you, but I fear we must leave sooner than planned. You have been delightful company as always, Tobias, Addison. Do visit with your new companion when you can." Agnes smiled at me like she wanted to pet my head, her fingers twitching, but she breezed past with Oswyn following in her wake. He winked at Jonathan, ignoring me, Tobias fast behind them this time.

I blinked at the quick exit, holding the cake fingers out to Edgar when our eyes met. He took one with a small nod.

"What was that then?" I turned to offer the cakes to Addison, who took one as he held his cup out for Jonathan to fill it.

Chance was the first to crack, stuffing his knuckles into his mouth to hide his laughter. Haddley was the same colour as his wine, while Garrett had his face buried in Haddley's neck and was shaking.

"That, my dear," Chance said, standing to saunter over and select a slice of cake, "was quite the performance. Given Addison's uncouth display we may not see them for another decade."

"Uncouth? It was a bit over familiar, yes, but it wasn't gratuitous."

"I'm afraid it was," Addison said. He nabbed another cake finger, smirking to himself.

"A kiss is that rude to them?" I asked.

Chance snorted, draping over Addison's chair to press their cheeks together. "Not simply a kiss, the staking of a claim. Daddy here did the vampire equivalent of taking you roughly on the dining room floor."

The temptation to throw the plate into Chance's face was only outweighed by my desire to eat cake. "Surely you're not such a puritanical lot? It was chaste. He didn't even feel my arse up, I've done worse for cover on a job."

"I am glad he didn't do that. Agnes may have flung herself out a window." Tobias was at my side, selecting the thickest piece of cake he could.

"We're downstairs," I said. I thrust the plate onto the trolley, so they could all get some, extricating myself.

Addison tutted. "She'd still do it."

"Why did you feel the need to be so possessive, Addison?" Garrett called, still snickering.

"Never mind that, where did all those manners come from? She cracks me in the groin for holding her shoulders and Oswyn gets to pet her thigh?" Chance stole a bottle of wine from the trolley, spinning the cap off with a flourish. He grabbed another slice of cake and flopped down beside Garrett and Haddley, legs splayed out in front of him.

"It was unusual. You're hardly a meek flower, princess."

"You said they didn't like humans. Better to play sweet than seem like a challenge." I shrugged, grabbing a cake myself before I sat on the settee next to Jonathan. He offered me tea and I shook my head.

"And you slipped into the role so well," Chance said.

"All of which was going fine, until Addison made their eyes pop out like a frog's," Edgar's snicker was barely kept in, rich in his voice.

"Oswyn was getting interested, despite Ena's attempts to put him off. We've fished poor Jonathan out of his clutches too often for me to want to attempt the same with Ena." Addison sipped his tea, eyes carefully elsewhere.

"They didn't like talk of the fire, that's certain." Haddley had disentangled himself from Garrett, gazing around Addison's head to inspect the cake.

"Their interest in me meant Jonathan got a clear exit," I said.

"And put you straight in between two very unpleasant individuals," Haddley added. His slice selected, he retreated again.

"It doesn't sound like they come around very often. They were last here a while since, she said? It would be considered rude to leave so early where I'm from."

"It is here, too," Tobias said, tipping himself back into the chair to scowl at their coach driving away.

"Addison may have helped with that." Edgar had leaned back against the wall now, watching the driveway as if they'd suddenly decide to return.

"He was thumbing his nose at my bore of an uncle. Though your reaction was an excellent addition, thank you for playing along." Tobias turned back, grinning at me. "I don't believe their story of just dropping in, either."

"Why were we lying about how long I'd been here?"

"Anything new is shiny to them, they'd want to try and steal you away." Tobias shook his head, looking ready to spit.

Like I was a pet. I knew she had that in her head, the little stroking touches like I was a cat. "Can they do that? Is that not also rude?"

"Thrall, or seeking to pull rank. Oswyn is technically head of the family, given my brother's death and my abandonment of the line."

"Oh, good luck with that. No thank you." I shook my head, cracking my knuckles.

Tobias tilted his head at me. "You don't approve?"

"Of him leading? It's like having a sheep fucker leading the clan. If he really thinks humans are the equivalent of cattle, why's he trying to get his hands on everyone? You don't see Jonathan dropping trews amongst the bread."

Addison nearly choked on his tea, setting it down on the trolly.

"Thank the gods," Garrett offered from the back of the room. "I need to know I can eat without seeing that."

"I'll endeavour to control myself," Jonathan replied.

"We should mention that next time he calls round, see if Agnes can still blush," Tobias said. "It might be nice to see her friendlier, too, given how sweet she was with you."

"I think she'd have had a collar on me if she could," I said.

"Not quite, that would get in the way." Edgar tapped his neck. "Maybe we should have you perched on one of their laps next time? The chairs are big enough."

"Peace, the lot of you." Addison sighed, finishing his tea.

# Chapter 38

I took to retreating into Addison's study in the afternoons, separate to our talk of magic, to sit with books and read in peace. It was an easy habit to indulge, and I was found less often here than in the little library upstairs. The timepieces were still here, despite the absence of one hourglass, and it was a calm point to centre myself.

That peace shattered with a hammering on the front door that shot me off the chair I had draped myself over, book in hand. Whoever they were, knocked like they were there on business, pounding the wood, and I came out into the corridor to see Jonathan going for the door.

"Expecting company?" I asked.

He shook his head as he wiped his hands on a cloth, tucking it into the back of his trousers. We went to the entrance way, the blurred shape of a body visible through the frosted glass. They banged on the wood again.

"Is someone trying to break in?" Addison appeared at the corridor, Tobias hanging behind him.

"Break the door down more like," Tobias said.

"They are rather insistent," Jonathan said. His shoulders tensed at another round of knocking. "Shall I ask Garrett to intervene? I believe he's the only of the sired here."

"No, if there's trouble we can meet it," Addison said.

The hammering began in constant earnest, no longer bunches but an increasingly frustrated escalation.

"Open this door!" The shout rippled through the room with a bark of authority.

"Fuck." They really wanted me back to send *him*. I glanced about the house—did we have any windows open that someone could come in through? There'd be others outside, but they weren't stupid enough to pour in without knowing the internals. I covered my mouth with my hand, trying to think of their plan. Secure the perimeter, find the enemies strengths, make a plan.

"Lambkin?" Addison came close. "Are you alright?"

"I know who that is." I screwed my eyes shut, plastering my back against the staircase.

"That good?" Tobias asked.

I sighed, dropping my head as I looked around the room. No way out. "I should open the door."

"What?" Jonathan bristled, his shoulders rippling in outrage. Sweet man, that would not help.

"He'll kick it in. Or blow it open. I can try to reason with him but he's not the calmest negotiator. More people will wind him up." It wouldn't work, but I owed him that.

"Who is it?" Addison took my hand, thumb stroking the back.

"He's called Ben, Benjamin. He's from the college. It would be better that door was opened rather than broken down."

"Temper on him?" Tobias asked. I nodded, flinching at another hit against the wood.

"Open it, Jonathan," Addison instructed. "If he's determined to be entertained he can do so without causing property damage, and allow a discussion." He made it sound reasonable. Like you could reason with fire.

Jonathan frowned but did as bid, snagging the handle before he hopped back, tugging the door open with him. Ben staggered into the room with enough momentum I wondered if he'd been about to shoulder the lock. Subtle as ever.

Ben was tall enough to take up the whole doorframe, travelling clothes further bulking him. Rougher than when I'd last seen him at the college: his chin gone to dark stubble and his eyes banked with darker circles. Travel never sat well on him. His hair was longer but nothing terrible, the wear of the road, and the sun had bleached the rich brown into a mix of tawny shades.

He glowered around the room, grey eyes slate with stormwater wash, until they alighted on me and tipped into a deep scowl.

I stepped forward. "Well met, Ben."

"There you are." He took two strides towards me, and Jonathan was in his way, broad shoulders covering Ben's view.

"You'll forgive my interruption, sir, but you were just trying to knock our door down. We'll need some introductions." Oh, the bite in that voice.

"Get out of my way, I'm here for her."

"Ena is a guest of this house, and she is under our hospitality." Addison moved forward, to stand beside Jonathan. Tobias stepped up to Jonathan's other shoulder.

"Got yourself a set of bodyguards, have you?" Ben sneered and caught my eye between the row of heads. "Smart."

I swallowed a sigh. There was no way to wind this down, I knew that. He was vibrant in his anger—cheeks flushed, eyes flashing—and there was a cocksure edge to his grin that I knew too well. "Where are the other lads, Ben?"

He snorted, having the decency to cover it with a cough. "Two on the front gate and one breaking in through the back."

"Who is it?" I asked. I wanted to come out from around the men but I was near shaking, fear and anger, the clench of my jaw barely enough to stop my tremor.

"Timothy."

"Right, Garrett'll be fine," I said, looking up to the ceiling as I blinked back the itch of tears. This could be worse.

"Tim'll be hurt you think so little of him."

"No, he won't. He knows I think he's all mouth and no trousers." I scowled at him, and that smug smile. Gods I wanted to knock that into the ground along with his teeth.

"Are you going to come out and talk to me properly or do I have to continue shouting over your companions?"

"You'll talk to the lady however she wishes." The sting in Jonathan's voice was like when he'd had the chap at the gate, steely warning.

Ben did not take that well, sneering further as he stepped closer. "I'll talk to her however I wish, she's mine." Gods above, here we go. "Has she not told you, her wee knights off to her defence?" Ben laughed, tilting his chin at me as he peered between Addison and Jonathan.

I stepped around Addison, my finger going up to push into Ben's chest. "There's nothing to tell. I've left the college."

"We're here to fix that."

Addison slid between myself and Ben like a dance partner stepping in, his back to me. "People do not belong to others."

"Oh, a rich man with a conscience, how quaint. What's the lapdog then, your adopted charge?" He jabbed a finger at Jonathan, spitting on the floor between them.

"Ben," I said, half warning.

"Shut up, I'm not for being lectured by some rich fool with a sweet spot for pretty faces."

Did he not realise? He was shouting in a vampire's face; surely the eyes must have given him a clue if the energy didn't.

"Princess, you alright?" Tobias asked, one hand on Jonathan's shoulder to keep him grounded.

Ben rounded on that, face going florid as his chest swelled. "You're on eke-name terms? Just a few weeks and you're their little whore, is that it?"

"Don't you dare!" Jonathan broke Tobias's grip and surged into Ben's space. Ben backhanded him away, the force enough to spin Jonathan's head. Shit. Tobias shot forward, getting hold of Jonathan to drag him out of the scrum, and Addison loomed up to his full height, fingers twitching as a swell of citrus flooded around us. This was about to go very wrong.

"Ben, have you checked the energy here?" I shot in front of him, between him and Addison, hands on his chest to shove him once, twice, back into the doorway and away. He had to be out, he would turn this into a proper fight if he kept his growling up and there were only two ways that would go.

He caught my left wrist, dragging me closer as he went with my pushing. "You're the only magic user here, don't try to scare me like some little loon."

"I'm fucking not, you numbskulled eejit!"

"Lambkin, you don't have to protect those who would harm you." Addison was at my back, one hand gripping my hip to keep me within the room.

"Hands off, fop, I'll be taking her back."

"Did you do any checks at all?" I cried, too many hands on me and too much yelling at my back. The scuffle of Tobias and Jonathan behind us was up to shouting, I was losing track of the voices with the noise, they were all too loud and Ben still had hold of me, as did Addison, one hand anchoring me each way.

Ben scoffed, frowning at me. "We acted as soon as we knew where you were."

"Of course, why would you do any preparation when you can come and kick the door down." I yanked my hand away, yelping when he pulled it back. The grip on my wrist tightened, painful even without my fear, and I bit back a cry. "It's a house of fangs! You're busy offending vampires."

He let go of my wrist, hopping two steps back to draw a blade. "What?"

At least he was outside the doorway. My wrist throbbed, the skin heated from his pulling, but if I could get the door shut he'd slink off to brood and make a new plan.

"I suggest you put that away, now, or I'll use it on you myself." Addison's voice held none of the usual warmth I knew from him, despite the heat of his presence at my back. His eyes glowed, the song of magic sparking off him like lightning from a thunder-cloud.

"Peace, Addison. Let me speak to him. Yes?" I put my hand on his fingers at my hip, hoping to ground him. I'd never seen a vampire go feral. I didn't want to. He didn't look my way, but his grip tightened in acknowledgement before he let go, nodding a little.

Ben laughed, folding his arms to shake his head at me. "So, you're shacked up with a bunch of leeches? Honestly, Ena, you leave us and stumble into depravity. Have you already fallen so far down that you have to whore yourself out for blood as well as the rest?"

"Why does everything you say have something to do with me fucking someone?" I asked, bristling at his revulsive smile. Of course he thought I was sleeping with one of them, or all of them. His brain never wandered far from the rut anyway, why would he assume anyone else's would.

"Because the only thing you ever had that was worthy of me was your quim. Why would this be any different?"

"I'm going to skin him, never mind Addison's threat." Tobias was at my shoulder, the door too small for all of us crowding in.

"You two, stay here. You!" I stalked out after Ben, abandoning the immortals in my own hot fury. I was going to belt him, never mind his fire, I was going to send him back up the road missing his fucking teeth! As if he was one to speak of being *worthy*, when he'd tied me to him with no chance of escape. "It's more than you've ever had, isn't it? All you had was that prick for a brain and your temper, neither of which got you any closer to the damn Council."

"I think you should come back inside," Addison said.

Ben was staring at me with something new in his eyes. It wasn't quite fear, I'd seen that in training, and there was certainly some lust, I knew that too, but this was more mixed.

"I'll deal with him," I said. "Check on Jonathan and shut the door."

"Princess, you need to calm down."

"I'm alright!" I bit it out, still staring Ben down.

"Lambkin, your hand's on fire."

I shook my head, unwilling to break the line between me and Ben. "I've not used my words."

"They're right." Ben tipped his chin to my left hand, balled into a fist at my side. I brought it up and found blue fire there, an impossible colour. My words brought orange fire, the heart and the hearth, not the cold fury of blue. That was...

"Shit." I opened my hand and shook it, licks of flame falling onto the gravel. They shed like a skin, tumbling and curling as it ate itself into oblivion before hitting the stones, and all my fury went with it. A cool pool of fear leaked in, settling low in my gut. I glanced up at Ben, his lips in a thin line as he stared back.

"Have you been dallying with some other school, sweet? That's not of our teachings." His voice was sheer spite, a poison I flinched from.

I showed my hand, a fresh line of crimson snaking over the thin skin at the back, cracked open. I'd never been happier to bleed. "This is new. It wouldn't hurt me if it was learned."

"Unless you weren't skilled yet."

"You know my studies, Ben, I'd have it learned if it was deliberate."

He scoffed, brows pinching together as I clocked steps approaching my back.

"You're injured." Tobias was at my side, hand on my elbow as he drew the bleeding hand closer.

"It's from overexertion, I'll tend to it." I couldn't take my eyes of Ben's grim face, a close-set wrath ticking in the way his jaw worked. He might kill me. I'd been running on his ambition being a guiding star to my survival, at least until he was fed up of chasing me, but if he thought I'd defected rather than simply run, I'd be in the river. A deep dread swelled in my chest; heart thudding too hard against my ribs.

"You just let them handle you?" Ben snapped me out of my panic, chin tilting to Tobias.

"I have my guard up," I said. My mouth was thick, tongue heavy as I tried to swallow against the weight.

"He's still touching you."

"She can speak for herself if she objects, friend." Tobias's whole body turned to face Ben, grip gentle on my arm.

"I didn't speak to you."

"Ben, for fuck's sake, behave," I snapped, half ready to slap him. Maybe I could divert matters that way, get a beating for insolence to distract him.

"Forgive me if I don't want my betrothed punctured through like a pincushion."

I closed my eyes, head dropping forward as I felt Tobias stiffen. "I've left the college. We're not betrothed."

"This tantrum doesn't stop our promise."

"My severing from the school does." I looked at him from under my lashes, all my fight burned out with that blue fire. "You can only marry a member. So, head back up the line and find yourself a nice wife to have your children. Try Tiffany, she always liked you more than she liked me." Truly, Tiffany deserved better than Ben. But Ben brought money, and no small amount of power, as well as his swaggering gait. That would get her more than I ever could.

"She's weak."

"She's perfectly competent, you just don't like her skills."

"We were due to be wed!"

I flinched at his shout, shoulders jolting as he reached for me.

"If you touch her, I'll break your hand," Tobias said, pulling me back into his chest. "Or maybe I'll bite her, and make her one of us. Would you marry one of us, Benjamin?"

"Tobias?" I whispered, rigid in his grip. His face was beside my ear, breath hot on my neck to highlight his threat.

"She's mine." Ben growled, stepping closer to grab my shoulder. Tobias's hand shot out, snagging the open fingers and wrenching them backwards. There was an unmistakable snap, then Ben was on his knees and howling.

I peered round at Tobias who shrugged. "I warned him."

"We should get inside, now." My legs shook, Tobias's grip the only thing keeping me up. If Ben started to use spells now, he'd be out of control. The pain might be enough to drive his focus off, but his anger was still there, and all he needed to do was get the incantation out.

"Are you going to let him do that?" Ben shouted, still on his knees.

"Ben—" I began.

"It's only two fingers, you'll be fine. A doctor in the city will set them for you."

"Tobias, we should go inside. If he uses his magic..."

"I think the pain will be a bit much for that." He pecked a kiss to my neck, nipping the skin to draw a bloom of heat. I squeaked, a hand flying to the trickle of red. "See, Benjamin? So easy for me to take her, and here you are on your knees. Run off back to your men, and see a doctor. Come back when you can behave."

"Stop." Ben forced himself to one knee, foot planted so he could push up, but he got no further, a sheen of sweat covering his face as he panted with effort. My heart twisted, wanting to stop the hurt, but I never was a healer.

Tobias span, me still in his arms, lifting me like he had the night. "Lay your head on me, like you've fainted," he muttered, hefting me in his arms a little more.

I bounced with the movement, letting my head loll against his chest as he said. I could hear Ben grunting, but he was obscured by Tobias's shoulder, and I didn't truly want to see if he was staring after us.

We approached the door and Tobias twisted, pulling me closer to him as we stepped over the threshold. There was an old magic in that, a claiming, and it wasn't lost on me as he kicked the door shut. I closed my eyes so I couldn't see Ben before the wood clacked into place.

# Chapter 39

"Jonathan, can you lock that please?" Tobias asked, still holding me.

"Are you going to set me down?"

"Not until Addison sees you."

I got a grip on his shoulders and he set off down the corridor. "Would him seeing me walking be detrimental somehow?"

"With you bleeding, yes, even if it's shallow. I just got him calmed from your boy hitting Jonathan."

"He's not my boy. And I did this, it's my magic."

"I understand, but indulge an old monster."

I scoffed. "You're hardly that."

He shook his head at me. "You'll see what I mean when we get there. His eyes will be different, and he'll avoid the light. He'll also be a touch affectionate."

"Like carrying me when I can walk?"

"Hush. You can deal with that and I'll take care of your wound."

That was kind of him, given he'd swooped in as my rescuer. "Thank you."

"You're welcome. And we're going to have a talk, once he's back to himself."

Inevitable, I supposed. "Alright."

We came to the door and Tobias kicked it open, the sound loud in the silence of the corridor. The study was dark: the curtains drawn and fire doused cold in the grate.

"We're here," Tobias called, thrusting the door shut behind him.

A hiss, barely more than a breath, came from the bed. Addison sounded pained.

"I'm going to set you down, and he's going to want to see you're in one piece. Here you go." Tobias put me on the bed, low enough that I could shuffle back.

Before I moved, Addison drew me closer, arms at my waist and pulling me along the bed, up to his chest as he enveloped around me. He was propped up against the corner, back tucked into the two walls, and he hunched lower as he pressed his face into my hair. I stiffened in the hold, trying to shift my hips so I could support my weight rather than drape across him.

He shook his head, voice low against my hair. "I smell blood."

"Tobias nipped me, it's nothing."

"Too much to be nothing." He was rubbing his face into my neck like a cat, a near growl low in his sighs.

"Her hand's cut from the magic. I'll tend to it." Tobias stood from his spot, going for the door.

Addison was still brushing into me, his hair soft against my throat, and I tried to shift again so I wasn't pressing into his chest. He grunted, hugging me closer. "No."

"I must be crushing your legs."

"It's nothing." He shifted so I slid down between them, his thighs bracketing mine. Pulling me flush against him he took a deep breath, stilling.

His arms were so tight my ribs pressed against them as I breathed, and he seemed to tremble. I slid a hand up towards his hair, trying to find his face so I could rest my palm against his cheek. "I'm here, Addison. I'm unhurt."

"You're bleeding. Both my humans are injured."

"I did mine to myself. And Jonathan's wound is my fault too, he thought he was defending me."

"Ben is lucky I didn't skin him with his own knife." There was a bitterness in his voice that went beyond the earlier cold into a real threat. "I would have ripped his throat out for harming my family, accords or not."

"You don't need to do that. Tobias scared him off with two broken fingers."

"Tobias is kinder than I. He made sure I was here before he went and got you. It's considered poor form to hurt a human. An unreasonable imbalance of power." I nodded, breath catching as he ghosted his lips over the point where Tobias had broken the skin. "We do as little harm as we can."

"I know." I slid my hand to cup the nape of his neck and scratch through the soft hair there.

"Will he come back?"

"After that trick with my hand, I've no doubt. Either him or someone more senior."

"Why?"

The door opened as Tobias came back in—backlit and with hands full of a basin, steam curling about him. The rush of light left me blinking but he closed the door, submerging us into the gloom.

"How are you faring?" He knelt on the bed, shuffling up on his knees until he was at the headboard and snug beside Addison. Twisting around, he sat back, setting the bowl down in the space between his crossed legs before setting a small box on my thigh. "Sugar cubes. Eat."

"Better," Addison said, face still buried in my neck, though he plucked the box up and tucked it into his side.

"I need her left hand, alright?"

"Hm." A crunch sounded around the grunt.

"Yes, I'm fine with that," I said. I didn't know if Tobias could see my frown, but I looked his way anyway.

"He's still winding down, princess, he might have hissed at me."

"Like a cat?"

Tobias snorted, taking my injured hand as he shifted his weight on the mattress. "Worse. Even a bucket of water won't scare him off."

"You said you thought he'd return, lambkin?" More crunches, close to my ear, and I would have laughed at the idea of him chewing sugar if it didn't make me want to hug him instead.

I rocked my head back, letting my cheek rest against Addison. Contact would calm him down, from what Tobias said. That's all it was. Tobias set a warm cloth against the wound on my hand, the sharp sting focusing my mind again.

"Ben doesn't like to lose. He has a reputation to build, defeats reduce that. He's always been focused that way."

"And he sees your leaving as a loss?"

I winced before Tobias began to swipe with the cloth. "We were meant to wed."

"What?" Addison's head shot up, his grip tightening around my waist. I wriggled a little, coughing around the interrupted breath.

"Easy, old dog," Tobias said, bumping their shoulders together. "She needs to breathe to speak. Chew some more cubes."

"We were promised to each other. His powers are aggressive; he's a great fighter. Excellent as a guard, or an escort."

Addison tutted, resting his chin on my shoulder, jaw bouncing with his bites. "Indeed."

"My powers could be considered to complement his. I don't have much active expression of them, but the passive perception is useful. I was usually taken along with him."

"And he fell in love with you?"

I laughed, jarring Tobias's hold on me. He grabbed my hand back and set it beside his bowl. "No. He's not known for love. There was a view that we would produce strong heirs—his active powers with my passive ones. The seniors agreed."

"And you?" Addison's voice was soft in the darkness, almost lost in the sound of Tobias washing the cloth out.

"I was fifteen and indebted to the college. The best I could do was buy time."

Tobias dropped my hand before he caught himself. "Fifteen?"

"We've been promised twelve years. I argued I should be allowed to make my own way first, improve my powers. It's easier to accompany clients without a mark."

"They still marriage mark you?" Addison's chin shifted, trying to catch my gaze, and I closed my eyes. It was dark anyway.

"Collarbone, or the back of your neck. Ben would want the bone."

"Would he be marked as well?" Addison crept his fingers up my free arm, sugar cubes abandoned, rubbing little circles at my bicep. I let him, the weight in my throat enough that I needed the distraction.

"You get matching scars like a ring, or a letter. A rune, depending on where you hail from. But it's obvious. Doesn't allow you to blend."

"Which you needed to be able to do." Tobias put the bowl aside, drying my hand.

"I put it off for some time. But at twenty-six we're expected to be devoting ourselves to the college or the cot. I wanted neither, kept pushing it off. Ben was getting impatient."

"Is that why you ran, princess?"

"Why does any dog slip the leash? The call of something better in the distance."

"You're not a pet." Addison tightened the arm he still had around me, shifting his legs so they held me closer.

"Says the dog petting her," Tobias muttered.

"I'm disloyal. Leaving is one of the worst things you can do, in our college. Crossing to another school of the craft, that's maybe the only thing that could be worse, because then you're both a traitor and a threat."

"Ben thinks you've done so?" Tobias's fingers snaked along the wound on my hand.

"Yes. That blue fire isn't a college skill, it was spontaneous. I know what we do for things like that."

"You kill your own?" Addison asked.

"First, we get someone like me to cause a soul wound, so their magic's unstable. Not safe for them to use because they could hurt themselves. Not a big one, just enough to hobble them, so they can be returned for the Council to judge. They might be left to heal, if they're suitably sorry. Or they might be killed as an example of what happens when you double-cross us."

"You think that's what they'll do to you." Tobias didn't bother to make it a question.

"They'll need to get someone like me down, but yes." I was the best knife in their drawer, but I wasn't the only one. I hoped they wouldn't make Tiffany do it, her powers weren't spirit. Air could work, though. Fire was too much.

Tobias huffed, clicking his tongue. "Twelve years is a long time. Are you sure he doesn't love you?"

"He'd wait twenty. He thinks powerful children will get him onto the Council and he's not been sufficiently victorious to guarantee it other ways."

"Victorious?"

"You earn your position. Ben works hard, and he's diligent, but he's nothing beyond a very thorough student. That's not enough."

I shivered as Tobias rubbed something into my wound, an ointment by the thick slide of it over the skin. He pecked a kiss to the knuckles when he was done. "What will he do?"

"Come back with more of us, or send someone else." Like George. I shivered at the thought.

Addison nodded, brushing his hair against my neck, and I squirmed a touch, opening my eyes to squint at him. "You were careful to get him out of the house."

"I didn't want bloodshed. And, with respect, I didn't know what would happen if he hurt one of you two."

"She was ahead of me on keeping you in line." Tobias sighed, going up on his knees so he could put the bowl on the floor. Stretching up, he collapsed back onto the bed, letting his weight rest on me and Addison. He shifted his legs so they tangled over too, trapping me between them.

I poked Tobias's arm and he huffed. "He's not the only one who was concerned. Now I know you're alright I need to calm down too."

I dropped back against Addison, no chance against the pair of them. "The two broken fingers didn't calm you down?"

"Did you see his face? And after I'd warned him too." Tobias chuckled to himself, shimmying a little higher so his arm could go around Addison's shoulders.

"Not many people get close enough to do that. He defends himself well. Did Garrett find the other man?"

"Scared him off, apparently. Showed his teeth and the man went racing," Tobias said.

"Good, that's smart of Tim."

"I thought you didn't like him?" Addison said into my shoulder. He tugged the wrap at my hair free, starting to run his fingers through it.

"I love Tim to bits, but he's too sure of himself. He'll leave an opening because he thinks he can cover it, put the rest of us at risk. He'll be great when he's learned."

"You sound fond." It wasn't said as an accusation, if anything Tobias sounded like he was smiling, but it landed like a blow.

"You grow up with folk, of course you get soft on them. I didn't want them to die because they didn't have the sense to gather gossip in the town."

"We won't kill them. I make no promises about pain, but I don't take life unnecessarily." Tobias's fingers slipped along my thigh to find my hand and hold it. He was so carefully soft, all his movements slow enough that I could stop them.

"Thank you. Why are we all in a pile here rather than upstairs?"

"The magic, to soothe him. Only way to get that hallion to calm down is sink him into a nest of bodies."

"I find myself needing reassurance. I tended to Jonathan's cheek, so I knew he was well." Addison sighed, leaning into Tobias. I was twisted between them, not uncomfortably but it was an intimate position.

"And I brought you back so he could check you over. By which he apparently meant drape himself over you like a great dog."

"Cat," I said, pleased at the feel of Addison's smile on my skin. "So you all cuddle after a fight?"

"Only when there's a real risk. Any argument can be settled, but if this one thinks there's a risk of blood he gets protective," Tobias said.

I laughed, relaxing under the weight of their bodies. "And here I am bleeding all over your house."

"You have displaced a remarkable amount for a mortal."

"Says the man who headbutted me."

Addison chuckled, turning a little so his chest curled more fully against my back, running his fingers through my hair. "Do you want to sleep? You must be tired."

"I could do, but I should apologise to Jonathan."

"Save that for later, princess. Stay here a while."

"Alright." I closed my eyes, letting myself sink between the two of them. This was not the strangest after-fight ritual I had met—the college had a number of them—but ending up in a pile on the bed usually had a different source. This was a nice one.

# CHAPTER 40

"We should declare her as one of the nest, undermine whoever's sneaking around. You already stepped out with that show for Oswyn, she could be considered one of ours. A paramour, or a student."

"I don't have students."

"You've been teaching her, whatever else you call it. She's precious to us, now, not bait for some experiment. What if we're right and she's harmed?"

"She's awake too, you pair are loud." Someone had been kind enough to cover me with a blanket which I shoved off as I sat up.

"Apologies, lambkin, we didn't mean to wake you."

I shook my head at him. "What are you arguing about?"

They both began to speak, spilling over each other.

"Given the concern about someone seeking to harm those close to one of us—" Addison began.

"There is someone with a dislike for one of us two. We don't know which, but it puts you at risk."

"Could be both," I said. I wiped my face with my uninjured hand, trying to shake off the fog of sleep. Their silence went on too long and I blinked over at them, outlined beside Addison's desk in the shadows. "What? You're a pair, why limit it to one of you?"

"We had anticipated it would be one or the other. Considering who would dislike us both is a smaller list."

"I can't imagine anyone thinking they could strike one of you without also going for the other. Why are we talking about formalising my role?"

"Given someone is sniffing around, declaring you as under our shelter means harm to you is harm to us. It's more restricted than your simply staying as our guest, but it would offer more protection."

Logical, despite the tightness it brought at my throat. I didn't need any more claiming. "What's brought this on?"

"If your college attacks again, and we move to defend the nest, such action would be considered reasonable if you were ours. And if whichever immortal was trying to influence you does so knowing you are ours, that would be a violent act," Tobias said.

"So you could retaliate."

"Yes," Addison said. "But that means an advancement of matters that are not currently how our relationship stands. Even if we don't act on it, a level of familiarity would be expected."

My stomach clenched, queasy unease settling around me. We had not yet set our boundaries for what this could be, if it were to be something. Establishing it under duress, for others' benefit rather than mutual enjoyment, didn't sit well. "I'd need to pretend I was yours. Either of yours. Both? How long was I asleep? I feel like I've had too many cups."

"Is that from the magic?" Addison asked. That set my spine straight, all tiredness lost to the memory of the blue fire.

"Probably, yes. I should have something to eat to make up for that." I stood, still shaky but able to stand.

"You don't want to know more about the suggestion?" Tobias pushed forward, coming towards me slowly so I could see his approach in the gloom. "It's not about claiming you, it's warning others off."

"It sounds like you need to argue it out. I'm sure you'll tell me when you've decided." I gave them a quick nod, darting around Tobias to go for the door. I managed not to bump into any furniture as I got there, more blind luck than acclimatised eyes. Slipping out the door, I pulled it closed behind me with too much force, my grip aching around the handle.

I shot down the corridor, almost a run, lest one of them come after me. I wasn't for having that tangled a conversation, about claiming and belonging. It didn't matter in the end. I didn't have patience to sit and talk through that with them when there were more pressing matters.

I found Jonathan in the kitchen, as I'd expected, thumping a dough into order at the table.

"Has that dough irked you?" I leaned against the door to give myself a moment to slow my heart, smiling when he looked up to me.

"Ena." He abandoned the bread, rushing over to pull me into an embrace. The cut on his cheek was still swollen but it looked less inflamed than my hand; Addison must have been gentle with him. There was the telltale cast of bruising lurking at the edges, but that would bloom then fade quick enough.

I hugged him back, patting his shoulder as he turned me into the kitchen and marched us over to the table. He ushered me onto one of the chairs and began pummelling the dough anew. "Are you alright?"

"I thought he'd hurt you. When Tobias took you off to Addison's room... I know better than to interrupt them in that mood, but I was worried."

I held my hand up to show the gash across the back of my hand. "Just this. And that wasn't Ben, that was me using magic wrong."

"How does one use it incorrectly when you're trained?"

I dropped my hand, barking out a laugh. That was too long a discussion. "Tobias took care of the wound, he made sure I was patched up. And he broke two of Ben's fingers."

He blinked at my avoidance but gave a small nod. "Good. Comes trying to kick the door in and then gets annoyed we won't let him drag you out by your hair. They want to take you back, I take it?"

I portioned off some of the flour dusted over the table, flattening it down so I could trace shapes in it. "Yes. Ben has a claim on me he wants to make good on."

"Marriage?" I nodded. Jonathan gave a particularly firm thump to the dough, shaping it into a rough circle and setting it on a board atop of the oven. A cloth went over it, tucked in at the edges before he turned back to me. "I'd kidnap you myself if you tried it."

"You disliked him that much?"

"The lad my sister married was like him. Wicked things, men who want to own women. They should be put in the stocks and beaten."

"I didn't know she was married."

"She were." He wiped his hands down, chewing his lip before he leaned back against the oven. He worked the knuckles of one hand with the fingers of the other, like he was counting them. "He wasn't a good man. Beat her black and blue."

"What?"

"Beat a baby out of her. He didn't want it. It was that that killed her, we thought. Damn near put father in his grave, too."

I started, the splay of my hand scattering the flour patterns. "Gods, no wonder. I didn't realise she was gone."

"Seems poor company to mention the dead, but I can't not speak of her. She's my little sister."

"I'm so sorry. What happened to him?"

"Nothing. He said she'd fallen down the steps."

"Folk believed that?"

"Not a whit, but there was no proof otherwise. I knew him though." His mouth pulled into a low line, no more a smile than my own. "His ladder slipped when he was doing the thatching that autumn. Shame that."

"A crying shame."

He nodded, something like a smile coming back. "There are enough bad men in the world without joining them, but sometimes you have to take action."

"Is that why you ended up here?"

"Aye. Had to be out of the town for a while after his accident and I came looking for work down in the city. Addison bumped into me during one of his many evenings out."

I swithered, trying to feel out my next question. "He liked your company?"

"He liked that I'd tell posh idiots to fuck off when they were handsy with the lasses in the theatre. He stepped in when one of them was trying to have me dragged out for a hiding."

"A lashing for a tongue lashing? Seems a bit overzealous."

"He was a duke or some such, I never kept track. They kept me for my muscle not my social airs. This one wasn't used to someone having hands on him, and was much too free with his own pair. I may have put a drinks tray down on them."

I'd been forming the flour into little mounds for something to do with my hands and they scattered as one hand planted into them, the other trying to cover a snort of laugher. "And Addison swooped in to rescue you?"

"Gave the man a proper dressing-down. Sent him out the door with a promise to call on him socially, which was almost as terrifying as the telling, and then told me I might want to consider a change in my work."

"That's a charming line."

"I thought he wanted me for his bed, at first."

"Oh?" I leaned forward, my flour abandoned as I caught his gaze.

He shrugged. "A lot of rich men like a bit of rough. Accent like mine, it wasn't the first offer. And he's comely enough."

"You came back for that?"

"Not just that, I also fancied not getting a kicking."

I sat back, grinning at him. "So, did you?"

Jonathan puffed air through his cheeks, turning to examine the bread. "When did you become a gossip?"

"When I thought you had some to tell me."

He came back to the table, starting to clean up the mess from his dough. "I came here anticipating he might want such things. But he didn't, at least in the usual sense. He wanted company, and company for those he'd sired. Human company."

"Did you get a cuddle as well?" I glanced back to the corridor, the little room with all those clocks.

"Yes. They like a lot of that when they want it, you can be with them for hours."

"It seemed a bit odd when he started hugging after threatening to skin someone, but it makes sense. They are like cats."

Jonathan hummed, mouth working like he was weighing something before he said it. "He was deeply concerned for you. I think the only reason it was Tobias out there was because Addison would have done real harm."

"Two broken fingers are real harm."

"I mean deathly. I've not seen Addison kill but they're both generational vampires. It would not be unreasonable to kill a threat."

"They'll come back once Ben's been seen by a healer."

"Not a doctor?"

"Some of us can patch up wounds. Nothing huge, but enough to fix something like that quicker than a doctor setting it."

"If they've brought someone like that with them," Jonathan said.

"They'd be idiots not to."

"Idiots like coming to the house without gathering word of who it belonged to?"

I blinked at him, denials on the edge of my lips. He raised his brows. "Yes. Idiots like that."

"Can you heal?"

"Gods, no, I wish I could. I could do some good with that."

"You don't like your magic much."

I shrugged, standing. "Do you need a hand with anything in here?"

"Not yet. I'll want a hand with the stew later but otherwise we're fine."

"I might go out for a bit, then, to the gardens."

"Stay away from the edges, hm? Garrett did a sweep but better to be safe." Jonathan caught my injured hand, inspecting the wound. "And take care of that, it looks sore."

"I can hardly feel it after Tobias cleaned it up."

"Cover it with something before you go out. That ointment looks grand, but you want to keep it that way."

"Aye, I will."

# Chapter 41

Marching around the front of the house I checked for something big enough to hide behind. The low border hedges would give some cover but not enough, and a few of the trees had adequately thick trunks to hide me if I stood but not sat.

My eyes settled on the willow, drooping branches still layered with summer leaves. It wasn't perfect cover, someone would still see me under there if they were looking, but it would do.

I dipped under the curtain of new growth and into the cool space underneath. It was light enough, the leaves diffusing what sunshine we had into the limpid tones of a stream. I suddenly missed the sea, my chest swelling with an urge to see the crashing certainty of the surf and tide. I wanted the clean, brutish wind that whipped sand and bubbles along as birds screeched overhead. I swallowed against the rush of it, shaking my head. I'd see the sea again.

I crept around the trunk, checking for the spot with best cover, and once I was satisfied, I sat with my back against the wood. Crossing my legs over, I held my hand out and let my guard drop down, unspooling it like a ball of wool. It was years since I knitted but the movement was the same, an easy spin around and around to let it gently pool out.

A lick of blue flame peeked from between my fingers, quivering like it was caught in a breeze, and as I turned my wrist it clung to the skin. The tug of fire brushing across my palm reminded me of having my hand in a stream, flame spreading out with a warm tickle. The wound on the back began to ache, pulsing in time with my heartbeat, and I twisted my arm so I could watch the blood well up. A deep-red cost to the blue wavering from my wrist to fingertips.

Heart-fire. Forbidden work.

I'd had my words since I was a child. Hidden, and safe, and close. They were mine. Heart-fire was a blended magic—fire and spirit, a truly magical substance—elements intertwined in a perversion of the order of things. Grotesque, in the eyes of the college. Abhorrent. It held an echo of the blessed fire Addison had given me details for—less refined, probably the closest a human could naturally create. Even that wouldn't be enough to save my neck from a noose. Ben had seen it. He'd come back to kill me, or he'd bring one of the Council members to drag me back up the road. At least it wouldn't be a drowning; I'd be strung up as a warning.

I dropped my hand into a closed fist, killing the fire, rocking my head back to rest against the trunk. The thickness in my throat returned, cold sweat breaking across my back and forehead as I quashed the panic down. I brought my knees up to my chest, stuffing a knuckle between my teeth to bite down on. I knew ways to keep the cries inside my throat. Pain usually worked, a bite enough to refocus the upset into something more direct, but I couldn't stop the tears already running free. Fuck.

My bleeding hand started to drip so I brought it to my chest, pressing a handkerchief to the wound. I sniffed, wiping my face with the square of cloth before I wrapped the wounded hand up.

I should run. They knew where I was; Ben would come back.

If I went now, I'd have a few days on him, try to make it to the coast. I could manage enough to get a ticket away on a boat, either to one of the farms looking for workers or some of the other jobs like a maid. I was hardy, I could work a field until I found somewhere to go in a new place. I didn't know how they would be for magic users, but other places had schools. I could teach, lie about my background and use my words. Pass for a wise woman if I had to.

The college would have to work hard to find me somewhere across the ocean.

"Forgive my boldness, miss, but you look dreadful."

"Gods above!" Edgar's voice startled me out of my planning, my legs kicking out automatically. He was peering underneath the leaves, almost upside down for the tilt of his face, and he dropped to his knees to shuffle underneath and join me.

"Apologies, I thought you'd heard me approach. Jonathan told me there's been an intrusion."

"There was. The lads from my college found out I'm here."

Edgar whistled, sitting beside me at the trunk. "Not smart ones if they attacked without a plan."

"Their leader acted before he thought. Too used to fighting."

"So are you, by the smell of it." He nodded to my hand.

I pressed the handkerchief harder. "He hit Jonathan. I stepped in."

"Now you're bleeding. And crying."

"A woman can be upset at causing trouble." It wasn't a lie, exactly.

"You've not been upset at trouble since Garrett brought you home. What's hurting you?"

"My hand's pretty sore." He frowned at me, waiting for further response. "Why are you pressing it?"

"Because you're part of the house. If you're hurting, we do, too. I want to know you're well."

"I fear what my college will bring with them."

"Don't be doing anything silly. We can all take care of ourselves." He took up his knife, showing me the well-oiled blade.

"Silly things like shouting at my previously betrothed?"

Edgar winced, nodding a little. "Jonathan mentioned that too. You don't like the man, do you?"

"No. I don't want him hurt but I won't go back with him."

"Good. Because things like running off, or going to meet that lot on your own, that would be foolish."

I sighed. "I could go, you know. Slip off in the night."

"Worked so well previously."

"Do you have some vampire cousins you think will abduct me too?" He smiled, shaking his head at me. "Staying brings danger."

"With respect, the nest is filled with old soldiers and magic users of uncertain ability. Whatever danger you may bring meets worse at our gate. You're one of us, our little band of chaos would march with you to worse places than Edinburgh."

The hushed discussion in the study came back to my mind. "They're wanting to do something about that. Declare me as partnered with them."

He hummed, a smile that was only half there catching his lips. "They wouldn't do that unless they thought it was necessary. I'm not fond of the thought."

"Means they'll bite me?"

He nodded, scratching his chin with his blade. "If they're talking about that, then they're afraid for you. From what I'm told the last one declared was Margery, and that was only until she turned."

"None of you lot?" I frowned at him.

"Must not be pretty enough."

"They may as well put a lariat on my neck." I'd seen some nice ones, in the big houses up North, but silver or gold, it was still just a pretty noose.

"They won't see it like that. Surviving the war, continuing after, they know what they'll do to defend their own. They forget the other side of that."

"Hm?"

"That those you protect must live, too, on their own terms. Addison has never been bad for that, sometimes takes a while to realise, and when he does, he acts. Hence Tobias shouting at him, and my collection of knives. They'll want to protect you as best they can."

"You think I should stay."

"At least until your college has been dealt with so you're safe in the city. Or wherever else you want to go. Lady like you has the whole world to explore, even without fangs."

"I'd like to go back to Caithness, sometime."

"Aye?"

I tugged my knees up again, resting my wrists on them. "It's wild. You get up there and it's bogs and forests, proper flow country. Sparking with magic. There's cliff after cliff, a coastline like a dragon's clawed its way out of the land, and all these little stone houses hunkered down into the heather."

"Sounds like you like it."

"I loved it up there. I got to go back sometimes. It's a long trip from the city, though, even with a coach, and the road's poor as a farm track."

"It's home?"

"I was born up there. You get sent to the college early."

He turned to look at me. "And your family let you be taken off?"

"My mam kept me hidden when I was wee. She was hidden too. She's who I get my words from."

"Was."

"I was little when she died. Got sent away soon after." My father had no interest in a devil child, despite granny's wails. She cried every time I went back South, even though she'd been the one to send for the college, before I wound up in the loch too. Better a distant grandchild than a dead one. "The college pays well for youngsters."

"Aye, same as the army. They own you?"

"The fuck they do. They consider me indebted, but they don't own me."

"That's what I like to hear. You going to come back inside?"

I laughed at his bluntness. "Is that why you're under here, to draw me back in? Alright."

"You should come with me to see the city, tomorrow," he said as we stood. "There are some new knives in, we can get you more for when your college comes back."

# Chapter 42

Tobias was waiting in the kitchen when we came back in—dusting ourselves off from the time under the tree.

"You're bleeding again," he said.

"Just the wound opening up, it's nothing much." I held the bound hand up, showing a small spread of red through the cloth.

"She was teaching me about magic," Edgar said. He steered me past Tobias with a small nod, directing me to the hallway so I could slip away while he turned to speak.

I took the opportunity, heading along the corridor and towards my room. It was a bit soon for dinner and I had a chance to be alone. Maybe sleep. If I slept now, it would be easier to waken later.

Edgar's words in the garden snagged at me, grated against my training like nails in a coffin. I knew it was wrong to seek comfort in their hospitality, despite my chest tugging with the desire to remain. There was someone pursuing the immortals, trying to hurt them. It was their problem, certainly, but I could help. I wanted to.

But Ben would come back. Now he'd his pride hurt, he'd be vicious. Or they'd send one of the Council members, and that would cause real havoc—something I couldn't divert with some cheap shouting match. Someone would get hurt.

The college only had jurisdiction to harm me, truthfully, but it depended on who they sent. Someone canny would drag me off by the hair, quick and simple. Someone cruel would make an excuse for a real fight; sling some magic to show the strength behind our name. It would be quite the victory to have bested one immortal vampire, never mind two, and they were a pair. We'd never usually go for them, but to reclaim property, well.

I wasn't going to be the cause of that.

My room seemed dim despite the large windows, the gloom of my mood stealing even the evening light. I could leave them a letter—I had time to write one if I was to creep off in the night. That would give them something to show whoever appeared from the college.

I crossed to the dresser, sitting before the mirror. I felt like I could weep, half guilt and half grief, none of the sharp certainty I'd had before I left Nicnevin. I didn't want to leave here.

I faced myself in the mirror, eyes watery, ready to slap some sense back in. One of the curtains beside my bed was closed. Turning on the seat I narrowed my eyes, holding my breath and licking the back of my teeth. The curtain swayed, as if caught in a breeze, or the window being open.

I didn't leave the windows open by the bed today. Just the one at the desk.

"Who's there?" I stood, keeping the chair between myself and the room. My knife was at the table by the bed. I could get to it.

"Ah, shit."

"Timothy?" I yanked the curtain back to see Tim stood plastered into the corner. He was sweaty and pale, holding his hand to his chest like it hurt, and his dark eyes looked worse in the fading sunlight. He'd never been big, but he was my height and had filled out well enough to hold his own, and it wasn't right he should be here, hiding. My heart lurched at the sight.

"Aye aye," he said.

"How the fuck are you in my room?" I held the curtain aside, pointing to the bed.

"I came in through the window after that leech scared me. I thought he'd have my arm off with that knife." No one had mentioned a knife, with Garrett scaring him off, but Tim always liked to run his mouth.

"So you broke into the house?"

"The room smelled like magic. Knew it would be yours."

"There are two other magic users. One of who is an immortal." I put a hand over my eyes, breathing through my nose. "Get on the bed, let me have a look at you."

"You'll make Benjamin jealous."

"I'll toss you out the damn window."

"I knew you'd missed me." His smile was strained, thin lips almost disappearing, but he pushed off the wall. "I'd rather be by the window."

"Sit somewhere and let me check you over."

"Fuss pot."

"Tim!" He nodded, moving to sit on the windowsill so he was backlit by the dying sun, the last colours of the day just brushing over the tops of the trees before night would swathe over everything. I brought his arm down to see a nasty cut, shallow but long, which must have bled a lot given how tacky it was. "What happened?"

"One of your charming companions, scaring me off from the garden." That certainly wasn't Garrett, he'd not slice someone.

"Did you cut it on the railings?"

"Shut it, they went for me. Anyway, why aren't you screaming bloody murder like you did with Benjamin?"

"Stay here, I'm getting water." I went into the bathroom, running a basin full and dropping the cake of soap into it. I plucked up my facecloth and set the items down beside him as I came back into the room. "We'll need something to cover that too."

He caught my hand, the uninjured one, as I turned to dig into my wardrobe. "Don't ignore me."

"I'm not, I want to get that covered before one of them comes to investigate the smell."

"Say you're bleeding."

"You're bleeding more than my wound. They'll worry."

"They that keen on your blood?"

"They don't feed off me." I shook my head, grasping his hand in mine briefly before I let go. "I need to wrap you up once you're clean. Let me get a shift, or a stocking. You can say you nicked it off a line on the way back to the lads."

"I heard Benjamin screaming."

I turned away, going to my wardrobe. "One of them broke his fingers. Only two, like."

"They what?" Tim whistled, snorting to hold back a laugh.

"Ben wouldn't leave. There're two immortals in this house, and he'd decked one of their charges. The more reasonable immortal broke his fingers."

"The more reasonable one, aye?"

"The other one would have skinned him." I tugged a cotton shift out of its spot amongst my skirts, before kneeling next to Tim and unwrapping my hand so I didn't get the hanky wet. He held his arm out, clicking his tongue as I pulled his shirt free.

"Why are you being so daft?" he asked.

I rubbed the facecloth with the soap before I answered, jaw working. "It's complicated."

"Did you and Ben fall out?"

"No more than usual. This'll sting."

"Aye, sure. If it's not that than—shit, ow!" He pulled his arm away and I tugged it back, tightening my grip. "Then what is it? Have you fallen for some fancy man? Is there a burden in your belly?"

"Gods above, Tim, what?" I slapped the cloth into the water, sitting back on my heels. "You think I'm carrying a wee ain?"

"Why else would you bolt? If it's Benjamin's it would make sense, he's always growling about getting the next lot out, but if you need free of one there's the nuns. Or angelica root, Tiffany would see you right there."

I covered my face with both hands, dribbles of cool water flowing down from my fingertips, over my cheeks. Once I knew I wouldn't slap him I looked back up, scowling. "I've not been tupped, for goodness' sake. I haven't been with anyone except Tiffany in a while, and keen as Ben is he wouldn't do much before marriage. I couldn't work with a bump."

"I thought you must be desperate, is all. Why else would you run?"

"There's a lot to it."

"So come back to where we're staying and explain it." He grasped my shoulders, frowning as he held me. "Trust us."

I picked the cloth back up, wringing it out and starting to wash his arm again. "No."

"What's so bad you can't come and tell us? Aren't we family, and the rest?"

"Because they wanted me to be with him, and nothing else. None of my work, or studies, none of my skill. Just a babe at my teat and another on the way, given how Ben talks."

Tim frowned, stilling my hand with his on top. "Most women want to be mothers."

"And it's a blessing, and I'm happy for them. But I don't want that. Tim, I don't want all I've done to be naught."

"It's not naught, you'd have a family."

I pursed my lips, tongue tight against the back of my teeth before I spoke. "If that's all I'm allowed to have, and it will be with how the college has mothers tethered down, then I don't want it."

He frowned as he let go of me, sitting back against the window frame and sucking his lower lip in to chew it. He'd done that since he was little. He'd always be little to me, even if he was only two years behind. I went back to washing his arm and he looked down at the bloody water, staring at it like he could scry some answer from the suds and swirls.

Once his arm was clear of blood and scabs, I checked the wound—clean enough, and shallow as I'd thought, he'd absolutely sliced it on something—then dried the skin off in firm pats.

Shuffling back, I tore the slip into strips, the ripping loud in the silence between us.

"Say something," I said. I came back to him, starting to wrap his arm.

"I'm thinking."

"Thought I saw smoke at your ears."

He snorted, holding still while I continued to wrap, and when I tied the ends, he turned it a little each way. "Thanks."

"You're welcome. Done thinking?" I sat back on my heels again, washing my hands in the basin.

"You're going to have to bloody me up," he said.

"Say again?"

"We'll have to make it seem like you've got away from me. I can say I followed you on the way somewhere. You've gone off to another town, or towards the coast to get a boat going to Ireland, that would do. I can limp in, play defeated, and it'll send them another way."

"I can't beat you up."

"You don't want to go back. They need to be looking elsewhere. I don't know why you're here, of all places, but none of them have come in to ravish you and you're not bedecked in bite marks so there must be something sensible happening. Yes?"

"None of them have bitten me."

"You seem safe here." He grimaced, shaking his head. "Safer than the city at least, with those dead mages. I saw the mess of one of them in the paper. I don't think I can send the college very far off, but it would let you get hidden, wouldn't it? Then, when you can't be found, maybe Benjamin will focus elsewhere."

"Tiffany."

"She'd maybe have him, and be the better of it. There are others after her hand, too."

I grinned. "Good. She deserves choices."

"They're always limited in the college, but aye." Tim nodded, standing and kicking the basin as he did. "Shit, sorry."

"Come here." I dragged him over to the bed, grabbing the remains of the shift to dry the water. He'd got it on the rug so I knelt to blot it, hoping the blood wouldn't stain. They'd know it wasn't mine.

"You'll still have to bloody me up, or it'll be too obvious."

"I'm surprised they're not looking for you." I turned to look at him from the spot on the floor, smiling.

"They know I'll turn up. I always make it home."

"That's an unwise claim to make." A voice from behind made me shoot forward, sprawling across the floor from my ungraceful flight. I twisted round, finding a tall man part way through the window. He was looking between me and Tim as he unfolded into the room. No face.

"Does everyone come through windows here?" Tim moved from the bed to beside me, offering a hand up.

I took it, pulling him close to whisper as I stood. "Tim, run."

"Hm?"

I kept him near, shoulder to his chest as a shiver ran through me like Mark had stroked my back. "I need you to get out of the door, yell your lungs out and get gone."

"I can hear you," Mark said.

I pushed in front of Tim, shoulders back to cover as much as I could. It was pointless, he was as big as me, but I needed Mark's attention. "He's nothing to do with the house."

"And you're bandaging his wound and telling him to run from me." Mark crossed his arms and I could feel a leer I wasn't able to see. "Excuse my suspicion, darling, but that seems connected."

"Here, I'm one of the College of Nicnevin, we're nothing to do with this house of fangs. I'm here to bring Ena back with me, and you'll not stand in our way." Tim ducked past me, walking to Mark, and I grabbed for his shoulder, cursing when he slipped my grasp as he moved to square up.

"What a bold little guard dog. Much more interesting than any of the pups in the nest." Mark tilted his head like a bird, unreadable face making my eyes hurt as I came closer.

"Tim, *please.*"

"Why can't I see his face?" He leaned back, so he could say it over his shoulder to me, and I strained to reach for him. My limbs were leaden, unfathomably heavy.

"Because I don't want you to, little terrier." Mark's hands went to his hips as he laughed, leaning to one side to look at me. "He's quite the defender."

"Oi, eyes on me." Tim slapped a hand across that unseeable face and my stomach dropped, swooping as the sound rippled through the room.

I couldn't make my hands move to grab him, pull him close, and a cold frisson of dread slid through me. My spine was frozen, my muscles cooling and solidifying like I'd been dropped in ice.

"And he bites as well. Bad dog." A thick, wet sound went through the room as Mark slapped Tim back, Tim's face whipping too far around on his neck. He didn't even blink, eyes simply going unfocused as they almost looked at me. He dropped to the floor.

Scalding hot tears slid on my cheeks, and I wanted to fall onto my knees to pull Tim close, but I couldn't move. I couldn't even duck my chin to look at him.

"Tim." Forcing the word out was like breathing through water, my lungs burning.

"Don't worry, darling, it was quick." Mark appeared before me, grasping one of my useless hands in his. "I didn't make him suffer. Now, I need you to sleep."

The word was like a blanket over my head, a wave of dizziness that turned my stomach. No, no, no, I couldn't. My hand tightened in his grip as I strained to push myself away, get beside Tim. He couldn't be gone. His eyes were always dark, always had shadows, if I could just get hold of him, he'd still be there.

"Tim."

"Goodness, you do fight. No wonder, with your raw little soul." Mark stroked two knuckles against my cheek, fingers cold as my own. "We must go. You're not going to like this."

He stepped away, a hand producing a knife from his belt. The handle was ornately carved, a pretty piece of work like a courting gift from back home. It was small enough to look like one for fruit, or food, less than the length of my finger, and he held it with the confidence of someone used to handling them.

Kneeling, he plucked Tim up and brought them chest to chest, tipping Tim's lolling head so his face looked away from mine. A sob creaked past my lips.

Once Mark seemed satisfied with the angle, he brought the knife up with a looping flourish, then buried the blade into the pale skin at Tim's throat. It jammed in the tough cartilage and he pulled it free in a quick swipe, bringing the knife up to lick.

Blood welled up; not the arcing spray of heart's blood but a rich pour, and Mark dipped his head to lap at it. My stomach yanked against itself, the urge for it to turn over lost somewhere between there and the rest of my body. I couldn't stop the tears.

His drinking was obscenely loud in the room. A gasping breath broke as he sat back, wiping a hand over his mouth. His mouth. I could see him.

"A user's blood is a fantastic boost, but does rather interfere with ongoing enchantments." He turned, smiling at me. A line of red fluid dribbled from one corner of his lips. He was beautiful now I could see him, in the way the immortals were, but there was a feral air to him—like a wolf, the promise of teeth sinking in. Golden eyes. I almost knew him.

I shook my head, eyes squeezing shut so I didn't have to see what he'd done, see Tim like that on the floor. "Why?"

"I need to take you somewhere else, and you're trying so hard to resist me." His body came flush to mine, hand cupping my cheek, and a wet kiss pressed against my forehead. The heat was more from what was on his lips than the man himself. "Don't struggle, darling. Sleep."

# Chapter 43

This place did not have hideous ceilings. It had a fire; the fluttering whisper off to one side from where I lay. A small bed, I thought, it was soft enough. I closed my eyes again, keeping my breath even and slow as I listened to the room. There was rain. No one else breathing. That was good.

I peeked an eye open, looking back to the wooden ceiling with its dark-stained beams. It was evening, by the shadows on them, and I had a good idea that a window would be on the far side of the room if I sat up to check.

"Are you always so guarded when you waken?"

The voice startled me into sitting, tucking my legs close, so my knees were to my chest. Mark sat at the end of the bed, his smile soft as butter in the glow of the fire. His face hurt to look at it, something itching at the edge of my mind. A hangover of the enchantment maybe.

The room was plush, large rugs covering most of the floor, the fire, tall windows at the other side. The bed had a thick cover across it, very comfortable, and a blanket had been placed over my legs, now tangled at my feet.

"Where am I?"

"My home. I've had this room prepared for you."

Manners first, manners until there was a reason to be rude. "My thanks for the hospitality. Why did you bring me here?" He killed Tim. I could not let that thought out of my mouth, much as it prickled on my tongue. My whole mouth buzzed, in fact, tongue thick against the roof. I brought a hand up to touch my face.

"I wouldn't do that yet." Mark leaned forward, catching my wrist, and I stilled.

"Why?"

"Rose healed you, but things will be painful."

"Healed me of what?"

His smile faltered for a moment, and I was struck by his beauty again. I knew him, except I didn't. He could have been a sculpture, marble left to weather to grow the shadows that shrouded his features. Sharp, sharp cheekbones. Like he'd been hungry. His whole being seemed steeped in hunger, a cold loneliness that poured from him despite the smiles.

I wanted to crawl into the fire.

"It'll all be clear soon. I need you to trust me, can you do that?"

I shook my head, pressing back against the headboard. "Absolutely not."

"I suppose that's my fault." He nodded, jaw trembling as if he might cry. He was always close-lipped, like the words would tumble out too quickly if he let them slip. "I'll have to ask your forgiveness again, then. You'll understand soon."

He grabbed my ankle, pulling me towards him with a strength that knocked me flat onto the bed. I shoved my hands up, meeting his chest as he came flush on top of me, body slotting over mine like we were lovers. I was frozen against him again, the same icy torpor as in my room, and he stroked my hair as he shushed me.

"Don't worry, don't worry. You are so precious to me, darling. It won't hurt for long." He tipped my chin back with one thumb, burying his face in my neck. I arched as a flood of spirit pierced through my guard, swamping me back into darkness.

# Chapter 44

It was an ungodly war.

What they did to the humans was unconscionable. Piles of bodies drained, butchered. Limbs cut off to share. Mages kept alive for longer, so their powers could be eked out over battles. It took so little to kill a human, but they could survive such devastation with the right methods. Torniquets. Spells.

I saw one who had slammed her own head into a stone wall, over and over, so she couldn't be used as feeding pot. Or at least wasn't aware of it.

I wasn't aware when they took my fangs.

"Get him up." I knew the voice from the battlefield; Henry, one of the seniors from the other families. An old one, even by our standards.

I was hoisted by the wrists—bound in magic chains, for nothing else would keep one of us—and sack over my head. They let me stand, once I was on my feet: the magic likely wouldn't let me hurt them, and when they took the bag off, I knew most of the men. Some better than others, I marked Edmund's broad shape, but they were all my generation rather than Henry's. We were in a large cell, the white stone walls made up of slabs as broad as my arm. They sparkled with the light of a fire, somewhere behind me, and there was a buzz of magic that seeped through the room like spilled ink.

It was quite bare, for a cell, just the area I was chained to and a table within my sight. There was more of the room behind me, must be for the fire, and the sound of someone tending it. No bed, no chair, not even a bureau for penning letters. So sparce for such a space.

"Henry." I greeted the speaker, ignoring the others. I owed him some little mark of respect: I had killed his sons. We're hard to kill, those born to the blood, and each corpse was a well-taken trophy. No one thinks that of their own child, though, even in war. Henry regarded me: wizened from the fighting, his skin was slack, with wrinkles etched deep into his brow. We don't age like that, usually, we reach our peak and anything further is a fathomlessly slow process.

"Jean." Of course he would go for my formal name. Boring.

"This isn't keeping with the usual terms." I jangled the cuffs, glancing around. "I knew your family had suffered in the war but surely you're not so bereft that you couldn't provide me a bed."

He laughed, nodding like a fox. "It is not in keeping, this is true. The honour of your family deserves more than bare stone."

"And yet here I am."

"Here you are." He glanced around the other men—sons of other noble families. "You killed my boys."

"They fought well."

"I raised good men."

"I was sorry to find us on opposite sides. I'd have loved to have studied with them." They had been strong mages. No match for Addison and me, but skilled.

"They would have enjoyed it. They valued knowledge. I value it too, in a different way. You have the same knowledge they did."

He was wrong but not too far off. "They used time, yes. We studied different matters, but I could appreciate their skill."

"No one was as good as them, in our ranks. They were the pinnacle." Henry touched a hand to his heart, fingers splayed wide to cover it over his loose shirt. Was he feeding? Such rapid weight loss was sickness or absence.

"I'm sorry to have taken them, then. If there's no one else, Addison will tear through the rest like a storm."

"He's in mourning, I'm afraid."

My heart stopped. Tobias. I'd seen him bloodied, seen the etch of death threatening on his torn throat, when he'd gone after Edmund in hot temper at their father's killing. Pushing the hoard back had been the only way to give him time to heal. "Who?"

"You." Henry held his other hand out, two glistening teeth sat in his palm. The roots were still bloody, a thin rivulet of red running along his lifeline, and by the curve at the point I knew them as fangs.

I slid a hand to my mouth. I couldn't feel it, when I touched my lips, and slipping them inside, I shuddered as a fingertip brushed against raw flesh. No pain, just the soft maw. "What have you done?"

"They worked hard on their magic, my boys. I never had the same aptitude, you understand. I know other things. Pain. Grief. Desperation." He stepped closer. "How good do you think Addison will be when he sees these? How well will he resist tearing the throat out of some weak little lamb that comes trotting along to help, so he can rend us limb from limb?"

"I wasn't even awake to defend myself." I shoved forward, chains be damned, growling when the magic surged from the binds, electric along my bones.

"When he's hurting, he'll show he's like the rest of us. The beast within always calls for blood."

"We're more than beasts!" I bellowed at him, chest out as I pulled up to my full height.

"We are. And we shouldn't debase ourselves by pretending humans are even close to our equal." Edmund shoved forward, chin tilted at me in defiance. His family did well off the southern ports, well enough to ensure his and Tobias's training.

"Your family wealth runs off humans, you'd be well to mind that on. Or did you forget it when you took your father's head?" A cheap shot, but it landed, his eyes flashing as he bared his fangs.

"Shut up, Edmund." Henry shoved the man away, turning back to me. "Addison will show his true self. Until then, we're going to have your magic."

"I won't do anything for you. You defile the law of the families."

Henry stepped closer, a half-step. "I'm a patient man. We'll convince you." The others shared a laugh like a gaggle of children.

Torture, then. Let them. We healed, and I'd have company soon. "He'll know I'm here."

"Not in this room, he won't. My sons made this for us, using our combined strength. A room hidden in time, a pocket of nowhere. An excellent spot for meetings."

My head span with the thought, sweat prickling along my temples. "That's against the oaths. The risks. It could crumble the boundaries, tear through into somewhen else. It could implode."

"Scare tactics to dissuade weak-willed practitioners from attempting it. You know it's possible." Henry was before me now, and even so depleted, I could see in his eyes the old, cold skill of an animal. He wanted me to suffer.

"Many things are. It doesn't mean they should be done. I could have drained your sons' throats and put their heads on a spike."

He hissed, bearing forward and I grabbed his shirt, throwing him into the wall.

"They got that temper from you as well, hm?" I kicked the back of his knee out, shoving his thin face into the white stone. Dark blood seeped, streaking the pristine wall as he sank lower. The magic in the chains spiked along my arms, fizzing through my blood like a lightning strike.

"They always took more from me than their mother."

"I'm sure she regrets that now." I tossed him back towards the others. I had no fangs to bite with, and strength alone wouldn't take his head off. "I can do that even with your magic against me. Imagine what I'll do when I get free."

Henry gathered himself together, hand still clamped around my teeth. "Rest. We'll have more to speak on later."

He walked past me, followed by his throng of conspirators. Edmund didn't meet my eyes. Once the stone had ground into place, sealing me in, I sagged against the wall, arms spasming from the suppressed shocks.

"He doesn't much like you." A voice came from behind me, frail in the echo of the space.

"He doesn't have much cause to."

"It's the nature of war." An older woman walked around the side of my vision, thin and drawn as a mourner.

"Well met, my lady."

"You don't need to say such things. I'm human." She turned her neck to show bite marks, little semicircle scars that loomed against warm skin. Her hair was long, tied into a tumbling braid that swung along her shoulder and slipped as she turned her head back.

"You're still company."

She smiled, gentle, before going to stand against the wall opposite me. "I don't know much of you, good sir, but I know the master seethes at your name."

"And has left you here with me."

"I'm to prepare things for your interrogation. Tools."

I blanched. "You're the torturer?"

"He wants you for himself. I'm a servant." She laughed, shaking her head.

"A strange house to serve in." A strange habit for those who would have humans as cattle, to use them throughout the house.

"My family was taken by the war." She smiled, the tight sort that hid other moods. "They took my husband off to the lines, to feed the army. I'm told my children were sent to other families."

"Told?"

"They taunt you. Tell you little bits to see if you flinch, or if it changes the taste of your blood. I'm kept."

"Without meaning to be a brute, mistress, what has brought you that honour? This house isn't known to keep humans."

"I have some magic."

"You're trained?"

"No." She shook her head firmly, wrapping her arms around herself. "My priest would have drowned me, rather than see me go off to one of the schools. It's only a touch. Easing a birth, or settling a horse. Kindnesses. It's of God, I know that. I can't think it's a wicked thing."

"Of course not."

"You have it, too."

"Different to yours."

"He hates it. Even as he feeds off me, and keeps me, he despises it."

"You're thralled?" She nodded, eyes downcast. "I'm sorry."

"There'll be more to be sorry for when he's at you. He howled half the night for his children."

I sighed, sliding down the wall to sit. "We're deeply loving creatures, even the cruel among us."

"I don't doubt it. I think he'll do his best to keep you alive."

"There's not much that gets us."

She nodded, rubbing her hands together. "I'm sorry for that. I'd kill you if it would help, but I'll not be able to."

"Don't feel obliged. It's a kindness to wish it."

"More a kindness to myself, sir. I'd dearly like to hurt him."

"My companions will do that. Addison, he's much stronger than I am. And Tobias, a great warrior. If they truly think me dead, they'll have revenge. It won't take magic blood and bodies to fuel Addison. His fury doesn't need anything but his own bright soul."

"You sound fond."

I smiled at her, shaking my head. "I love him, so I know the measure of him. He's a better sort than Henry."

"I'll have to prepare the things now. I'm sorry."

"What's your name, mistress?" I asked as she pushed away from the wall.

"Alma."

"Don't worry for me, dear Alma. I'll have had worse than they can pull from their little minds. I'm a trained fighter."

She set a thin hand on my wrist as she moved past, bowing her head. "As you say, sir."

"Jean-Luc. Luc, to those I like," I said as she shuffled off. Metal clicked behind me as she started her tasks.

It was a wicked thing to thrall a human so, bind them to a master with no grace and no choice. I'd take her with me when I left.

# Chapter 45

Torture is a middling troublesome thing to an immortal. Or an indulgence, depending which end of the knife you were on. Henry indulged, providing me with a variety of ways to sample pain. Hot iron, knives, magic. Magic is the most effective, in the sense of lingering potency. Our healing doesn't counteract that. It's easy to rend flesh that heals over and over, but pain that ekes its agony out for days at a time is more spiteful.

"Do you know why my teeth are still missing?" I asked. Alma was shuffling around in the background of our special room, her frame wilted as a neglected flower. Sometimes she washed the stones around me, so the sparkling white was not stained rust red and I could sit outside my own filth.

The sound of her tasks stopped before she spoke. "Yes."

"Will I like the answer?"

"I fear not."

"Best tell me before he gets here then, temper the blow."

She came around to see me, painfully thin. Henry had fed from her in front of me, he made no secret of boosting his strength before he came to play his games. He brought her food and drink then, but little else.

"Magic. They wanted to be sure you couldn't get them back. I don't know if there's a particular trick to your healing, forgive me, but I know the same magic they used to catch you was used for your teeth."

It had been a forbidden snare that had caught me, a sudden bubble of power that ricocheted me from the battle to torpor-like sleep. They were a filthy weapon of the war. Sired soldiers would be torn through; burned into ash at the sheer expression of magic. A loss for their side as much as taking me.

"That's troublesome."

"I'm sorry for your troubles." Alma came closer, her brow slick with sweat. "I fear there are more coming. Something's wrong in the house."

"Oh?"

"I can feel it. Like a tide." She tapped her chest, looking to the door. "I don't know how to leave here. They wanted me here as eyes on you, not to leave."

"I know, Alma. I know it's not deliberate."

"But if there's something wrong, I can't help you." She turned to me, hands shaking as she gripped one of my broken wrists. They were stitching back together slowly, the lack of blood making the healing gradual. "I don't know enough to get you out."

"You don't have to."

She shook her head, cheeks wet as her whole body began to tremble. "I think I do. Something's very wrong, Luc."

"Speak to me. Tell me about Dennis." Bringing her husband up was a painful memory, but it was someone she loved; something bright to set her mind on.

"I haven't seen him in so long. I have to do something terrible." She brought a shaking hand to her chest, nodding a little to herself.

"What are you saying?"

She passed a small knife into my hand, only a few inches long. The handle was carved bone, the engravings warm from her grip, and she curled her fingers around mine as she pushed our foreheads together. "I know you can't end yourself, but may it serve you well. If you take one hand off at the wrist it would free you from the chains, and this will be quicker than gnawing."

"Alma, look at me."

"I cannot." She pecked a kiss to my forehead, then she was gone. Behind us was the collection of tools, and the fireplace, but little else from what she had told me.

"Alma, come back to me."

"I cannot." The sound of scraping and clattering grew, a *woosh* from the flames taking over.

"Alma?" The crackle of the fire grew into a roar, too loud in the space, then the scent of burning blossomed. I knew the smell. I'd passed the piles of bodies in battle. The acrid curl of scorching hair crept out. "Alma!"

A groan of something came but nothing more, other than the fizz and pop of wood and fat mixing. I closed my eyes, sinking against the wall while the sounds of the fire abated, back to the usual growl.

A fully thralled human will kill themselves on the death of their master. It is one of the many reasons thralls are so wicked. It was a compulsion, like salmon leaping up the river. I'd seen Alma bitten enough times to know the strength of her connection to Henry. She didn't even scream as the fire took her.

Henry was dead. A small victory in the overall war, though my heart swelled with satisfaction. I'd rather have taken his head myself, admittedly, but true death was good enough.

It did leave me in the room. Alma's knife would work well enough for getting my hand off; there was a grim certainty in cutting myself free. I could saw through the healing wrist and grow the hand back in a week or so. Do the other once I could hold the knife again. Slower due to the lack of blood, but they'd never been willing to risk me feeding.

What then of the door? Depending on the chain, I could check it while regrowing the first hand. I gripped the knife, biting my lip for resistance. I'd been naked for months now, no shirt collar to grit my teeth with, so flesh would have to suffice. Maybe Alma had left the shawl she wore at night.

The knife was kindly sharp. Once I'd jammed the cuff as far down my wrist as I could, it was no hard task to sink the blade between the bones. With a bit of wiggling, and a hearty spurt of dark fluid, the blade sang through. It took a level of sawing to get through the side and free the blade, but by that point the pain was a bright, fresh thing, different to Henry's machinations. I leaned into the vivacity to finish the job.

Popping the cuff free was easy. I clamped the knife between my teeth, crushing the stump closed so I could ease the bleeding. I would lap the spilling blood later. The chain clattered to the floor, loud over the sizzle of burning muscle. Only the one hand lost, then.

The smell from the fire was making my mouth water, much as it turned my stomach, and I peered around the wall. She'd laid down in the fireplace, a hearth for a pyre. A thick layer of logs and what I took to be oil, from the bottles discarded before the stones, was underneath her. Her arms had drawn to her chest, a pantomime surrender to the flames, skin blackened and gnarled.

I would not do anything to her body, other than wrap what was left. Her red shawl was discarded, tossed aside on a long table with the implements I knew well, like fresh blood across their points. I scooped it up for a distraction as much as any semblance of decency.

I stuck my head under the chimney to see the familiar heather grey of a barrier, probably one of the wards keeping the room suspended. No option there, then. Breaking the ward would not only send the room stumbling through time, but the magical rebound would have nowhere to go except directly to me. A sure death, one could hope, but the alternatives were bleak—shattered consciousness, fractured into pieces of oneself and tossed through time. Maybe to become one of the grains in the currents we manipulated. The idea of being conscious in that state, unwilling and unable to change anything, made me retch.

No, I would use the same way Henry had.

The door was more substantial than I had anticipated—a single, huge block of marble. It was easily six times the size of the other stones that made the walls, and there were no hinges or seals.

I knew the sound of it moving; the slow grind of stone against stone. Was it simply a large slab? Sliding my fingers along it, the stone sang with power, near leaking out as I splayed my fingertips to catch the sparks. There was magic through the stone, weaved into it like the veins of cream and grey that glinted in the firelight. Magic that spoke to my magic, but was not the same.

I took a few steps back and pulled my power together, leeching sparks from the door to give myself traction.

Nothing.

I let my work dissipate, walking back to the stone. It was huge and heavy, would have made a grand sculpture in the hands of someone with skill. I shoved it, hard, growling when my fresh stump bumped against the cold surface.

Nothing.

# Chapter 46

*We are more than beasts. More than hunger and teeth in the night, more than the desperate thirst. But the beast is there, and in hunger it howls. Long and loud.*

I came back to myself from another surge, knelt before the marble. Again. It sparked in the darkness; slips of magic diffusing like mist. It was the only light left in the room. The first few weeks in the dark had been the worst. Now it was common.

The slab was wet from my blood, and when I stroked it, my left hand sang with agony. Clawing again. I sucked the fingers, habit more than any sustenance. I did not remember eating my severed hand, but it was gone when I returned from the first frenzy.

Sometimes it was slamming. Pounding my fists. The desperate waves came and abated like a drunken tide, pulling me under as instinct forced up. My hunger wanted to live.

I got flashes sometimes. My fingers raw, nails buckled and hanging as I dug them in, over and over, dropping off as I scrabbled against the stone. My shoulder hanging at an angle after I'd popped it free on the seam of the edge. Resetting it was easy, but the pain lasted.

Given enough time marble's no longer smooth—the imperfections will out. The beast knew this as well as I did, for it was me, it shared my knowledge.

It didn't have the finesse to use such knowledge well.

I sank down, twisting so my back rested against the damn stone. In the privacy of my dark prison, no one could see me weep, but I resisted the urge. Pain was no stranger, and I would heal. It was slow, and the hunger so deep, but we were creatures of survival.

# Chapter 47

I kept two piles—blunted instruments and those yet to be used. Blunted ones were discarded to my right, and those yet to be used were company to my left.

The intimacy of their use made them easy to adapt, a familiarity of form and shape that I could employ. They didn't last long against the cold stone, days at most, but I had time. The pieces of stone littered the floor around me, my own snowfall.

The *chip chip chip* of each attempt was a slow clock for my imprisonment. I had no company but Alma's body, long fallen in her improvised grave. It was oddly naked, her resting place, a poor form of respect. I hoped she joined Dennis.

Her children were probably dead now. Either from the war or age.

*Chip chip chip.* I would get through the implements before the stone, but I would make as much leeway as I could. After that I would need other tools.

The grate from the fireplace. I'm sure she'd not begrudge me that. She gave me her courting knife. Dennis had carved it for her—some men made their love spoons, to show their skill at carving, but hers had made her a knife. He was a practical man, she'd said.

I missed her voice.

*Chip chip chip.*

I'd blunted the tools. Their handles were mostly used as well, carved into the stone as long as I could.

Dragging myself into standing I closed my eyes, picturing the room as it was before. The fireplace housed Alma, and underneath her was the grate.

"I'm sorry, Alma. I must be a brute again." My voice was so misplaced in the darkness, creaking and dry. I would've frightened her to death if she heard me.

I walked to the fireplace slowly, feeling along the wall so I didn't kick the jutting stone. My limbs had a constant ache, the healing eked out to weeks at a time from hunger. The surges didn't help.

I leeched energy from the stone, and it yielded to me, but it was cold. Not the warmth of blood. Not even the indulgence of food. I didn't fear drawing too much from it—time does not run out for us, and this magic was of time—but instability was a risk.

Maybe it would all crumble into time. Maybe I would spin out across the ages, scattered amongst stars and galaxies. I missed the stars.

The fireplace was long cold, and her bones were colder from resting against the metal. I cupped her skull, hugging it close for longer than was reasonable. Her children didn't get to do this. I cradled it higher, dipping my chin to rest against the smooth, cool dome.

When the bone had warmed from the meagre heat of my skin I set her down at the far side of the fireplace, turned so she could watch me at the slab. Digging through the remaining ash I found the long bars of the grate. With a roaring tug I yanked it free, falling backwards when it popped from its housing in the stone.

I laid in the dark, listening to the thud of my pulse and the creak of metal under my grip. I would get the bars separated, fashion them into makeshift chisels for attacking the marble. I needed to do as much as I could before the hunger rolled up again.

At a certain thinness, marble let light through. You could see this in some of the classic sculptures; women bedecked in shawls carved so thin that candlelight spread through and made the skin glow, as if the statue were alive. Like it would stand and greet you. Embrace you.

We were often called statues, Addison and I. Pale warriors, still and serious in the scrum, slinging magic like vengeful angels. His dark hair like a raven's feather, a poor omen for our enemies. We turned no one to salt, but he was biblical in his wrath, whereas I was more intimate. Hot-blooded.

Was.

I hoped Addison had been, at the end, as well. I hoped he had killed Henry. Or that Tobias had; my other love could be so very *vicious* when it suited him. He wore his heart ragged on his sleeve and he'd tear a throat clean through with his fangs.

I didn't know if they still lived. We had no thralled women to watch burn themselves, no soul bond to tie us to each other. If we'd that, they would know me alive, even locked out of the world as I was. They would have looked for me. Someone would have.

I could not think they'd end themselves, so it would have to be the war that took them.

I sat before the slab, my efforts showing a deep well in the stone—I could place the whole of my hand into, past my wrist. Slow progress, but progress. I had bars left that I could keep using, and though the beast within howled and growled, when I came back I could restart my work quickly. My healing had slowed; days and weeks for nails to regrow, flesh to knit together.

Clawing was the most common trait in the frantic blackouts, the stone painted slick when I came back to myself. I dreaded it now. The surges were less distant, instinct twinning with my sorrow and pushing close to awareness. I would not be given the luxury of forgetting much longer.

There was so much stone.

Once the metal was used up there were few options. I needed something pointed, something sharp to eke the most out of each crack. There couldn't be that much more of it. I could feel the swell of the magic between the slab and surrounding stones, the ebb and flow as it trickled between them. Once I reached the outside I could get more traction. Access my magic properly. Shatter the damn slab into gravel.

I took a deep breath, rearranging the dregs of the shawl around my shoulders. It had long gone to straggling pieces, held together at the seam. Much like myself. I was depleted, shuffling around like a lost ghoul. I was close to gnawing the stone, even without fangs.

This was a more constrictive option, though I feared it would drive me into another frenzy. The beast protected me, as much as it drove me to blind pain, and this activity needed both.

I brought my left hand to my right arm, gripping hard at the back of my wrist. Taking a deep breath so I could scream, I slammed the arm down into one of the larger marble shards, the sharp edge waiting for me among the rest. It sliced through the flesh and the crunch of it cracking through the bone moved within me like a wave.

I dropped to the floor, panting, the blood making me dizzy with the richness of it. One down. This was the worst of the two, the thicker bone by the elbow, and we were through that, my beast and me. The wrist would be easy.

The first slam was agony but not success. I opened my hand so I could push with the full breadth of my palm as I drove the wrist down into the marble again. A clean snap echoed out.

I laid on my side, shivering, so I didn't retch up my empty stomach. My fingers sank into the gash near my elbow, digging until I found the leaking crack inside. Getting purchase was easier than I'd anticipated; the wound was long and uneven, so I could get my fingers in deep. I sank my teeth into my lip as I gripped the broken bone, twisted it within the muscle. Starvation had made my muscles weak, and they yielded the thin prize with the softness of a carved roast.

Once I had it, I rolled onto my back, panting stale air. I was so used to pain, so familiar, that sometimes it no longer hurt. Sometimes it was just tears, or the prickling loneliness nestled deep in my chest. Sometimes it just hurt, and even my beast curled its back before it snarled.

I had my tool. Sticky and jagged, it would serve to get me through the marble. I had to be close to the end. I could stretch my arm into the hole, now, and the magic stirred in a different way.

# Chapter 48

"It took me three bones to get out." I was propped in someone's lap, head on their thigh, as they stroked my hair like I was a precious thing. "Three bones, with over a month for each one. Always the right arm. I almost gnawed it off at one point, the smell of blood was so much."

I shook at the words, and Mark pulled the blanket up over me, gentle, ever gentle. It was heavy and soft, a well-made thing. Strong colours. I focused on the weave of the wool. I couldn't scream.

He returned to stroking my hair. "I'm sorry. That was indelicate of me."

I couldn't move. It wasn't the same cold as before, his influence, but I was trapped in my skull, curling into myself.

"My magic changed, too. You'll have seen that. The well ran dry, and what I poured back in wasn't the same." He laughed, light and high. "I didn't know that was possible. We weren't told of it."

He lifted me, hands plucking me up by the shoulders to rest my hips on his thighs, my side to his chest. My head bumped his shoulder, dipping like I was asleep. Turning my chin with his fingers he smiled, finally showing his teeth and the gaps where his fangs should have been.

"You did so well, darling. Over a hundred years, spirit to spirit, and here you are. Still in one piece. None of the others managed it, but I knew you would. You work with spirit, you're strong, of course you would."

He wrapped his arms around me, hugging me close as he settled back on the wall. "Sleep, and in the morning we can talk."

There was no push of his power, but my mind went willingly into the dark.

# Chapter 49

I awoke to the same dark, wooden beams. I stared at them, pondering their height and the length of the bed-sheets. My body felt a long distance from my mind, a chasm between them, and I had no wish to traverse it. But I could fashion a rope from a torn sheet.

Better dead than what had happened. What could happen next. I should move, tear the sheets with my teeth.

My teeth…

Someone knocked on the door and I froze. The door opened, then soft footsteps came in, halting.

"Are you awake, mistress?" A woman came beside the bed. I turned my head to her, nodding. "I'm here to help with your morning."

She was young, younger than me at least. The dark dress she wore seemed like a governess; elbow sleeves and a high collar, neat as a pin, and her red hair flowed down her back. Pale skin, deep marks under her eyes. Not a sleeper. Scars on her arms—a human.

"How long did I sleep?" I asked.

"A day and two nights. You've been with us three days, and Mark held you the day you arrived. Is it alright if I sit beside you?"

I nodded. She sat at my hip so I could look at her. "What's your name?"

"Rose."

"You're the healer."

"Aye." She fiddled with her skirt. "I have to ask you something, miss. I know what he did was... I don't think he should have done it the way he did."

"You know?"

"I know what he's told me. What he wanted to share. I'm not like you, I only have the healing. I couldn't understand. He tried, before, but it hurt me, so he stopped."

At least he'd stopped. She was too young for that, that wasn't right. I pushed the cover off me, ready to sit up. I was clothed beneath it, my modesty preserved by a nightdress, and I swallowed a shudder as I swung my legs over the edge. "Healing helps the world."

"You're kind." She set a hand on my arm. "I don't want you to think he's monstrous. He was so desperate for someone to know."

The cold focused sharp in my chest. "What?"

"I can't even imagine a hundred years, oldest anyone in my family reached is seventy. And he rushed on and did that, and it's not alright. I know it's not alright. But please don't think he's wicked."

"He killed my friend."

She bit her lip, nodding, started playing with a long strand of her hair. "He said the man attacked him."

"Tim slapped him."

"I believe you. But Mark wanted you so badly. And drowning men take others into the deep."

I nodded, swallowing the reply. Her arms were littered with scars, little white lines that overran each other in disarray. "Were you hurt?"

She crossed her arms, shaking her head. "It's nothing. You need to eat. Or even tea? I can make a good brew, I'm from Lancashire and we like it good and strong."

"Why did he take my teeth?" I clenched my hands in the material of my nightdress. It was a fine thing, and close to my size, which I didn't like.

"I don't rightly know. He'll tell you, if you ask. He's been dreadfully worried. Had me come in over and over, see if you needed healing. I tried to make sure you could sleep."

A kindness within her power. I looked at her properly, tried to smile. It felt wrong on my face. "How come you're here?"

"He took me in when I was young."

"Young? You're a slip of a thing." What age had she been when he tried to bond with her? She was barely out of being a child.

She laughed, looking away to the window. "I'm eighteen, been here since I was thirteen. He saved me from someone. Killed them in front of me. He was very apologetic."

"Someone wanted to hurt you?"

"Healers are a commodity, in a city. People want them for a lot of reasons. Female ones get the most attention."

I crossed my arms, anger heavy on my tongue. "Serves them right, then."

"I'm sure he'd be pleased to hear that." Rose smiled, catching my hand. "Please try not to hate him. He's not all bad."

"Neither are executioners." I patted her hand, forcing myself up. A wardrobe sat in one corner, a proud thing with beautiful wooden detail. "Are there clothes for me?"

"Yes."

I shouldn't have been surprised. The nightdress fit. Crossing to it I opened the door: it held a bursting selection of dresses, tops and skirts, colours to suit any mood. All expensive, and beautiful, and I itched with the desire to set it alight.

"Do I have to talk to him?" I pushed some of the dresses aside, looking for something tolerable. No trousers.

"He's worried for you. But he would settle for me confirming you're up."

"I would appreciate that. Do you want to do that, and I'll get dressed?"

"Do you not need assistance?"

"I grew up in a college. I'm quite capable. And you can call me Ena, I'm not a scholar."

"You are the lady of the house, though."

Cold went down my back like a dousing. I turned to her, frowning. "Pardon?"

"Mark's confirmed you're the mistress of the house. Or to be treated as such, at least. It's not like you're married." Her strangled laugh was enough for my heart to dive into the bottom of my ribs.

"I suppose I'm the only female guest?"

"Yes!"

Fuck. Fuck, no. None of this was good. The clothes and the room, the set-up to slide into the household like I was here in a role. I smiled at her, gripping the wardrobe to keep myself still. "That's kind of him, then. Let him know I'm hale, I'll get something on. A dress I suppose." I'd no other bloody choice.

"He would enjoy that. He was very careful choosing these for you. I could braid your hair, if you like? While you drink your tea."

The thought turned my empty stomach, but I kept the stilted smile, nodding. "That would be lovely."

She nodded and left, shimmering hair fluttering behind her. There was a wave and curl to it, despite the frizz, and with some care she would be a beautiful lass. I should be grateful for human company.

Once I was sure she was gone I shot back to the bed, grabbing the pillow. Burying my face into it I smothered the sobs wracking my chest, breaths flitting in and out like I'd been running. This was a trap, a beautiful and carefully pulled together snare, and I was stuck within it.

I couldn't even feel the despair I knew was there, trapped in the ice of my heart, only the trembling terror that it *was* there, would break at some point and sweep over me. I couldn't take another view of what had happened to him. I would rather find the roof, or use one of those lovely beams. There had to be a way to get separate from him.

I had to get out.

Bringing my head up, I gulped air as I wiped my face. There was limited time, I had to get myself together. I slapped my cheeks a few quick times to get my head clear, gripping my skull to shut everything else out.

Secure the perimeter—I couldn't do that yet, I didn't know how to get out and Mark had something that could freeze me, so running unawares would leave me vulnerable. But I could get dressed and follow Rose, look for a door I could sneak out of later.

I turned the pillow, so the wet side was down against the covers, and went to the wardrobe. Better to look like I was able to be calm, make it seem like I would co-operate. I could do this, this was no different to a job. Treat it like a job and get through it, plan what to do when there's a break in the armour. I knew this backwards.

I blinked at the wardrobe again, peering at the options. A dark green dress was close to the door, the weave strong and the details neatly sewed in—it was more ornate than day ware, for but it would suit me.

A modesty screen stood off at one side and I took the dress behind it, grateful for the little slice of privacy. I had no idea if he wanted to drink from me, or if he had already. He'd had ample opportunity, unconscious and unguarded around him for days. I slipped out of the nightdress, pulling the green piece quickly up my body. It fitted me well. Another grim kindness.

Mark couldn't bite me, certainly, but he could cut me. It seemed like he did Rose, if those scars were what I suspected. Maybe I could bargain with that, offer it in return for an exit. Maybe he simply wanted my blood, a battery for his revenge on the others.

My heart lurched at the thought of the nest. I didn't know who would take it worse, that Luc was now Mark, that Mark was how he was. They'd be shattered. Gods, what if he was as touchy as them? I brought my energy up, seeking to wind it tight, but it wouldn't hold, wouldn't stop running away like water through my fingers.

I stepped away from the screen, towards the cold fire. A long mirror was hooked above it, reflecting light back into the room; I had missed that before. With a focused effort I forced my energy to show. My reflection swelled with light, blue as the fire from my hands. A deep gash showed at my neck, where he had forced contact, the energy misting out like rain. I brought a hand up to trace the shape, the leaking power.

My chest tightened. A soul wound. The ones I made were never so ragged; I was careful with those we brought back. He'd wrenched me apart. It could heal, but it was a slow process without help. Months, at minimum, maybe years.

Months of being a risk in my sleep, or being found by the college—I had no way to hide from them like this. I couldn't use my magic safely. My options for running dwindled like the unspooling thread of my power, everything slipping through the scar at my throat.

The door opened behind me and I saw Rose coming with a tray of tea, and some small slices of cake. I dropped my energy, turning to look at her as she came in.

"How do I look?" I asked, holding the skirt out to show the length.

"It's a fine colour on you. I brought the pot, in case you wanted more than a cup, and I brought some parkin. Mark was pleased to hear you had wakened." She hovered at the door, still hold of the tray.

"Will he expect my company?"

"Yes. He's in the library. I could take this through there, if you like, and have the fire lit?"

"I am chilled. I suppose it's the way in these houses."

"Often." We both knew it was not true, but little lies eased the unsaid things.

"Let's do that. Are you the only person he keeps?"

"No, there are others, but they stay out of the way. Not everyone finds him comforting." She nodded to me and I followed her.

"Does he feed from them?"

"No, he's not that kind of man. I know he's been ungentle with you, but he doesn't hurt us."

My response stuck on my tongue, Tim's name between my teeth along with all the rest. I smiled around it, trailing behind her pretty hair.

# Chapter 50

The library was substantial, large as a church and tall enough to have a walkway around the upper half with a short ladder leading up. More dark wood, the same tall windows and rich layers of rugs and carpets as the room. It was all familiar: money everywhere, in quality and adornment. Deathly quiet, though, not even the ticking of a clock. The silence was thick, far off from the bustle of Addison's study. I strangled the thought before it continued, lest I start to cry. That would help no one.

Rose left me beside a large table, tray set down, while she disappeared into the bookcases. There were stacks of books on the table too—art and language, tomes of fiction. I bent lower to inspect the spines: well-preserved, the gold-thread titles gleaming.

"He'll be with you shortly. I'll get the fires lit too." Rose pointed to a short distance away, into the bookcases, and I nodded.

The door clicked closed and I checked over the room again. I could go up the ladder, keep a distance between us. There would only be one way down, from what I could see, but I could always jump. It was about one-storey. I'd jumped worse. No cushion this time, though.

I wrapped arms around my torso, hands up under my armpits to stave the chill. It was sunshine outside, it should be a mild day, but my fingers were ice. I went to the window, checking for an open one. We were a long way from the hedgerow, a broad drive leading up to the house from a dark tree-line at the end: too far to run without being spotted.

"Contemplating your escape?" The voice came from up high and I turned to see Mark on the long gangway. There must be another ladder then. Good. Options. He was in a short-sleeved shirt, almost relaxed, and he seemed buoyed compared to my last time with him. Lighter. Bastard.

I worked my jaw before I answered, trying to speak well. "I don't think I'd get very far."

"You're right. Would you run if you thought you could?" He smiled, leaning forward on the rail so his elbows sat on the metal.

"Why did you take my teeth?" It was rude to answer one question with another but I couldn't help it. It leaked around the space where the teeth used to be.

He laughed, looking almost embarrassed for a moment before he stood straight again. "I could tell you the truth, which will be uncomfortable, or a lie which may sit better. Which would you prefer?"

I blinked at him; words scattered at his offer. It was alien to have someone be as forthright as me. Explicit. I could do this, though, work the dance of words back and forth. "The truth."

"As you wish. Come to the seats for that, it'll take some time to discuss." He moved to the ladder, much too fast, and then he was down on my level and offering me his arm.

I shook my head, nodding for him to lead me onwards, and he stepped off through the bookcases. He brought us to a scattering of overstuffed armchairs, in a rough semicircle around a large fireplace. It was stocked for burning.

"Can I start that?" I asked.

"Rose said she would send someone. Using your powers would cause you to drain more energy, and you're still recuperating." He sat on a low love seat.

It was hard to argue with the logic, much as I wanted to. A word of power wouldn't drain me, they weren't my power being used, but he didn't seem to know that. Or didn't want to let me have fire in my hands. Either way I nodded. "Alright."

"Good. Can you come here?" He patted his thighs, arm open for me to curl into.

"I'd prefer to stand. Do you not like me looking at you when we talk?"

He laughed, the same laugh as when I woke up to my head on his thigh, light like a silver bell. "You're right. I was much bolder when I could obscure myself from your gaze."

"You still could, if you wanted to?" It might be easier to speak if I didn't see his face.

"I couldn't. We've touched spirits, I can't obfuscate away from that."

"I wasn't aware that was a consequence." I wasn't aware of any of the consequences, except the one I had found in the mirror.

"Come, sit here and I'll tell you more."

"I don't trust myself to do that."

"Scared your powers will hurt me?"

"I might try to scratch your eyes out." He was stronger than me, he could subdue me, but still. I'd no idea where this bravery was coming from, other than that I wanted to make him bleed. To inflict something, *feel* something, other than that cold void that had swollen within me.

"That would hurt, but it wouldn't get you away from me. Would you prefer a knife, carve something into my chest? Slit my throat?" He said it so reasonably, like placating a child, and I swallowed twice before I could speak again.

"I'd like that very much, but you're not really going to let me, are you?"

"I would, if it settled you down."

"Settled me?" My voice went before I could stop it, a hot rush of anger melting something in me enough to laugh. "You killed my friend. You mutilated me! And my power! How do I settle, to that?"

He grabbed me before I could breathe in again, a hand at my head and another at my hip, pulling me back down against him and into the chair. I held still, rigid in his grip, eyes closed, waiting for more. He was so tall, even compared to my unusual height, and I crooked my head into his shoulder so I rested on the material. An inch, already, but he could snap my neck with his hand there.

He seemed to like my resting against him, humming in approval and stroking my hair. At least it was braided.

"You can hug me if you want something to do with your hands."

"I might need them to gouge my eyes out too."

He laughed, scooping me closer to press a kiss to my temple. "So sparking. You should use lightning rather than fire. I am glad to see you awake."

"Why did you take my teeth?"

"I sent them to Addison."

I sat up, meaning to look at him, and he tugged me back close. His grip was no tighter than before, but a tension sang in the muscles around me—the promise of more if I resisted. I stilled, hiccoughing around a breath. Treat it like a job, Ena, work with what there was on the table. "I think that will cause distress."

"Do you?" He let his head rock back, his shoulders bunching up closer to his neck. I set my head back down on them, hands fisted in my skirt.

"I'm not a vampire, so it's not a guarantee I'm dead. I could just be being tortured."

"Just?"

"There're worse things, evidently."

His laugh was more of a puff of air than any real mirth but he brought his face back close to me, raising a hand to tilt my chin. Our gazes met, his eyes yellow as a cat's. They held bands of gold, little chasing rings that settled near his pupils. More like a wildcat than a tabby. Feral.

"You know it, too. You know everything about me." He kissed my cheek this time, his lips cool. I tightened my grip in my skirts to resist pushing away.

"Did you want him to know it was you? Because they think you're dead." I turned a little in his lap, so my chest almost faced his, and set an open hand below his collarbone. They liked contact, needed it, this was direct contact. Me touching him, not him grabbing me. His shirt was good material, rich under my skin, and his heart kicked away under his ribs. He felt warmest there, as if even his heart didn't want to be chased by the cold.

"I don't know. I like the idea of it hurting him."

"Tobias too?"

"In a way. I love them both so much, but not like you. They're still in love with a memory."

"It's a beautiful memory."

"Oh?" He began to rub my back, slow circles around my shoulder blades. Soothing. Soft.

"I caught a glimpse of it. I saw how Addison saw you. A smile like sunshine."

"He showed you that?"

"He didn't mean to, it was an accident. Most people will kill you for knowing their secrets. Hate you at least."

"I could never hate you." He hugged me close again, resting his chin on my shoulder so he could speak close to my ear. "How could I hate someone who can finally understand me?"

My stomach turned and I drew a shaky breath. "What will you do if they come looking for you?"

"They won't look here. You have a variety of enemies who could have stolen you off."

The darkening of Tim's eyes flashed through my mind. "They would have done it differently."

He inclined his head for a moment, gasping when he seemed to realise. "Yes. Well, your college would. You did annoy the thieves too. Anyway, they'll be too distraught that you've been hurt to do anything."

I shook my head, letting myself curl into him. Mark accepted the affection. This was all wrong but it bought time, bought chances to learn more. No point in spitting a word; fire alone wouldn't kill him. Haddley had said you needed blessed fire and I didn't have the ingredients for that memorised recipe. Maybe my heart-fire, but that was only a maybe. If it failed, there'd be worse than a bloodied nose.

"I don't think so. They were fond of me, but mortals are brief creatures. I'd be another death in a line of us stretching all the way back," I said.

"You do yourself a disservice, darling. I saw Tobias's fury when that braggard tried to take you from the house. That was honest anger. And he ensured Addison didn't do something worse."

"He'd know."

"What do you mean?"

I opened my mouth to speak, chest tightening at the edge to his question. "Well, Tobias pulled Addison back in the war. When he was killing other immortals. You know what happened." It was a beseeching question, not really a statement, no matter how I tried to harden my voice.

Mark shook his head, light stubble scratching against my cheek. "When I got out the world had moved on."

He didn't know. Should have made a fucking noose of those sheets before the girl came in. "Do you want me to tell you?"

"I'm curious, so yes. You've had such a reaction to it."

"Promise you won't hurt me." Again.

"If your answer angers me it will not be at you or directed towards you. You have my word." His word had meant a lot to him before. Fuck.

# Chapter 51

"Addison killed Henry in a particular way. The way he thought you'd been killed." My voice was small, barely myself. "Tobias had to kill others to protect him. Hide what had been done."

"What do you mean?" Mark gripped my shoulders, gentle, like I'd shatter, moving me back so we looked at each other. His eyes were so open, the gold almost glinting.

"Addison fractured him. I don't know a better word. Tobias said there was one, but Addison broke Henry's soul up and tossed it through time. He still had a piece in one of the hourglasses in his room. I hurt myself looking at it."

Mark blinked twice, mouth open like I'd slapped him. "That's very much forbidden."

I nodded, unsure where to look. I settled for his brows, so I could watch his reaction but not the pain of his eyes. "Tobias made me swear not to say anything. The consequences."

"Oh yes, there are strict consequences for the forbidden things. A fate worse than the forever death."

I licked my lips as if it would ease what I said next. "That's what Addison wanted." My knuckles were straining where I gripped his shirt, hands fisted in the material. I was shaking. His grip on me tightened and I shivered more. "I didn't want to know and now I can't even hide."

"No worry, my dove, only Rose has magic and she won't harm you. She's wonderful at healing."

As if that was the only risk. I kept my eyes on his brows. "She speaks highly of you."

"I feel a debt to her. I killed her father, it's a terrible sight for a child."

"Her father?" I caught his eye at that, the word snagging.

"He'd taken her from her school and was to sell her off. A monstrous thing to do. I hadn't realised he was her kin until she was crying. Of course I had to take her in."

I sighed, slumping into his chest, head to his neck. He was slightly warmer; I didn't know if it was real or the reflection of my breath across his skin. "Couldn't leave her to be hurt."

"Precisely." He brought a hand up to stroke my hair, trailing his fingers all the way down the braid. "You think the same. I knew you would. I knew before I'd even joined with you. I saw it in your eyes when you pushed back beside the tavern."

Should have kept my mouth shut. "I'm glad she was safe with you. Healers bring a lot of good to the world."

"You sound sad." He pushed my shoulders, enough to bring me back up. The cold rush of air on my face meant I'd been crying. Everything was starting to buzz, the trill of adrenaline and tiredness pushing against me.

"I often wished I could heal."

"You can. You offer clarity and insight, bring honesty when someone would lie to themselves."

"That is not often considered healing."

"Let those who doubt it lick their own wounds." He said it with a venom, a bite I hadn't even heard from him when he was at the tavern. It killed any response I would have, so I shrugged, and smoothed my skirt for something to do with my hands.

"What should I call you, by the way?" I asked, looking around the library. Anywhere but that yearning gold. "Rose calls you Mark. I know a different name for you. What do you prefer? Names hold power."

"I think you're beyond making a poppet of me with my true name. Luc's long dead, and I'm marked by what was done to me, so I am Mark."

"Alright." I nodded, looking back at the dark fire. "Can I ask some less nice questions?"

"Why do you preface them?"

"I don't know you well enough to know if you'll get angry. You were calm about Addison and Tobias. You might not be about other things."

"You aren't usually so cautious. I've seen you be much bolder with the pups."

"No one else has done what you did."

"You sweet thing, stepping so carefully around my thorns. I won't be angry at your questions." His fingers returned to running along my braid, up and down my back. Soothing, almost.

"Why am I here? If you don't mean to taunt the others, why take me from the nest?"

"I took you because I saw the opportunity and couldn't resist. I was going to wait until you'd run off in the night, fleeing your college. But then you were hiding that lad I'd taken a slice at, and it was so easy to slip in."

The wards, of course, we'd not feel him coming. Tim had been right. "Why the room I'm in, then, and the clothes?"

"Once I had you I couldn't keep you in poor care. I got the clothes while you slept. With Rose's aid, she changed you. The room is small, but now you're awake, you can share mine."

I jolted at his comment, refusing to budge in his grip. "Why would we do that?"

"Since we're joined, it will be better to do so. I'm not going to put myself upon you, but we're already so intimate. Cuddling won't be too scandalous for you, will it?" Scandalous, he said. Was it the only word they knew for matters under the covers?

"I cuddled those at the house." They gave me comfort when I was scared. He was not comfort.

"So much trust in us leeches?"

"I know what I thought when I woke up there, but they're not that." I looked at him, willing him to say the thing on my tongue.

"You think I am."

"You drank Tim. You drink from Rose."

He shook his head, turning my chin so I looked at him. "I don't drink of her. She's a charge under my care, I wouldn't take blood from her."

"She has all those wounds."

"They're not my doing. And while I won't deny I'd find drinking from you enticing—" He took a moment to move my braid away to my right shoulder, so my neck was bare to him, and let a fingertip linger at the pulse point. "—I would never do so without consent. You're much more valuable to me than being a battery."

I knew this talk. I pressed my lips together, grasping his shoulder as a distraction for us both. He couldn't think this would work, that I'd be some doll for him to pet and fuss over. "I don't understand."

"You will. And if you would offer your blood freely, I'd not refuse. But I don't want you to feel it's an obligation. This is not transactional, I want you to give yourself willingly."

"How do you—" I stalled, brain somewhere between a scream and a sob, heart loud in my ears as it kicked into a galloping pace. Willingly? None of this was willing, none of this was my choice.

"How do I what, sweet?"

I scrabbled for words, to untangle the terrifying conclusion of what he was saying. "Do you mean to turn me?"

"Eventually. I'm in no rush."

I sat back, squeaking when he brought me closer again, pressing my head into his neck. "Have you noticed how you can touch me with no pain, after we shared a connection? Despite your magic, spirit work, we're level together."

Shared, like I had a choice. There'd been no choice in what he forced onto me. I nodded; I'd scream if I spoke. Maybe I would set us both on fire. He wouldn't die but it would hurt.

He waited for me to speak, until I ground out a word. "Yes."

"That's because we're connected now, a soul bond. It's very rarely formed with vampires and mortals. This isn't thrall, like poor Alma, this is something much purer. Like love. And when you turn, you won't be my lessor, even without true immortality. We can be joined through the ages."

"I don't know what to say." Fuck no, I'd kill myself.

"You don't have to say anything. I can feel your railing spirit. The fear, the panic, the warmth, all those cascading things within. I can feel you." He brought a hand very slowly between us, resting it at my heart. "And you can feel me too, though you may not know it yet."

The chasm. He was that yearning maw within me. Surely there had to be more, he couldn't only be a void. Gods above. Did he see me like I'd seen him? No, if he had he'd know about my words. The thought nagged through me, as chill as the wind on the cliffs, and I blinked up at him. "I need time to get used to that. This is overwhelming."

"Of course, darling. I'm in no rush. You'll have time to get used to the house, and to me. Though, if you were in Addison's bed so soon maybe I should have you in mine tonight. I find myself disliking the idea of him getting to hold you close."

"He's very, uh. Soft. Likes to hold hands or rest together. If you like that too, I could do that." It was a mercy to be saying it into his shoulder. But I could make that work. Make him think I was working on his level, go along with the touches, get some slack in his suspicion so I could get out. That was almost a plan.

"Share my bed?"

"I've not laid with him, or any of them. As long as you understand that."

"Neither of them has had you?"

My gut twisted at the surprise in his question, indignant at the curiosity. "Why is everyone convinced I've been fucking that pair?"

"In the noble houses it's common. Not with any of the charges, of course, you wouldn't do that to a child you'd raised. But for a human who joined later, as an adult, well. It wasn't rare to declare a companion of the nest, so other families wouldn't seek to claim them."

"Before the war?" I asked. He nodded, hand resting at the base of my back to keep me sat on him. That's why Tobias suggested it: an old echo of their traditions. Sweet, foolish man. We were only taught about the war, being a battery. No one mentioned being cherished. Companionship. I swallowed a gag.

"You seem troubled."

I shook my head, trying to bring a natural smile. "I think I'm overtired. I should probably lie down."

"Eat something first, if you can. Hunger doesn't suit you."

# CHAPTER 52

Mark's room was bedecked with art—paintings crowded for space on the walls. They crept around the furniture, almost overlapping, and I was afraid to look too closely lest I bump any off. I inspected them while Rose made plans to move my items through.

"Fond of paintings, is he?" I asked.

"He has an appreciation for art. Not all to my taste but he likes variety."

It was a reasonable statement. "Seems like he just buys what he likes."

"He pays well."

"Good." It was meaningless chatter, nothing more than noise to keep my mind distracted, but she indulged me.

"If you want to keep looking at them, I'll start moving things over?"

I nodded to her, inspecting a long seascape. The coast was almost familiar, an oil rendition of a lighthouse with crashing waves and a lone boat being tossed about.

"Do you like that one?"

I yelped, nearly bumping into the painting from the shock of the voice behind me, and an arm snuck around my waist to pull me back against Mark's chest. "You startled me."

"You were so absorbed I couldn't help myself. Your focus is impressive."

"I didn't know you were in the room."

"I saw Rose passing and thought I'd join you. You'll need peace to get settled, but if there's anything I can do to assist, let me know. I want you to like it here."

"Where is here?" I'd only seen the inside of the house, but the trees looked unfamiliar, and I had no anchor.

He tilted his head at me, so like Addison it made my heart yank, once, before he smiled. "You don't know?"

"I do not."

"Would you like to?"

The nature of the question gave me pause, too leading. "I think so, but I'm wary. I have no way to protect myself from old things. Much as I'm safe with you, I might not be so lucky with other energy." Safe. Gods it was a blessing I could lie with a straight face.

"I'll protect you. Come with me."

He took my hand, still cold but not as cold as his, and we launched off down a different corridor. It was a struggle to keep up with him, those long legs striding ahead as I near trotted behind. Flashes of rooms went past, and when we crossed a large hall, something about the space made my stomach tighten, a dizzying coldness shooting through me. I stumbled and he caught my shoulders, pressing us on.

"You're enthusiastic," I said.

"I must confess I'm delighted. I thought you'd realised and were simply too shy to mention it. Being able to show you makes my heart skip."

We shot past tall windows; the beautiful garden ignored in favour of a broad, dark set of stairs that I had not yet discovered. I must get an idea of the layout of the house. This staircase had neglected lamps studded into the walls, barely piercing the gloom of a long corridor at the bottom.

"Mark?" We were descending into darkness, my eyes unable to see much beyond his back leading me on. "I can't see."

"Trust me, darling."

I had little choice; he was pulling me along anyway. "Alright."

He shivered, his grip on my fingers tightening. On we went, into the basement or passage, and after a few turns I was entirely unable to see. I nearly held my breath, lest it disturb his focus.

We stopped, arms bumping together as he stilled. "I'll need to guide you. Come closer."

I stepped up to his back, so he could turn and grip my shoulders. "What is it?"

"You'll see soon."

"I doubt it."

He giggled, tugging me close for a hug and turning me to one side. "Quite right. You'll realise soon, though. I'm going to guide you forward then you should feel the energy. Can you do that for me?"

"Alright."

"Perfect, good girl." I struggled to keep my shoulders down at the comment, letting him push me forward while one hand ducked my head a little. "That's it, a couple more steps and you'll be there."

I took two steps forward, arms out to feel for my surroundings. Nothing. I was alone in the darkness which could have gone for miles. Eyes open or closed it seemed to make no difference, but I kept them open in case. "Like this?"

"Perfect. Now reach out with your gift, what do you feel?"

I had no guard so whatever was there could simply rush upon me. If it noticed me. This was a dreadful idea. My shoulders dropped as I began to feel out, ungainly without my usual skill. I could still do some direction though, and as I scanned around, little sparks began to unfurl like flowers in the morning sun.

They were silvery white, quite alien to my magic, and as I drew closer one of them lanced towards me like mercury. I yelped, hopping back, but it struck home and a wave of shock rocked through me. The scars on my stomach jolted with recognition.

"This is Henry's house." The hall had been familiar because I'd seen it, in a very different way. Gods above.

"You're such a clever girl." Mark was beside me, his voice low and proud, and I stumbled into him as I twisted around in fright. He tugged me close, wrapping his arms around me. "I have you."

I grabbed onto him, for balance if nothing else, and the slips of energy continued to reach out like grasping fingers. "Why?"

"Why am I still here?" I nodded, hugging him closer. I didn't know if I wanted to run or scream but I needed him to get out of this hellish place and I would not let him slip away. "I didn't want to go back to my family. No one wanted this cursed little spot. I suppose if they had I'd have been found, eventually."

"If they could have moved the marble. You got yourself out."

"I did." He ran a hand over my cheek, chest bouncing in a laugh. "You say that without much venom."

"I'm glad you got free. What you suffered was a wicked thing."

"The torture?"

I shook my head. "No, that is what it is. War does those things. The being alone. Yearning. I can still feel some of it, and it's terrible." I loosened one arm to pat my chest, the ache like a hollow through me.

"You sweet thing, don't cry for me." He scooped me closer, tender, pressing kisses to my cheeks and forehead. I was crying for him, rather than me; for who he had been. Who was here now. This had been his cell. Despite the dark, I recognised that energy, that sickly glow, from the memories of him carving. Little wonder he broke free as someone new.

My hands trembled as I set them on his chest, trying fruitlessly to meet his gaze in the dark. "Why didn't you rip it down?"

"And waste a perfectly good house? I think not. I admire your spite, but I was always better than Henry. What better evidence than taking everything he had and making it more. Making it mine." His arm tightened around me, low at my back so we pressed together.

"I'd have burned everything."

"Righteous anger burns bright, but it burns all. I prefer your compassion. It's one of the things I love about you."

"Compassion?"

"Your empathy. No one else could have taken my story. They all broke underneath it. I did, too."

I hugged him to me, frowning into his chest. "Survival is a bloody thing."

"Said like a survivor. Do you want to lie down on the bed?"

"I would appreciate that," I said. He pecked a kiss to my forehead and took my hands, leading me away.

# Chapter 53

He was a cuddler too. He tucked in close to my back, sliding one arm under my neck and the other tight around my waist, so he could hold me.

I laid still in his grip, listening to his breathing turn slow and regular and watching the colour of the sky change through the window. It was a parody of intimacy, an echo of something that could be tender.

"What are you thinking?"

I jumped at the question, soft and close to my ear. "I thought you were asleep."

"I wanted to make you more comfortable. What's keeping you awake?"

I took a breath in, holding it for two, three beats of my heart before I huffed it out. "I know there are some conversations one shouldn't have. I'm curious about certain things but if I ask you, we must have that conversation. Or not. Either way it means something."

"What a busy mind. No wonder you couldn't sleep." He turned onto his back, tugging me along with him so I had to twist and roll over. "Rest your head here and tell me what's bothering you."

I turned to see he was patting his chest and a hot little coil of spite rolled through me. The idea of cuddling up to him like a lover, more blatant than the last position, stuck against my teeth like gristle. "I'd rather not."

"Come on." He sat up a little, weight perched on one elbow, before pulling me closer until our heads nearly bumped together. With a quick twist he sank back down, dragging me with him so I was laid on top of his chest, legs tangled together. Just like with Tobias, but less blood. I shoved my head down to rest on his left shoulder, hard enough to knock that thought away.

"This is intimate," I said.

He ran his fingers through my hair, playing with the links of my braid. "What questions were you avoiding, darling?"

"I don't know much about vampire magic; I've only learned the basics. But why have you been taking blood from mages in the city? You still have your magic."

"I do, you're right. What do you notice about it?"

I swallowed, tracing my fingers along the back of his arm in mindless patterns. False intimacy—it was a useful tool. "It's different to how it was in the war. Your powers aren't the same."

"Quite so. You know what I was before?"

"One of the archmages. He was as well."

"You can say his name, I won't be upset. But yes, we were archmages. Power over time and distance, able to transport and transform. Not an easy skill, I assure you. Addison was always the more scholarly of us, I confess, I wanted to get more experience."

I didn't dare mention the notebook, still on the dresser in the nest. Or my questions. He tugged me up, so my body slid higher and I was nestled into his neck. "You were more practical."

"That's a kind way to say I was stupid." He chuckled, pecked a kiss to my hair. "It meant my magic was less precise than his but had a wider reach. Preferable in a battle. It also meant when I was depleted for so long there was less structure to draw back from. When I recovered my strength physically, the magic was different."

"Your skills didn't match your connection," I said.

"Exactly. What I use now is hungrier than it was in the war. I can still use my skills, and thrall, they haven't departed me, but the costs are higher. To balance that, I need more power."

"Why do you kill them?"

"I don't have fangs, darling. As you know." He tapped my upper lip, against one of the gaps. My whole core seethed with the need to punch his fingers away but I kept still, nodding. "Getting blood requires more direct methods. And for those who I tried to bond with, the results were poor. It was a mercy to let them end and take my energy back. Arif was the last one. He couldn't do anything but weep."

He hadn't even done that when I'd seen him, just stared. I swallowed down my sickness, sadness, screwing my eyes closed. "He was in a poor way."

"You tried to help him. I saw you scream at Garrett, roar him down despite being so scared."

"You were that close?"

"I'd gone to instruct my men and there you were, causing havoc. It caught my curiosity." I shrank at the fondness in his voice.

"Does it not seem wrong to you?"

"Killing to help myself? No more so than fighting the war. I killed then. You've killed, to protect yourself."

"You saw that too?"

"Easy to watch from the shadows. I've been close to Addison, on and off, for years." They'd been right about Arif, then. Taken because of his link to them. I nodded for him to continue, his voice almost wistful. "Less so Tobias. He's so wrapped up in his guilt he might recognise me, even with henna in my hair. The hunger changed me, but there's enough of me left for him to know."

"Would that hurt you?" I wanted it to. I wanted something to rend him apart the way he had me, but that wasn't going to happen. He was barely whole to break up again.

"Before I had you, yes." He leaned closer, curling up from the bed so he could kiss my forehead. "You know both sides of me. They only know their cherished memories."

I shook, unsure what to say to him. "Killing humans didn't seem to be something you liked, before."

"I don't enjoy it now; it's simply a necessity. Are you afraid I'd do the same to you?"

Yes. "No. I find it hard to balance the two stances."

"Then put it aside and don't think on it now." He wrapped his arms around my back, hugging me to him. "You've had much upheaval in the last few days. You should rest."

"Don't thrall me." It was out before I could stop it, the fear in my voice alien. I'd shook off Addison's, but his had been suggestion, not the cudgel of Mark's will. Poor Tim.

I'd hunched against him, wound tight like a cornered cat, and he shushed me as he stroked my back. "I won't, darling. You fought so well against my thrall last time I wouldn't want to exhaust you. You're much better than I expected from one of your school."

"What?"

"Nicnevin, while doubtless strong, have always been quick to fold. They could have helped, in the war, but they closed their doors and bolstered their defences, admitting none. Helping none. Too focused on protecting their mages to sacrifice anything for the cause. They've always been brutes, even to their own, but they were smart there."

We never went to table at the war, that was known. Because of the risks. Because of how many could have been killed. "We always welcome other mages, even if only for a night."

Mark chuckled, reaching up to pet my hair. "I'm sure they do now."

His grip did not lessen but he returned to stroking my back. I closed my eyes and tried to make my breathing slow and even.

# Chapter 54

The days became quiet and steady in the strange new house, passing in an irregular blur. Mark was the only vampire here, the humans made up of Rose and a few other servants who seemed to take to my arrival in stride. It was a huge space for so few people. I could go all morning without seeing someone, eat breakfast alone with no one calling out for me. No experiments or spell discussions, no trips out to the city.

I'd spent a few days mapping the house to my mind and Mark let me. No room was out of bounds, no space locked to my hungry curiosity: it was all laid out for me to root through like a truffle pig. My Bluebeard had no forbidden door with tell-tale key, just a yearning gaze and a bloody cellar.

Mark left in the morning, up with the lark and out the door. I laid in the blushing dawn, feeling the sparse warmth from his body dissipate. Then I rose and began my own day.

I made a routine as the days bled together. Practicing with my energy in the mirror had yielded nothing but tears, and I needed something to distract me from worrying the wound like a fresh bruise. In the morning I took to the library, picking through the shelves and taking books to my little room, now a sort of study. A large desk had been placed underneath the window with a chair to accompany it, and piles of papers and ink.

I wondered if this was what the nuns in the college experienced, shut up with nothing but the burden of research and the certainty of the coming night, I didn't linger long in that thought. I wasn't making discoveries for the colleges, but I had access to texts about vampire history and family lines, most of which I could read.

A knock sounded at the door, along with my name. "Ena?"

"Come in."

Rose poked her head into the room. Her eyes were watery, red around the corners, and there was a low tremble to her voice. "There's someone at the door. I wouldn't usually trouble you, but they seem quite insistent to speak to someone and Mark's away."

I blinked at her then stood, shaking myself out of the shock. "Who is it?"

"He says he's from one of the colleges." My heart leapt to my throat, unruly as a colt. "I fear it'll be about me, I daren't meet him."

"About you?"

"Healers are usually accounted for after they leave the schools. When my father took me out, there would be a record that I left but not one of where I went. What if he's here for that?"

Unlikely, given it had been so long, but an excellent excuse for me to see someone sane. I nodded, crossing to her. "Don't fret. Take my lead, and we'll tell Mark together when he gets back."

"What if he's angry?"

"He won't be. Let's go and see who it is."

She led me quickly down to the front door where I saw one of the servants, David, arguing with someone at the threshold. David was a solid man, but bookish, not at all suited to blocking a door.

"You cannot come in, sir," he said, pleading.

"I can and I shall." My stomach sank. Descending the steps, the open door revealed Ben, dressed up in formal attire and shaved. He suited it better than the scruff of the road.

"I am here on official business, and I will come back with a constable if I'm prevented in executing it." He puffed his chest out, scowling when he saw me. I understood what he meant with that line, the threat of bringing authority, and from that I could guess the act he was playing at. Alright, we both knew the steps to this dance.

"No need for raised voices, I'm sure. Why don't we go through to the drawing room and talk like reasonable people over a cup of tea? I'm sure we can do that, can't we, Mr?"

"Joseph Finnemore."

"Well met, Mr Finnemore. Can you spare us the time for a cup? The master of the house is out for the morning but I'm happy to assist."

"I'm sure that will serve as a start." The loathing in his eyes was real enough, no act there.

"My thanks." I inclined my head, all easy, closed-mouth smiles. "If you come this way. My companion will act as chaperone."

"I would prefer privacy for the nature of the discussion." His tone was clipped, another scowl sent at Rose who had her chin tucked to her chest. She trembled, despite the iron grip she had on her own arms, and it would be cruelty to make her endure the entire meeting.

"You can see why that might give a lady pause, no?" I asked, leading us to one of the front-facing rooms. All the better for seeing the drive, and any approaching company.

"I'm not interested in excuses; I merely want to be about my business."

"Alright. Why don't you help with the tea?" I set a hand on Rose's shoulder, winking, and she shot off. "The drawing room has the most sun this time of the morning, so if it's too bright for you please say."

We entered the airy space, the curtains swept back from the long windows, and I pointed him towards a chair where the sun would be warm but not too bright, letting him sit before I took the one opposite. They were upholstered and fussy, more effort to keep clean than they were worth, but offering him the best spot in the house was polite.

My chest was tight as he stared at me. I wanted him to take the lead in whatever this was, so I waited for him to speak.

"There doesn't seem to be many staff for such a house," he said.

"The master keeps a small retinue. For an immortal he's less ostentatious than some."

"An immortal with at least two women who are trained under his roof. Your magic's clearly visible." So that was how he'd found me. I was right that it would give me away.

"I was injured recently, my ability to shield's been damaged. I don't know the time for recovery yet, I'd need to speak to a healer. I've taken steps to isolate myself, meantime, so it shouldn't impact anyone else." He'd be able to pick up enough from that. We had done similar dances before on jobs, the need to speak between lines lest there be listening ears.

"That must have been a significant injury." His smile was thin, cruel.

"Yes. Worse than the time I broke some fingers." His jaw tightened, eyes dark, but he kept the act going.

"A painful event, I'm told." He flexed his hand, showing a healer had helped him.

"The master of the house is away until the afternoon, so if you require anything from him, I must ask you to return. Or I could ask him to stay back tomorrow morning, though I'm unsure of his plans for the week."

"You're left to tend the house so frequently?"

"My companion is a diligent worker, and healer."

"I'm sure you're kept busy, then. If I were to return later, there would likely be a colleague." Two of them could come and get me. That would be him and one of the others, though I'd never been told who else was down. The risk of them against the risk of Mark sat like severed heads on a scale in my mind, neither appealing.

"I wouldn't want to inconvenience you, making a colleague travel as well."

"We often travel together. One of our colleagues was killed, alone, so we don't visit alone anymore. I came here today as I noticed your energy, it was unusual enough for an enquiry." He'd not brought backup. Stupid, stupid man.

My heart wavered; the memory of Tim livid behind my lids. "I'm sorry for your troubles."

"Such is the nature of our work. He was a valued member."

I looked out at the window to blink away wetness in my eyes, when a knock sounded on the door. David brought the tea in on a small trolley, the cups rattling as they bumped over the carpet.

"Would you like a bite to eat, mistress?" he asked.

"No, thank you, just tea is lovely." I brought my best smile up, taking the offered cup.

"Mistress?" Ben repeated after David had left.

"I'm considered the lady of the house. I do ask them to call me my name."

He snorted, putting the tea down with a clatter. "A fine step up."

"It suits the owner."

"And you're here as his companion?"

"I joined the house unexpectedly. My injury finds me so I can't leave."

His gaze narrowed at that, eyes ticking over my shape. "You do look unwell, if I may be so bold. Would you prefer to seek treatment?" The college could heal me quicker than waiting for the wound to resolve. I knew that.

"I'm not sure the current plans for the house allow such." I took a sip of tea to warm myself—I was chilled despite the sunshine.

He stared me down, tongue slipping out to wet his lower lip. "If you have an ailment it would be better to seek treatment. There's no benefit in letting a matter linger."

"I fear it's not one with a swift remedy."

"A better reason to seek treatment sooner. If you remain unwell then it could be a cause for other visits." So there were more people than Ben looking. That could mean a Council member was down, they would easily track me.

"I'm unsure how wise that would be. The household is busy and it's not easy to seek—"

The door opened with a loud thud, the shaking figure of Mark filling the space. He was pale, as ever, but slick with sweat like he'd been dipped in a river.

# Chapter 55

"Run," I hissed, my heart freezing with fear.

"Well met, sir, I'm Joseph Finnemore and I'm here with—" Ben rose, striding forward, only to meet Mark's hand around his throat. He lifted like a doll, and Mark slammed him into the wall with force enough to bounce paintings on their hangings.

"I know who you are." Mark's teeth were bared, the words barely a growl around them.

"Mark, he's not a threat." I was up, my legs unsteady as I ran to their tangled figures.

"You're not the judge of that." Mark's fingers tightened around Ben's throat. Ben was kicking, trying to pry the hand from his neck but to no avail. He punched Mark once, twice, scrabbling for purchase, but it was like beating stone. I yanked Mark's shoulder, but trying to pull him off was useless.

"I know him better than you do, and I know his powers. He's not a threat to you." I put my hand on Mark's wrist, trying to draw his ire my way, to dispel it. "He thought he was being clever sneaking in."

"He means to take you from me."

"She's mine, we're betrothed," Ben squeaked and I kicked his shin. A petty spite. His face was a hideous red and I feared the blood vessels in his eyes would pop if he didn't get air.

"You said that at the nest as well. Like you could even earn her." Mark squeezed tighter. Ben's eyes started to roll.

He was going to kill him.

Not another one, I couldn't see another one. I had nothing to bargain with, but he only had one arm on Ben—I could work with that. I tightened my grip on his wrist, screwing my eyes shut. *"Briseadh."*

The crunch of bone under my fingers was loud, disgustingly familiar, but it loosened the grip on Ben's throat and he sucked in air.

"And who is he to you that you'd do that for him?"

I was against the wall, wrists pinned above me. My head smarted from an impact I hadn't even registered, pain distant compared to the fear narrowing my vision. Mark's face was so close I could see the bands in his eyes, the wide, dark pupils that bored into mine.

"His absence would be noted," I said. I hated the tremor there. Ben was discarded on the floor, gasping like he'd been underwater.

Mark barked a laugh, bitter. "You didn't do that for the other one."

"I would have if you had let me." I surged at him, anger usurping my fear. "You gave me no choice!"

He sagged a little, still pinning my wrists but his shoulders and head dropping. His left hand was at an odd angle, twitching as it healed. "You love him."

"I don't."

"Why should I not snuff him out then? He's come here to take you, to hurt you. Why are you defending him?"

"Because I don't want you to murder him! A college coming here would draw attention. Please, if only for Rose, think about this."

"Think about this instead." Ben grabbed Mark's ankle, stabbing a small blade into his thigh, deep enough to kill a human.

Mark howled, dropping me to pounce on Ben and start beating him. It was horribly one-sided, Ben's attempts to defend himself batted away. He had no fire to draw from, he couldn't use his powers without an incantation and there was no let-up to allow him to growl one out. I heard an ugly crack of bone before I could shake my voice free.

"Mark, *please*. I'll stay."

He stilled, one hand gripping Ben's shirt. "What?"

"I'll stay. Willingly."

"Ena, no." Ben groaned and Mark punched him again, a wet squelch coming from Ben's nose.

"Tell me again," Mark said. He dropped Ben, stalking back to me and crowding me against the wall. "Repeat what you said."

"If you let him go, alive, I'll stay here with you. I could get out, now, I could leave, but if you let him go I won't try to run."

He leaned down close, so our noses nearly touched. "How could you leave? Your magic's unruly. Wounded. *Useless*."

"Broke your wrist, didn't it?" His eyes narrowed and for a few agonising heartbeats I met the stare of a predator, something inhuman and strange evaluating my words. "You can feel me like I feel you, you said. So feel. I'm not lying."

"Ena." Ben was still on the ground, bloodied but able to roll over. He crawled closer.

"Quiet." Mark tracked over and kicked him once, hard, in the face. I flinched at the moan Ben gave, his hands over his mouth. Blood splattered to the floor when he looked up. Mark came back to me, pressed up like he had simply been distracted. There was nowhere left to bargain between him and the wall.

I gripped his hand tighter, pressing it against my chest again. "Feel."

His eyes flicked between his hand and my eyes, like he was trying to weigh up what was there, or he might dig in to examine it. His left hand was fine now. Like I'd done nothing. "You have something else nestled in there."

"I was sent to the college late. I got more knowledge than most children before they're taught. I won't use it, if you let him go."

"How can I trust you when you've been lying to me?"

"I never lied." I tilted my chin at him, matching those calculating eyes. "I offered to start the fire for you in the library, first day I woke. Let him go."

"Don't listen to her," Ben said, hitching himself up on his elbows. His face was a mess, swollen and covered in red, one eye nearly closed. "She was to be mine for years, she loved me. I'll come back for her."

I tried to tear away from Mark, near overcome with an urge to beat Ben's face in. Was he so idiotic that he couldn't see I was keeping him safe?

Mark kept a hold of me, arms around my waist despite my thrashing until I was draped over, leaning down towards Ben. "I never loved you! You were a bully, you hated me. You only wanted to fuck me because of the kids it could bring you."

"That's not true." Gods, he sounded small. I recoiled at the pain in Ben's voice, clear despite the swollen lips. "We were promised. Your ambition was always as hungry as mine, whatever you tell yourself. You achieved like I did. We match."

"I said I'd marry you because it was that or the nunnery. And I ran, rather than be stuck with your child on my hip." Mark laughed and if I'd had my knife I would have stabbed him. I was rotten, tongue heavy and stomach churning from such cruelty, but I needed Ben to leave.

"I accept your offer—" Mark's words snapped my attention back to him. "—subject to two additional terms."

"What?"

"One, I want to know more about your magic. And two, I want to marry you."

I looked back at him, his grin smug, my heart heavy. "Marry me?"

"Yes." He nodded, hands slipping down from their grip on my waist to my hips, pulling me closer to him.

"I'm human, I'm going to die."

"That's not guaranteed." He meant to turn me, of course. Married for eternity. I'd need to read more of those books on lore, see if there was vampiric divorce. Or just suicide. Gods above.

"I'm not letting you do this." Ben began crawling over, dragging himself by the elbows, and I couldn't stand to look at him.

"Yes, just let him go!"

"Excellent." Mark pulled me forward into a kiss, surprisingly gentle for the bitterness in his eyes. It was brief, more a show for Ben than anything else, but his hand cupped the back of my head to hold me in place. When we parted, he was grinning and bright-eyed, sighing happily.

"Was that necessary?"

"I always was a romantic." He wrinkled his nose at me, almost playful, before he turned to Ben. "Now, my unlucky Benjamin, we must deal with you. Ena has bought you your freedom, and that was her doing not yours. Remember that. However, there's still a price for what you've done. I always take my prices in blood."

"Fuck you." Ben spat, panting against pain. A rib in the lungs, his face, that kick, any of it could have pained him. I kept my eyes on Mark, unwilling to look for more agony.

"You're not to my tastes. Though since we're betrothed, now, maybe Ena and I will, soon." Mark threw a wink my way but there was nothing of him in it—I knew this voice, this bravado. This was Luc down in the dungeon and throwing empty threats. This was performance.

Ben snorted, gagged, spat blood. "She'll never love you."

Mark knelt, fisting a handful of Ben's hair so he could yank it back, bring them face-to-face. "She'll never love you. I've a long time to build my relationship with her. Even more than your precious years together. Now, shall I take your greedy eyes, or your lying tongue?"

"Mark!" My throat clenched at the threat.

"You bought his freedom, darling, but I never said he'd leave unharmed. Just like you never said you didn't have magic." He looked back at me, grip tightening in Ben's hair. "Now, he can pick, or I can. I don't like you, Benjamin, so I'd pick whatever I thought would make your life worse, but I'm a fair man. You can choose. I'll even be sure it doesn't hurt."

"You can't." I was begging, again, begging not to have to see this, to know this.

"Go and get Rose. I'll be sure he doesn't bleed out. I might even use the pieces if I think they're of good enough quality."

I couldn't move, legs useless under me as I stared at them. Ben shook his head, trembling from the unnatural arc in his neck. "Rose, is she the healer?"

"Yes," I said. My fingernails dug into my thighs; the material of my skirts gripped until it could tear. I couldn't fight Mark, not in hand to hand. I had no knife, and breaking his bones had lasted minutes, I couldn't get them separated.

"Go get her. My ribs will get me if he doesn't."

"I did hear one crack. Maybe more. I was distracted by the knife in my leg." Mark yanked the hair in his fist and I ran from the room, heart in my throat as I called for Rose.

# Chapter 56

Like a coward I didn't return to the drawing room after I found Rose. I fled to the library, shot up a ladder. There was a snug spot between two bookcases, almost in a corner, that I squeezed myself into. I brought my knees up to my chest, arms on top to hide my face, and hunkered down. A fine place to sit and cry, to shake until my muscles gave up.

After the shaking stopped I stayed where I was, watching the sky change colour as I shivered from the cold stone and wood around me. At some point the sound of a carriage leaving came through the window. My leg cramped from being folded up so long, the pain short and vicious, and after a while that faded, too.

Hiding here would not fix what I had done. It wouldn't fix whatever happened to Ben. It would only stall the inevitable. But sometimes that was enough, a little room to breathe away from this vice of a man. It had to be a relationship now. Gods.

"I'm coming up, darling." Mark's voice floated towards me in gentle warning. He didn't need to give me one. He was being careful.

Mercifully he moved at a human pace. I counted his footsteps as they approached, habit more than anything—I couldn't run, my legs were numb, and there would be no point. He sat in front of me, taking up the whole walkway with his long legs; I could see them from the sliver of space at my sides.

"I wanted to talk to you."

I brought my head up to look at him. His clothes were different, both shirt and trousers, so he had cleaned up before he came to find me. A kindness. I nodded for him to continue.

"I've sent Benjamin back to the city. We know where he was staying, and one of the staff will ensure he's left with someone." He paused and I nodded at him, inclining my head in thanks. He trailed his fingers over mine, testing. I didn't flinch. Maybe my arms were numb too. "I'm sorry you had to see me like that. I should have tempered myself."

I coughed as the words caught in my throat, dry from crying. "What did you take?"

"His tongue. I put him to sleep and Rose healed him so he wouldn't choke on the blood." It was so quick, that slip back into ordered viciousness. Not cruelty; he was carefully considerate, just ruthless.

I nodded and looked down at my knees, taking a deep breath to steady my words. "That's the better way for it."

"He was braver than I expected, for one of yours. He never sought to bargain, though he never used his magic either. If your Council had come with even half of that energy in the war, rather than holing up, things may have been different."

"The Council are their own sort. We're different."

"I don't mean you, my dove, I'd never mean you. You're the cuckoo in the nest, hiding with your extra magic. You're better than them."

"I left." It was all I could think to say. I left, and now I was here. Now Ben was maimed, and Tim was dead, and gods above I hoped Tiffany was still in Edinburgh, still working stupid, old men with her charms and spells and not the next one I had to see bloodied. Please, please.

"I wanted to apologise for something else too." He shuffled closer, so he could lean in and cup my cheek. "I'm sorry that our first kiss was out of spite. I regret that."

"It was for show. Hardly counts."

"Look at me, sweet." He tugged lightly at my cheek, a suggestion rather than an order, and I peered up at him. "I shouldn't have done that."

"Thank you for apologising." I ducked my head, though his hand stayed in place.

He was quiet for an awful, stretching moment. I counted my heart-beats, willing him to speak, and when he did it was little above a whisper. "Are you afraid of me?"

"I was. When you had me up against the wall."

"I thought you loved him. I failed to see how this was different to the other man."

"Timothy. I'd grown up with him since I was seven. He was my friend. I would have begged for him, if I could." My voice crackled and I covered my face, elbows down at my hips so I could be as small as possible, hide from him. "Gods, I would have, and you snapped his neck."

"I'm sorry. I'm sorry, darling, come here." Mark took my shoulders, pulling me up and around so he could nestle me into his chest. I shook my head but there was no real fight to it, I had no hate left to throw at him. He shushed me, rocking me back and forth as he stroked my hair. "I'm sorry I hurt you."

I cried, covering my face against his honeyed words, the slow thaw of my frozen emotions threatening to rush out over me. Absolutely not. I would not break before him. I would not be shards like Henry, or a twisted creature like him, changed into someone I was not because of a long, slow agony. I took a shuddering breath, wiping my face down and giving myself two sharp slaps with both palms before I sat up to look at him properly. We were tangled up, my arse on the floor but my back and legs supported by his opposite thighs, so there was nowhere to go but his chest or the wall he had pulled me away from.

"It was a shock to see you so like you were in your memories. I'm glad that you made sure he was healed, thank you," I said.

Mark looked at me carefully, brows down low and lips pressed together in a crinkled line. "Why did you hit yourself, sweet?"

I laughed, shaking my head. "That's not a hit, just some slaps to focus the mind. It's one of the things you learn in the training. If you shake a bad mood off before it takes root it can save hours of tears."

"Hours." He repeated, swallowing around the word. "I would let you cry for hours, if you need to."

I smiled, setting a hand on his chest. "That won't remedy anything, so best not."

He held me like one did a snake in the evening, when they might bite or might lazily curl up, unsafe until some unknown decision had been made. "Will you come and eat with me?"

I wrinkled my nose. "I don't have much of an appetite."

"I know, but it's almost evening. We can share something if you don't feel well enough to eat a full meal."

"Alright."

He stood, taking my hands and pulling me up with him. His hands were warmer than mine for once.

# Chapter 57

I found Rose in the kitchen the next morning, trembling as she washed a tea-set.

"You alright?" I asked. She jumped, teapot leaping out of her hands, and I scooped to catch it before it hit the floor.

"I'm sorry." She clamped a hand to her mouth, eyes wide as the cups drying beside her.

"It's alright, it didn't break." I set the pot down, upside down so the water could drip out. "What's wrong?"

"Nothing." She yanked up a quick smile, more of a grimace.

"You're not a great liar, chicken."

"Chicken?"

"Chicken Licken, the sky is falling. I used to read it to the younger ones. What ails you?"

Rose frowned at me and turned back to the sink, shoving her hands in the water. "I don't wish to speak about it. I'm sure you're already furious enough with me. And I'm quite livid with you."

"Why's that then?" I took a towel and started drying.

Her nostrils flared but she kept her tone civil. "You could have told me you knew the man."

"I didn't know what he was coming to do. If it was something stupid, I wanted the chance to talk him out of it. Or be sure you were safe. My school is subtle but not kind."

"Meaning?"

"He'd slit your throat if he thought you were going to scream. Or burn your voice away. I didn't want that."

"How can I believe that?" she spat, water sloshing in the basin when she tossed the cloth down.

"I could have gone out the window with him after David gave us tea. If I wanted to be gone from here, I would be, no matter how sweet you are." It was a half lie.

She stilled, shaking her head, then sobbed. It was a hiccoughing, broken sound. "Don't say that. I had to heal him. After his tongue was—" She broke off, one hand going to her throat. "It goes so deep into your mouth."

"Come here." I pulled her to me, hugging her close. "It was a grim thing. You shouldn't have had to do that. Mark's temper got the better of him."

"The man just kept laughing. He knew his tongue was going, he'd chosen it, and he kept laughing until Mark put him to sleep. I've never seen Mark so incensed."

"He's probably shielded you from that. He wouldn't want you to be scared." I stroked her hair and rocked her like I would one of the youngsters in the college. She deserved some softness, even if it was a role to play.

"He fears you're scared of him." Her words were muffled into my chest, her head tucked beside my chin.

"I'm not scared of much."

"You should tell him that. He was sick with nerves after he did it. I think he knew it was a bad thing."

"He was sending a message. Those aren't pretty things."

"You talk like you've been to war."

"Never war, no. Politics, or marriage talks, things where you need a read on people. That's me."

"You've killed people, though."

I jarred at the comment, stepping back from her. "What makes you say that?"

"Mark mentioned it. That you killed like he did, in the college. That's why you were such a good match, you both understood the need. He argued with that man about it." Her head ducked down, looking at her shoes as she twisted her hands.

I opened my mouth but none of the tangled words would come out, snaring together into a mess. I took a deep breath and shook my head, managing a small smile. "It's probably different between immortals and mortals, but yes. I know sometimes a life must end. It's not easy."

"You shout sometimes in your sleep. I heard you then, too." I should sleep in the stable at this rate.

"Sorry. Are you preparing this for the company?" I nodded to the tea-set. He'd mentioned a visit in passing last night.

"Yes."

I nodded, fingers tracing over one of the knives in the drying pile. It was different to the others, the flat blade about half as wide as my thumb and with a line of notes engraved across it. I picked it up, holding it to the light to read the small words there too. The sharp edge was keen, wet from the suds. "This is beautiful."

"I'm fond of it." Rose took it from me, smiling as she slid it into a pocket. "It was a gift. I like to take care of it."

"It looks old, you must have taken good care of it."

"I have. I don't know if he's told you who is coming, I forget their names quite often, but they're nice. Mark sometimes gets cross with them because they talk about the war, but they mean well."

"I'll be nice."

She nodded, catching my hand. "You've always been nice with me. Can you do the same with him?"

"You've only known me a few weeks," I said, shaking my head. "I might be pretending to be nice to get your guard down."

"You didn't bargain for that man in deception. That was desperation."

I huffed out a laugh, unable to argue as I let go of her hand. "Can I help at all?"

"They're not due for a little while. I'll serve when they do. Mark will want to show you off I'm sure, so don't feel you have to do anything."

I left the room, heading for the library. I would read until I had to present well.

# Chapter 58

The carriage arrived a little before noon. A rude time to arrive, to me. I had no idea of rightness anymore, some part of me was still spinning on the ice of repressed feelings and expectations. Treat it like a job, keep the focus on the goal. I could find a new goal once this meeting was over.

"Ena?" Mark's voice called through the library, and I set my book down, walking over to meet him.

"I heard the coach."

He grasped my hands in his, running his thumbs over my knuckles. "Do you feel well enough for company?"

I laughed, but it sounded brittle even to me. "Why do you ask that?"

"You're drawn, sweet. Did you eat breakfast?"

"I didn't have much appetite. I'll have something with the tea, though."

His face pinched as he stroked my hair, tucking some behind my ear. "Will you eat with me later? I like us taking meals together."

"Of course." I squeezed his hands, our cold fingers overlapping. He was almost warmer than me again. "Is there anything I should know about these folk before we see them?"

"They're not best pleased with me currently, but they should be civil. They'll want to talk about some things you may find distressing. If you need to leave at any point, let me know."

"Distressing?"

"They're not fond of humans. Or too fond, depending on the human."

"Right. Will I be safe, given..." I trailed off, waving a hand to my throat.

"Your magic is tempting, but I'm sure they'll control themselves. And if they don't, you're my darling, I'll remind them to behave."

"Of course." I smiled, accepted the hug he pulled me into.

"Don't push yourself too hard today." It was so earnest, the way he whispered it into my ear like a lover. The way he held me a little tighter like I'd slip away.

"I'll soon let you know if I need to leave. Have I been meek or mild thus far?"

He grimaced as we parted but shook his head. "No. Now—we're being terrible hosts. Let us go down."

He offered his arm, and I slipped mine into the waiting space, stepping up close to him. We looked like a good couple to anyone else. It was expected to be gracious and warm to guests, so I could be that. Reading on vampire history hadn't given me much other insight but at least I could play to known standards.

Mark kept me on his arm as he opened the door to the morning room.

Honey-warm hair and amber eyes greeted me, and my stomach sank low into itself as I spotted the accompanying man's dark, unruly hair. It didn't suit him as well as he thought it did.

"Oswyn, Agnes, a delight to have your company," Mark said. Straight into showmanship, a bright smile that didn't show his teeth. I matched it, grip on Mark's elbow tightening a little as I set my shoulders back.

"So that's why you're gallivanting around, is it?" Oswyn scowled at me, wrinkling his nose. "The pair in that wretched nest weren't enough for you, girl?"

"Her magic is out. Did you do that on purpose to spook us, little lamb?" Agnes asked, half rising towards me. Oswyn put a large hand on her wrist, tugging her back down.

"My apologies. My magic hasn't calmed to being here yet." I smiled at her, joining Mark on a love seat so we were sat across from the other couple. It could have been any family friend visiting a newly engaged pair, good wishes and good company, but the scene made me swallow a heave.

"I'd love you to join us again." She patted the space between them.

"I'm afraid not." Mark wrapped an arm around my shoulders.

"Wrapped around her finger just like the others," Oswyn grumbled.

"Please don't be mistaken, I'd never done anything romantic with either Addison or Tobias. They simply didn't want you to touch me anymore." I leaned into Mark's chest briefly, hand brushing over the weave of his shirt. "It was a vulgar method, but he's protective of his humans."

"Wouldn't you know."

"Oswyn, behave. I think it's wonderful that she's with Luc. It means we get more of her company." Agnes smiled, fangs on show.

"I'm pleased we can be so civil." Mark took my hand, entwining our fingers, and I let my free hand slip onto my lap and towards the pretty knife at his hip.

"Civil is the least of what I'll be if we don't get matters back on track. You've been neglecting your end of our arrangement," Oswyn said. Agnes nodded, eyes lighting up when someone knocked on the door.

Rose entered with the tea service on a large tray, carefully giving everyone their cup and saucer, leaving the milk and sugar on a small table beside the chairs.

"Pretty little thing," Agnes cooed.

"Thank you, mistress." Rose took two quick steps backwards, out of reach, and curtsied before she retreated out the door.

"She knows her place," Oswyn said. He wrinkled his nose at the drink but sipped it anyway.

Mark coughed, refocusing the group. "Forgive my lack of attention. We had an intruder at the property yesterday." No blood on the carpets at least. That was either Rose's skill or someone's cleaning. I didn't know which was better anymore.

"She attracts more trouble than a bed warmer's worth," Oswyn said. He nodded at me, and I smiled silently back. Be nice. Polite. Docile would be too far in a room of predators but I could be nice until he gave me a reason otherwise.

Idly, I imagined what it would be like to thump him, crack into that square jaw. I hadn't fought an immortal, yet, but one solid hit would be satisfying. Probably wouldn't break a bone but I could try, aim at that lovely hinge under the ear and shatter it. Terminal, once he realised what I'd done, but I'd go out smiling.

"No more than my bodies in the city. You were indulgent of them." Mark smiled over the lip of his cup. This was fun, his voice was as sweet as syrup. If we were all going to be playing that game I could keep up.

Oswyn tutted. "You need to take power, it leaves packaging. But if we don't do something soon this impromptu opportunity will be lost."

"They are wracked with worry about her. Beside themselves. Distracted," Agnes said.

"Strike in haste and retreat in speed, Oswyn. You aren't a match for Addison. You need to be patient. Our methods will have to change given Ena's removal."

"I don't see why they should, use their anguish against them," Oswyn said.

"That didn't work well last time. Was it five Tobias killed, or six? I know Addison took Henry's head, so it must have been five nobles, yes?" I looked to Mark, keeping my face as open as I could.

"He killed his brother," Agnes said. "Poor Edmund, he was my sister's favourite child."

Edmund who had killed their father. Edmund, southern port holding, one of those that had been there when Henry trapped Luc. I'd seen him in the sliver of Henry but hadn't brought the items to bear in my mind. The way Tobias had talked about the war…

"Sister?" I repeated, glancing between the two of them, gaze settling to Oswyn. "I thought you were the blood relative?"

"No. They took after their father more than my sister, but I am the familial link." Agnes still had her fangs out. I took Oswyn in again—the chest, the shoulders, the unruly hair. The eyes, so similar to be unsettling.

"Forgive me, I failed to see the likeness in you. And I'm sorry for all your losses, it must be hard to see Tobias so often with that in your heart. But Tobias did kill his brother, because he thought my sweetness here was dead. Grief spurred him on." I gripped Mark's fingers tighter, my hand on his thigh for a light squeeze there too. "I don't think leveraging grief will work as you anticipate. You need to wait for the depression, that takes longer."

"And how would you know that?" Oswyn asked. He was glowering at me, almost a shine in that tabby-cat gold.

"Have you heard of the College of Nicnevin? I'm not sure if you will have, we're not fond of vampires. We're popular consultants for wedding negotiations, professional contracts and bodyguards. If you think power dynamics are so different for the immortals, I'm willing to learn, but in my experience thus far it's remarkably similar."

"You think your little tricks work with us?" Oswyn scoffed.

"I think Addison made you flee his house using the same tactics I've used to get rid of overeager suitors. You vanished quite quick after that." I tilted my head to one side, looking him over. "I can tell you how I'd do it. With the nest."

"Ena." Mark's warning was gentle but firm, a squeeze of my fingers accompanying the words.

"Oh no, let her go on. I'd love to know how she would hurt them," Agnes said. She leaned forward, eyes on me as she licked her lips. She was ravenous, a starved dog on a chain, and I wondered if that slim figure was her choice.

"Addison's easy—hurt the nest. He prides himself on what he created, so you destroy it. We'd probably use fire to draw them, then take out the soldiers, the untrained mage next. Leave the doctor and the human alive, though. There must be something to lose, otherwise they'll go feral."

"How do you mean?" Agnes asked.

"People with nothing to lose are very dangerous. You keep something they love, and you use it as the screw to tighten their binds. The human would be the obvious one, Addison loves him, but the doctor might work. Tobias has more of a soft spot for him. Then, once that's taken care of, you move on the immortals."

It was utter tripe, largely, but a believable line. Addison would wreak bloody vengeance on anyone who touched his sired, and I'd witnessed how ruthless Tobias could be with a sword. Anyone trying this plan would be torn apart. I found myself enjoying that.

"Tobias must be left alive." The yearning in her voice made my throat tighten, almost as much as the light in her eyes brought a roil to my gut, but I smiled, nodded, leaned into Mark's arm again.

"You've given this some thought." Oswyn was practically sullen, sitting back in the settee like he was a child bored at church.

"It's natural I'd consider my options, given my training. You have different issues though, don't you?"

Oswyn's brows quirked. "Such as?"

"Legitimacy. Tobias is your rake of a nephew, but he fought in the war. Killed many. Apologies, again, for that reminder." I inclined my head to Agnes, a conciliatory smile. "But he's proved his merit. You're the default. You want something more prestigious than that, don't you?"

He was in front of me, one hand at my throat as he leaned in close. "Say that again."

"Oswyn, be aware of your place," Mark said. He didn't rise to challenge the hand on my skin, though, and I brought up my prettiest smile, baring teeth, as I leaned into the grip.

"You haven't proven yourself and it itches under your skin, doesn't it? You're the head of the family and Tobias could sidle in and take everything from you." I glanced to Agnes again, winking. "What a curse to bear, for such a very long life."

"Insolent bitch." The bright sparks of his fist against my nose were a marvel—a glorious familiarity from the college—and I revelled in the urge to fight.

I surged up against his grip, grabbing his tunic so I could drag him closer to me, spit the blood flooding into my mouth across his face with a cackling laugh. "That's all you can do, isn't it Oswyn? Be a nasty little bully. No brave sacrifices for you. No wonder you have to break him to be sure of your place."

"It would be best of you to go back to the settee. Now." Mark had his knife out, twirling the handle between two long fingers and flicking his wrist so the blade swung in a lazy figure eight.

"You'll let her speak to me like that?" I let go and Oswyn stepped back, wiping his face off with a corner of his tunic.

"Ena, go find Rose to heal your nose."

"It's not broken." I pushed it either way, showing him the clean movement. Tears prickled in my eyes, already swelling skin flaring in protest: a pain that was pure and bright. I couldn't care for the tears, it was such a relief to have something tangible to cause the pain. I turned back to Oswyn. "See how a silly little human can do this? You're not smart enough to get behind Addison and Tobias. You should listen to Mark."

Oswyn gawked, spinning on his heel to sit beside Agnes. She was grinning like a cat, swaying in her seat as she leaned to kiss his cheek. I looked away before I could see if she licked him.

Glancing to Mark, I met his frown. His voice was calm, but his eyes had that same anger as yesterday. "You should listen to me, too. You need to conserve your strength."

I acquiesced, leaning in to kiss his jaw. "As you wish. It was lovely to see you both again." I stood, curtsied low enough to be polite and left the room.

# Chapter 59

I veered away from the kitchen, going to our bedroom instead. I'd wash up in the bathroom and wait for this disaster to be over.

It had been foolish to taunt Oswyn into hurting me but the thrill, the elation, was running through me like starlight. And why should the little toad not be reminded what he was? It would have been wiser to learn more of their plotting. If I'd held my tongue, I might have managed it, but it was too late to change that. I'd have to speak to Mark instead.

Pushing into the bedroom I went to the bathroom and turned the tap, letting it fill the sink. It wasn't a poor bathroom, nicer than some in the nest house. The sink and bath were pleasant enough, and the mirror, while small, showed me in stark form.

I was pale, and the blood across my mouth and chin was a vicious streak of red that painted me even whiter. A stupid clown with a miserable smile. Dark eyes, bags there despite the sleep I got cradled into Mark, and my collarbone was sharper than it used to be. I was never a frail thing but I could be mistaken for one like this. He was eating me up from the inside.

Shaking my head, I twisted the tap into stopping, dragging my eyes away. I soaked the washcloth in the water and let it steep for a few minutes, droplets of blood tapping a pattern into the trembling surface. There was a similar tremble in me, an inevitable flinch that would break this bubble of despair and let it flood out, but I couldn't afford to sink into pain and darkness while there were three immortals in the house.

Focus on it like it's a job. Get to the next breathing space, then regroup. Survive.

The facecloth was soaked and well chilled, so I plucked it up, wringing the excess out before I wiped the coating of blood from my chin then lips. I washed it out after each swipe, bringing my face back to myself. I lasted a few minutes at the quiet task, until the swirling in the water reminded me of the last time I had been cleaning blood, and I couldn't stop the sob that burst forth.

It was just a little thing, a creak from my throat, and I slapped a hand to my mouth lest more come. That jarred my nose, which began to bleed again, and between that and the unfurling blood in the water I sank, hands clasped over my face to stifle the cries that wracked me.

They kept coming, my shoulders hiking up as I curled into myself, tucking into the wall. Blood and tears coated my hands and stained my skirt, but I couldn't stop them long enough to stand and change.

# CHAPTER 60

"Ena? Ena." Someone was shaking my shoulders—Mark, knelt before me. We were in the bathroom, my hip and shoulder sore from being against the wall. My head was thick with crying. I must have fallen asleep after the sobbing finished. I patted my face, wincing at the layer of blood now sticky. Mark's eyes were wide as he stared at me, gripping my shoulders enough to hurt.

"Sorry, I must have lost track of time," I said, dizzy from the sudden awakening.

"Why didn't you go to Rose?"

"I wanted to wash myself up." I unfolded from my spot, wobbling as I tried to stand. Mark tugged me close to him, helping me up and manoeuvring me so I was stood before him. His shape blocked the door, and I shuffled on my feet for a way to get out. He grasped my chin, leaning close to inspect my face, brows low as he turned my cheek either way.

Dissatisfied with what he found, he sighed, plucking the discarded wash-cloth from the floor. "Why are you doing this?"

"What?"

"All of this. Stand there and let me clean you up." He filled the sink with fresh water, rubbing the cloth under it before lathering the soap.

I closed my eyes, swallowing the tightness in my throat. I wouldn't watch the water turn again. "I don't understand your question."

"You refuse to eat unless I make you. You're exhausted. You taunted Oswyn into lashing out at you, despite the fact he could have snapped your neck."

The laugh escaped me before I could stop it, and I flinched when he took my chin in hand again. "Oswyn was rude. Calling you the wrong name, talking like he was in charge. He can't overwhelm Addison without you, and he can't take Tobias on his own."

"He could have done you real harm." Mark's touch was disgustingly gentle, as if he were afraid he would break me. I bit into the side of my cheek, hard, focusing on the pain to keep still.

"Then he'd have to deal with you. And his wife. While he's rude, he's not entirely stupid."

"That isn't an answer." He kept wiping at my face, cleaning me with kitten swipes and an aching softness that made my stomach roil.

"I don't like the man or his arrogance. Just because Agnes wants to fuck her nephew he takes it out on you?"

Mark almost laughed. "Please, don't. I prefer not to think on it."

"Worried she'll get jealous because you managed what she hasn't?"

He huffed air, breath soft over my lips. "She won't allow Tobias to be killed, so we must do something else. Addison's the natural target, given the upset he's caused. Tobias would have to return to them if the nest was harmed. I didn't want to hurt them at first. I wanted them to be alone, as alone as I was. They can hardly look at each other without knives in their chests. It seemed right."

"Love like a hook in their heart. I saw it." I shivered. They deserved better than that. They all had, once.

"You don't seem upset." His grip softened enough to make me look at him again.

"You were stalking the nest. I'm hardly surprised you had ill intent. If the college had given me sanctuary, I might've been one of the mages you killed. You clocked my power enough to come and spook me off, maybe you'd have thought me a useful battery if you saw me alone in the city."

"Don't say it like that." He dropped the cloth in the water.

"That you would have killed me? You might. I don't know when you began to view me... differently."

"I could tell you." That hope in his voice, that softness, it made me want to claw his eyes out. As if he had the right to treat me like some wayward lover and not a trapped, fluttering thing.

"Spare me. It would seem trite given you're planning to kill your previous beaus." My chin was cold and the bathroom felt too small, Mark's frame taking up all the space as he stooped to care for me.

His smile was thin, stretched tight, but he shook his head. "That was enough to begin with. Then, Oswyn recognised me. He was the first for a long time. I don't mix with others much."

Hardly surprising. "What did he do?"

"He told me about Addison's efforts. How he was a nest head, bringing good humans into the fold. Trying to correct the horrors of the war, like it could be made better by siring new ones. Like he could replace what was lost." The last words were barely there, a whisper of wind on sand. He took my hands in his, broad thumbs rubbing over my knuckles. "And the way he looked at you, like you were sunshine. I saw that in the city. Even if he was trying to distance himself, he was fascinated. Worried. I hated seeing that, until I understood why."

"He's only fond because of knowledge. He agreed to teach me about his magic if I taught him about mine. He even gave me one of his notebooks, I was that poor a student." I kept telling myself that's what it had been. Research, a ticket elsewhere. Two students exchanging things.

His thumbs stopped their pattern, his head tilting. "Do you believe that?"

"Why would he be interested in a human? We're like dogs to you, we age and we die. I was a curiosity." It stung to say, a lie sour on my tongue, but it was easier than the other thought. The press of their bodies, safety in their tangled limbs. Laughter in a house. I couldn't think of it.

"That's not true. We've always had a weakness for humans. He's risking a lot of ire with how many he's turning, and it works well for Oswyn."

"They come as a pair. If you're aiming for one, easier to take both."

"Do you think me wicked?"

"We're all creatures of desperation at times, you've had longer to steep in yours. And you brought me into it with you, because you needed someone to hurt as much as you did." I laughed; the sound as weak as I felt. "I was a poor choice. I wonder if you're disappointed in that?"

"I didn't expect you to cope as well as you have."

"Yet you did it anyway?"

"I did. I worry it was wrong of me, given how you are now." He frowned, a finger skimming along my chin. The movement was worse over the wet skin, much too intimate, and I looked away to the door again.

"Obstinate? Been that way a long while, I'm afraid."

"That's not what I meant. Stay still." He brought a towel up to dry my face, rough compared to the soft cloth, and I peeked back to inspect him. He was focused on what he was doing, gaze firmly on my swollen nose, and so careful as he dried me off. His eyes flicked up to mine and I looked to the mirror rather than the red-tinted water.

"Speak plainly, then. I'm too worn-out to talk around a matter."

"Worn-out, exactly. Why are you endangering yourself? My home should be a solace for you and you're pushing yourself to every edge you can find."

My gaze went back to him, brows up and lip bitten. That only made it worse: the uneven pressure a reminder of what he'd done. What I was now. My heart sank, and a quiet fury slipped in its place instead—my skin prickled with it, the back of my hand thumping with pain in time with my pulse.

"Solace?"

He winced, setting the towel down. "This is your home. You keep pushing yourself further and harder and I fear what it'll do to you."

"If I wanted to do myself harm there are things I could have done. Take your solace in that."

"What are you talking about?" I shook my head, moving to leave the bathroom but he caught my shoulders again, face stern. "What do you mean?"

"You have long bedsheets and bare beams. I could have taken myself out of this place the first morning I woke up. I considered it, in fact, after what you did. Better dead than a pet. Throwing myself off the roof wouldn't work, it's not tall enough to be certain, but there are knives too. I could probably find something in the garden. I'd bet you're still in yarrow country down here."

"Don't say that." He yanked me to him, so hard it knocked the air out of my lungs. "Don't say such things."

"Or what, you'll lock me in the cell downstairs? You'll chain me up?" I shoved his chest, separating us so I could flee the stifling space. I was whittled down to the last of my fear—the pain from earlier had brought focus and my own hot hate, and I didn't want to be rash.

He followed, snagging my wrist to turn me. "Ena, don't speak like this. I don't want to have to restrict you, but I will if you're going to do something foolish."

I rounded on him, barely out of the bathroom door but full of my vehemence. "Foolish? Foolish like sleeping in the same bed as someone who pulled out two of your teeth? Someone who took the tongue of a man he was jealous of? Someone who took the closest thing you had to safety and tore it apart? Which of those choices should I revisit, Mark? Which of them were mine to be foolish with?"

"I didn't do those things to hurt you." He grabbed my arms but I wrenched away, my focus oversharp, pulse thudding in my ears. I was getting too angry to keep everything in check, to keep a lid on the simmering disgust pooling between my teeth.

I didn't want to be around him. To give him that reaction, overspill from my carefully won balance. He caught me again, grip tight on my wrist.

"Let go of me!" I shouted, regretted it, ground my teeth together to keep the rest of my venom in.

"Talk to me, please." He tugged me towards him again, arms open as if to hug me.

I turned, tried to bolt for the door but he pulled me back, the momentum toppling us towards the bed.

He came with me, his body over mine as he fought my flailing arms. It was too much like before, when he'd brought us together, and an animal fear flared up. I twisted my hips to try and buck him, clawed for his face until he pinned my wrists above my head and flattened his body against mine. There was nowhere to move, not an inch he wasn't pressed against me, even his arms fixing my elbows down.

Our breathing was heavy—puffs of hot air in each other's face—and I closed my eyes.

"Go on then," I said.

"What?"

"You have me pinned on the bed, what else would that be for? Run out of patience for the idea of me falling for you?" I knew I couldn't get him off but I could make it hurt him as much as it did me. I wouldn't look at him. I wouldn't give him the satisfaction of seeing me weak. He could do what he was going to, and I'd hate him even more, and that venom could poison us both.

"How can you think I'd do that?" A hand left my wrists, the pair still held easily by the other, and, trembling, he cupped my cheek.

I gave in despite myself, leaning up to look him close in the eyes. "What other things are there left for you to take?"

"I would never do that. I wouldn't force you like that." His voice broke, a coughing sob stealing whatever else he had to say.

"Don't you dare, don't you dare." I tried to twist away but he collapsed onto me and wrapped his arms under my back, pulling me against him with bruising strength. His head was buried into my chest, hidden as he wept into my blouse.

"I'd never. That's not who I am."

"How can I believe that?" My voice betrayed me, a waver that spoke to the wetness in my eyes, the fear sliding through my blood.

"I know it's hard, darling. It's hard because you're human and I've hurt you and I'm sorry. I'd never do that to you. But you can't leave me. You can't know me as you do and leave me alone."

His shoulders heaved with cries, his large frame rocking against me. Gods above. I tentatively pulled an arm down, laying it across his back. If nothing else it anchored me against the violence of his sobs, the weight of the shaking. He quivered at the touch, his head popping up to look for my gaze. I met it, bringing the other hand down to stroke his hair.

"That's why you didn't go back to them. Because you couldn't show them this side of you?" He buried his head into my chest again, crying harder, and I continued to stroke his hair. It was such a deep red, coppery in the afternoon light. Like a splash of blood across my chest. A wound would have been easier, at least I might die quick. "It's alright. You can cry."

He howled at that, wrenching me closer to him, my back protesting at the way he bent me. "I can't lose you. Don't try to take yourself off like that, please. I can't."

"Hush, I won't. I'm here. I promised to stay." I curled closer to him, let my cheek rest against his crown. It wasn't a lie. I *had* promised.

It was a babble of reassurance, though, whatever he needed to hear to make the pain stop. His edges were just as frayed as mine, and there was little I could do to stem the tide except false promises. Cruel, really, but I'd heard his threat. Better to be a liar than trapped down in the dark. Not a second time. And crying men made unsafe women. This was all familiar.

"I love you." He rocked back and forth, his grip on my ribs painful.

"I believe you." I kept running my fingers through his hair like he'd done when I woke up, soft against his scalp, over and over. It wasn't too far from comforting one of the young ones in the college. I knew how to do this. I could be this.

We lay in silence once his cries had stopped. The light on the ceiling changed, gone from solid afternoon sunshine to the ruddy glow of evening. I pondered, in some far-off spot at the back of my skull, if I could kill him. I didn't want him to hurt the nest. Tobias had cut those men's heads off, burned them. I was lacking a pyre, but the kitchen had knives. Break his neck, saw through the flesh, try to make blessed fire. An unlikely plan. I couldn't fight an immortal.

"We should go and get something to eat," I said eventually.

He shook his head. "I don't want to let go of you yet."

"Alright."

# Chapter 61

The splintering shriek of wood being torn asunder rattled me out of sleep with a spike of fear.

Mark sat up, throwing the cover off. We were still dressed for the day, tangled together from the earlier argument, and while it was dark outside it wasn't deep into the night; the moon was low and starting to creep into the long journey across the window.

"Stay here."

He was gone before I could argue and I shoved up off the bed, glancing around for a weapon. The kitchen—a knife.

I slipped out of the bedroom, stealing about the corridor to take the long route around. It sent me through the moonlit halls, empty rooms now looming threats in case there was some intruder within. Improbable, given I was going away from the sound, but I was taking no chances.

The back stairs were clear and there was no one else in the kitchen when I reached it, not even servants. Was Mark diligent enough to have given them a way to get out? I picked up a knife from the drawer and glanced back towards the quarters. No sound, nothing to indicate they were awake and escaping. I knew where David slept, roughly, he would have sense to get the others hidden out in the garden.

A woman's scream ripped through the dark and I raced from the kitchen with the knife tucked flat against my wrist. Everyone would have heard that.

The front door was torn open, sagging off its hinges, the wood burning with a jagged light. The sound of bodies broke from the next room, the morning room, and I tore towards it in search of Rose.

Throwing the door open, caution abandoned to fear for her, I saw two shapes bent over someone on the floor, long hair spilling out to cover her face.

"Step away from her, now," I shouted, all the bravado of a job in my voice. If they were thieves, they were idiots, and if they were worse, I'd make them regret hurting her.

"Princess?" One of the figures looked up and I near sobbed at the voice.

"Still one for eke-names, I see." Mark appeared at my side, one arm snaking around my waist to take me with him as he walked forward. "You've injured my charge, Tobias, I expect you to deliver her over. Now."

Tobias recoiled, his face passing through a grimace and heave as he stepped closer. "Luc?"

"Stay there," Mark snarled. I grabbed his wrist, tapping the back of his hand in reassurance. I had to get Rose. A tumble of the three of them would be vicious—inevitable that Rose and I would be hurt in the overspill.

"He uses Mark now," I said.

The other figure was Addison. I knew the shock of hair before he stood from checking her, and his face was unreadable as he looked us over. "That's why you sent us her teeth," he said.

I closed my eyes for a wavering moment, willing myself not to cover my mouth. They'd had them, then, he was honest.

"A touch dramatic, wasn't it? She said it was. You were right, darling." He pressed a kiss to my hair and I let him, schooling my face as I opened my eyes again. Tobias bristled but Addison set a hand on his wrist, the shake of his head barely enough to let his eyes off us.

Rose groaned and Tobias scooped her up, shushing her as he turned and placed her on one of the settees behind them.

Mark hummed, his arm around my waist tugging me closer. "Return the girl to me, she's human and she's not thralled."

"You were dead! Your fangs! We mourned you!" Tobias shouted.

"Addison, she's precious young, she shouldn't be around a fight." It wasn't clear if he was calmer than Tobias or in shock, but I had more chance of getting his attention than Tobias. Both their eyes glowed like cats in the dark.

Addison's gaze caught on me, flashing. "What has he done to you?" He took half a step closer and Mark growled, baring his gapped teeth.

"Addison, focus! What's happened to her?" I asked.

"Let Ena come and get her." Tobias cut in, pointing to the settee. "She can see the girl out of the room. Us three can finish this."

"How did you know to come here?" Mark let go and I went, slowly, to the other side of the room. The two men parted for me, Addison brushing his fingers against my arm as I went past. I could have wept.

"Oswyn. He hadn't cleaned her blood off well enough when he came into see us. To gloat." Tobias shook with the telling of it, large hands flexing in and out of fists as I passed. "I knew her blood as soon as I smelled it. Wasn't hard to get it out of him with the right pressure."

Mark sighed. "I thought it might have been Agnes. She's so giddy after a little blood."

"We left her with his neck open," Addison said.

I was through the two of them, shaking as I got to Rose, kneeling beside the settee. An ugly cut leaked at her forehead, her eyes glassy, and for a horrible moment this was my first day in London all over again, and there would be blood on my hands when I touched her. But she blinked up at me, and almost cried when I touched her cheek. Her knife was out, glinting at her waist, and I tucked it back in.

"We need to get the others, alright?" She nodded, sitting up. I held my arm out and she stood, shaky as a new lamb, leaning against me. "I'm coming back over."

Addison reached out to my hip but pulled up light of a touch as I turned the two of us. I ached to go to him, only nodding before we went back towards the door. Creatures of yearning, all of us.

The walk across was agonising, the weight of three gazes pressing down as I led Rose. She was drooping, but more stable as we moved, her weight on me lessening as we approached Mark.

"Are you well, little dove?" He stepped before us, lifting her chin to inspect the wound on her head.

"Yes. I startled him. I don't think he knew I was human."

"I didn't," Tobias said. I looked back at him, his face grim as I'd seen it in the memoires. No sword this time. He nearly panted, teeth bared around his pain.

"Rose, listen. Get the others. I want you to go to the best spot in the garden and wait for us. You can do that for me, can't you, my special girl?" Mark's hands went to her shoulders, holding her closer for a minute. His voice was tender like he spoke to a child, softer than he'd ever been in my time here, and she nodded like she was half asleep.

"She needs healed, she doesn't need thrall," I said.

"Go." He pecked a kiss to her forehead before he looked at me. "It'll only last until she gets the others to safety, I don't use thrall on her except for urgent matters."

She stepped around him, back straight but eyes unfocused, and walked out. I looked back to him and saw he had her knife, the flat blade glinting in the uneven flames from the door. The fire was spreading, eating towards us.

"Ena should go with her," Addison said.

"No." Mark dipped towards me, looping his arm around my waist and pulling me flush, my back to his chest. The knife flashed in front of me, up to point at the other two. "I'm not letting her out of my sight. I'm not as foolish as you two."

"How are you here?" Tobias said, lips curled back over his teeth. "You were dead."

"Hidden. Pushed out of time by Henry. She told me what you did to him, by the way, Addison. I didn't know you loved me enough to break your vows."

Addison flinched, tongue slipping out to wet his lower lip. "I loved you more than that. Let her go, and let us talk. I need to understand."

"No. Ena knows me now, and she's such a good match. Just perfect." He stroked my cheek with the back of his fingers, the knife sliding perilously close to my skin. I kept my back rigid so I wouldn't shake.

"What do you mean?" Tobias started closer and Mark flipped the knife, now pointed at my neck.

"Steady, Tobias. You always did rush in. And not even a sword, I'm insulted." Mark tutted.

"Others needed it more than me, and I wasn't for risking it being used on her. I'm not unarmed." He tugged his jacket, a flash of a handle at his hip. One of Edgar's knives. My throat clenched, joy and fear strangling me in their intertwine.

Mark snorted; the bounce of his chest violent against my back. "Do you remember our last battle? How you'd run in after Edmund and I saved you. I thought about that a lot, in the hundred years on my own. Locked in a cell."

"Ena, look at me," Addison said. I did as bid, meeting his gaze which shone so soft, so pained. "He has fed from you?"

"I didn't do anything so based. We have a soul bond."

Addison opened his mouth with a snarl, eyes bright.

"You joined with her? She could have died." Tobias went to Addison, and they bumped shoulders like they were magnetised, couldn't help but crash and repel. I couldn't focus, the flash of light on the blade a shiny distraction. My heart thumped in my ribs, but the whisper of the knife near my neck kept me still. He'd promised he wouldn't hurt me.

"She lived. I knew she would. I was waiting for her to adjust, before I sired her."

"You don't have fangs," Tobias said.

"There are other ways to exchange blood."

Addison stepped forward, one hand up and open. "Luc, let her—"

"*Mark!* Luc has been dead since Henry imprisoned him with magic from his own dead sons!" The knife was mercifully pointed at them again, enough to let me breathe a little deeper.

"Mark, then. Let her go. She doesn't need to see this as well as what you've shared," Addison said.

"A century," I said, voice thin. "The time of him being tortured and the years it took to carve himself out. He worked so hard at it, all alone."

"Oh, my love, no." Tobias came two steps nearer and Mark had the blade at my neck. They'd made it some way closer. No retreat either. "She's human, you can't do that to her. It's a cruelty."

"She's strong. I won't let you have her back, the pair of you, she's not yours to share. We're bonded. She's promised to stay with me, *chose* me. And when she's turned, she will be like me in every way, even down to her teeth."

My heart stalled in anticipation of the blade. A crackle of magic ripped through the room in echo: Addison had something in one hand, a pale-blue ball of light that fizzed like trapped lightning.

"If you harm her, I'll use this." Addison held the ball higher, so the lances of energy arced out towards us.

Mark laughed, back to the high and unsteady giggle I knew. "You're pulling out old things there, Addison. That must hurt to bring out again, especially in this house. Did Henry beg you not to? I won't beg."

"It should be her choice. You knew that. That's why we fought." Tobias's forlorn words were low underneath the crackle of flames and magic but my heart clenched. This was all wrong.

"Stop," I said, eyes on Addison. "He's not going to hurt me, he's just scared." The others had to get away from this. Rose would be getting them out of the back, hopefully she was with them and they were clear by now.

"I can't let him do this to you," Addison said. His face was so flat, so angry, nothing of the love I knew. His eyes were molten.

He understood desperation. Maybe he understood what I was doing, buying time. He still held the magic, that old curse, high, though. It hissed like an angry cat. I hadn't heard it make that noise with Henry.

This was all wrong.

"He's not going to. He took my teeth so I didn't feel it, and he took care of me after we connected." Killed my friend, kidnapped me, maimed me. "He's not going to hurt me."

"You are hurt, love. You're so gaunt. Your magic is leaking." Addison had pity, maybe worse, in his eyes and I couldn't take it.

"I know that!" I patted my throat, sobbing dryly at the mark wrought against me, the hole where I should be, but there was no part of me there. "But I would rather be injured than dead."

"Dead like the man left in your room?" I recoiled at Tobias's question, twisting in Mark's grip to hide my face in his chest. A blunt opportunity, but I would take it.

"Cruel, Tobias. She loved him a lot. I regret that death." He stroked my hair, the arm around my waist now up my back to hold me close as I brought my hands up to his chest, inching my wrist higher. It was a weak plan, I knew, but I needed to get my hands together.

"You killed him," Addison said.

"And drained him. It took a lot to get her to sleep, she wanted so badly to go to him." He stroked my cheek, the knife sharp at my temple, and I looked up to meet his radiant gaze. Even that witch-light was dimmer in him.

"Sorry." I smiled as I pulled the knife from my sleeve, barely sure of what I would do except slide it into him, get Rose's pretty blade away from me. I jabbed for his neck out of practicality as much as proximity; there was always an instinct to protect your throat.

"Ena!" Tobias shouted as Mark cackled, flashing forward to grab my wrist and yank it high. The knife went through him, smattering my face with hot blood. It felt obscene—like a brand over my skin. He squeezed my wrist until I let go of the blade and I sobbed.

"Tricky, darling, tricky. Are you so keen to get my blood that you'd take it for yourself?"

"Let her go!" Addison shouted, the first time I'd heard such a frantic sound, and I screwed my eyes closed at the animal fear it drew down my spine.

I was going to die between them. All the running and squirming, my rigid patience, and this would be my end. A dead man's revenge. The certainty of it was gossamer against my skin, a perfect kiss of the reaper coming for me.

I opened my eyes to Mark's smile, wide as a hungry cat.

"All we have to do is share blood. We've shared so much more than that already." His eyes were peat-fire wild, barely seeing me as he stared at the others, but that knife was still above me.

"Mark, it doesn't have to be like this. You wanted me to have time. Think about how we were last night. We can be like that more, but I need to heal."

"You don't suit begging, darling. You didn't when you did it for that mutt of a human but it's worse when you're like this." He brought his arm around, no longer pinning me against him, so he could cup the back of my head. There was no reason in that loving gaze, nothing to grasp onto. I couldn't fight an immortal. "No one else will make you beg."

I hugged him, one-armed, pressing myself into his chest. "Is Rose safe?"

"Yes, our connection's faded. The others will keep her from coming back in. It's only us." He pecked a kiss to my hair and I heard the others move, the crackle of the magic launched at us. Felt the way his arm dropped my pained wrist to bring his knife down.

I was going to die. Fuck this.

I couldn't fight an immortal, but I didn't need to. I wrapped my freed hand around my right arm as the knife sank into my shoulder, wide of the mark because of my tightening the grip around him. *"Briseadh."*

My arm split open with a magnificent burst of white pain, vivid behind my eyes as bone pushed free of flesh, and blue fire tumbled out. I had no shield, no way to keep myself safe, but he couldn't get away from me. I tightened my grip, the bone slick under my thumb, and he didn't even scream.

"Fire?" He cupped my face, knife abandoned in my muscle, tilting my chin up to look at him. The flames licked around us, not even hot despite the way my hair smoked and curled.

"Heart-fire. Together in the end, I suppose." I didn't know if he could hear me over the flames. We were in our own blue cage, bound together as the world fell away.

It was better like this. Addison hadn't had to be the worst of himself again. Tobias hadn't been powerless. Mark would be dead, hopefully, and I would be free. In a way.

It was worth running from the college just to be sure I had that.

"Together." Mark smiled, folding over to hug me against him.

# Chapter 62

Shouting. It was rotten the afterlife should be filled with angry voices. No one shouted in a mortuary, that would be wailing, so I must still be alive. I worked to open my eyes, and took in the canopy of the bed above me. I knew that green.

"You with us, princess?" Tobias was in a chair beside the bed, Addison's bed, his long fingers playing with the edge of the covers. His hair sat lank around his face, eyes bloodshot and deep-set in circles that outlined them like bruising. I gawked at him, blinking a few times before I nodded. "Should've known it'd be a fight that woke you."

"Who is it?" My voice was disgusting, dry as the grave, and he passed me a cup of water before he said anything else. I sipped, letting it warm on my tongue. The air was cold at the back of my neck and I slid one hand up. It took much too long to find the fuzzy remains of my hair, jagged from someone's earnest efforts at chopping it. Slick patches of skin rolled against my fingertips. No braids for a while.

"Addison's dealing with some uninvited guests. As are most of the others."

"Who?"

He looked away, biting his lip before he answered. "Some of the men from your old place. Older ones. Self-righteous pricks. When they heard you were injured chaos broke loose."

I sat up, grateful someone had put me in a nightgown. My right arm ached, wrapped in thick bandages so I couldn't see the wound, and the hand was sheathed in a glove. I was damn near swaddled. "We should get me down there."

He was between me and the door immediately, that same swift movement Mark had done around his house. "You're in no state."

"When they see what I'm like they won't want me back."

"You're not that bad." He was a terrible liar.

"I am here." I tapped the spot on my neck, where Mark would have stabbed me. My fingers slipped along to the shoulder, where he had succeeded. A thick ridge of scar tissue welcomed me. "I'm a broken tool."

The shouts got louder and Tobias sighed. "This is a terrible plan."

"They'll make one of the sired throw a punch, or threaten to burn Haddley given he's untrained. They'll make Addison step in and claim it was aggression." I pushed the covers off, grateful the gown went low enough that I didn't have to look at my skin as I shuffled to the side of the bed. "Who dressed me up like a granny?"

"Addison needed to check your wounds, so we did it. Rose wanted to. She's a great defender of your honour." He laughed but there was no mirth, shaking his head. "Too fond of knives, that one."

Rose was safe. My heart swooped at that, one good point in a constellation of disasters. "She heals herself up."

"Do you want me to carry you?"

I shook my head, grateful when he kicked shoes my way. Standing took effort, pushed my breath out of me in agonising pants, but I managed. Walking might be easier. "I think I'll make it."

"How about I get you down the stairs? They're in the drawing room, you can walk that bit." He'd scooped me up before I could argue, holding me against his chest like he had my first night in the house. I put my arms around his neck, wincing at the jolt of pain it brought, and he took us out, opening the door with his hip.

"Did Oswyn survive his wife?"

"Yes. He's going to be ugly for a long while in his healing, but she didn't kill him."

"Shame."

Tobias started down the stairs, clicking his tongue. "I'll do worse if he tries anything like that again."

"Is Mark dead?"

He almost missed a step, pulling himself up before we toppled. At least we were nearly at the bottom. "Yes. I couldn't even take his teeth for you, your fire burned him right up."

"Good. I didn't want it to be Addison's spell that got him."

"You were thinking about that?"

I wrinkled my nose. "It would have hurt him too much. I didn't want that on either of you. Put me down, I'll walk with you the rest of the way."

A clamour of voices spilled from the drawing room, and though Tobias knocked, no one seemed to notice.

The room was anarchy—three men in the Council's dark blue robes stood up and shouting, pointing at Addison who was also stood, separated from them by a tea trolley, with his shoulders back and lips in a thin line. Chance was at his side, smirk like a blade out on show, and Haddley was holding Garrett back as he surged towards the Council members. Edgar was assisting in pinning Garrett, with some effort, whispering something by the proximity of their faces.

"Did you start the party without us?" Tobias called. They stilled, all eyes on the door.

"Ena!" Chance shot around Addison, throwing himself across the room to skid in front of me. "You shouldn't be up."

I held my hands up, palms open. "You lot can't even behave when I'm almost in the ground."

"She's in tatters."

"Well met, George." I was at least willing to pretend to be cordial as I limped forward and took Addison's chair.

Sinking down was mercy, my legs knocking together as I sat, and I crossed my ankles to keep them still. George, late into his forties and wearing his age on his face, looked as miserable as I'd ever seen him. His longer hair was frizzy, spooling around his head in curly tangles, and his stubble had patches of white he usually shaved clean every morning.

"What have you done to her?" I didn't know the man to the right of George, not well enough to remember his name, but he was similarly wrinkled and equally grim. They must have travelled recently. I knew the one on the right was a financier, he was always there at meetings for the budgets of the dormitories.

"This nest did nothing to me. The vampire who took Benjamin's tongue did."

George's face hardened. "Would that be the same one they say killed Timothy?"

"He did. Snapped Tim's neck, drank his blood, used it to overpower me. He was responsible for the death of several mages in the city over the last few months, too. It's a wonder any of us escaped."

"He tortured Benjamin," George said. The accusation was in there, the question as to why he hadn't done the same to me.

I let it sit in the open, unwilling to give him anything without an explicit request. "Yes. He made Ben choose between losing his eyes or his tongue. Ben chose wisely. Someone can give him a voice, or he can learn to speak with his hands. He's resourceful."

"Ena, you don't have to talk about this," Addison said. He was hovering at the back of the chair like a worried hen, chest puffed up. Chance flanked the other side, knelt beside it like the bodyguard to a throne, crackling with something unsaid.

"We need to know what happened so we can inform the healers. She'll have to travel at half the normal rate, she looks fit to shatter at a bump in the carriage." That was the other one, I think he was Alastair. He looked like an Alastair.

"Have you not checked my magic?" I leaned back into the chair with a sigh as deep as my bones. "You should, George. You know me."

He frowned, stepping closer to inspect me, and I stared back at him, tapping the space at my neck where the mark had showed. His eyes were the hazel green of bog-water, things stood too long in stagnation. "How did they do that to you?"

"The vampire forced our souls together. A bond, so he could always find me, and he took these, too." I smiled wide, pulling my lips up to show the gaps at my teeth. The three men shifted away a good two steps, the back pair bumping into the settee. Haddley whimpered.

"Mutilation wasn't reserved for the men, then," Alastair said to the others. He had the decency to try and be quiet, but it was no use in such close quarters. "That does make it less likely."

"Less likely what?" Tobias asked. He'd taken up duty beside the doors, arms crossed over his broad chest.

"There were concerns she may have been thralled. Or that she'd given the men over willingly, to save herself. Extracting teeth makes that less likely."

"You thought what?" I sat up, leaning towards them.

"You deserted your position. The idea that you'd taken up with a vampire was startling enough, but with an entire nest, and with a mage-killer? Of course we thought you might bargain with them," George said.

Of course. The words rolled around my mind, tightening my stomach like I would throw up the water. I swallowed against the press up my throat, shaking my head. Bargains. I'd bargained for Ben. Not that he could tell them that.

"This can be dealt with at a Council trial. We should hasten back up the road," Alastair said.

"I'm not going anywhere."

"You still have to return with us," George said.

"No."

"Ena, this isn't a discussion. You could be used in a move against us with how damaged you are. Someone could try to study your skill. Has there not been enough bloodshed already with Timothy dead, and Benjamin maimed?"

"Wouldn't try that," Tobias said. He was smirking, but I couldn't begrudge him it.

"George, do you remember how you used to beat me for speaking the old words? The little smattering of Gaelic I had."

He had the decency to look chagrined, bobbing his head before he answered. "You were particularly stubborn about that, yes."

"I got so careful I barely need to say them anymore." I held up my bandaged right arm. "Did they tell you how I got out, from the vampire who ravaged my soul?"

"Easy, petal," Chance said.

"You don't have to tell them anything else," Addison added, stepping around to block me.

"Yes I do." I shoved his hip, plucking the glove from my right hand. Blue flame flickered then burst into life, richer than it had been before. Hungry. "I broke my arm to get blood, and I burned us both up. Heart-fire might be obscene but it's very effective against immortals."

"That's forbidden work," Alastair said.

"I don't know if it was his influence that brought it out, or if it was a desperate reach, when I knew I'd die. But it killed him. These men rescued me. I owe them a debt. I plan to repay it." I closed my hand, letting the fire drop, and tugged the glove back on. My skin was shiny and red but not bleeding, at least. It didn't even hurt.

"You owe them a debt?" Oh joy, the financier spoke. "You're contracted to the College. Your bed and board, your training, the absolute decimation of your team through your own stupidity, *that* is a debt."

Addison chuckled, cold as a chain falling. "Is that why you're here, you twitchy little man? Because of what you consider her owing?"

"All members of the College are under contracts. While I'm sorry that such... indelicate matters happened, she broke her contract."

"Donald, don't say it like that." George scowled at the financier. Some little humanity in the man at least. He didn't meet my eyes.

"I'll buy her contract from you." Addison crossed his hands over each other, shoulders settled.

George coughed, scowling at Addison. "This isn't some slavery chattel, it's a long-term agreement that's been in place since she joined the College. We—"

"How much?" Tobias asked, pushing from the wall to stand beside Addison. "You're here to claim her, how much is she worth?"

Donald faltered, tripping on his words. "There're costs for the others as well. The dead man and the maimed one."

"Did Ben tell you about this place?" I leaned to one side, so I could look at George. "When he could, I mean."

"We received reports that it was a nest," George said. He still wouldn't look at me, not really, and a little part of me revelled in that. That I'd become so ugly, so broken to him, that all my shiny potential had been obscured.

"Yes, he rushed in. Tim's death would overtake the discussion. Those two are born vampires, as I'm sure you can tell, but that one in particular—" I pointed to Tobias. "—he's one of the enders of the Immortal War. Heir to one of the families. Don't try to be canny."

"We'll need to evaluate costs and confirm a figure," Donald said. "We can return with that tomorrow."

"Sent on will be adequate," Addison said.

"You can't be thinking to sell her, surely?" George asked, rounding on the others. "She's not a beast!"

"She's compromised, and clearly not in her right mind if she's deciding to stay in a house of fangs. Let us at least recoup the costs of her misadventure," Alastair said.

"We'll discuss the figure and revert to you. Who should I address matters to?" Donald asked, turning from George and Alastair to look at the immortals.

"Him. It's his house." Tobias tipped his thumb to Addison, who was working his jaw like he had something to say. He kept his counsel, staring the men down, though he joined hands with Tobias.

"We'll be in contact shortly. Thank you for your hospitality." Donald gave a neat bow of his head, grabbed the bag on the settee and made for the door.

"I'll see you out." Chance was up and next to him, teeth on show as they bumped together at the threshold.

George came closer to me, skirting around the immortals to take my hand. "You should come back."

I looked up at him, trying my best to smile. "No."

"You don't belong trapped in a hungry house."

"Just trapped in the College, shut up with the nuns? Spare me."

He shook his head, lips pursed, but let go to join the others. I leaned forward to watch them pass out of the door before I flopped back, eyes closed. I might throw up. There wasn't enough in my stomach to do so but even the emptiness sat heavy.

"Can I come over, Ena?" Haddley called.

I cracked one eye open to look for him, frowning. "Yes."

"Good. I wanted to come and give you a hug but you're all hurt and I couldn't and they were being so obscene with what they said and I'm glad you're alright." He was beside me in a blink, not touching me but buzzing with energy.

"Thank you, Haddley. We'll have to catch up about research when I don't look like I'm fresh from a coffin."

"You should go back to bed and rest," Addison said. His fingers ghosted over my shoulder.

"Your bed, you mean?" I asked.

"It's a good bed. I'll come join you once those men are gone."

# Chapter 63

"Ena?" Rose stuck her head through the door, a tray balanced between her hands. I smiled at her as she came in, skirting around Tobias, who hadn't left his perch at the end of the bed since I came back upstairs. Playing guard dog.

"I'm happy to see you," I said. She looked healthy. Still slim, long hair still wafting behind her, but her eyes were bright and her smile solid.

"I'm glad too. I heard you awoke to the row."

"Did you stay out of the way?" She'd been so scared when Ben came.

"Addison's vouched for me to stay. I don't know if I will, but it's nice to have the option." She set the tray down beside me—chicken soup. She wrinkled her nose. "I thought it might help."

"It will. I think I have you to thank for healing me?"

"It wasn't right you should die." She shook her head, and frowned at Tobias before she continued. "I don't know them well enough to like them, but that pair were beside themselves with fear for you. They let me heal you and gave you blood, too."

That was why I was as well as this, then.

"That's a conversation for Addison to have with her. Let her eat her soup." Tobias shifted on the bed, arms crossed.

"Rose makes good soup. You should try some."

"She's a good cook."

Rose chuckled at him. "I'll leave you to it, but have him come and get me if you need anything. I'd like to talk."

I nodded, holding the bowl up to my chest so I could soak in the heat. Even through the glove it was wonderful, the warmth spreading over my hands like stepping into a fresh bath. She dipped her head to Tobias and left, closing the door quick behind her.

"Want to keep my company while I eat?"

"This isn't company?"

"You could sit next to me."

He laughed, twisting up to his knees and shuffling over to prop himself beside me against the headboard. "Better?"

"Yes." I leaned into him, shifting the bowl to one hand so I could get the spoon from the tray. "I'm glad Rose is here. She needs somewhere soft."

"You think we're soft?"

I swallowed a spoonful. "Absolutely. Soft as your pocket, the whole lot of you."

"I'm not sure everyone will take well to that."

"Shouldn't have been soft." I ate some more soup, grateful for the familiarity of this. A moment to simply exist, and eat, and have the world be still.

"I didn't know if you would want any of us near you. After what happened." His head was back against the headboard, eyes on the canopy. Careful, gentle man.

I took another spoonful while I thought of an answer. "Don't try to bite me."

"I never would."

"I know. I didn't know if you would want to be near me either."

"Why?"

"I killed someone you loved. Tends to make meals a bit tense."

"I went there ready to kill for you, even if I left my sword with Garrett." I raised a brow at him. "In case Agnes got ideas."

I managed about half of the bowl before I set it down. "My stomach hurts."

"Little and often. You've lost weight, will take a while to come back."

"I'll soon get it back."

"If you eat. Rose said that was an issue."

I opened my mouth, licking my top lip to speak, and gaps where my incisors were bumped along my tongue. "He took my teeth. I didn't feel it, but he did. How could I..." I trailed off, a cry hiccoughing up my throat. I covered my mouth, shaking my head.

"It's alright, lovely, cry if you need to. It's alright to cry." Tobias put an arm around my shoulders. It would be easy to sob into his chest, let myself fall back into the pit I had been on the precipice of.

"Beloved, you are a menace." Addison's voice held no real heat as he came into the room. "You have her crying already?"

"We were talking about soup," Tobias said.

"My fault." I pulled myself up. "I'm sorry."

"Don't apologise, lambkin. You can cry as much as you need to. Here." He handed me a little square handkerchief and I buried my face in it, wiping my eyes. "We can take things at your pace. Talking, magic, all of it."

"I don't know if my magic's safe, with that wound. I'll have to experiment." I kept the handkerchief, breathing deep. It smelled of him.

"Haddley will be delighted to hear that. He loves an experiment," Addison said. He scooped the tray off the bed, together with the discarded soup, and set it on a chair. Returning, he perched on the side, one thigh crossed over the other so he took up as little space as he could.

"Why are you so far off?" I asked.

"I wanted to give you a chance to speak without being crowded. A feat I see Tobias has failed at the first challenge."

"I asked him to come sit. I missed you both. That house was nothing like here."

Addison smiled, a pained thing. "It wouldn't be. We'll need to talk about that at some point, but I don't want you to feel pressed. When you're ready is soon enough."

I nodded, playing with my hands. Questions hung on my tongue, heavy in my mouth, and I was half afraid of the answers. "Do you want me to leave, when I'm hale? Given what I did."

"What you did?" Addison repeated.

"Luc. Mark. The fire," Tobias said. He squeezed my shoulder, nuzzling closer. "She thinks we'll want rid of her."

"Not at all. Please don't go." Addison came along the bed, catching my hand. "I am so sorry that you were dragged into our pain. If you feel safer elsewhere, we would both understand. I'll pay for a house for you in a heartbeat. But, we dearly want you to stay. If you would wish it, we'd declare for you. It only seems right it would be both of us given you have both our hearts."

Tobias nodded, batted his lashes at Addison. "It's uncommon to be declared for two, but not wrong. As long as you were comfortable with us as a joined lot, we would love you to join."

"There's no need for an immediate decision, of course. You need to heal. But when we received your teeth, thought you gone, I—" Addison cut off, shaking his head as he looked down. Wetness dropped quickly from his chin, and he wiped his face with the back of one hand.

Tobias coughed, fingers combing through his hair. "He was in his room for two days, inconsolable. Whereas I wrecked mine, and Jonathan scolded me for the damage. Once he'd finished hugging me."

"You're hopeless," I said.

"When we thought you lost, it focused how precious you are to us. Fond, as I said before, was an underestimate I'm ashamed to have used." Addison's eyes were so soft, open as a new morning's golden light.

I frowned, looking between them. "This is unexpected."

"We've been throwing ourselves at your mercy since you got here," Tobias said.

"That was me and the window, as I recall."

Addison squeezed my hand. "It's an offer with no pressure. The first thing to focus on is healing. Rose worked hard to help you, and we have both given you blood, but it will take time to recover physically."

I twisted the fingers of my free hand through the fuzz of my hair, shorter than I liked. There would be more scars underneath the nightgown. "I'd like to stay. I'll need to see what I can do with my magic, that's a slow thing. I'd feel safer staying with you two while that heals. And I'd want it to be both of you, if we do the other as well. You're both hopeless, of course, but I'd not be without either of you."

Tobias laughed, burying his head in my shoulder.

"You can stay in this house, and in this bed, as long as you like. Though, I'd appreciate the chance to return to our previous sleeping arrangements, if we could."

"He's been curling up on the love seat since you got back, lest you woke and were afraid." Tobias leaned in to whisper it to me, lips brushing my ear. "He looked like a little lost dog."

"I can still hear you, heart of mine," Addison said.

"That's so sweet," I said. The laugh was barely stifled but I tried my best.

"I didn't know how you'd feel. I couldn't stand not being close, but I didn't want you to awaken scared. We don't know what happened, with how long you were away."

"Well I learned to whistle a new way." I hissed air through the gaps in my teeth and neither of them laughed. "You're going to have to perk up, I'm allowed to make jokes. There was always a risk I'd lose some teeth with my work. I survived. I'll get upset at it again later, and cry a lot, but for now I'm alive. That's enough, no?"

"Of course it is, lambkin. Now, might I join you? I've been desperate to give you a hug since I saw you downstairs."

"Yes." I held my other arm up so he could join us at the top of the bed, his long legs tumbling over mine as he pressed in like a cat. "You're going to own me shortly. What will we do about that?"

"It's absolute rubbish. Even their own leader didn't agree with it. I'll have no claim over you that you don't explicitly grant. Anything else would be abhorrent."

"He'll trade you it for a kiss," Tobias said.

Addison leaned over, grabbing Tobias's shirt to pull him in for a quick press of lips. There was such a simple joy in it, bare love, that I couldn't stop the smile it brought. Parting, Addison sat back and planted his head at my neck, breathing in. "I'd do that if you wanted. But only if so. Buying your freedom is nothing. If you choose to leave afterwards, I'll respect your choice."

"Too many choices, we should sleep." Tobias shucked down on the bed a little, slipping his arm lower so it looped around my hips.

"Really?" I asked, poking his head.

"Sleep is good for recovery. I'll keep guard while you rest." Addison went to stand and I tightened my grip on him, shaking my head.

"Stay. I'll feel safer with the pair of you beside me."

"That makes me very happy to hear, sweet."

# Epilogue

It was all for love. Is all for love.

The wrong sort of love for my darling, but she has time to come around.

So sweet that she would worry for them, even at point of death. So unlucky she wasn't quick enough to stop his spell.

I am too weak, and too little of myself, to do much but hide. But I'm very used to being constrained, and as long as I'm undetected in her, I'll have Ena for company. I couldn't have hoped for anything better than joining with her so purely. That I have to share her with them, well. Undesirable, certainly, but not intolerable.

Once I'm able to be more than this, I'll remedy that.

# ABOUT THE AUTHOR

Charlotte Platt is a dark fantasy and horror writer based in the very far north of Scotland. When she isn't out beside the river looking for herons, she can be found walking her parents' rescue dog, Joe, or tending to her garden—both of which feature heavily on her socials. Outside of writing she likes live shows, comedy, and music, as well as researching deep dives for her next novel.